Praise for Z.A. Recht's

PLAGUE OF THE DEAD

"Z.A. Recht's *Plague of the Dead* is an awesome zombie novel. A literal, intelligent thriller filled with a cast of strong, believable and well-drawn characters, this is a story that will grip you and, at the same time, fill you with an uncomfortable sense of dread."

—David Moody, author of *Hater*

"Zombies . . . military . . . global devastation . . . Z.A. Recht has engineered a virus so infectious even die-hard zombie critics will get down with the sickness."

—D.L. Snell, author of *Skin and Bones*

"*Plague of the Dead* is the perfect combination of viral thriller and zombie nightmare, the kind of story Tom Clancy might write if he had the balls to tackle the undead. Thankfully for us, Z.A. Recht has those balls, and he pulls out all the stops in this action-packed zombie extravaganza."

—Ryan C. Thomas, author of *The Summer I Died*

"Hypnotically readable . . . [*Plague of the Dead*] is one of the most believable zombie stories I've read in quite some time. There's hardly a moment to catch your breath as Recht deftly moves the narrative in directions that seem quite plausible in today's post-9/11 age. I'd like to commend Permuted Press for discovering another fine author!"

—R. Thomas Riley, author of *Through the Glass Darkly*

"Intense and action-packed! Recht aims for the head with this one!"

—Geoff Bough, *Revenant Magazine*

"*The MorningStar Strain* is a zombiefied *Out of the Ashes,* a blend of *28 Days Later* zombies and Romero zombies, with a climax so intense it literally had me shaking. A FANTASTIC book!"

—Travis Adkins, author of *Twilight of the Dead*

"A truly epic novel that deserves your immediate attention!"

—Pain @ Allthingszombie.com

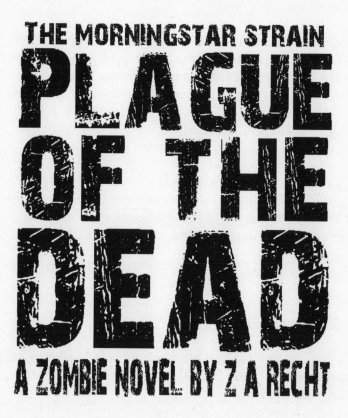

THE MORNINGSTAR STRAIN

PLAGUE OF THE DEAD

A ZOMBIE NOVEL BY Z A RECHT

with an Introduction by Bowie Ibarra

Pocket Books
New York London Toronto Sydney

Pocket Books
A Division of Simon & Schuster, Inc.
1230 Avenue of the Americas
New York, NY 10020

This book is a work of fiction. Names, characters, places, and incidents either are products of the author's imagination or are used fictitiously. Any resemblance to actual events or locales or persons, living or dead, is entirely coincidental.

Originally published in 2006 by Permuted Press

First Pocket Books trade paperback edition January 2010

Interior design by Travis Adkins

Manufactured in the United States of America

10 9 8 7 6 5

ISBN 978-1-4391-7673-3
ISBN 978-1-4391-7728-0 (ebook)

INTRODUCTION

WHAT IS IT about being eaten alive that bugs everyone?

Wait. Scratch that. Never mind. I know the answer.

Flesh being torn away from bone. Appendages being removed with no anesthetic. Perhaps spending the last moments of your existence watching your entrails being removed and devoured by total strangers. It's probably kind of stinky, too.

Yeah, I guess that's why being eaten alive can be a real bummer.

So what is the appeal and importance of the zombie genre in the new millennium? Perhaps its importance is in two key concepts.

Let's start with our fellow citizens both in the U.S. and in the world. It could be argued that an artificial disconnect has been implemented by the overly commercialized U.S. through electronic media like Internet, wi-fi, and video games. These forms of entertainment (distraction?) put us in our own virtual world for hours at a time. The price, though, is that it separates us from our families, friends, and potential new amigos. More in a moment.

The second is the cynical perception of the role of the U.S. military in responding to (creating?) the zombie apocalypse. In this new millennium, a second renaissance, so to speak, is occurring. Those same people spending time away from their families and friends are sharing reliable information about global happenings.

It has been dubbed an 'information war', a struggle between forces who are trying to enlighten and those trying to enslave. Though many might deny it, there is credible information in regards to U.S. government involvement, planning, and execution of national emergencies in an effort to command and control the populace. Whether it's 'bird flu', 'anthrax', 'terrorists', or 'smallpox', the government has already put in our heads that a 'biological attack' was inevitable, and we should all be afraid. Smallpox is all but eradicated, with the exception of several vials at Fort Dietrich. For those Internet junkies out there, simply doing a Google search of 'Fort Dietrich' brings up some interesting hits on the aerosol dispersal of pathogens.

So why are these two concepts important and a key to the re-emergence of zombie popularity? A zombie apocalypse would do something that some might claim we have forgotten how to do: interact and work together with other people. Suddenly, the stranger across the street becomes your best friend. The 'crazy' man who everyone thought was a terrorist because he had a gun collection becomes an asset. And now you have to work with your rival to fight a common enemy. The zombie apocalypse, as terrible as it seems, actually brings people together.

Since September 2001, not only the United States, but the world, has not been the same. And though the five-year mark has passed since that despicable day, the perception of the events of that day have changed drastically. People are becoming more and more skeptical by the day about the government version of the events. And with the reputation of Fort Dietrich, a zombie apocalypse by an artificially manufactured virus is something that is within the realm of possibility.

Z.A. Recht's *Plague of the Dead* brings these two themes together with fantastic precision and magnificent eloquence. I have to say I'm really rather envious of the attention to detail and his patience in telling his story. Z.A. Recht has a clear vision of the zombie apocalypse and communicates it with all the details, gore, and struggle for survival that every zombie fan wants and needs. It is an awesome addition to the ever-growing zombie universe.

My fellow zombie fan, you have done yourself a great favor in purchasing this book. It is now time to gird up your loins for one of the best zombie adventures out today. Rest assured the eating, disemboweling, and dismembering are only a product of your imagination.

Let's just hope the boys and girls at Fort Dietrich don't get any funny ideas.

Sincerely,

Bowie V. Ibarra

To Ben. You should have lived.

And to Barbara. They are still coming to get you.

PLAGUE OF THE DEAD

PART ONE:

SMOKE

START INTERCEPT_

Electronic Mail Window 

From: Anna Demilio <ademilio@usamriid.mil>
To: Francis Sherman <fsherman@pentagon.mil>
Date: September 02, 2006, 10:24:32
Subject: Re: Epidemiological Recommendations Regarding New Finds/Current Outbreaks/Rural Specific

The first stages of an epidemic are as subtle as the early symptoms of the disease itself. Early outbreaks will be in remote locations, nearest to the source of the virus or bacteria causing the sickness. Deaths will be few, as will cautions. Few cases are not worth the time or attention of the CDC or USAMRIID, as almost all of such outbreaks burn themselves out within a week or two. Most of the world's deadliest diseases come out of the jungles of Africa, and the land there is fortunately sparse as far as population goes. Villages are separated by miles of inhospitable rain forest, making direct travel a nightmare, and most roads are nothing more than muddy potholes. On my last expedition to the Congo regions, our Land Rovers became mired so often it would have quite easily been faster to walk. Such conditions make excellent natural deterrents to the spread of outbreaks and many African villages have adopted policies of self-seclusion in the event of such cases. They will block the roads with tree trunks and set guards at the edges of the village to keep out all strangers until the plague is cleansed from their midst.

Today's advancing technology makes such practical steps harder to accomplish.

With our network of intercontinental flights and travel routes, a single infected person has the ability to spread disease throughout the face of the planet in a matter of hours. Imagine the possibilities. If a man who has contracted Ebola Zaire boards a flight in Mombasa to Rome, he may infect one or two of his fellow passengers. He and the newly infected passengers may then take connecting flights to Moscow, London, and Paris, each of these persons infecting one or two more each step of the journey. As these people take the newly contracted disease along their own travel routes, it is easy to see how in a matter of hours a disease could easily spread across entire continents. In this particular case, we have chosen to use Ebola Zaire which has an incubation period of roughly one week. During that period, the infected can spread the disease but show no symptoms of their own, until the headaches begin around day seven. In this manner a devastating disease can effectively ambush a population. By the time the original carrier takes ill, thousands could already be carrying the virus in their bloodstream.

It is therefore my recommendation that international travel

Electronic Mail Window

policies be placed higher on the list of governmental priority for reform. Travelers seeking to return from foreign countries should be delayed in an acceptable manner to observe the possibility of contagion. If this is deemed unacceptable, international arrivals should, at the very least, be given a physical before readmittance to the country. I should cite the example of the discovery of Ebola Reston in Virginia; for a moment imagine if this had not been a new strain, but rather of the old Sudan or Zaire varieties.

On a more personal note, I should add that the number of new diseases discovered each year has been rising steadily as our travel and technological capabilities rise. While most of these are harmless or parasitical in nature, some are downright frightening, with almost unimaginable prospects of destruction. I do not need to cite examples, as I am sure we all know those of which I speak.

Of particular note is the viral infection I have been studying. For details see folder for Project Morningstar [Top Secret/eyes only]. What I can say about Morningstar is that this virus is an evil bastard, if you'll pardon the expression. On lab tests we found that some mammalian species react horribly, and judging from the virus' genetic preferences it is likely that human beings will also be susceptible. So far, dogs, cats, horses, and goats have reacted, and we have also achieved a response from dolphins. Avians seem unaffected. However, we have found that some bats are susceptible. Some species show no ill effects; we believe this to be due to a natural genetic immunity. We're looking into it; possibly a cure in there somewhere.

As I was saying, the virus shares some qualities with known diseases as far as symptoms go. It is similar to Malaria and Ebola in that the first symptoms involve muscle pain and nausea; later stages include tissue deterioration. We've found that Morningstar is a host-lover, and will not kill its victims outright. In this manner we are somewhat blessed; victims may live long enough to see a cure found. However, it is strongly recommended that victims be placed under close observation and restrained. Tissue deterioration is moderate in most cases, equally light and heavy in others. Heavy tissue deterioration makes the option of euthanasia look promising. It includes loss of smaller extremities such as fingers and toes, severe skin/hair/fur loss, muscle and bone rot. See folder for Project Morningstar for photos. This seems to be an unwanted effect of Morningstar, as in most other areas the virus tends to sustain the host in order to continue its own existence and guarantee procreation of the strain.

Seasoned epidemiologists are already well-versed in virus transmission tactics. In this sense, viruses could almost be called intelligent. Some viruses are airborne, and symptoms usually include coughing, as if the virus knows that it can travel through

Electronic Mail Window

the air and tries to make its host be an unwilling accomplice in spreading it. Ebola, meanwhile, is not airborne and is rather contracted through blood and bodily fluids. Final stages include the crash-and-bleed, in which the victim enters a seizure, bleeding from nearly every orifice, guaranteeing that blood will be strewn around the immediate vicinity. In this manner Ebola hopes to find a new host even as its old one dies.

Morningstar is far darker, perhaps even evil, in its own methodology. My studies have shown a dramatic rise in the aggressive nature of the host. Infected canines became feral shortly after showing symptoms and autopsies confirmed a large concentration of virus in the saliva of the hosts. Morningstar is transmitted through bites, similar in function to Rabies. The host is meanwhile running a high fever. This effectively boils the brain of the host, and in essence is a biological lobotomy. The host is no longer able to make distinctions between friend and foe, and likely loses all higher brain functions completely. We will not be certain until a human host is available for observation.

I have outlined Morningstar to the extent I am able without first having command permission to discuss more in-depth facts and figures, and so I will close. Allow me to reiterate that Morningstar, along with Hanta, Lassa, and a slew of other deadly strains, give us more than enough reason to begin travel and epidemiological reform in the United States. Will be waiting for reply.

Lt. Col. Anna Demilio
US Army Medical Research Institute of Infectious Disease

/end

CONTINUE INTERCEPT . . .

ADDITIONAL DATA INCOMING_

Quick Reply click MENU for more options

From: Francis Sherman <fsherman@pentagon.mil>
To: Anna Demilio <ademilio@usamriid.mil>
Date: 09.14.06 - 15:12:06
Subject: Re: Epidemiological Recommendations Regarding New Finds/Current Outbreaks/Rural Specific

Doctor,

Firstly, allow me to congratulate you on your outstanding achievements in the field of epidemiology. We've gained many useful insights from you and your staff at USAMRIID and we hope to continue that relationship in the future.

However, at this time we cannot impose any travel reform on our international airlines or shipping lanes. Such a move would be disastrous economically. I am sure you can understand the President's reaction to such a suggestion. I should add that he does agree with you as to the serious nature of a biological threat, be it from Africa or South America or the Rocky Mountains of Colorado.

We have increased surveillance of viral hotspots in Africa as per your suggestion, but as of today we will be taking no steps that could hinder growth of the economy.

Maj. Gen. Francis Sherman
US Army, Pentagon

Electronic Mail Window 

From: Anna Demilio <ademilio@usamriid.mil>
To: Francis Sherman <fsherman@pentagon.mil>
Date: September 14, 2006, 17:48:45
Subject: Re: Epidemiological Recommendations Regarding New Finds/Current Outbreaks/Rural Specific

General,

Frank, how many senators were looking over your shoulder while you wrote that patronizing piece of crap?

Lt. Col. Anna Demilio
US Army Medical Research Institute of Infectious Disease

/end

Quick Reply click MENU for more options

From: Francis Sherman <fsherman@pentagon.mil>
To: Anna Demilio <ademilio@usamriid.mil>
Date: 09.14.06 - 20:11:09
Subject: Re: Epidemiological Recommendations Regarding New Finds/Current Outbreaks/Rural Specific

Anna,

Three, and a very pissed-off ambassador from Kenya. You lose a lot of popularity when you start talking about things that'll cost people profits in this country. I'm probably going to get ripped a new one when they find out I've been corresponding with you over this. You owe me one for not letting them go out there to USAMRIID and shut you down completely. If there is a storm brewing out there, I'm sure they'll do what's right, but only after they can see it for themselves.

Maj. Gen. Francis Sherman
US Army, Pentagon

Electronic Mail Window

From: Anna Demilio <ademilio@usamriid.mil>
To: Francis Sherman <fsherman@pentagon.mil>
Date: September 14, 2006, 23:54:23
Subject: Re: Epidemiological Recommendations Regarding New Finds/Current Outbreaks/Rural Specific

General,

The mistake the first two little pigs made was letting the wolf get close. Smart thing to do would've been to blast him when he started up the path. But I'll let them do it their way, and we'll see.

Lt. Col. Anna Demilio
US Army Medical Research Institute of Infectious Disease

/end

INTERCEPT COMPLETE_

Mombasa Airstrip
December 09, 2006
1032 hrs_

A LONE FIGURE was running towards the control tower, waving his arms. In the tower, a tall man held a pair of binoculars to his face, focusing on the man. He frowned.

"What the hell is that guy doing?" said Mbutu Ngasy to one of his co-workers. "Call security. Get him off the runway."

As the shift director of air traffic control, Mbutu was responsible for the smooth takeoffs and landings at the Mombasa regional airport. The rogue figure was dead-center on the main runway, blocking traffic.

Mbutu flicked on his radio and said, "Flight 931, hold position. We've got a trespasser on the ground, over."

"Roger, control. Holding pattern, over," came the static-laced reply.

Below the tower, Mbutu could see two security vehicles powering through the dirt alongside the runway, blue lights flashing. They slowed as they got near the man and the man then stopped in front of them, gesturing wildly at the tree line where he had originally emerged. Mbutu raised the binoculars again and focused them beyond the security detail and trespasser, towards the tree line, curious as to what the man was so excited about.

Fifty yards further, four more people had appeared and were walking steadily towards the group on the runway. Mbutu grimaced, holding the radio microphone to his lips.

"Got four more coming your way out of the trees, security. What is this, a party? Over."

"We see 'em."

One of the security vehicles peeled off from the other, heading towards the four new figures. Behind it, the lone trespasser was being placed in handcuffs. He wasn't resisting.

Mbutu watched the other vehicle as it pulled to a stop in front of the four figures. He saw the two guards climb out of the truck. They held up their hands, pointing at the woods, ordering the trespassers to go back the way they came. However, the trespassers continued to advance.

Mbutu saw one of the guards take a step back, shaking his head in disbelief as he drew his pistol. The other guard soon did the same. Though Mbutu couldn't hear the words being spoken, he imagined one of the four trespassers had made a threat or two.

The gunshots—unlike mere spoken words—were easily audible, echoing across the runway. Mbutu saw the flashes of fire as the guards fired their pistols, then saw the sprays of blood popping from the backs of the victims.

Then his jaw dropped open in awe.

The four trespassers *kept coming*.

The guards were firing quickly now. Mbutu saw one of them drop an empty magazine to make room for a fresh one. One of the trespassers took a round to the forehead and dropped to the ground, twitching. The other three were almost on top of the guards, who had backed up against their own truck, cut off from escape.

Mbutu saw the trespassers encircle the guards, and then lost sight of the action, blocked from view by the security vehicle. He cursed and tossed away the binoculars.

"Call the police!" he shouted to his co-workers.

One of them had already picked up the telephone. "This is Mombasa Air Traffic Control, reporting shots fired on the runway. We've got trespassers—definitely dangerous, probably armed!"

The other security vehicle had motored over to the group of trespassers, the original lone man still handcuffed in the back seat. The guards climbed out, weapons already drawn and primed. Mbutu watched carefully. The guards down there had a much better view than he did, and they obviously didn't like what they saw behind the captured truck. They opened fire.

In the distance, Mbutu heard the sirens of the approaching police. There was always a detachment on hand somewhere at the airport and their quick response was welcome in situations like this one.

By the time the police cruiser had arrived at the scene, the security guards had put down the trespassers. The police looked over the bodies, took photographs, and were in the process of booking the handcuffed man when Mbutu made it to the scene on foot.

"What happened?" he asked, slightly out of breath from the run.

One of the cops answered him. "Don't know for sure, yet," he said. "From their clothes they look like rebels, but it's way out of character for them to come into a town like this. Quite a distance to travel, too. No weapons either. Probably some cannibals, the sick bastards. Wish they would stay out in the wild."

He pointed at the bodies of the two security guards.

Mbutu looked, then wished he hadn't. Chunks had been torn from the flesh of the guards. Raking wounds from teeth and fingernails scarred the corpses and both lay in pools of blood.

"*Dear God*," he uttered. "What brought them to this?"

"Hungry maybe," one of the cops replied. "With the ban on cannibalism and the population situation in the jungle, it's no wonder they tried to get a meal in town."

Mbutu looked sick. "How can you joke about it?"

"Who's joking?" said the officer. "We've been seeing those tribes in town more and more often lately. They're protesting the prohibition, chanting about how *they* need to eat too."

"Here comes the coroner," said the officer's partner, gesturing into the distance. An ambulance was trundling down the runway, lights and siren off. After all, there was no real rush when all the patients were already dead.

"Here! Back her up here!" directed the officer, waving the ambulance into position. The back doors swung open as it came to a stop, and white-coated medics climbed out, dragging stretchers behind them.

"How many?" they asked.

"Six," said the officer.

"Holy shit," one of the medics breathed, spotting the bodies. "What happened?"

"Don't worry about it," the officer told him. "Just get 'em out of here. There's a flight waiting to land."

Mbutu felt his lip curl at the officer's apparent disregard for the lives that had been ended, but said nothing. Here, as in many places on Earth, life was cheap.

The medics loaded the corpses onto the stretchers, zipping them into dark plastic body bags and stacking them like so much cordwood in the back of the ambulance.

"We'll be sure to let you know what we figure out," the officer told Mbutu before climbing into his squad car to follow the ambulance.

"Right," Mbutu said under his breath as the cars receded into the distance. He was left standing alone in the hot sun on the runway, the only evidence of the recent violence a few smears of blood on the edge of the pavement. "You do that, officer. You do that."

Mombasa Hospital
December 09, 2006
2013 hrs_

Dr. Klaus Mayer was a general surgeon on staff at Mombasa Hospital. He was in his mid-thirties and had traveled to Africa from his home in Austria to do a year of pro-bono work. He felt he was able to make a real impact here. He saw evidence of this every day when patients thanked him or when he would see a nurse using one of the techniques he'd been teaching.

Tonight he was pulling morgue duty. The hospital was severely understaffed and all the doctors took turns filling in the vacant positions. Dr. Mayer was sitting at the check-in desk in front of the morgue's double swinging doors, scratching notes into a patient's file. He was expecting a visit in a few minutes from the police. They were bringing him six bodies. Apparently there had been an incident at the airport. The police had refused to give him any details.

Like that's going to matter, he mused. *I'll find out when I do the autopsies.*

He sighed, tapping the pen against the file. This was one of his tougher cases. An older woman had come down with a case of malaria, and her immune system was having a tough time fighting back the disease. She had nearly recovered twice now, but relapsed both times. She had two daughters, each with their own families, and they were destitute. The extended family relied on the income she made as a seamstress. Even with all the adults and some of the children working full-time at whatever odd jobs they could find, they barely made ends meet. They simply couldn't afford to lose their mother, as cold as that sounded.

But I've become used to these kinds of things, Dr. Mayer thought. *I don't know if that's comforting or frightening.*

He heard the chime of the elevator bell down the hall, then heard the doors slide open. He lifted his eyes and saw uniformed officers exiting, accompanied by paramedics. They pulled gurneys between them.

"Ah, *sehr gut*," Dr. Mayer said, standing and switching to the local dialect as the officers approached. "Bring them right inside, please. Do you have any specific time you would like the autopsies finished?"

"As soon as possible," said one of the officers, (the same that had talked with Mbutu on the landing field.) He didn't elaborate, and Dr. Mayer didn't ask him to. Here, it was best to let the officials go about their business, and mind your own.

"Please leave them here," Dr. Mayer instructed, leading the police and medics into the morgue. The room was cool and sterile and smelled of antiseptic. There were two stainless steel autopsy tables in the center of the room, with light fixtures perched overhead. As they entered, Dr. Mayer flicked a switch on the wall and the lights hummed to life. One of the bulbs flickered on and off, buzzing quietly.

The medics wheeled the gurneys against the far wall and handed Dr. Mayer a clipboard. He let his eyes scan over it, then pulled his ballpoint from his chest pocket and swiftly gave his signature, adding a flourish under the Y in his last name. The police didn't bother to tell him anything else, but he overheard them talking about taking a prisoner up a few levels to be treated for wounds.

Dr. Mayer knew what was expected of him and didn't press the issue.

"You might get a bit of a shock when you open 'em up," one of the medics said as the police were leaving. He spoke conspiratorially, glancing over his shoulder at the officers to make sure they weren't watching. "Cops think its cannibals or rebels. Heard 'em talking."

"Thanks," Dr. Mayer said, eyeing the medic. For a man who had seen all manner of injuries on the streets of Mombasa, he seemed unusually shaken. Dr. Mayer was now hopelessly curious as to what he was going to find.

Once his company had departed, Dr. Mayer got down to business. He snapped a pair of latex gloves over his hands and pulled a surgical mask over his face, adjusting his glasses around the rubber straps. He rolled a cart of instruments up to one of the shining tables and retrieved a blank file and pocket tape recorder from his desk. Finally he pulled the first gurney alongside. Ideally one other person would have helped him lift the body from the gurney to the autopsy slab, but he made do by shifting the head and shoulders over, then moving to the other end of the corpse and pulling the legs onto the table as well.

Dr. Mayer clicked the tape recorder on as he stood over the dark body bag. The writing on the black plastic bag said that this was one of the perpetrators of whatever crime had occurred at the airfield.

"First subject, received December the ninth at eight-twenty p.m.," he narrated, pulling back the zipper on the bag. He flipped the plastic back and raised his eyebrows. "Subject is an adult male, estimate between twenty-five and thirty years of age. Appears to have been in moderately healthy shape. Some signs of malnutrition are apparent. Two lateral scars on the upper left thigh. Wounds appear to be old."

Dr. Mayer lifted the body's head in his gloved hands, turning it gently under the bright white light of the fluorescents. The bulb that was shorting out continued to buzz and crackle as it flickered.

"Cause of death appears to be from trauma to the skull. One, maybe two gunshot wounds, entering through the frontal lobe and exiting through the rear. Skull appears to have shattered, most likely due to calcium deficiency."

Dr. Mayer halted here, frowning beneath his mask.

"Interesting."

He pulled a long-necked cotton swab from a jar on the instrument tray and dabbed it at a wide slash on the body's shoulder. It came away covered in black, syrupy blood that had congealed on the skin around the wound.

"Subject appears to have suffered wounds from an animal. Pattern suggests biting, perhaps a monkey. The blood surrounding the wound implies it was pre-mortem. It doesn't appear to be either life-threatening or infected."

Dr. Mayer let his eyes roam to the corpse's chest. Here he found his most confusing item yet.

"Three gunshot wounds to the chest," he said for the benefit of the tape recorder, but then his voice trailed off. He stared at the wounds for a moment, then grabbed the corpse firmly by the shoulder and lifted it up on its side. He inspected its back and found two exit wounds. One of the bullets had lodged inside the man somewhere. But the wounds themselves were not what interested him—it was the lack of blood surrounding them.

He coughed, clearing his throat.

"Gunshot wounds to the chest appear to be post-mortem," he said, again letting his voice trail off. After a moment he reached over and switched off the tape recorder.

"This is strange," he said to himself, eyes on the corpse. "Why shoot a man in the chest when you've already killed him with a shot to the head?"

Dr. Mayer seemed to ponder this for a minute, and then seemed to throw the thought away. He clicked the tape recorder back on.

"Moving forward, I'm going to open the first subject for confirmation on cause of death," he said, pulling a scalpel from the instrument tray. He lowered the blade over the corpse's chest, and then stopped just inches from the flesh. Along with the bullet wounds, there were other puncture marks on the man's chest. These were smaller, neater, and also bloodless.

Dr. Mayer had seen these types of wounds before. In Europe, they might be associated with a stabbing wound from a stiletto or other thin, cylindrical blade. Here in Africa, there were certain rural tribes which used a lightweight hunting spear. He didn't know what they were called or how they were made, only that they were of a thin, flexible wood that reminded him of the branches of weeping willows. Occasionally he would get a case where a tribesman had been speared on accident while hunting—or intentionally by a rival tribe. The wounds he saw on his current subject were identical.

This presented Dr. Mayer with a riddle within a riddle. This man had been stabbed and shot after he was killed—but Klaus Mayer knew for a fact that the police here in Mombasa went better armed than their rural counterparts. They had no such spears to stab this man with. And why would they even want to after they had already killed him?

The answer was simple enough, though it still made little sense: this man had been attacked by tribesmen after he was dead, and then had somehow found his way to the airfield, caused trouble and had been gunned down—all while already being dead.

"There must be some rational explanation," Dr. Mayer said. He looked over at the tape recorder and realized he had broken his continuity. "Located small puncture wounds in the chest of the first subject that appear to have been caused by a stabbing weapon, not a firearm. These wounds are also post-mortem. I cannot explain how these wounds occurred."

Dr. Mayer was already thoroughly frustrated and he hadn't even begun the meat of the autopsy procedure.

Hopefully some of the other bodies would shed some light on the matter.

2234 hrs_

Dr. Mayer had completed three of his six autopsies. He still felt discouraged. He had found similar post-mortem wounds on two more of the attackers. Some were gunshot wounds, others inflicted by spear. He'd moved on to one of the dead security guards, hoping that maybe one of the victims of the attack would have some new evidence for him.

"Fourth subject is male, early to mid-thirties, in good condition. No noticeable identifying marks."

Dr. Mayer examined the guard's wounds. As he did, his eyes grew wide. These guards were wearing the uniforms of the airfield security details. Obviously the crime in question was the murder of these two men by the other four that had been brought in with them. The method of the murder, however, was grisly and revealing.

"Cause of death seems to be loss of blood, or shock trauma. Too early to tell. Wounds are apparent in the neck, shoulders, and forearms. Subject appears to have attempted to defend himself from the attack that killed him. Wound patterns are similar to those found on three previous subjects. They appear to be bites."

Dr. Mayer rubbed his eyes with the back of his hand and took another look. He rose to his feet, walked over to the desk and lifted the telephone from the cradle. He dialed.

"It's Dr. Mayer down in the morgue," he said. "Are my x-rays ready yet?"

He listened.

"Good. Could you have someone send them down as soon as possible?" A moment passed. "As soon as possible, I said. The police want their autopsy reports."

And I want them too, he thought.

He hung up the phone and returned to the stool by the autopsy table. Using a small camera and a tape measure, he took the dimensions of the bite marks on the security guard's shoulder. There was one very clear imprint he focused on, simple blackened tooth marks in a nearly perfect bite pattern. He was planning on using those marks to verify his hypothesis.

As he was jotting the measurements onto a legal pad with his ballpoint pen, the attending nurse pushed open the swinging morgue doors and handed him two thick manila envelopes. He thanked her before she left, then unwound the string from the tab of the folders. He got up and shuffled over to the wall, pulling the black and gray x-rays from the envelope. He popped them onto a dark screen. He chose one from both folders, and then dropped the envelopes into one of his voluminous coat pockets.

Dr. Mayer ripped the sheet of measurements from the legal pad and stuck those to the screen as well before turning on the light behind it. It flickered to life after a few seconds. He leaned over it, comparing the x-rays of the attacker's jaws to the bite marks on the guard's shoulder.

He mumbled to himself, scratching figures and notes onto his pad as he looked back and forth at the images, recording the width of both jaws, the shape of the teeth, and which teeth were missing or damaged.

"*Looks close*," he commented, eyes darting back and forth between the photos and the notepad sheet. "Could be human. Maybe the final subject has the correct jaws."

Behind him, the arm of the security guard seemed to shift. Dr. Mayer glanced at the table, but the body was motionless. He went back to his x-rays.

"*Wait*," he said, pulling one of the x-rays loose. He laid it out on the desk and plucked the notepad sheet down. He carefully compared a slight gap between the left canine mark on the guard with one on the x-ray. "They match. They match!"

The guard on the autopsy table had slowly turned his head away from Dr. Mayer. His eyes were now open, but glazed and lifeless. Dr. Mayer still sat with his back to the table as he looked at the papers in his hands with a furrowed brow.

The guard slowly and silently pulled himself upright. He sat for a moment and tilted his head back to look up at the light hanging overhead. It was the fixture in the light that was shorting; it flickered on and off, bathing the guard's face in a kind of greenish quasi-strobe. He seemed captivated by it.

Then Dr. Mayer clicked his ballpoint pen. The soft noise caused the guard to turn his head in that direction. He opened his mouth as if to speak, but no words came out. He managed a sound like a sigh.

Dr. Mayer had come to the only possible solution: the guards had been bitten to death by their attackers, the four unidentified men. Those same men were (if the evidence was correct) already dead at the time they bit the guards. If he was any less rational a man than he was, Dr. Mayer would have cracked right there. He reasoned that there was simply some small piece of evidence he had missed that would allow him a nice, logical, safe conclusion to give the police—and himself. After all, there was absolutely no such thing as the *undead.*

That was when he heard the sigh behind him.

Dr. Mayer felt a shiver run down his spine and was tempted to look over his shoulder. He chuckled to himself suddenly, brushing the feeling aside and delving deeper into his notes, looking for that missing clue. Surely the sound was nothing more than the morgue cooling system kicking on, that was all. His imagination was getting the better of him.

As Dr. Mayer chuckled, the guard slid off the autopsy table and landed awkwardly on his feet. If the good doctor had remained silent, he would have heard the soft slap of flesh against ceramic tile when the guard hit the floor.

The guard took one careful, lurching step forward. His toe tag skittered along the tiled floor.

This time, Dr. Mayer *did* turn around.

His eyes widened and he fell back onto his desk, knocking the cup of pens and pencils over. They scattered. The x-rays and folders were pushed off as well as Dr. Mayer scrabbled.

The guard was right behind him. Dr. Mayer felt hands grip his arm and neck and pull him back onto the desk. He saw the glowering visage of the dead guard scowling down at him.

Dr. Mayer screamed.

This isn't possible! The dead can't live! They're dead! They're DEAD!

The guard scratched at Dr. Mayer, leaving angry red marks down both arms. The guard wrapped his teeth around one of Dr. Mayer's hands and bit down. Dr. Mayer screamed again, kicking furiously. The doors to the morgue burst open and the nurse that had brought him the x-rays earlier dashed in once more. However, she took one look at the scene within and turned on her heels, fleeing and screaming for help.

"Don't leave me here!" Dr. Mayer called out.

The guard perching over him seemed to growl in response, a deep guttural groan issuing from the slashed remains of his neck.

The doors to the morgue swung shut, and Dr. Mayer had one more chance to scream before his voice was cut off. The fluorescent light above continued to hum and flicker, creaking slightly from side to side.

PART TWO:

SMOLDER

START INTERCEPT_

Electronic Mail Window

From: Anna Demilio <ademilio@usamriid.mil>
To: Francis Sherman <fsherman@pentagon.mil>
Date: December 12, 2006, 11:10:05
Subject: MORNINGSTAR

General,

We have recently acquired a victim of the Morningstar strain from a contact in Mombasa. Apparently the man was bitten by another victim and fell ill shortly after. I wouldn't have bothered writing you with this update unless I thought it was important—in fact, I'd call it vital. We have identified the victim as one Dr. Klaus Mayer, late of Austria. We have confirmation of the time he was infected, as well as a sample of tissue from the original host. In this particular case, it took only a matter of hours for Dr. Mayer to succumb to the disease. My hypothesis is related to the wounds he suffered in contracting the virus, made about the head and neck by the original host's teeth and fingernails.

As you know, in our laboratory experiments we inject our subjects with a dose of the virus, usually in the haunch or hindquarter, and observe the reaction. In Dr. Mayer's case, a much larger amount of the strain was transmitted directly into the carotid artery, giving the virus an instant route to the Doctor's brain and central nervous system. In our experiments, the virus would have infected vessels and capillaries near the injection point, multiplied, and spread slowly toward the brain before symptoms occurred. I believe that Dr. Mayer's quick deterioration was due to the size and location of his point of infection. Notable is the original host's apparent choice to attack Dr. Mayer in those particular areas rather than in the chest, for example, or Dr. Mayer's head itself, which was left alone entirely.

I have a theory about this as well, but without further evidence I cannot in good conscience reveal it.

Hope this comes in handy.

Lt. Col. Anna Demilio,
US Army Medical Research Institute of Infectious Disease

/end

ADDITIONAL DATA INCOMING_

Quick Reply - PAGE 01 of 02 click MENU for more options

From: Francis Sherman <fsherman@pentagon.mil>
To: Anna Demilio <ademilio@usamriid.mil>
Date: 12.13.06 - 13:17:34
Subject: Re: MORNINGSTAR

Colonel,

You're saying that a large wound, in the right place, by an infected person, can drop the incubation period of Morningstar from a little over a week to less than a day?

You had better be shitting me. And you're about to find out why, even if disclosing it costs me my stars.

There are more cases in Mombasa, and we've gotten reports of victims in Kinshasa and the Lake Victoria vicinity as well. Looks like we've got us an outbreak on our hands. Virus seems to be centered on the Congo River basin. Somewhere in there is the Morningstar strain's home. Anyway, so far, almost three dozen confirmed cases. God only knows how many unconfirmed ones are hiding out there in the jungle, praying they'll get well without having to go to a hospital. You know how most of the rural-types there feel about hospitals, Anna. They think you only go there to die.

Actually, they're not far off this time around. Seems the originator of the Mombasa outbreak was a trespasser the police arrested on the runway at the airstrip. He took ill a couple days after Dr. Mayer was attacked. No one was watching him; he was resting in a hospital bed surrounded by sick, injured, or otherwise defenseless patients. You see what I'm getting at here?

The bastard went ape shit on them; just seemed to snap a day after he took ill. He'd fallen into a light coma about an hour beforehand, then just came awake, running about the place, tearing stuff up. He got three or four of the patients in the process, bit 'em good. They're currently under observation in the ICU there. Armed observation, if you get my drift. With a little luck Mombasa will be able to hold the outbreak at its current point.

I'd love to get you more than a sample from the host that got Dr. Mayer—that guard—but his body's been burned. Police gunned him down as he was trying to leave the morgue.

Yes, that's right, Anna. I said the morgue. Dr. Mayer was the coroner on duty at the time he was attacked. I'm sure your generous benefactors neglected to tell you that little jewel of information, didn't they? Deduce what you want to. I'll just flat out tell you if you keep reading.

That man was dead, Doc. He was legally, certifiably, completely dead. He'd bled out from bites and scratches caused by another group of carriers—bet they didn't tell you about them, either—and somehow found it in his corpselike self enough energy to jump up off the autopsy table and have a go at Doc Mayer.

PAGE 01 of 02>

Quick Reply - PAGE 02 of 02 click MENU for more options

I'm not a religious man, Anna, but unless you and your science can get me an explanation pretty fast, I'm going to start dusting off my field bible.

Now, assuming Morningstar hosts become aggressive enough to bite the nearest person, and assuming that type of bite can cause the disease to manifest within a few hours, are we shit out of luck, or do we have a shot at beating this thing?

Maj. Gen. Francis Sherman
US Army, Pentagon

PAGE 02 of 02

ADDITIONAL DATA INCOMING_

Electronic Mail Window

From: Anna Demilio <ademilio@usamriid.mil>
To: Francis Sherman <fsherman@pentagon.mil>
Date: December 13, 2006, 20:19:21
Subject: Re: Re: MORNINGSTAR

General,

We're shit out of luck.

The spread of the disease could be controlled easily if we had more time between manifestation of symptoms and the original bite, but if we assume most infections will occur through massive trauma, we could be looking at an uncontrolled outbreak within the span of a few days. And let's not forget infections through more subtle means—touching contaminated blood and then rubbing your eye would infect you, but you wouldn't show symptoms for nine or ten days, as the virus would need to multiply considerably before it gains dominance. Who knows where such carriers could be? And how can we identify them before they succumb?

I have to tell you I was highly skeptical of your claim about the host that infected Dr. Mayer being dead at the time of the incident. This is medically impossible. But I trust you to a degree, and so I decided to test the theory.

We've performed an experiment that I don't think you would condone. Neither would the American public, for that matter, or the international community. But I'll make you a deal, General. You don't tell anyone about this and I won't tell anyone about you disclosing classified material to me.

Electronic Mail Window

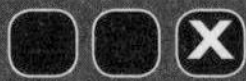

After what you said about the security guard and the morgue, it got me thinking. The bites and scratches would have transferred Morningstar to the guard before he bled to death. There might have been enough blood pressure remaining to carry a massive amount of virus to his brain. Over the next few hours, though the guard was physically dead, the virus must have changed... *something.* That could be the cause of his apparent revival. Or maybe he wasn't dead at all, merely close, and the virus gave him enough rage-fueled strength to bring himself to his feet again. You know how undersupplied and undertrained some of those EMTs are down there—they might have misdeclared him dead. But there was really only one way to test that theory.

We secured Dr. Mayer to a gurney today and took some vitals. This was tricky; Dr. Mayer has completely succumbed to Morningstar and is quite hostile. He's strong, quick, and doesn't seem to care much about pain. We got his standard heart rate, respiration, blood pressure. Then we shot him in the chest with a hunting rifle Jack brought in. He died pretty quick—painless, too. His vitals zeroed out. We monitored the corpse for a couple of hours, and were about to give up when we caught a heartbeat. Just one, and the cardiograph flatlined after that. We waited, and a minute or so later we got another beat. After that, the ECG lit up like a nuclear Christmas tree. We'd shot Dr. Mayer in the chest at point-blank range with a .30-06, and he'd been legally dead for almost four hours, but we were getting brain activity and a heartbeat—albeit a terribly slow one. Respiration remained at zero.

Within a few more minutes Dr. Mayer was fully awake. I should tell you he seems much slower. Could be rigor mortis; most of his body seems to have begun the decay process before he re-awakened. Can't be sure until we observe him longer. In any case, he's a lot less dexterous than he was before we killed him.

Maybe this information can help you. All I know is, I've seen the dead return to life, I've seen the infectious qualities of this disease, I've tried to warn the administration about it, and I've seen them completely ignore me. Now it's starting and we're totally unprepared. I'm going to leave the lab now and go get a martini.

Or ten.

Lt. Col. Anna Demilio,
US Army Medical Research Institute of Infectious Disease

/end

INTERCEPT COMPLETE_

Cairo
December 21, 2006
1734 hrs_

CAIRO BURNED.

The fire spread through sixteen city blocks in a few short hours, consuming building after building. The conflagration had begun when an army convoy fuel tanker headed south towards Lake Victoria had gone through the road, breaking into a sewer pipe buried too shallow beneath the pavement. Main battle tanks had gone before it, treads chewing the road to pieces, and made the route treacherous. The tanker's caps had broken loose and petrol had washed across the highway.

Soldiers immediately blocked off the section of road near the spill and began cleanup, but a spark had ignited the vaporous fuel emissions and the area went up in a white-hot flash. The buildings nearest the spill site had caught fire first, and prevailing winds had carried the blaze across the city blocks. Hundreds, maybe thousands, were lost and presumed dead. Thousands more were injured.

Rebecca Hall wiped sweat from her brow, taking a moment to breathe. The twenty-two-year-old volunteer wore a dirty, stained t-shirt and had a band strapped around her arm that bore the Red Cross symbol. She had been bringing water to the burn victims for nine hours, offering words of comfort, cleaning wounds, and injecting painkillers into those who needed it most. She was exhausted. Her patients got water, but she didn't think to drink any herself.

Rebecca could feel the heat off of the fire just a half a mile away. It was moving parallel to their position, but fire crews and soldiers had warned them to be ready to evacuate on a moment's notice if the winds shifted. The fire and the daily heat of Egypt—even in December—was enough to make her feel dizzy.

"Becky! We need more gauze from the truck!" yelled a doctor. Rebecca was too beat to look up to see who it was. "Becky! Hurry!"

She spun slowly towards the surplus deuce-and-a-half that served as the little relief station's supply depot. Medics were handing out packages of bandages, morphine, and canteens of water to dozens of other volunteers, who were swarming around the back of the truck with outstretched arms. They jostled and shouted at one another as they grabbed at the supplies being tossed out over the small crowd.

Rebecca elbowed her way through the crowd towards the truck. She reached the vehicle and pulled at the leg of one of the medics inside.

"Sarah! Sarah! I need gauze! We're running low on gauze!"

The medic looked down and rummaged through the supplies. She returned, "Becky, we're almost out! There's only three boxes left—and maybe twenty canteens of water! What are we going to do?!"

"Keep working until we're out, then make do!" Rebecca shouted back, grabbing the gauze before one of the other volunteers could snag it. "Cut the coats and other gear into bandages! Send some runners to fill the canteens!"

"The plumbing's out!" Sarah yelled.

"Then send them to the river! I've got to get these back to the doctors!" Rebecca paused, tucked the gauze under her arm, and looked up at her friend. She added, "Are you going to be alright?!"

"I'll be fine!"

Rebecca fought her way out of the crowd and stumbled back towards her post. Her mouth felt like sandpaper and her vision swam. Unless her eyes were playing tricks on her, the fires seemed to be getting closer. And so did the refugees. An unending stream of them poured down the street toward the Red Cross aid station. Egyptian army soldiers armed with assault rifles pointed them towards the posts that could help them. Some argued with the soldiers or tried to push past them.

Rebecca saw one man get whipped with the buttstock of a rifle. He collapsed to the ground and a woman screamed, kneeling over his unconscious form. The soldier who had clubbed him was yelling and gesturing towards the fire. Police with riot shields were trying to corral the uninjured from crossing into the aid station, and the uninjured were trying just as desperately to get to their wounded family and friends.

"Help my baby! Someone help my baby!" sobbed a woman, stumbling towards Rebecca.

She tossed the package of gauze bandages onto a bloodied and soiled gurney and walked over to the woman, holding out her arms.

The woman was carrying a child who looked around five, maybe six. Its face was blackened and cracked, burned almost beyond recognition. The child wasn't crying.

"Let me see!" Rebecca yelled over the crowd. The woman handed her child off into Rebecca's outstretched arms.

Rebecca laid the girl on the gurney and pressed two of her fingers against the child's throat. There was no pulse. The child had already died.

"Doctor!" Rebecca called. One of the three doctors working at her post paused for a moment and fixed her with an inquisitive look. "Have a look at this one!"

The doctor came running over. Rebecca turned to the mother and put her arm around her shoulders, leading her away from the gurney.

"Come on, come with me, let's get you some water, the doctor's going to take care of your little girl . . . Don't worry."

The mother was still sobbing, looking over her shoulder at her child, then back at Rebecca. She was confused, hurt, and panicked, but she allowed herself to be led away.

Behind the pair, the doctor glanced subtly to make sure the mother wasn't watching, then pulled a sheet over the child's head. He waved to a pair of local volunteers, who ran over and pushed the gurney swiftly away.

This was a technique that had evolved over just a few hours. The bereaved were simply causing too much disorganization. The volunteers had started lying to people shortly after the first fight had broken out between a mourning father and a soldier who needed him to make room for new patients.

Rebecca hated the lying. She hated telling people their loved ones were fine, when in fact they were dying or already dead. She imagined how she would feel if someone told her that, only to find out the truth later. These people were going to be devastated. They were already hurt—and their wounds were only going to get worse.

She pulled a canteen from the back of the deuce-and-a-half and sat the weeping mother down by one of the truck's massive tires.

"Here," she said, twisting off the cap. "Drink this. You'll feel better."

The woman quieted long enough to take a small sip from the canteen. She sputtered and coughed, then tried again, this time taking a deep drink. When she finished she returned the half-full canteen to Rebecca with a grateful look on her face.

"There," Rebecca said. "Better?"

The woman managed to nod.

"I'm going to go check on your little girl. Stay here and try to rest, okay?" she said, leaving the canteen by the woman's side. She stood up and swayed back and forth on her feet for a moment. She became acutely aware of her thirst once more, but reminded herself of the other wounded people still coming in to the station. She turned, running back towards her post. She had lost count of her trips for supplies hours before. Her feet felt like they were tingling as they slapped the pavement and her vision blurred a little, then snapped back into focus.

She slowed to a stop by her post, leaning on her knees, trying to catch her breath. She'd only run a hundred feet or so. Why was she so tired?

The world seemed to phase in and out of focus, and Rebecca shot out a hand to steady herself.

"Rebecca?" asked a voice. It was one of the doctors. "Rebecca, are you alright?"

She looked up at the source of the voice, but couldn't make out the face. The doctor was silhouetted, and behind him rose a curtain of fire. Rebecca felt the world spin around her, and then her vision went dark entirely.

She crumbled, unconscious, to the ground. She'd become one of the victims she had been trying all day to save—a victim of heat stroke and dehydration. The doctor who called to her ran over, then knelt. He called for help.

"She's burning up! Get her out of here and back to base camp! And for God's sake, someone get more gauze up here!"

Behind the aid stations and refugees and shouting soldiers, Cairo still burned.

Washington, D.C.
December 27, 2006
1342 hrs_

"Stick to the script! Don't put in anything that isn't written on those prompters, or the FCC'll have our asses," growled the station supervisor from the control room overlooking the news studio. "And remember to look confident, Julie. America's watching. On in five, four . . ."

In the studio below, news anchor Julie Ortiz straightened her back and cleared her throat. The cameraman in front of her counted down silently with the supervisor, flashing fingers. Two, one . . .

The studio silenced, and a backlit sign bearing the words 'ON AIR' lit up. The buffer music began to play from the control room.

A pre-recorded tape announced, "Welcome back to Channel Thirteen News, bringing you around the clock updates on the crisis in Africa. Here's news anchorwoman Julie Ortiz!"

Julie smiled into the camera.

"I'm Julie Ortiz, thanks for joining us. Our top story this afternoon—the biological crisis in Africa has reached new heights of destruction, when earlier today we learned that rescue and relief stations in Cape Town, South Africa were contaminated by carriers of what is now being called the Morningstar Strain by government officials. While many refugees were able to escape by boat, thousands more were left behind on shore."

The station supervisor cued footage they had received of the event. The screen beside Julie began flashing images of helpless refugees standing waist-deep in the ocean, waving frantically to the boats at sea. The video footage was grainy and shaky, taken from a home video camera. The image pulled back, showing the railing of the boat the videographer was standing on.

Cape Town was more or less intact in the background, though here and there plumes of dark, oily smoke rose up from the city.

Julie continued, "What happened next was captured by amateur photographers. Channel Thirteen has decided to air footage of the fall of Cape Town, and warns viewers that the footage may be considered disturbing. Parents, use discretion."

The footage cut to a different cameraman, this one closer to shore on a smaller boat. Voices in the background seemed to be coming from the other passengers, looking at the helpless refugees trying desperately to get to a ship.

Suddenly, the crowd on shore took up a shout, and the mob almost seemed to boil as the people splashed madly into the water, trampling one another into the sandy bottom.

"Infected carriers of the Morningstar Strain become violent and homicidal, hostile to the point of actively seeking new targets to attack," Julie said as the video played. "The Cape Town refugees drew the attention of nearby carriers, and the crowd's reaction cost many refugees their lives."

The video showed the knot of refugees on the shore splitting in two, with half of the group running one direction down the beach, the other half in the opposite direction. A scattered few still tried to swim toward the boats, and a sickening number of bodies floated in the water, drowned or trampled by the mob.

The mob scattered to reveal hundreds of carriers of Morningstar.

They had plowed into the group of refugees from behind, and caught them unaware. Several people were down, clutching bloody wounds caused by the scratching, thrashing limbs of the carriers or their bloodied, gnashing teeth.

A couple of the carriers stumbled about quietly, as if in a daze. Most flicked their heads about, spraying blood and bits of flesh from their mouths as they growled and ran after the surviving refugees with fevered speed. The cameraman zoomed in, trying to capture the action as closely as he could. One refugee was tackled hard by a carrier, and his head was pulled up by the hair as the carrier sank his teeth into the back of his neck. Another's back was flayed as a carrier dragged her nails across the refugee's skin.

"More carriers were coming to the site than the refugees expected. Most were cut off and infected before they made it to safety. The death count is estimated at twelve thousand," Julie said.

The video cut to a new angle. The sun in this tape was lower in the sky and the clouds were beginning to turn red in the early evening hours.

"Four hours later, the destruction was complete," said Julie.

On the tape, the survivors on the shore had vanished completely. There was a new mob standing on the beach, waist-deep in the water.

Carriers.

Thousands upon thousands of them.

They pawed at the sky and each other, a teeming mass of infected humanity. Here and there, the carriers turned on each other, snarling and grabbing one another, falling into the water and rolling as they hissed, scratched, and bit one another. Most, however, stood fixated by the boats offshore. Their heads turned back and forth as if they were looking for some path that would lead them to the survivors onboard. They seemed reluctant to try their hands at swimming. One or two plunged into the water, but quickly resurfaced and dragged themselves back into the shallows.

The tape cut out and Julie took over the screen again.

"U.S. government officials have authorized aid to be sent to the survivors of what is being called the *Cape Town Slaughter*. The USS *Ronald Reagan* left home berth today to set sail for South Africa, acting as the flagship of a task force that will rendezvous east of Bermuda. There is still much to be decided in the matter of containing the Morningstar Strain, and fighters on the aircraft carrier are on standby, waiting for an order to destroy contaminated areas. Joining us now via satellite link to explain the threat of the strain in greater detail is Lieutenant Colonel Anna Demilio from the US Army Medical Research Institute of Infectious Disease. Colonel, welcome."

The studio supervisor split the screen into halves. Julie's smiling face occupied one half, and the other half showed the grainy image of Anna Demilio. She was in her early forties, still attractive, wearing BDUs. She, unlike Julie, was not smiling.

"Thanks, Julie."

"Colonel, the spread of the disease has reached epidemic proportions. Is the speed of contamination something that could have been predicted, or prevented?" Julie asked, shuffling sheets of notes on the desk in front of her.

"Well, Morningstar is one sick puppy, if you'll excuse the expression. It has the potential to transmit itself in an amazingly short period of time, under certain conditions. It is likely, however, that we've seen the fastest period of the epidemic already. In nature, the disease would take over a week to incubate within a host before symptoms first appear. The zero case, or the person who originally contracted the disease at the beginning of the outbreak, probably walked around for that entire period of time, spreading the virus to people he or she encountered, before he or she took ill. Then, a week after that, all the carriers that were infected by the zero fell ill. The second generation is probably responsible for the minor outbreaks in Kinshasa and Mombasa we saw earlier this month, but they had already infected numerous others before they developed symptoms, and so on. Now that Morningstar has dominance on most of the

African continent, contamination should slow somewhat, as most if not all infected people are still on the continent, and the threat of hidden contamination is reduced significantly. So, to answer your original question—yes, we could and did predict the spread of a virus like Morningstar, but there is no real way to prevent such outbreaks from occurring."

"Could the CDC or USAMRIID have sent teams in to contain the disease in its early phases?" Julie asked.

"We could, and we should have," Anna said, folding her hands. "We didn't, simply because the disease was too new and mysterious to accurately judge the threat it presented. If we had sent a team in without a full bank of knowledge, a team member could have become infected and brought the disease home with him or her. Now that we know how it's transmitted, we can better deal with it."

"And how does Morningstar spread from host to host, Colonel?" Julie asked.

"Well, it's not airborne. Viruses like influenza tend to be airborne—that is, you can spread them by coughing or breathing on someone. We should thank God or luck or whatever we believe in for that. Morningstar is transmitted through bodily fluids. We have examined cadavers and found that there is a high concentration of virus in the saliva of carriers, as well as in seminal and vaginal fluids. Then, of course, there's blood."

"So you're saying a person could contract the disease through any contact with infected fluid?" Julie asked.

"Not through *any contact*. Theoretically, you could put your hand in infected blood, and providing you have no cuts or breaks in your skin, you could wash it off and be fine. But most people who come into contact with contaminated material don't take the threat seriously enough and either fail to sterilize their skin thoroughly or assume water will do the trick. Then they might rub their eyes, or even pick their nose, and contract the disease."

"One final question," Julie said, pulling a fresh sheet of notes.

"Okay," replied Anna, leaning forward slightly.

"Do you believe there is a significant risk of Morningstar outbreaks in the United States?"

At this, Anna halted. She opened her mouth as if to speak, but held back. Her eyes flicked to the side and hovered there a moment before darting back to the camera.

"No, Julie," Anna said. Her voice was heavy and subdued. "I don't think we have any reason to worry."

"Well, thanks for joining us, Colonel."

"My pleasure."

"That was Lieutenant Colonel Anna Demilio from the US Army's Medical Research Division. After a word from our sponsors, we'll return with more breaking news from the front lines of the war on Morningstar. This is Julie Ortiz. Thanks for watching Channel Thirteen news!"

The cameraman held up a finger, signaling Julie to wait. She sat patiently, a smile on her face, until he dropped the finger.

" . . . And we're off the air!" he said, letting the camera sag on its base. He pulled the headset from his ear and grinned. "Nice broadcast, Julie!"

But Julie Ortiz wasn't listening. She glared up at the control booth over the studio floor.

"What the hell was that bullshit, Jim?!" she demanded, standing up from behind her desk.

"That bullshit was exactly what the people needed to hear, Julie," said the station supervisor through the intercom.

"And that last question—the one about outbreaks in the US—that doctor's answer was so blatantly false I don't know how I can find the guts to even call myself a journalist after airing it!"

"That's enough, Julie! We air what the Feds tell us to air! We're in a crisis here! The last thing we need is rebelling anchorwomen messing with the flow of information!"

"You know what, Jim?" said Julie. "Air *this*."

She flipped him off.

"You're on thin ice, Julie," the supervisor replied. "Sit down, smile, look pretty, or go find yourself another job."

Grumbling to herself, Julie sank slowly back into her chair.

"I don't know how much longer I can do this," she said.

The cameraman looked sympathetic. "Don't worry. The Feds know what they're doing. They're probably already getting it under control over there."

Julie grimaced. "You know, I'd really love to think that."

Suez
December 31, 2006
2043 hrs_

A steady stream of ferries worked their way across the Suez Canal, bearing loads of terrified refugees and rear-guard soldiers.

The evacuation was taking place as scheduled. General Francis Sherman took a deep pull off his cigar, the coals glowing orange in the darkness. He was almost sixty years old, but was no worse for the wear. General Sherman took pride in passing the same physical fitness tests as eighteen year-old recruits. Now, he was glad for it. He'd been almost two days without sleep and weariness was threatening to overcome him. Before rest, however, came work.

"How long until the last load crosses the Suez?" he asked, breathing a cloud of smoke.

"Another day at most, sir," said Commander Barker, the Naval officer in charge of the transport barges the task force was using to ferry refugees. "We're not having any problems."

"And the bridges?" Sherman asked.

"Planting the demo charges now, sir," said Colonel Dewen, US Army. "We'll be green in thirty. Just give the word and we'll light 'em up."

"We're not expecting any more traffic from the railway or roads, are we?"

"Nothing scheduled, sir, but you never know . . ."

"Barker, get a few of these ferries up to the El Ferdan crossing and El Qantara. If any civvies show up after we blow the bridges, get 'em across by boat."

"Yes, sir."

"There's one snag in the plans, General," said Sergeant Major Thomas, a scarred veteran of Vietnam, Grenada, and Desert Storm. "These refugees—there are more than we thought. We're not going to have enough food or shelter for them all."

"*Damn it*," General Sherman said, frowning. "Well, there's nothing for it, at least for a little while. Distribute what we've got, and dispatch a request for more gear."

"Right, sir."

"Commander, Colonel, come with me, please," Sherman said,

beckoning the two officers to follow him. He led them to a camouflaged pavilion near one of the makeshift docks the Corps of Engineers had built. The pavilion was well lit. A generator hummed nearby. The sounds of the diesel ferry engines, shouting soldiers, and the *whup-whup-whup* of helicopter blades in the sky overhead forced the general to raise his voice slightly to be heard.

"Gentlemen," he began, looking down at a laminated map of the area, "We're in a tactically sound position."

He illustrated, pointing down at the thin blue line of the Suez Canal on the map.

"Here, we're less than five miles from El Ferdan. That's the most probable crossing point for civvies we missed. If any of them show up, we'll be ready to get them across the canal. The tunnel to the south and the crossing farther north will be demo'd, and we'll leave a small contingent of troops to watch for survivors at each point. The canal itself is our most valuable defensive tool." General Sherman then folded up the laminated map to reveal a second map underneath. This one covered less ground, and features such as the railway bridge—the longest in the world—were plainly visible on the grid-lined satellite image. He continued, "If we learned anything at Cape Town, it was that carriers don't like to swim. We've got eggheads working on a hypothesis for it as we speak. Personally, I think they just don't like getting wet. In any case, once the bridges are gone, we'll have successfully cordoned off the Middle East from infected Africa. Commander, are the Seaguards in position?"

"Yes, sir. Battle groups are stationed outside every major port on the continent. The Brits have North Africa covered—there's a task force controlling the Nile delta, another off Tunisia. Germany sent ships a day ago. They're still en route, but when they arrive, they'll take up positions in the Strait of Gibraltar and off Morocco. We've got Cape Town, Port Elizabeth, Mombasa, and the Congo delta blockaded. The *Reagan*'s battle group is steaming toward the Red Sea, with an ETA of thirty hours."

"Good. Let's hope you Navy boys can keep those ports closed. God only knows what would happen if one—*just one*—contaminated person got in a speedboat and made his way past the barricades to another city port."

"And not just the virus, sir," added Commander Barker. "Remember Cairo."

"Yes. There's a lesson for the historians down the line," General Sherman said.

Cairo had been a complete disaster. It was thought originally that the Egyptian city would be the best base of operations for the cleansing and containment of the continent, but panic and disorganization had quickly brought that idea crashing down. Half the city had been consumed in a massive conflagration shortly after soldiers and relief workers began to arrive. Rather than being one of the last bastions of humanity on the continent, it had been one of the first to be fully evacuated. Ironically, there hadn't been a case of Morningstar within five hundred miles. Cairo had torn itself apart. If similar panic was induced in other cities, the destruction could be just as wanton. Sherman shuddered to think of a massively overpopulated city like Shanghai becoming compromised. More people would die at the hands of their fellow panicked humans than at the hands of the virus itself.

"As for us, here at Suez, we've got a tough job too," Sherman went on. "We're the vanguard, gentlemen. This is the only land-based link from Africa to the rest of the world. Gibraltar comes running in a close second, and we've got a similar garrison stationed there. Assuming the carriers are brave enough to test the waters and try to swim across, it'll be our job to hold them at any and all costs." Here General Sherman paused. The two officers looked up at him expectantly. He went on, "And, gentlemen, I do mean at *any* cost." The pair nodded. "I just want to make that abundantly clear. If your own child was scratched by one of those things, I would expect you to kill that child without hesitation. If your own dear mother showed up and tried to get you to stop, I'd expect you to kill her before turning back on those carriers. Nothing—and no one—is to interfere with the defense of this canal. The penalty for interference is death. No court-martial. No juries. No trials. You shoot the person or solve the problem, no questions asked. Understand?"

"Yes, sir," both echoed in unison.

"Good," Sherman said. "Now look here. We're entrenching along our side of the canal. We're putting up razor wire along the shore on both sides—that ought to slow them down and let our sharpshooters take 'em out. We've got demo boys laying down minefields beyond the wire nets—*early warning*, if you will. There are nine artillery batteries ready to fire to the east of us. If any of your boys spot a group of carriers coming at a distance, call in death from above."

Sherman turned his back on the map, facing the canal. A group of refugees was just debarking from one of the ferries. He watched them, puffing on his cigar, before continuing, "We're working with worst-case scenario situations. Assuming the carriers somehow breach the canal lines and get across the water, we're setting up two more lines of defense we can fall back on. The Corps of Engineers is setting up a system of trenches two miles east—defense line one. Beyond that is the First Cavalry—defense line two—consisting of fast attack helicopters and Abrams main battle tanks. Defense line two is a last-ditch, all-out assault. If the enemy gets that far, we're probably already fucked. There are no fences, no wires, no trenches past the canal and line one—just armor and ammo." General Sherman turned back to the two officers under the pavilion. "But we don't have to worry about defense lines one and two. Why? Because we're not letting the damn infection get carried across this canal."

The two officers nodded silently. Colonel Dewen's radio squawked. He mumbled an apology and clicked the handset.

"Echo Lead, reading."

The voice over the radio was slightly garbled, but the words came through clear enough.

"Sir, Echo Two here. Demo set and primed at El Qantara. Echoes One and Three reporting same, over."

"Roger. Hold position and wait for further instructions, over."

"Roger that, sir. Echoes One through Three holding for orders. Out."

Dewen released the handset and turned to the General.

"The bridges and tunnel are ready for demo, sir," he said, grinning slightly.

"I heard," said Sherman. "Let the men know we're about to light up the night."

Commander Barker picked up his own radio and began talking, telling his barge captains to hurry under the railway bridge before it came crashing down. Dewen was on the horn ordering troops near the bridges to move away and take cover. The process took a few minutes, but the two officers finished shortly and nodded to Sherman, who took the radio from Dewen.

"Gentlemen, let's blow up some bridges," he said, allowing himself a rare moment of mirth. Barker remained impassive, but Dewen grinned—the man honestly enjoyed explosions. It was one of the reasons he had chosen to become an infantry officer in the first place. Dewen lifted a pair of binoculars from around his neck and raised them to his eyes, looking in the direction of the railway bridge. Even five miles away, the outline of it was distinctly visible in the night.

Sherman clicked the handset, paging the demo teams.

"Echo Two here."

"Echo Two, this is General Sherman. You are green to go. I repeat, you are green. Give us a count and fire when ready, over."

"Yes, sir!" came the reply. In the background of the transmission, Sherman, Barker, and Dewen could hear Echo Two shouting commands to his men before turning his face back to the mouthpiece of the radio. "Charges primed, safeties off, blowing in ten. Nine. Eight. Seven . . ."

"Here's to containment and a carrier-free Middle East," Dewen said, still looking through his binoculars.

" . . . Three, two, one. Mark."

The night vanished in a brilliant white-hot flash of light. It lasted no longer than a second, and when it faded, the officers under the pavilion could see the roiling orange and black flames that marked where the world's longest railway bridge had just been. The light from the flames illuminated flying metal debris shooting high into the sky. Then the noise hit them, a deep, basic rumbling that first shockwaved through the camp, then shook every item that wasn't bolted down.

Finally, the fire receded until only licking tongues of flame were visible, and the noise vanished entirely.

The radio squawked.

"Echo Two here. Demolition successful. All objectives destroyed. Out."

The entire continent of Africa was now completely contained. Any plane that tried to fly off the landmass would easily become prey for the Superhornets patrolling the airspace.

Any boat that tried to steam out of the area would be sunk by one of the dozens of destroyers, frigates, and attack subs that prowled the waters.

And any vehicle that tried to make its way to the relative safety of the uncontaminated Middle East would find that all three Suez crossings were now nothing more than smoldering piles of rubble.

The largest maximum-security prison in the world just had its grand opening.

Inmates?

Just one.

Its name?

The Morningstar Strain.

PART THREE:
SPARKS

Electronic Mail Window 

From: Anna Demilio <ademilio@usamriid.mil>
To: Francis Sherman <fsherman@pentagon.mil>
Date: January 03, 2007, 09:14:45
Subject: UPDATE

General,

The shit's really starting to fly over here in Washington. The Dems are accusing the Reps of covering up the initial outbreak. The Reps are saying the Dems are holding America back by trying to place blame instead of helping. The Dems counterattack by saying the Reps are too busy shouting down the Dems to be doing anything productive anyway. And so on and so forth.

Nero's fiddling and Rome's burning.

I can tell you that both parties aren't doing jack to help out anything. I went on national TV a little while ago and had Senators dictating my answers to me the whole time. I really wanted to just tell the truth—especially about the dead victims returning to life. But the reporter never asked me directly, and I was ordered not to say anything I didn't have to. Then, right at the end, she asked if I thought America would be contaminated. I really wanted to tell her I thought there was a good chance of it happening, but there was basically a gun to my head. Not literally, but there were guns in the room, and they could have theoretically been pointed at my head if I'd said that. I feel like shit, Frank. I'm lying to the entire country.

I called the journalist who interviewed me a few hours after I finished. She's just as pissed as I am. Seems she had a gun to her head, too. We're collaborating on getting the truth out. I know the government really doesn't need any more pissed-off idealists shooting their mouths off right now, but the people have a right to the truth, don't they?

Anyway, that's what I've been up to. Research is revealing absolutely nil in the way of progress. We've hit a few stumbling blocks in the genetic encoding of the virus, but we're working overtime on it.

How's the desert?

I hear the sun's nice out there.

Lt. Col. Anna Demilio,
US Army Medical Research Institute of Infectious Disease

/end

Quick Reply click MENU for more options

From: Francis Sherman <fsherman@pentagon.mil>
To: Anna Demilio <ademilio@usamriid.mil>
Date: 01.03.07 - 13:51:21
Subject: Re: UPDATE

Anna,

The desert blows Cong chunks. There's sand everywhere—and I do mean everywhere—and there's an infinite number of refugees to look after. We've got an army here in the desert, almost a quarter million troops from all over the world, but a quarter million soldiers to eight million refugees isn't a nice ratio. We're low on food, water, and supplies, and the natives are restless.

We've got the area nice and cordoned, but we just don't know what to do with all these people. Our biggest worry is that some of them may be infected, so we've had to quarantine all of them in camps. We're already being called Nazis. I guess it doesn't matter that the Israeli military is just as gung-ho about keeping the civvies contained as we are; we're simply Nazis for putting them behind barbed-wire fences and keeping our eyes on them. We've got medics clearing refugees, but it's a slow process. As we clear them we let them out of the camps and they're free to go, but it'll take months to check them all, and if any are infected, we'll know within a couple more days.

Despite being undermanned, undersupplied, and outnumbered, we've got a great team here. I'm getting my hands dirty along with everyone else at Camp Forty-Nine near El Ferdan. I've met a lot of great people. You know Colonel Dewen, of course. He's busy keeping the Army grunts in check. Commander Barker has been a godsend. He's made sure every refugee had a ferry to board for the past week.

Then there's a girl named Rebecca Hall I just met two days ago. She's a medic with the Red Cross, and a damned good one. She was at Cairo, and I had dinner with her last night and got her to tell me her story. Can you believe she actually went almost a day without water in this damned desert heat looking after civvies before she finally dropped from exhaustion? If I can find a medal for that, I'll see she gets one. She's got a lot of good insights into the disorganization that took place in Cairo and elsewhere. I'll be faxing a memo to the Pentagon with her thoughts soon.

We've got a functioning airbase here at El Ferdan now, thanks to the Corps of Engineers, and we've even got civilian inbound planes from airstrips in Africa. We're pulling survivors out every minute by land, sea, and air. I met a fellow named Mbutu Ngasy today who's taken over running our makeshift control tower—seems he was one of the first people to run across carriers of Morningstar, if his story is to be believed. He's a damn impressive physical specimen, too. When I first saw him he was hopping out of a Cessna with three full packs of gear

PAGE 01 of 02>

Quick Reply click MENU for more options

and two children sitting on his shoulders. When I get that medal for Rebecca, remind me to get one for him, too.

Mbutu says at first the police thought the problem was cannibals, due to the bite and scratch marks the carriers like to inflict. That makes sense, and explains why they didn't react quicker to the threat down in Mombasa. We haven't had any contact with that city in a while. Mbutu brings news:

Mombasa is a graveyard. No burning, looting, or pillaging, he says. Just death, and lots of it. Apparently a man was bitten near his airstrip in Mombasa and turned at the hospital, infected a few more, and so on and so forth. It's amazing how many macabre stories you get out of these survivors.

Anyway, I've got to go, Anna. Millions of refugees are waiting for lunch, and we don't even have enough MRE's to feed ourselves.

Lt. Gen. Francis Sherman
US Army

P.S. - I've been promoted.

PAGE 02 of 02

Electronic Mail Window

From: Anna Demilio <ademilio@usamriid.mil>
To: Francis Sherman <fsherman@pentagon.mil>
Date: January 03, 2007, 18:01:34
Subject: Re: Re: UPDATE

General,

Or should I say Lieutenant General? Three stars, eh? Congrats. Hope you've got enough spunk left in you to get the fourth.

A young, attractive girl who's also a medic and is into telling war stories? You sound like you've got a crush, Frank.

A strong, tall, African man who's into saving children and surviving outbreaks? Ooh. Be still, my heart.

Lt. Col. Anna Demilio
US Army Medical Research Institute of Infectious Disease

P.S. - I still haven't been promoted.

/end

El Ferdan
January 5, 2007
1522 hrs_

THE SUN WAS beginning to set and the sky was a brilliant hue of orange. Things had settled down along the canal as the soldiers dug in and waited. Here and there came the distinctive pop of an M-16 round being let loose from the confines of a chamber. Carriers kept approaching the canal, one or two at a time, and were systematically put down before they even reached the line of landmines protecting the far bank. The sharpshooters were chuckling amongst themselves, placing bets and taking turns shooting at the infected as they approached.

Some were easier targets than others. Every third or fourth carrier shambled slowly across the sand, dragging its feet and looking more worse for the wear than most of its companions.

The remaining three-fourths of the infected proved harder targets. As soon as they drew within sight of the entrenched soldiers across the canal, they broke into a full-out run, arms outstretched, teeth gnashing. These carriers usually took several attempts to hit, and it was not uncommon to hear a curse ring out directly after a missed shot, and see money change hands. Though gambling was technically against regulations, General Sherman couldn't bring himself to put a stop to it. Hell, he'd participated in more than a few games of craps in his day—why rain on the soldiers' parade?

"There's three more," said Rebecca Hall, looking through a pair of binoculars. She was languidly stretched out in the sand, back against a crate of MRE's.

"Where? Oh, I see 'em, just past that dune, there," said General Sherman, looking through his own pair of binoculars. A shot rang out and one of the carriers fell to the ground, twitching. One of the sharpshooters had drilled the figure dead-on. Sherman grinned. "A fine hit! A palpable hit!"

"What?" asked Rebecca, lowering her binoculars and fixing the General with a curious gaze.

"Nothing. It's from Shakespeare," said Sherman, still grinning.

Rebecca and the General had formed a fast friendship. It was an odd pairing—one, a three-star General who had seen combat spanning four decades, the recipient of almost every military decoration the United States offered, and a commander of armies. The other, a twenty-two year-old young woman fresh from college with almost no real-world experience other than ideals, hopes, dreams, and a little white armband with a Red Cross. The General felt as if he'd gained a daughter, or at least a pupil. The medic felt as if she'd gained a mentor.

"Oh, and I wouldn't know anything about Shakespeare, is that it?" Rebecca asked.

"Not as much as I know. An old general has to have hobbies."

"Alas, poor Yorick, I knew him—"

"Hamlet," said Sherman.

Rebecca felt challenged. "*All the world's a stage, and—*"

"*All the men and women merely players.*"

"Dammit, General! Alright, how about . . . *Cry Havoc! And let—*"

"*—Slip the dogs of war*. Julius Caesar. Third act, first scene, specifically. Don't try to test your elders, Rebecca. We've had a lot more time to memorize the lines of a dead playwright than you have," said Sherman, again chuckling.

"Ever read Heinlein?" mumbled Rebecca.

"Who?" asked a distracted Sherman, looking through his binoculars at the remaining carriers.

"That's what I thought," said Rebecca, a touch of triumph in her voice. A second shot rang out and another carrier fell to the ground, kicking up a small cloud of sand. "It's really too bad these are shamblers. I'd like to see your sharpshooters have a little challenge."

The soldiers and relief workers had taken to calling the slower carriers *shamblers* after their hesitant, swaying walk. The faster carriers were being called *sprinters*. All in all, they estimated they'd shot about a hundred shamblers and sprinters in the past few days.

"I wonder why some are slow and others are fast," Rebecca commented.

General Sherman glanced at her from behind the lenses of his binoculars, but said nothing. It was true he could reveal what he knew about the Morningstar Strain and the positive proof they had of clinically dead bodies reviving, but he chose not to burden Rebecca with the knowledge.

As it stood, the only people who knew about that aspect of the virus were the powerful elite and whichever refugees from the continent had witnessed one of the deceased victims reanimate. Sherman had already lassoed several of the soldiers and workers who had heard the stories from the refugees and told them to keep it under wraps, and to spread the word to the refugees to do the same. He knew there was no way to keep it secret forever—or even for much longer. The survivors of the contamination of Africa weren't under anyone's orders. Tongues would wag.

"It doesn't matter," he finally said. "It's an entire continent. They'll probably just keep coming like this, in scattered groups. They're mostly mindless, I think. Probably just wandering around. We'll just keep 'em contained and let 'em starve to death."

"How long will that take?" Rebecca asked. "I mean, a person starves in about a week. The infected people on the other side of that canal have been about for weeks now."

"Maybe a lot of them starved days ago. Maybe we're just seeing the new recruits," Sherman replied.

Rebecca let herself delve into the possibilities.

"Well, maybe it alters their metabolism. Can a virus do that? I really don't know. I can splint a broken leg but I don't know thing one about viruses."

"I don't know either. We've got eggheads who work on that stuff," Sherman said. "They build the saw and hand it to me. I do the cutting."

Rebecca glanced askew at the General, who was studiously ignoring the girl. "So you *have* read Heinlein."

The General smiled wordlessly.

"General!" came a gruff voice. Sherman swiveled his head and spied Sergeant Major Thomas jogging over to them. The sergeant slowed to a walk and saluted. From the ground, Rebecca smiled and waved at him. Thomas didn't acknowledge her existence.

Sherman returned the salute. "What's the news, Thomas?"

"Satcom's got an update for you, sir. They think you might want to come have a look," Sergeant Major Thomas said.

"Oh, for Chrissake, Thomas, I don't need to verify every time a city on the continent catches fire or put my signature on bad weather reports."

"They strongly recommend you have a look, sir," Sergeant Major Thomas said, features expressionless. General Sherman had known Thomas long enough to know when he was being deadly serious.

"Alright, alright," Sherman said after a moment, pulling himself to his feet with a heavy-winded sigh. "Lead on."

"Have fun," said Rebecca. She lifted the binoculars back to her eyes as a third shot rang out. The final shambler in the group pitched face-first into the sand. "*Oh, got him*," she whispered.

Thomas opened the door to the trailer that held the satellite communication equipment for the encampment and propped it open with one arm, letting the General enter. There was a young lieutenant in charge, leaning over the shoulder of one of his subordinates as they studied a display. As Sherman walked in, the lieutenant spied him and snapped to attention.

"Group, atten-HUT!"

The soldiers began scrambling to their feet, but Sherman waved them off.

"As you were," he said quickly. "What's the problem, lieutenant?"

"Sir!" said the young officer. "We've got a few interesting images off the continent from one of our spysats. We've been working on cleaning it up."

Sherman pulled up a folding chair and propped one leg up, folding his arms across his knees as he looked at the screen the lieutenant was gesturing at.

"This is the east bank of the Nile near what's left of Cairo. We've been monitoring the delta for the British battle group stationed there, trying to give them advance warning of any ships trying to clear the delta and hit the Mediterranean Sea. We've picked up trawlers, tugs, and even one kayak, and that lets the Brits—"

"Get to the point, Lieutenant. I was busy doing nothing when you called, and I'd like to get back to it."

"Yes, sir. Anyway, our spysat's delicate enough to pick up a single person from space. We tried focusing on Cairo to test it out, and we got this."

The officer punched in a few commands and the image on the screen flicked to a closer-in shot of the burned out city. The streets looked strange, as if there were ants crawling all over the pavement. The image zoomed in closer, and Sherman saw that what he had thought to be ants were actually carriers. Thousands of them.

"We backtracked through the spysat memories and found out

these infected are the refugees that stayed behind in Cairo after the fires. Morningstar must have reached them. We're thinking one of the sprinters made good time and started spreading the disease from further south. But that's not the disturbing part."

The image changed again. Sherman noticed the timestamp was dated only a couple hours before.

This one showed the multitude of carriers flowing across the bridges, heading east. Heading straight towards the Sinai desert—and the Suez Canal.

"At first we thought they'd actually grouped together, formed a battle plan, and decided to head for us," explained the officer. "We double-checked and realized there was one more refugee who decided to make a run for it. He's in a semi trailer headed our way now. Unfortunately for us, half the city noticed his exit and decided to chase him."

The Satcom image switched to the overhead view of a truck barreling through the desert. It was halfway between Cairo and Suez. The carriers were miles and miles behind, but they had a single-mindedness about them. They'd head in the direction their prey went until they ran him down—or found new prey.

Sherman now knew why Thomas had insisted he see what Satcom had to say.

"How long until they reach Suez?" he whispered.

"The sprinters slowed down once the truck was out of sight," the officer said. "They're moving at a nice walk, about two miles per hour. We've got some time on our hands. But they'll be knocking at the door very soon."

"Where?"

"Suez, down at the Red Sea end. The truck driver's thinking of using the tunnel, I think. Too bad we blew it up, sir."

They were at El Ferdan now, north of where the carriers would approach the canal. The soldiers were dug in along the length of the canal, but if there was going to be a duke-out at a certain point, he wanted to be in the thick of it. No, more than that. As the ranking officer present, it was his *duty* to be in the thick of it. Sherman looked at the images a moment longer before turning to face Sergeant Major Thomas.

"Thomas, let's pack up. We're going to Suez."

Washington, D.C.
January 5, 2007
2045 hrs_

"Is all this cloak-and-dagger stuff really necessary?" asked Julie Ortiz from behind her oversized aviator sunglasses. She was sitting in the booth farthest from the door in a mom-and-pop restaurant. The place was dimly lit and the waitresses were surly, but the food was decent. That was one of the only things keeping her from leaving. The other thing keeping her from running to the nearest three-star establishment was her companion.

"Yes, it is," said Anna Demilio from the opposite side of the booth, her back to the door. She was dressed in civilian clothes and wore a faded baseball cap. "I already found three bugs in my apartment. They're really watching everyone who could spill the beans about Morningstar."

"How do you know they're not watching us right now?" asked Julie, smirking.

"They probably are. But I wanted to take some precautions anyway," said Anna. "What have they been feeding you about Morningstar?"

"The usual crap," Julie replied, sipping on a mug of coffee. "How it's completely contained now, casualty figures, cost estimates on rebuilding an entire continent once it dies down."

"Hmm," Anna murmured, spreading butter across a slice of toast. "Maybe I'm deluding myself with the idea that the virus is going to jump continents. Maybe I'm underestimating the military's ability to contain it."

"Now you sound like them," Julie said, frowning. "It's a fucking *virus*. It's not an enemy army. You can't shoot a virus or aim a missile at it. You can't lock your door and hope it'll knock first. It'll find a way in."

"I know, I know! I'm the epidemiologist, remember?" said Anna. "But this virus really needs a host to spread. We've been doing experiments. Some species are natural carriers and never develop any symptoms. Remember Reston?"

Julie gave Anna a blank look.

"Ebola Reston?" Anna prompted.

Still, Julie looked blank.

"Ebola Reston is a strain named after Reston, Virginia. A primate house there noticed a few of the monkeys were becoming sick with a kind of hemorrhagic fever. They sent samples to the CDC and USAMRIID, and it came back positive for Ebola. At first it was completely hushed up, and we sent biohazard teams in to sterilize the facility and quarantine the workers. You media types got suspicious, but all you got were pictures of us in containment suits and a little speculation from onlookers. We killed all the primates inside, disposed of the bodies, and nuked the place with chemicals. For a couple days, the Reston primate house was the only place on Earth where absolutely nothing lived."

Julie shuddered a little at the thought of the place being completely devoid of any kind of life, even viral.

"Turns out we were lucky. The strain only manifested in certain simian species. The workers in the house contracted the virus, of course, but never developed any symptoms. Today, in the U.S., there are probably thousands of people carrying around Ebola Reston from that one little outbreak. God knows what would've happened if it had been any other strain."

"So you mean there could be monkeys carrying around Morningstar? So what? They'll stay in Africa."

"Exactly," Anna said through a mouthful of toast. "It needs human hosts—the ones susceptible to it—to really spread. So, I mean, theoretically, if we contain the human hosts, maybe we really can contain the virus."

"Yeah, but if just *one* of the carriers got past the blockades—"

"Let's not think about that. But let me say that while the theory of containment is sound, Africa is a huge fucking continent. There's no way to cover every little egress port without stretching ourselves so thin that the line would become unsound. We do have all the ground routes off the continent covered well, though, so unless a carrier knows how to operate a ship or fly an airliner, we might be okay."

"Right, right. I already know all this," Julie said. "We've been debating it with the talking heads on all the major networks for weeks now. What's this big secret you wanted to tell me?"

"Alright. You might want to put down that coffee cup first," Anna began, nodding at the mug in Julie's hands. Julie set it down slowly. "Ready?"

Julie nodded, leaning forward in anticipation.

Anna announced in a low voice, "*Morningstar reanimates dead hosts.*"

Julie blinked at the doctor. After a moment, she chuckled.

"You've got to be shitting me. I was hoping for science *fact*, not *fiction*."

"It *is* science fact," said Anna, pulling a folded manila envelope from her pocket and laying it out on the table. "Look."

Julie pulled out the contents of the folder. There were medical charts, x-rays, graphs, and a few glossy black-and-white file photos. She focused on these, setting aside the other items.

The first picture showed a thirty-something man strapped to an examination table. His face was contorted into a feral snarl and he shimmered with sweat. His hair was unkempt, and he was drooling slightly. One of his hands was bloody and his skin was scratched all over as if he had run through a thicket of thorn bushes.

"This is Dr. Klaus Mayer," said Anna, explaining. "He was brought over by the Air Force from Mombasa hospital in the first days of the epidemic. What you're seeing here is a man who has succumbed to the Morningstar strain. At this point he was running a fever of around one hundred and six Fahrenheit, his pulse and respiration were rapid and his brain waves were highly erratic. He was openly hostile to anything around him that was alive. We experimented and found he wasn't just hostile towards human beings. He reacted the same way to lab rats we left in the room—rabbits, goats, anything with a pulse. This is the side of Morningstar you're familiar with."

"Yes," said Julie, scrutinizing the photo. "I've seen pictures of other victims. They look just like this Mayer guy."

"Look at the next one."

Julie flipped to the second photo. This one showed doctors in surgical gear gathered around Klaus Mayer. Julie recognized Anna in the photo, even behind her protective glasses and face mask. There was a man in the foreground cradling a .30-06 rifle in his hands. Julie felt her stomach knot up.

"We had some new information at this point in the study from a military official who's rather high-up," Anna explained, not mentioning General Sherman's name. "It seemed rather unbelievable, but I trust my source, so we decided to test the theory. Next picture."

Julie flipped. The third photo showed a close-up of Klaus Mayer on the examination table. There was a bloody hole center mass, and his eyes were no longer hostile—they were glazed over and half closed. His head had rolled limply to one side and his arms and legs no longer fought against the restraints that held him to the table.

"We shot Dr. Mayer through the chest at almost point-blank range," Anna said.

"I can see why you've been keeping this a secret. The humanitarian groups would be all over you for this."

"No," said Anna. "I'm not so much worried about shooting Mayer as I am about what happened next."

Julie flipped to the fourth and final photo. She gasped. Dr. Mayer was struggling against his restraints again, mouth open in a growl at the cameraman. He was no longer sweating, but he was definitely alive and animated.

"Dr. Mayer reanimated a few hours after we killed him," Anna explained. "He had a pulse and his respiratory system was functioning, but at almost undetectable levels. His brain activity, on the other hand, went off the chart. It's as if his brain went into hyper-speed when he reanimated, with synapses firing at around six times the normal rate for a healthy human."

"He's a zombie," breathed Julie.

"I suppose by definition he would be," Anna said. "But we at USAMRIID don't use sci-fi terms. We prefer to call him a *deceased ambulatory viral host*."

"So he's a zombie," said Julie, still focused on the picture.

Anna rolled her eyes. "Whatever."

"Are all the carriers like this?"

"No," Anna said. "Most of them are living victims. They exist in a kind of fever-dream from what we've learned. Think rabies crossed with some of the early symptoms of traditional hemorrhagic fever. If they're killed, they die like anyone else. I don't think that Klaus Mayer is aware he's still moving around. Before we shot him, I'm sure there was a shred of consciousness left within him. No, Dr. Mayer is truly dead and gone. His body, on the other hand, is still making the rounds. We think the virus assumes direct control of the host if the host itself kicks the bucket. Sort of like switching from autopilot to manual."

"Is this why . . ." Julie began.

" . . . Some of the carriers are so slow? Yes," replied Anna. "The virus seems to play off the reflex actions of the host body to keep it moving. That's why they seem so drunken and hesitant in their movements. Also, the body's dead. It's beginning to decay. The viruses can still reproduce in the cells that haven't died and decayed, but the body loses more and more mobility every passing day. We tested Dr. Mayer's corpse. He still reacts to stimuli as he did when alive, but it's like he's really high, or mentally retarded. Just as hostile as ever once you manage to get his attention though."

Julie said nothing for a minute, then suddenly blurted all at once, "This is beyond amazing. This is the story of a lifetime. No, this is the story of the century—*millennium*, even! This is the story to end all stories!"

"Be careful what you do with that," Anna said sharply, nodding at the envelope. "You can do what you want with it. It's yours to use. But think of the ramifications of publishing that story."

Julie's star-struck expression faded slightly.

"Yeah. I see what you mean. There'd be the religious groups who would call it the end of the world, fanatics would snap, people would organize mass suicides . . . I remember what happened when the comet passed by Earth a few years ago."

"Hale-Bopp," said Anna. "Organized suicides all over the world. People thought it signaled the coming of the messiah. The morons."

"Not to mention the riots," Julie said. "Anytime there's news that even hints at something destabilizing there's always a rush to the stores to stock up on toilet paper and skim milk."

"There would be people getting trampled to death, killed for a loaf of bread, shot for a gallon of gasoline," agreed Anna. "So it's my advice to you to weigh your options. On the one hand, you can keep this a secret and keep lying to the world about the seriousness of this virus."

"And on the other hand, I could tell the world and maybe kill thousands in the process."

"Yeah. Funny how when you finally know the truth, the

temptation to keep it secret starts to nag at you. So I guess the question you have to ask yourself now, Julie, is this: *how many lives is the truth worth*?"

Julie looked down at the manila envelope and photographs in front of her. Her coffee mug sat forgotten on the table, tendrils of steam winding their way into the air. Finally, she looked up and fixed Anna with a stare.

"I guess I really don't have much of a choice," Julie said. "I know what I have to do."

Sinai Desert
January 7, 2007
1302 hrs_

The ancient cassette player duct-taped to the dashboard of the deuce-and-a-half that was rumbling through the desert suddenly died, fading quickly to silence.

"Fucknuts!" swore Private First Class Ewan Brewster, beating on the recorder with the flat of his palm.

"Could you maybe watch the road?" said the man riding in the cab alongside the private.

"What? Oh, yeah, you got it, bro. Got any double-A's on you? This sonufabitch eats batteries for breakfast," Brewster said. "You're a photographer, right, Denton? Don't you guys have batteries for your flashes?"

Freelance photographer Sam Denton grinned wryly behind his dark sunglasses. He wordlessly reached into one of the pockets of his sand-colored utility vest and pulled out a small plastic box.

"Couple watch batteries and three double-A's," Denton said, waving the box under Brewster's nose. The private flicked his eyes between the road and the box. Finally he made a grab for it. The photographer snatched the box back, shaking his head.

"These go in my expense report. I need to be in the black after this assignment—I've got a motorcycle payment to make next month."

"Ah, shit, man. You're telling me you'll go the rest of the way to Suez in this empty-ass desert without any tunes just to save yourself a buck? Look, there's a Metallica album duct-taped to the bottom of your seat. No real American can say no to that, eh, comrade?"

"I'm Canadian," Denton revealed, smiling.

"Double fucknuts. The Captain didn't tell me I'd have a Canuck in my truck. Damn, man, no respect at all for us low-ranking types, I swear . . ."

"Hey, you want these batteries or not?" Denton said, chuckling at the private. "Even a Yank like you can appreciate that I've got the power in my hands."

"That's a terrific pun, *mon frere*. But fuckin' A. No, make that fuckin' double-A," Brewster said, beating one hand against the wheel of the truck. "Bring on the metal."

Denton fumbled with the cassette deck. Brewster watched as the photographer slid the backing off the old player and popped out the dead batteries.

"Be careful, man, the wires in there are loose ever since I—"

Denton glanced up in time to see the deuce in front of them slowing sharply.

"Brewster! Brake!" he yelled.

The private's eyes shot forward and he cursed, slamming the brakes on the heavy truck. Sand kicked up all around them as they skidded to a stop, and the tape player slid out of Denton's hands as he scrambled for something to hold on to. Brewster managed to spin the truck's wheels to the right and they came to a rest beside the truck that had been in front of them moments before.

"I think you'll listen the next time I tell you to watch the road, eh?" Denton said, laying the Canadian accent on thick, just to irk the private.

Brewster coughed Sinai dust from his throat. He fished a handkerchief from his BDU pocket and held it over his mouth.

"That's not funny, man. I'm responsible for this piece of taxpayer junk," he said, voice muffled by the cloth.

"Brewster! What in the name of all that is holy and democratic are you doing to my truck?" came a voice from outside the cab. Brewster swung the door open, still coughing, and looked into the livid face of Colonel Dewen. He seemed impervious to the dust cloud that still hung about the deuce.

"I couldn't see through the sand, sir?" Brewster said tentatively.

"Bullshit!" yelled Dewen. "You've been driving this deuce for a month now, and this is your third bang-up! I'll article fifteen your sorry ass, soldier! Get it together!"

Denton decided he was staying out of it. He said nothing, and instead picked up the tape deck from the floor of the cab, inspecting it for damage.

"Sorry, sir," Brewster said, dropping the funny-guy act. "I let myself get distracted. It won't happen again."

"That's more like it. Now dismount and get up-front. We're having trouble raising Suez," Colonel Dewen said, scowling at Brewster before moving on down the line to the next truck in the convoy.

"Come on, bud, step lively or face the wrath of Dewen," Brewster said, slapping a hand against Denton's shoulder.

Brewster landed deftly in the soft sand outside, slinging his M-16A2 over his shoulder with practiced ease. Denton slid out the opposite side of the cab with a little less luck, catching a camera strap on the door and cursing as he struggled to untangle it. He met up with Brewster in front of the vehicle.

"What's this all about?" Denton asked, wiping sweat and dust from his forehead. The convoy had ground to a halt all along its mighty length and soldiers were climbing out of vehicles in confusion.

"Don't know," Brewster said. "Hey! Darin! What's the Sitrep?"

"The Sitrep is this sand blows camel balls, and your mother's blowin' em, too, Brewster, you honkey bastard!" came the shouted reply from a few trucks over.

"That means he doesn't know," Brewster translated.

Denton spied a group of figures near the head of the convoy, the heat waves making them appear distorted. There was a radioman Denton made out easily enough—the bulky field radio on the man's back gave him away, as did the wobbly metal antenna that bobbed over his shoulder. The only other man Denton could identify had to be General Sherman—the older man held the radio's handset to his ear and had his other hand on his hip. Even from a distance the photographer could tell that Sherman was frustrated.

"Looks like the party's up ahead," Denton said to Brewster.

"Let's crash it," replied the private, making Denton flinch. The mention of crashing so soon after the overzealous private's driving wasn't reassuring.

The pair shuffled through the sand towards the lead truck in the convoy. Other soldiers had already gathered around, waiting to hear the update on the situation. The convoy had been traveling for almost two hours—slow going on the dirt and sand roads of the Sinai desert. Most of them were glad for the chance to stretch their legs.

As they approached the head of the convoy, Denton could make out General Sherman's words.

"Suez, Suez, this is Echo Lead. Do you read, over? Respond on any channel. Suez, Suez, this is Echo Lead . . ."

Denton had seen enough military campaigns in his years as a photojournalist to know that losing contact with an advance base was never a good thing. He wondered what had happened in Suez. Thoughts began to race through his mind, most of them unpleasant. Maybe the carriers broke through. Maybe there had been an ordnance malfunction. Or maybe the radio operator just wasn't paying attention.

Brewster took a knee near the edge of the group, motioning for Denton to join him. The photographer declined, instead popping the lens cap off his Nikon camera and lining up shots while he could.

General Sherman gave up on trying to reach Suez and dropped the handset into the radioman's pack. He sighed heavily and turned to the officer next to him. Denton glanced at the uniform, saw it read 'U.S. Navy,' and surmised this was Commander Barker. He tried to get in closer to hear what they were discussing, but Sherman and Barker had lowered their voices. The murmured conversations of the gathered soldiers weren't helping either.

Colonel Dewen came marching back up from the rear of the convoy and joined the conference. Denton was getting annoyed at not being able to hear the words of the three officers. He tried to edge his way around the semicircle of enlisted troops, but didn't want to appear too nosy—his press credentials were limited and the state of affairs in the world wasn't the best for messing with Lieutenant Generals.

Denton had an idea of what they were discussing, however. Two other times he'd seen advance bases go down—once in Bosnia, when a guard post had failed to check in, and again in Mogadishu, when a forward intersection stopped reporting. Both times the decision had been made to hit the spot with armor and artillery.

Just as Sherman seemed to be wrapping up the conversation with a grim look on his face, the radio clicked on. All the soldiers, including Denton, jumped a little. It was the last thing they had expected.

"Echo, Echo, this is Suez. Are you still there, over?"

General Sherman snatched the handset from the radio pack and held it to his ear.

"Suez, where the hell have you been? We've been trying to raise you for a quarter of an hour. Be advised we were two minutes from shelling your position into dust, over."

"Sorry, sir. We had a bit of a situation here," came the reply. "Area is secure now. It's safe to proceed, over."

"I expect a damn good story when I get there," said General Sherman. "Start thinking up a good sitrep. We're on our way down."

"Oh, man, this isn't good," Brewster said out of the side of his mouth to Denton. "Sounds like Suez is a clusterfuck. Sherman's gonna be pissed."

Denton frowned. He asked, "Clusterfuck?"

"Everything's gotta be FUMTU in Suez," Brewster explained.

Denton raised an eyebrow.

"*Fucked Up More Than Usual*," the private said, groaning. "Come on, man. Everyone knows FUMTU."

"It had better not be," Denton said. "I'd love to see how well we can defend the canal if our defenses aren't up to snuff."

"Oh. Yeah," Brewster said, fingering the strap of his M-16. "Forgot about the whole virus thing."

Denton cringed. The cream of the United States Army, indeed.

PART FOUR:

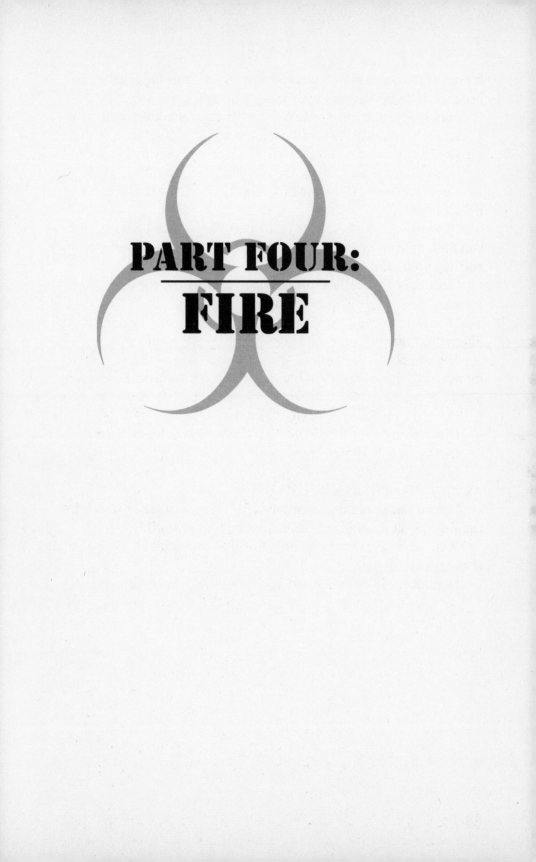

FIRE

Suez
January 7, 2007
1634 hrs_

Suez Base was a mess.

The first thing that the convoy from El Ferdan noticed as they rolled through the security checkpoint was the pile of burning corpses near the water's edge. Thick black smoke poured from the macabre bonfire, blotting out the sun. Soldiers supervising the burning turned to look at the newcomers, faces obscured by heavy Middle-Eastern style handkerchiefs they'd tied around their noses to help guard against the stench of roasting flesh.

Wire fences had been overturned, sandbagged bunkers were half-collapsed, and the sandy streets were pockmarked with black rings of carbon and debris from hand grenade explosions. The buildings were peppered with bullet holes.

"Fuck," breathed Brewster as the convoy pulled up to the base HQ. "What the hell happened here?"

The ranking officer present was a sergeant first-class named Decker. He had greeted the arriving convoy at the edge of the HQ's perimeter, waving them down as they approached. He cradled a wounded arm and his face was grim.

"Glad to have reinforcements," he'd said. "There's only fifty of us left."

General Sherman had balked at the number, and had asked just how they had taken so many casualties without command getting wind of the situation.

"It was the refugees, sir," Decker said. "We had a ship arrive out of the Red Sea this morning. We saw people on the deck. We helped them off and then sent a team onboard to clear the ship. They opened a bulkhead to a lower deck and were overrun. There must have been sixty, maybe seventy carriers in that ship."

Decker went on to explain how the carriers had almost immediately brought down the boarding party. The shore guards had tried to cut the ship loose and set it adrift on the Red Sea, but the carriers were too fast. They'd run down the gangplank and spread like angry hornets through the camp, attacking the nearest living, breathing thing they set their eyes on.

"That ship was the *Charon,* and opening that bulkhead let the demons loose right in the middle of us," Decker said, eyes distant.

The soldiers had mounted a resistance, shifting the razor-wire fencing that surrounded the base to block off access from the docks. They'd formed a firing line behind the relative safety of the wires and hammered down.

"We killed them all. It only took us a minute or two," Decker said, casually referring to the deaths of nearly a hundred victims of the disease. "And then we started gathering the bodies for burial."

Decker and his fellow soldiers had donned their MOPP gear and began neatly lining the bodies up. They slung their rifles, gritted their teeth, and took care of the dirty work. They also let their guard down.

"Sir, you can chapter me if you want to, but I swear I'm not insane," Decker said next.

"Nobody is saying you're insane. This isn't Vietnam, and these weren't innocent civilians," General Sherman said.

"You did good, sergeant," chimed Colonel Dewen.

"No, wait, listen," Decker said, eyes flashing. "We killed them, but . . . we didn't kill them."

"What?" asked Commander Barker.

General Sherman said nothing, but knew in his heart what he was about to hear.

"They got back up," said Decker. "They got back up, and they *slaughtered us.*"

At first it was just a couple. The soldiers had figured they had wounded—but not finished—the targets. They had put three-round bursts into the chests of the risen carriers. It didn't even slow them down.

"At that point, sir, order disintegrated," Decker said.

Some of the soldiers had lost control immediately, screaming about the impossibility of what their eyes were seeing. Others flung their rifles into the sand and had run off into the desert. A few kept their heads and had emptied entire magazines into the shambling dead, rocking the bodies with lead, but those that were knocked down crawled back to their feet and continued the slow, relentless assault. Soldiers were surrounded or trapped, then pulled down, shrieking, as grasping hands scratched at their skin and teeth clamped onto their arms.

And all the while, more and more of the carriers were re-awakening.

"Soon the whole lot of them were back up and moving," Decker said. "Then me and a couple others noticed that some of the infected personnel weren't getting back up. Those had head wounds, broken necks, that sort of thing. Thought that might be important intel, sir."

Decker had organized a last-ditch offense near the edge of the base camp. He was certain the soldiers had been routed and the day belonged to the Morningstar strain and its victims. He armed his soldiers with the remaining ammo and told them to aim for the head.

The soldiers turned the tide.

It had taken nearly an hour of bloody fighting through the dusty streets of Suez to kill the remaining carriers. When the attackers were down, Decker and the other soldiers had performed a tent-by-tent, house-by-house search of the base, finding and eliminating six more carriers, each one a potential death sentence for the parts of the world that remained uninfected.

"This time we made sure, sir," Decker said.

"Made sure?" Commander Barker asked.

Decker fixed him with a gaze. "We shot the bodies in the head, sir. All of them. Even our own. Then we piled them up, doused them in kerosene, and torched 'em."

For a moment, the new arrivals were silent. Finally, General Sherman spoke up.

"Where'd you get that arm wound, son?" he asked.

Decker flexed his right arm. His bicep was sliced, and blood coated the arm of his BDU top. The wound was superficial, and someone had tied a bandage around it.

"Can't rightly remember, sir. I believe it was shrapnel, friendly fire. Accidental," Decker said.

"You weren't bitten, scratched, anything like that?" Sherman asked.

"No, sir. None of them got near me. I made sure of that," Decker replied.

"Good enough for me," Sherman said. "Now I need you to assemble your men, sergeant. I've got bad news for them. The fight's just started."

1911 hrs_

The battle lines were drawn.

The soldiers had spent the past two hours reinforcing their foxholes and dragging the broken remnants of razor wire to the edge of the canal to bolster the fence line.

The Satcom operators had set up their mobile transmitting station and were working on downloading updated images of the desert east of Suez. Ammunition and grenades were re-distributed. Wounded soldiers were given a painkiller and told to walk it off—every rifleman available would be needed on the banks of the Suez Canal.

Brewster grunted as he heaved another sandbag onto the rim of his newly-dug foxhole, pausing for a moment to wipe sweat from his forehead. Denton crouched nearby, taking the opportunity to snap a photo of the soldier.

"Picture this," Brewster said, flipping the finger to Denton.

Denton snapped a second picture in response.

"You could be helping instead of taking Polaroids," said Corporal Darin, another soldier from Brewster's unit.

"I don't get paid to fill sandbags," Denton said. "You guys do."

"You won't be getting paid to shoot the carriers of Morningstar, either, Denton," said Colonel Dewen, surprising all three men as he loomed up behind them. "But you'll be doing it anyway."

Dewen tossed a rifle to the photographer, who caught it deftly with one hand.

"I haven't fired one of these in years," Denton said, working the bolt of the M-16 and checking the chamber before slinging it over his shoulder in one swift motion. His familiarity with the weapon startled Dewen, Brewster, and Darin. All three had assumed him to be entirely civilian. "I'm not sure if I'll do any good."

"Try," said Dewen. "If you only hit one of those shamblers, it might be enough to win the day."

"Can't argue with that," Denton said. "I'll do what I can."

"How's it coming, soldiers?" Dewen asked, switching the focus of his attention from the photographer to the two enlisted men shoulder-deep in the sand.

"Slow, sir," Darin replied. "Ground's a little sandy."

Brewster smirked, but cut himself off when he noticed Dewen glaring at him.

"Dig in good. The carriers might not be shooting at you, but you'll be glad you've got a stable firing position when they come over those dunes," Dewen said, glancing across the canal at the seemingly infinite sandy expanse beyond.

"Yes, sir," replied the two men.

"I'll be back in ten. Denton, come with me," Dewen said, turning on his heel and heading toward Suez HQ. Denton rose from his crouch and followed the Colonel, struggling a little to keep up. The man was a fast walker.

"What's up, Colonel?" Denton asked.

"Let the General explain."

Denton couldn't get anything else out of the recalcitrant officer, and gave up trying after a few more futile attempts. The pair reached the base headquarters—nothing more than a ripped and battered tent surrounded by sandbags—and pulled the door flap aside. It took Denton a few moments to blink the sudden darkness away when the flap fell closed behind him. As his eyes adjusted, he saw that the Satcom team had settled in nicely. Computers hummed and keyboards clicked away as the soldiers synched their machines with the satellites orbiting somewhere overhead.

General Sherman was standing in the corner of the tent, resting one hand on a folding table while he spoke with a third party over the field radio.

"No, one of each," he was saying. "I'm not looking for a strike force, I'm looking for a rescue team. Yes, that's right. One Huey, one Apache. That should do. Can you manage that?"

Denton couldn't hear the response. The radio could be set to broadcast replies through a speaker so soldiers could hear responses in the heat of combat, but the General had turned that function off, using the handset like a telephone in the relative safety of the headquarters tent.

"Good," Sherman said. "And be ready with the rest of that squadron. I may need to call in a real strike at any time. Have them hot and ready to fly. Out."

The General replaced the handset and sighed, rubbing his temples.

"Sir, Denton's here, as per request," Dewen reported.

"What? Oh, yeah. Denton. Let's take a walk, son," General Sherman said, leading Denton back out of the tent. The photographer craned his neck at the screens the Satcom soldiers were working on, trying to catch a glimpse of whatever it was they were looking at. Of course he and the other soldiers in the convoy, as well as the soldiers left in Suez Base, had been briefed on what was coming their way—an entire city's worth of infected carriers—but he wanted to see for himself. Before he could register anything useful, he found himself outside.

General Sherman heaved another heavy sigh and pulled a cigar from his breast pocket. He took his time lighting it. Denton stood next to him, hands in his pockets, saying nothing. The general puffed on the cigar until the cherry glowed red, and he blew a contented cloud of smoke into the darkening sky.

After a moment Sherman said, "Denton, there's a hellstorm headed this way."

"I know."

"You sure you want to be here when it hits?"

"I'm sure."

"Why?"

"This is where I've always been, General. Right in the middle of the shit. Now here I am, right in the middle of the biggest shitstorm of them all, and there's no way I'm missing the show," Denton replied.

"You could be back home, having a cup of coffee and watching it on the evening news," Sherman said.

"I help *make* the evening news, General."

"Why? Why is war so interesting? Why is seeing thousands of infected people being gunned down something newsworthy?"

"Are you trying to say you don't want anyone taking pictures of what's going to happen here, General?" Denton said, narrowing his eyes almost imperceptibly.

"Not at all. I'm asking why you would want to take pictures of it in the first place. I don't make the regs. I just follow them."

"Someone's got to show the world, General."

"Call me Francis. Or Frank. You're not enlisted, after all."

"Alright, Frank. Someone's got to show the world. Like you said, tonight thousands of people are going to die. I don't know what all this is about them getting back up once they're dead, but if they really do then we'll see thousands of people die twice tonight. That's something that has to be recorded somehow. We wouldn't have history if no one bothered to report it."

"You'd glorify the massacre of these people?" Sherman asked.

Denton felt his stomach churn, and anger boiled within him.

"I don't know where you get your ideas, Francis," Denton snapped, "But I'm no dirt-digging stereotypical journalist. I've watched just as many soldiers bleed and die as you have over the years. The only difference between you and me, Frankie, is that you make the wounds. I show the world the wounds you've made."

That seemed to hit the mark. Instead of taking the bait, however, General Sherman let a smile spread across his features.

"That's what I wanted to hear, son," he said. "You can stay for the shitstorm if you want to. You have my blessing."

Denton was taken aback. He hadn't expected this after the general's other comments.

"Thanks, General," he managed.

"No problem," replied Sherman, puffing on his cigar. "And just one more thing before you go back to the line."

"Yes?"

"I'd like to clarify something. There will always be folks who will be willing to go out of their way to '*make wounds*' on the souls and bodies of their fellow people. I'm not one of them. I'm here to wound the sinners, not the innocents."

Denton managed a grim smile and said, "The people coming at us tonight aren't all sinners, though."

"It's a unique situation, son," Sherman said. "It can't be helped."

"No moral quandaries?"

"No," Sherman said. "They've been drafted by the enemy. There's only one real course of action—kill them, or be killed."

"Then we'll kill them," Denton said. "And we'll let God sort them out."

2102 hrs_

With the loud humming of controlled voltage, the floodlights on the west bank of the Suez Canal came online, illuminating the battle lines in a kind of ghostly, flickering white light.

Beneath the floods were the soldiers, hunkered in their foxholes.

Their rifles were aimed at the bank beyond, shifting barrels nervously in the diffuse light. Their line stretched off into the darkness in both directions. No one spoke out loud, but here and there came a whispered query.

"Where are they?"

"They're coming soon."

"Keep your eyes open."

"Anyone got a smoke?"

"Those things'll kill you, man."

A new sound grew above the hum of electricity—the sound of distant chopper blades cutting through the night air. They grew closer. Some of the soldiers craned their necks back, squinting beyond the brightness of the floodlights, trying to fix the aircrafts' position.

With a shuddering roar, two helicopters flew over the defensive line towards the eastern desert. They stayed within view, and pulled about, circling. One of the choppers was large and bulky, slower than its companion, but deadly in its own right. The UH-1 flicked on its own spotlights, trying to pinpoint something on the ground out of view of the soldiers on the bank of the canal.

"What're they doing?" asked one trooper.

"Quiet! Just watch," said another.

The second helicopter was painted as black as the night it flew in. Narrow and vicious in silhouette, it stabilized and dropped closer to the ground, facing away from the defensive line.

"What's the Apache doing? Are they landing?"

The sound of a magnified voice loomed out through the darkness. The Apache pilot was speaking to someone on the ground.

"Civilian! You are entering a containment zone! You must submit to decontamination before proceeding! Stop your vehicle and dismount!"

The Huey had fixed its spotlights on something behind one of the sand dunes. The soldiers on the line were shifting now, curious as to what was going on.

The Apache backpedaled in the air, keeping its weapons trained. Whatever it was that they were focused on was moving.

"Civilian, halt! You are entering a containment zone! Stand down now! This is your final warning!"

Now the soldiers on the line could hear a new noise. The sound of a diesel engine drifted to their ears, and grinding gears followed. Someone was driving toward them. They steadied their rifles.

The Apache circled overhead, pulling over the canal and positioning itself above the soldiers. The Huey hovered over the target, spotlighting it. For the first time, the soldiers noticed the rope and harness dangling from the side of the Huey. They were trying to get the driver to climb onboard.

The driver wasn't having it.

A semi truck burst over the crest of the nearest dune, spraying sand in a wide arc. The gears ground again, and the truck accelerated towards the waters edge. It was clear the driver had no intention of stopping.

A screech from overhead drew the attention of the soldiers and for a second they were bathed in the orange light of ignited propellant from the rear end of a Hellfire rocket. The Apache had fired.

The truck wasn't built to take a missile to the front grille. It exploded, sending metal shards flying in every direction. The soldiers ducked into their foxholes as the remains of the vehicle came clattering down on the sand and with splashes in the canal.

Brewster raised his head slowly, adjusting his helmet as he peered over the edge of his hole. The ruins of the truck were on fire on the eastern bank. He grinned, nodding his head and turning to look at Corporal Darin next to him.

"Now, that had to be a foreign truck," he said. "Sure wasn't built Ford tough."

Sitting on a pile of sandbags behind the foxhole, Denton spoke up. "You don't feel sorry for the driver?" he asked.

"Hell no, man. The guys in the Huey tried to lift him out of there. The dumbass was running dead-scared."

"The stuff he was running from is right behind him," Denton said, pointing.

The Huey had circled the debris of the truck twice before its spotlights flicked off into the distance, once again illuminating ground beyond the view of the soldiers. The Apache joined it, and the pair flew further east. They began to fire at the ground, hovering in the air as they did so. The Apache let fly with more rockets, and the soldiers could hear the dull thumps of the distant explosions as the Hellfires hit and detonated. The two choppers were raining death from the sky.

"I hope they leave some for us," Brewster said.

"Don't worry," Denton replied. "There'll be plenty for everybody."

The choppers soon stopped firing. They hadn't run out of targets. They'd run out of ammunition. The two aircraft roared over the defensive lines once more, this time vanishing into the west. The sounds of their blades grew distant, and then faded altogether. The battle was left to those on the ground.

Silence.

In the quiet, the soldiers felt themselves growing nervous. Whatever the helicopter pilots had been firing at was still out there, beyond the dunes, out of sight, but coming closer. Safeties were flipped off and equipment rattled as they shifted in their foxholes.

"Hold your fire," whispered Sergeant Major Thomas, the grizzled veteran, as he ran up and down the line checking his men. He held a weathered Colt 1911 in one hand and a flare gun in the other. "Wait for them to crest the dune. Get a good sight picture before you hit 'em. Aim for the head! Remember to aim for the head!"

Minutes passed. The soldiers began looking back and forth at one another. Where was the enemy? Why hadn't they crossed into sight? What was waiting out there, beyond the comforting ring of brightness the floodlights provided?

Brewster wiped sweat from his forehead and pressed his eye back up against the night sight of his rifle, gritting his teeth.

Denton sat silently, rifle across his lap, camera around his neck, waiting.

Commander Barker nervously tapped his foot against the sandy ground, scanning the dunes with his eyes. He checked his watch and folded his arms, then checked his watch again.

Colonel Dewen chewed on the end of an unlit cigar, grimaced, and spit out a piece of tobacco. He went back to chewing.

Inside the command tent, the Satcom troopers had finally synched with the spy satellites.

"Quick! Quick! Pull up a view of our area, infrared, zoomed-in," said the lieutenant in charge. "Sharpen! Sharpen it up! Where are the carriers?"

The image flicked into focus, and the officer's face drained of blood. "Oh, shit."

Sergeant Major Thomas looked over his shoulder at the small

tarp General Sherman and the other brass stood under. The General nodded.

Thomas holstered his pistol and held the flare gun out at arm's length, aiming over the canal at the dark expanse beyond. He fired. The flare whizzed into the sky, leaving a light trail of white smoke behind it. It popped a moment later, bathing the desert in warm orange light.

—And illuminating the teeming horde of infected just beyond the perimeter of light.

There were tens of thousands of them, a mob the likes of which the world rarely saw, pushing and shoving one another like an army of agitated ants. The carriers closest to the defensive line seemed to notice it for the first time as the flare drifted overhead. They roared at the defenders.

"Hail Mary, full of grace," Corporal Darin whispered, sweat trickling down the back of his neck.

They charged.

The soldiers opened fire, hundreds of rounds thudding into the bodies of the carriers. Dozens fell, rolling down the sandy slopes of the dunes, but hundreds more ran over the bodies towards the water. Machinegun emplacements went full-auto, emptying drums of rounds at the infected. Here and there a head shot dropped a carrier permanently, but most of the shots went rogue, knocking a carrier to the ground only to have it rise up again minutes later.

"Ammo!" soldiers began to yell from their holes. Runners sprinted up and down the line, dropping satchels of magazines into the holes of the troopers who needed them.

"Backblast area clear!" yelled a man, aiming an AT-4 anti-tank rocket balanced on his shoulders. He fired, and the rocket blast cleared an area of infected, sending many flipping into the sky and leaving an open, blackened pocket that soon filled in again as the hordes advanced relentlessly.

The carriers had reached the minefield. They were packed shoulder-to-shoulder and every mine that had been buried began to detonate as the teeming mass ran forward, blasts enveloping them. The ones in the ranks further back kept coming, detonating mine after mine. Some of the carriers were enveloped in fire, running aimlessly about, trying to bat the flames down. Their anguished howls echoed over the canal and in the ears of the defenders, but they kept firing. And the horde kept advancing.

The carriers reached the razor-wire fences and ran full-on into them, slicing themselves to ribbons. As before, when the infected in front died, the ones behind kept pushing forward. The wire fences were a small obstacle, and were soon buried underneath the bodies of those they were meant to stop. The horde kept advancing.

"Ammo! I need ammo!" the shouts rang out up and down the line. The runners doggedly tried to keep up, throwing satchels of ammunition to those who requested it, but they were tiring, and the ammunition stores were beginning to run low.

The carriers had reached the water. They splashed into it, writhing, as they tried to push themselves towards the far bank. The canal was wide and deep and was the soldiers' best defense. They focused on the carriers still standing on the far bank. The ones in the canal swiftly floundered and stopped moving, floating face-down in the water. More joined them every second, splashing in and drowning as they tried to cross.

Soon the canal looked like a macabre logjam, with hundreds of floating bodies bumping in to one another as the firefight went on unchecked above them. The carriers splashing into the canal were pushing the bodies away as they thrashed about.

General Sherman noticed a few carriers had managed to pull themselves on top of the floating corpses. They were dragging themselves across the surface of the water, using the bodies as floats.

"Artillery!" he shouted. The radioman held a hand over one ear and began shouting orders into the handset.

"Thor, Thor, this is Suez with a fire mission, over . . ."

On the line, Denton found himself out of ammunition for his camera. The film rolls he had brought were used up and tucked tightly into his vest pockets. He let the Nikon rest around his neck, brought up the rifle Dewen had given him, and took aim.

"They're moving across the river!" Brewster shouted, noticing the same thing the general had moments before. He shifted his fire to the canal, picking his targets. Soldiers on the line joined him, and the infected crawling across the floating bodies began to fall off into the water. The soldiers were inadvertently helping the carriers build their bridge.

A whistling noise filled the air, and heavy blasts rocked the soldiers as artillery rounds began to slam into the desert on the east bank of the canal, lofting carriers left and right. One of the infected was tossed end over end high into the sky, arcing over the canal and landing with a sickening thump directly in front of Brewster's foxhole. He jumped back, startled, then thumbed his helmet higher and squinted at the body.

"Fuckin' A, man," he breathed, then raised his weapon to his shoulder and resumed firing.

The carriers were still madly scrabbling across the bodies in the canal. Some were more than halfway across. One of the soldiers pulled a grenade from his pistol belt, yanked the pin, and wound up to throw it. It slipped out of his hand and rolled back into his foxhole.

"Grenade!" he yelled, pulling himself up and rolling out of the hole. His battle-buddy spun to look for the threat, saw his friend rolling clear, and had enough time to mumble a curse before the foxhole exploded in a shower of dirt and debris.

The first of the infected put his foot on the dry eastern bank of the Suez Canal. A moment later, Denton dropped him with a shot to the forehead. The photographer was picking his targets, firing once every ten or fifteen seconds, sniping carefully. Dewen had only given him two magazines.

The canal was boiling with carriers now. Their reinforcements seemed to be cut off as artillery continued to bombard the dunes, but there were already thousands past the protective curtain of indirect fire. Soldiers pulled themselves up and out of their foxholes to get a better angle, firing down into the infected.

The second—and final—line of razor wire stood in the path of the carriers. This time they were going uphill, and they were less clustered than they were on the western bank. Many threw themselves into the slashing teeth of the wire, shrieking and pulling at it with their bare hands, trying to free themselves and only succeeding in tangling themselves further. What the razor wire began, the rounds from the soldiers' rifles finished.

The fire from the defensive line was becoming more and more sporadic. The soldiers were running dry. They settled for flinging hand grenades down the slope toward the wire fence, while the soldiers with ammunition remaining slowed their firing and picked their targets. Blasts cut through the air.

One of the grenades bumped to a stop against one of the wooden support legs for a section of fence. It sat there a moment, rocking gently back and forth, before it exploded. The force of the blast lifted the section of fence and flipped its end over. It landed on top of a group of infected on the shore, knocking them to the ground and entangling them.

It also left a section of the fence line wide open.

The infected poured through the gap, running up the slope toward the line of foxholes.

"The line's been breached!" Sergeant Major Thomas shouted. "Hold them! Keep them back!"

General Sherman's head snapped in the direction of Thomas's voice.

"No," he breathed, drawing his pistol.

The living carriers and their dead brethren swarmed through the gap in the fence line like a biological hourglass, and they were the sand.

Sergeant Major Thomas surveyed the situation briefly, then made a judgment call.

"Fall back!" he yelled. "Fall back to the outer perimeter! Abandon your holes!"

The call was shouted up and down the line. The soldiers began levering themselves out of their positions, scrambling away from the bank of the canal. The foxholes closest to the breach in the line found themselves directly in the path of the horde of carriers. The soldiers tried to get away, but grasping hands pulled them back into the pulsing horde. Their screams were drowned out by the roars of the rage-filled infected.

The remaining soldiers booked it to their final line of defense—nothing more than a line of sandbags three feet high on the east side of the Suez base.

"Get the trucks running!" shouted General Sherman, striding into the midst of the confused soldiers. "Where are my drivers? Drivers, get in those vehicles! Give me a firing line along the wall! If you're out of ammo, get on a truck!"

Sherman knew that with the canal breached, their hopes of

holding the eastern bank were gone. He didn't want to sound a full retreat—the soldiers would likely panic and run for it into the desert. They wouldn't last long once the sun got overhead and they were lost with little water and no food.

Brewster clambered up the side of the deuce-and-a-half and turned the ignition. He tucked his rifle beside him and hung his head out the driver's side window.

"Come on, guys, get on! Get on!"

There wasn't much time. The carriers were absolutely relentless. With the line of foxholes abandoned, they had quickly torn through the remainder of the razor-wire fence and made their way up the sandy embankment to the camp proper.

The soldiers on the firing line took aim. As the carriers ran into view, they opened fire, controlled single shots that knocked carriers back or dropped them permanently with a wound to the head. One of the rounds took a carrier in the temple, spraying blood and gray brain matter back onto one of the camp's floodlights. The blood coating gave the light an eerie pinkish-red quality, bathing the campground in a dusky hue.

The deuce-and-a-halfs that were loaded with soldiers began to roll out of the camp with all possible speed, grinding gears.

"Man, I wish I had a Bradley right about now," said Brewster, tapping the steering wheel nervously as soldiers clambered into the back of his truck. The passenger side door swung open, and Brewster snapped his rifle up, thinking perhaps a carrier had gotten past the wall and was looking to make a snack of him. But it was only Denton.

The photographer dropped into the passenger seat with a heavy sigh.

"Where's your weapon, man?" Brewster asked.

"Lost it. One of you jarheads knocked it out of my hands," Denton said, nursing a bruised wrist.

"Hey, asshole, we're Army. Jarheads are Marines. *Muscles Are Required, Intelligence Not Essential*. Remember that."

"Leave it to you to keep your levity in a situation as bleak as this one," Denton replied.

"My incessant jocularity comes from an innate talent to rationalize even the most depressing of scenarios," Brewster said.

Denton flashed him a surprised look. Brewster just laughed in reply.

Outside the truck, most of the first wave of infected to come up the slope to the camp had been wiped out by the careful shots of the infantrymen. Still, General Sherman knew the battle was lost. Out of sight, down in the canal, there were still thousands of carriers making their way across. They had neither the manpower nor the ammunition to win the fight.

He surveyed the scene one final time.

Most of the soldiers had climbed onboard the deuce-and-a-half trucks parked around the outskirts of the encampment. Only he, a few riflemen, Commander Barker, and Sergeant Major Thomas remained on the ground.

It was time to bug out.

"Alright, men! Retreat! Fall back to the vehicles! Let's get the hell out of here!" he shouted, taking a shot at one of the carriers with his pistol. The round took the carrier in the shoulder, spinning him and dropping him to the ground.

"You heard the General! Fall back!" Thomas yelled, letting fly with two rounds from his Colt that tore into the chest of a target. He dropped the empty magazine and slapped in a fresh one before turning to retreat.

Commander Barker was handling himself well. He held a rifle to his shoulder, popping off round after round, skipping backwards towards the trucks as he fired. Out of the corner of his eye he saw a soldier get tackled by one of the sprinter-type carriers. He spun, firing a three-round burst. Two of the rounds took the target in the neck and the third snapped its head back, impacting just under the nose. It fell to the sand, twitching. Barker ran over to the soldier, who was laying on the ground panting, furiously scanning himself for bites or scratches.

"You're fine, soldier!" he shouted, reaching a hand down to help the man up. The soldier looked up at his rescuer. His eyes widened.

Barker saw the man's expression, then whirled around. He found himself face-to-face with a carrier.

Barker swung his rifle up, but the carrier was too fast. It leapt on him, knocking him backwards, and sank its teeth into the commander's face. Barker screamed, feeling his own blood flow into his mouth. He managed to get the barrel of the rifle up and under the carrier's chin, and he fired. The top of the carrier's head exploded outward, sending a shower of brain matter all over the ground behind him.

"Barker!" yelled General Sherman, hanging on to the back of Brewster's truck.

"Go!" Barker retorted, pulling himself to his knees. He reached a hand up to his face. His cheek was terribly lacerated and his nose was not much better. "Get out of here! I'm infected!"

"We can try to stop it!" Sherman called out, beckoning with his arm for Barker to hurry to the truck.

"No!" Barker replied, reaching down to his pistol belt. He pulled a grenade free and held it up so Sherman could see it.

Sherman's face went blank for a moment. He nodded grimly, then swung himself up into the truck, pulling the flap closed behind him.

"*Godspeed, General,*" Barker breathed, watching the truck begin to move off into the desert.

He was the last soldier standing at Suez base.

He pulled himself to his feet and turned to face the carriers.

There were hundreds gathered in the base proper now. They were staring at Barker with undisguised hatred in what was left of their fevered eyes. They issued guttural growls, murmured challenges to the final human combatant.

"Alright, you bastards," Barker hissed. "You want me? Then come and take me."

The carriers roared, covering the distance between themselves and the commander within seconds. As they pulled him to the ground, Barker yanked the pin on the grenade in his hands.

Before the white blinding flash took Barker away, he heard himself laughing.

PART FIVE:

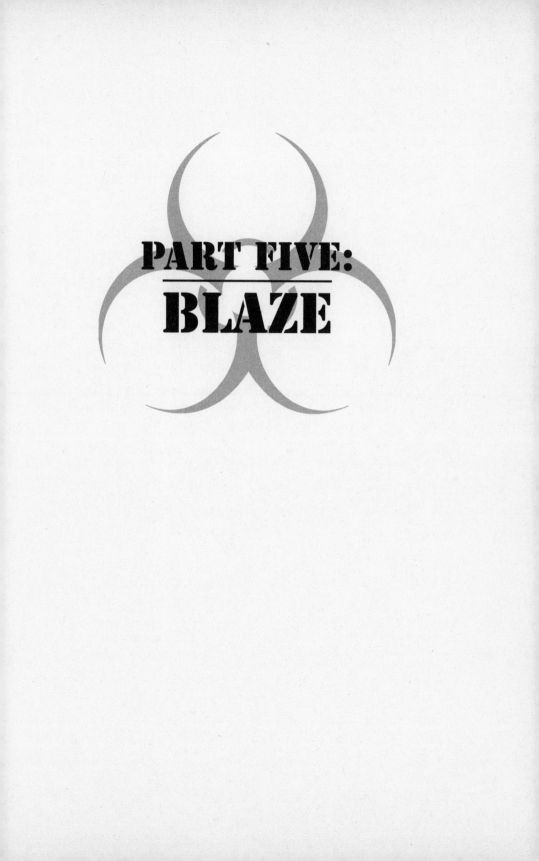

BLAZE

Washington, D.C.
January 8, 2007
1234 hrs_

"This is Channel Thirteen News, bringing you around-the-clock updates on the crisis situation in the Middle East. Here's news anchorwoman, Julie Ortiz!"

Julie smiled into the camera lens.

"Good afternoon, I'm Julie Ortiz, thanks for joining us. Our top story today—do the dead walk? The information that was leaked to the press anonymously yesterday says that they do; a morbid side-effect of the Morningstar Strain. Government officials have vehemently denied this allegation, calling it '*blatantly false*,' and that it was likely to '*cause undue panic and speculation*.' Congress has also called for a bipartisan commission to investigate the leak, which is believed by the FBI to have originated from right here, in Washington."

Julie glanced down at her notes before continuing.

"The public reaction to the news was both swift and widely varied. Religious groups gathered in their respective places of worship, and some said that if the reports were true, that the Apocalypse had arrived. Many families have begun stocking up on various food supplies, and grocery stores nationwide are reporting shortages of necessities such as sugar, flour, and canned products. Still, a vast majority of Americans have expressed disbelief in such a report. Should we be taking this report seriously?"

Julie glanced off-camera for a moment to get a thumbs-up from her supervisor, then turned back to the camera.

"Tonight Channel Thirteen hosts Central Intelligence Agency chief Tim Daley, and Dr. Vladimir Peshnikov, a respected virologist best known for his work in the treatment of malaria. Gentlemen, welcome. We hope your insights tonight will be helpful."

A pair of dour faces appeared over Julie's shoulders on the inset. Daley was middle-aged, and had a hard look about him, like the kind of man who was used to giving orders rather than taking them. Peshnikov was a bit less intimidating behind his glasses and thick black moustache.

"Thanks for having me, Julie," growled Daley.

"Good afternoon," said Peshnikov.

"Gentlemen, let me first ask you what your initial reactions are to the allegation that the dead are reawakening in Africa and the Middle East," Julie began, shuffling her notes.

"Well, I can answer that one," Daley said. "It's manure. Crap. This is not the kind of stuff you expect to hear your fellow Americans saying in the middle of a crisis. We have no delusions about this disease—it's dangerous. But it's not bringing the dead back to life! Why, that's blasphemy at its worst. God-fearing American citizens know in their hearts that there is no way in this universe the dead can somehow magically wake up—"

"Perhaps you are being too hasty, Mr. Daley," interrupted Peshnikov. "I was cynical as well, but my research has shown—"

"Oh, you scientists are always touting this research or that research and it never gets anyone anywhere. The dead are dead. It's not that hard of a concept to figure out," Daley responded with more than a hint of disdain in his voice.

"As I was saying," went on Peshnikov, "My research has shown that an organism can die, whereas parts of it continue to live. It is entirely possible that the creatures described in the leaked information are not reanimated humans at all, merely their bodies."

"Oh, that's helpful," snorted Daley.

"The allegation states that those infected by the Morningstar Strain are driven or compelled to spread the disease," Julie said quickly, before her guests erupted into a full-scale argument. "Do either of you believe that these reports of undead bodies may be directly related to the virus?"

"Of course," Peshnikov said before Daley could respond. "I see no other discernable connection between the two factors. Information such as this had never been reported before the outbreak of the Morningstar Strain. It is difficult not to see that the two are connected."

"Now wait a second," Daley said. "We haven't even established that this dead-bodies-rising thing is true or false yet, and you're already talking as if it is."

"Considering the new and vicious nature of our foe, Mr. Daley, I would be hesitant to deny new data offhand as it arrives simply because it conflicts with my religious views."

"The dead don't rise from the grave!" Daley shouted. "It's fiction."

"So you do not believe there is a connection between the virus and these allegations, Mr. Daley?" Julie asked.

"No. Well, it's possible," Daley said. "I don't know for sure either way."

"That's very scientific of you, Mr. Daley," sniped Peshnikov.

"What we need now more than ever is a sense of who we are, and what we stand for," Daley said. "We don't need to have mumbo-jumbo shoved down our throats at this time. We don't need to be talking about these godforsaken ideas of zombies and undead bodies walking around. What we *do* need is to come together as a nation and combat this threat through proper education and preparedness, so if this disease *does* hit America, we'll be ready in plenty of time."

"We may no longer have the luxury of time, Mr. Daley. Epidemics on this scale are rarely predictable," Peshnikov said. "What needs to be done is to understand the virus rather than running around making preparations we may, in the end, not even need to make. What if we issue protective garments to the citizens of this nation only to find that the disease is airborne?"

"But it's not airborne," Mr. Daley said.

"Yes, I know. It was merely an example."

"So, Mr. Daley," Julie said, "You believe that preparedness should be number one on America's list of priorities?"

"Yes. We have to be ready to stand and deliver if that virus finds its way across our borders."

"You have no understanding of the virus. How can you claim to be able to properly prepare *anything*, much less an entire nation?" asked Peshnikov.

"All I know is that we must take steps to preserve our lives and the lives of our children, not spread panic with blasphemous stories!"

"How trite a response—"

"Listen, you commie bastard!"

The insets of the two men vanished and Julie composed her expression. She said, "We'll be returning to the debate momentarily. Afterwards, Trent Dennison will take a look at the district's falling crime rate. We'll take a break, and return in a moment."

A moment later Jim the cameraman flashed her the all-clear signal. She relaxed, leaning back in her chair.

"Man," Jim said, letting the camera fall slack on the tripod, "Those guys sure got heated!"

"What do you expect?" Julie replied. "The world across the Atlantic is falling apart. They're getting spooked."

"What do you think about this zombie thing?" Jim asked. "I mean, now that we've heard the opinions of the experts."

He said it with enough veiled sarcasm to bring a smile to Julie's face.

"I don't know," she said after a moment. "Something tells me there's a grain of truth to it."

"Makes you wonder who had the guts to leak that kind of information—"

"Miss Julie Ortiz?" came a voice.

"Yes?" Julie said, blinking back the bright lights of the set. She couldn't make out her addresser.

A moment later the men—three of them—stepped forward into the light. Jim cast them a nervous glance. The three were immaculately attired in dark suits. Julie knew what was coming next before it even happened.

The leader of the group pulled out a badge and flashed it in front of her eyes.

"I'm Special Agent Sawyer, these are Agents Mason and Derrick, FBI."

"And?" Julie asked.

"You're under arrest, Ms. Ortiz."

"Wait a second," Jim said, stepping forward. "Why? What for? She's been right here for hours!"

"The charge is treason," said Sawyer. "And if you don't move back, we'll arrest you, too—for *obstruction*."

"Let me go, Jim," Julie said, standing. "I had a feeling these guys would be here sooner or later."

1345 hrs_

Julie was once again in front of the bright lights. This time, however, she was not on a set. She was handcuffed to a chair in a dim interrogation room. *Dim* was a relative term—it was dark everywhere in the room except for the bright triangle of illumination cast from the spotlight that was tilted directly into Julie's eyes. She tried to squint, to see around it into the murky darkness, but failed. She knew she wasn't alone. She could hear murmuring voices behind the light, shuffling papers, and soft footsteps.

Finally, the light was tilted up sharply and out of her eyes. She found herself face-to-face with Special Agent Sawyer, who was holding a manila envelope. Julie recognized it immediately as the one she had been given by Dr. Demilio, but forced herself to block that thought out of her mind.

"Well, Miss Ortiz, seems you've been a busy little bee lately," he said, unwinding the string that bound the envelope tab. He slowly upended the envelope onto the floor. Photos and documents spilled out and scattered. "We knew you used to be an investigative reporter, but we never guessed you'd be the kind that would sell out her own country."

He rested his foot on the lower rung of the chair Julie was bound to and leaned in very close to her face.

"You're in one hell of a shitpile, Miss Ortiz," he snarled, baring his teeth. "What you do now will help decide how clean you are when you finally get out from under it. Understand?"

She fixed him with a calm gaze. "I understand that this is the part where I call my lawyer."

Sawyer's snarl faded into a grin and he stepped back, folding his arms and casting a sideways glance at the other men in the room.

"Did you hear that? She thinks she gets a lawyer," Sawyer chuckled. Julie could hear muffled laughter from the other agents. Sawyer looked back at her. "I'm not sure you really understand your position, Miss Ortiz. Let me enlighten you—and I'll be sure to explain it in simple terms so I can be certain you'll understand."

Sawyer walked to the back of the room, behind Julie and out of her field of view. She heard shuffling papers. Sawyer reappeared over her shoulder, thrusting a folder in front of her eyes. It was unassuming and plain, except for a small orange tab in the corner.

"Do you know what this is, Miss Ortiz? It's a top secret document. That means it's classified. That means that your average Joe on the street is to know nothing—*nothing*—about what is inside this folder." At this point he pulled a second metal chair away from a table near the wall. It grated harshly along the concrete floors. Sawyer turned it backwards and sat down, looking at the folder in his hands. "When someone tells Joe what's inside one of these folders, we don't like it. We don't like it at all. You *told*, Miss Ortiz. You told Joe. And that, my dear, is when *this*—" (Here he held up the folder,) "—turns into something else entirely."

Without warning he wound his arm up and viciously backhanded Julie. She cried out, mouth hanging open in shock. Her calm gaze changed into one of fear, and a bit of blood slowly trickled from her lower lip.

"Pain, Miss Ortiz," Sawyer said, dropping the folder. "It turns into pain. At our hands. But don't get me wrong, Miss Ortiz. We're not sadists. We don't like seeing you in pain, even if you betrayed your fellow Americans. All we ask is that you tell us how you got these documents, and this can end before it even begins. Of course, we won't be able to let you go free, but a cell is much better than this room. And much less hazardous to your well-being."

Julie licked the blood from her lip. The coppery taste spread across her palate, as sickening and alluring as the agent's offer. The thought of turning in Dr. Demilio was quickly banished from her mind.

"My sources are protected by law—" she began.

Sawyer backhanded her a second time, then a third. This time Julie didn't cry out. She had been expecting it. She was no less fazed by these attacks than by the first one, however, and her vision swam as she tried to shake off the pain.

"We are the law, Miss Ortiz. Don't fuck with us," Sawyer said, voice going hard. "You've only been getting my good side. Don't make me show you the bad. I'll ask one final time—who gave you the information about the Morningstar Strain?"

Julie said nothing.

Sawyer stood, sighing, and brushed his jacket with his hands.

"Very well, Miss Ortiz. Derrick. We'll start with the sodium pentothal."

"Right," said Agent Derrick, turning and popping open a metal case. He withdrew a syringe and plunged it into a medicine bottle, carefully extracting a dose.

"You're just too stubborn to learn," Sawyer said to Julie as

Derrick tapped the needle. "We'll see how dogged you are after we try a few more *professional* methods."

1621 hrs_

Julie was thrown roughly into a tiny, damp cell. She slumped to the ground with a moan. Behind her, the federal agents slammed the iron bars closed and locked them.

"Have a good rest, Miss Ortiz. We'll be back soon to continue our little chat," said Sawyer.

Julie heard them walking away, chuckling and ribbing one another. Their voices grew fainter until finally there was silence. Julie tried to pick herself up, but her arm gave out with fatigue and she crashed back down to the floor. She rolled over onto her back slowly, blinking her eyes in the dimness.

The past few hours were a blur to her, but she remembered certain details all too well. The sodium pentothal had worked at first—but the agents had made the mistake of trying out a few control questions first, namely simple ones about herself and her childhood. The drug had warmed her, made her feel incredibly good about herself and her situation, and so she answered the questions. She refused to move on to their pressing questions until she had told them nearly every detail of her young life—including stories about her cat, Pogo, and the disaster that was her tenth birthday party.

When the agents had angrily demanded she answer their questions, she had become pouty, insisting that they didn't need to know because they didn't want to hear about Pogo.

Perhaps, she thought in retrospect, *I should have just told them then.*

As the drug began to wear off, they switched to other methods.

As Julie lay on the damp floor of the cell, she gingerly reached a hand up to the side of her face and touched it. She gasped, pulling her hand quickly away. The right side of her head was burned—not terribly, but second degree. She remembered the agents pulling the spotlight closer and putting it almost against her head, leaving it there for most of an hour. The heat had been agonizing.

There had been other attempts to get the answers out of her. The agents had developed an incredible talent for finding new, creative, and painful uses for paperclips. Julie flexed her fingers slowly, barely able to make out the red lines of blood under her fingernails where the agents had used those paperclips.

She knew she had gotten off light today. Aside from her red face and the dried blood on her lip and hands, she was virtually unscathed. She'd heard stories about interrogations—real ones, not the Hollywood dramatizations. There would be no cutting off of limbs or serious damage—they would keep their suspect alive and in good health while they tortured them.

Electrocution. Sleep deprivation. Starvation. Isolation.

Outside, the world was slowly coming apart at the seams. Inside—*wherever she was*—Julie Ortiz was beginning to be taken apart as well.

Sinai
January 8, 2007
1523 hrs_

Mbutu Ngasy blinked the brightness of the desert sun from his eyes and squinted into the distance.

"I do not see them," he said. His English was excellent, and though his accent was thick, Rebecca Hall could understand him perfectly. He spoke Swahili naturally, but in Kenya, English was the official language, used in government and education. He had learned it at an early age, and it aided in his old duties as the air traffic controller in Mombasa.

"They're supposed to be here already. I hope nothing happened," she said, pacing back and forth. She kicked a small stone across the ground and folded her arms across her chest.

"They will be fine," Mbutu said, as if that explained everything.

"Soldiers aren't superhuman," Rebecca replied.

"They are running late, maybe. But they will be fine," Mbutu repeated. "This is a blessed place. No harm will come to them here, or to us."

"What? Not more of that religious mumbo-jumbo, Mbutu! I've had about enough of it from the refugees, yammering about the end of the world . . ."

"Not religious. Well, maybe religious a little. I believe in spiritual power, though not in God as many do," Mbutu explained. "This place has much power."

"*Why*? It's nothing but sand and rocky hills. It's desolate and hot and empty."

"There," Mbutu said, pointing over Rebecca's shoulder.

She turned and looked.

"What?" she asked, spreading her arms wide. All she saw was an expanse of dust and rock. They were in the foothills of the desert, and here and there outcroppings of boulders sprang up from the sand as if by magic.

"There," Mbutu said again. "That mountain is Mount Sinai. In your mythology, this is where God spoke to men. So, I say there is much power here."

"Oh, yeah. *The Ten Commandments*. Charlton Heston," Rebecca said. "I remember now."

"Charlton Heston?" Mbutu asked slowly. "This is another name for the mountain in your country?"

"No, we call it Mount Sinai, too. It's just . . . *never mind*," Rebecca said. She resumed pacing.

Mbutu watched her from the corner of his eye.

"You are very impatient," he said after a moment. Rebecca glared at him, and he smiled broadly in response.

"I'm used to doing things, not standing around," she told him. "I need some action! That's why I came over here in the first place!"

"Your country," Mbutu began, "It is boring?"

Rebecca laughed. "You have no idea."

"You do not have fun? There are no games? No books? You do not have a husband?" Mbutu asked, ticking the items off on one hand.

"A husband?" Rebecca interrupted. "Are you kidding? I'm only twenty-two!"

"No, I am not '*kidding*'," Mbutu replied with a straight face. "You are not married?"

"Hell no!"

"Ah. I forgot—many in your country choose not to marry until later. Yes, now I can see why you are bored."

Rebecca laughed. "Shut up."

"Perhaps I will," Mbutu said, falling silent.

"Oh, you know I was joking," said Rebecca, punching him softly on the arm.

"Yes. Though now is a bad time for such things as joking."

"No," Rebecca said. "Now's the best time for such things. I can understand being humorless when everything's going just peachy. There's no need. You have everything you need, the world's perfectly sane, you've got a car and a house and two-point-five kids and there's no real reason to joke about stuff. I think when things are falling apart or you find yourself in a tight spot is the perfect time to make fun of stuff. I keep hearing the soldiers talk about facing death. If I have to face death, I'm going to laugh at him. Otherwise, I'll . . . just fall apart."

"Death is not a laughing matter," Mbutu said.

"No, it's not, it's serious, and that's why we should laugh at it."

"I do not follow your logic."

"Oh, hell," Rebecca said, brushing her strawberry blond hair out of her eyes. "How can I explain it? It's sort of like a way of saying '*I may be about to die, but I'll laugh and go out with dignity.*'"

"Laughing is not a form of dignity."

"Jesus, you're stubborn," Rebecca said. "It is in *my* book, okay?"

"If you insist."

"Why? Let me ask you something. If you were dying, or knew you were going to die, how would you want to go?"

Mbutu seemed to ponder the question for a long time. He then answered, "I would want to die in my sleep, like my grandfather. He did not know, so he felt no regret or grief at having to leave us behind. And those of us he left felt comfort in knowing that he died at peace, dreaming, perhaps, of something good."

Rebecca nodded slowly.

"That is a good death," she said.

Mbutu looked over at her expectantly.

"What?" she said, after a moment.

"It is now your turn to answer the question."

"Oh," she mouthed. "Well . . . I guess I'd like the whole dying in my sleep thing, too. But I mean, it's not guaranteed. I could go out in a car wreck or be shot or drown or be electrocuted. If it had to be like that, if I had to be awake and aware of it, I still say I'd die laughing."

"Perhaps. You have made me think of something my mother said to me when I was a child, after a roofer died in Mombasa. He had fallen from the roof because he did not tie himself down. She said he was foolish, and this was his reward. She said to me, 'In deaths like this, fools die screaming, and nobles die laughing at themselves.' Perhaps you are not really laughing at death, Rebecca Hall. You are laughing at yourself for maybe dying in such a foolish manner as falling from a roof."

Mbutu put a hand over his eyes, shading them from the sun, and squinted into the distance.

"They are coming," he said finally.

Rebecca spun, staring in the direction Mbutu was looking. She could make out several tiny specks in the distance, wavering in the heat. They looked like ants. She knew from her short time in the desert that the flat, open expanses created a kind of optical illusion. The convoy she was looking at was still dozens of kilometers away, but it was definitely the one they had been waiting for.

After they had received word of the battle at Suez, the soldiers had broken camp at El Ferdan and El Qantara and moved southeast towards the heart of the Sinai desert. It was out of the way, almost a hundred kilometers to the south of the last-ditch defensive lines the Corps of Engineers had set up for the sole purpose of ensuring a safe, secure rendezvous point for the defenders. They had enough fuel to spare to make the decision worthwhile and no one minded the extra effort expended in return for the added safety from carriers of the Morningstar Strain.

Behind Mbutu and Rebecca, the call was taken up in the makeshift camp that the survivors of Suez were approaching.

Sharm el-Sheikh
January 10, 2007
1203 hrs_

Rebecca Hall was tired, dirty, hungry, thirsty—and most of all, *hot*.

The trip from the base of Mount Sinai to Sharm el-Sheikh had been in haste. The remaining soldiers of the battle at Suez had linked up with the small company that had been waiting for them in the desert, and General Sherman had promptly ordered a retreat.

Rebecca wanted nothing more than to head for home, but her options, unfortunately, didn't include a trip stateside—*yet*, anyway. Apparently the situation in the desert was deteriorating. The carriers had broken the coalition's best line of defense, and at the last second the final lines had received word from Washington to pull back. Defensive lines one and two had been abandoned.

Sherman had been furious, making calls all day to try and convince the politicos that it was not in their best interests to abandon the defense of the Middle East.

He had been right and wrong in his assertions. Over the past day, reports had been coming in that the carriers were weakening and slowing from the heat and uncompromising landscape of the desert expanses. Satellite images and recon flights had reported that there were numerous carriers falling by the wayside as the horde advanced, this time staying down permanently. It seemed extreme exposure to the elements was an effective way of dealing with them.

Sherman had been skeptical.

"I've seen these things take a round to the heart and get back up a few minutes later," he had said. "What's to say the dead ones won't start walking around again here soon?"

Either way, the United States was now betting that the wires, minefields, and trenches they had dug as the second line would at least slow down the carriers long enough to allow Israel and the other Middle Eastern states to form a solid defense.

Rebecca had been surprised to hear about the apparent truce between the two ancient enemies, but only mildly so. Disaster always brought out both the best and worst of human nature. Apparently, in the Middle East, the best was showing through. She regretted being so out of touch with the soldiers in the desert—she would have loved to have seen an Israeli soldier and an Arab militiaman fighting side-by-side instead of with each other.

Sherman had plotted the route to Sharm el-Sheikh as the best possible exodus from the continent. There was a naval battle group stationed at the south end of the Red Sea that was going to send a destroyer over to pick up the remaining soldiers and refugees like Rebecca and Mbutu. The plan was to rendezvous with the battle group and catch a flight back to civilization.

Rebecca would have liked to have talked with Sherman about the battle at Suez, but his duties had kept him occupied during the trip. Instead, she spent her time kibitzing with Mbutu and a soldier named Decker. He was a sergeant who had been part of the original group stationed at Suez. She and Decker had become fast friends. As a medic, she had helped re-bind the wound on his arm.

Sitting in the back of one of the trucks as it rumbled out of the mountains toward the coastal town, Rebecca remembered her first meeting with the sergeant. She had been helping the Army medics as they tended to the battle scrapes and scratches of the soldiers at Sinai when Decker had sat down in front of her.

"Hi," he said. "I've got a small problem."

He had held up his arm, bound with a dusty and dirty bandage that was half-soaked through with blood. Rebecca had grimaced.

"What are you trying to do, suicide by gangrene?" she asked, pulling on a pair of latex gloves before gingerly unwrapping the bandage.

"Yeah. Thought it would be better than catching the virus," he replied.

"So debilitating, blinding pain that slowly spreads throughout your whole body while you watch your arm rot off piece by piece is a more appealing fate?" Rebecca asked, dumping the used bandage into a sterile container.

"No, actually. Think you can save me, doc?"

Rebecca laughed.

"I'm not a doctor. I'm not even a nurse," she told him as she cleaned the wound with hydrogen peroxide. He winced as she poured the liquid over the slice.

"You have a doctor's touch," he uttered through gritted teeth.

"It can be a lot worse," Rebecca said with a grin. "I could dump the whole bottle in there."

"I'll pass," he said. "What's your name?"

"Rebecca."

She smiled at him. He smiled back.

Then his grin had faded as she held up a needle and thread.

"That's a nasty cut," she said. "And I think it could use a few stitches."

Decker taught her a few new ways to swear before she finished re-binding his wound.

The truck hit a rock and the occupants in the back were jostled roughly. Rebecca managed to use a few of those new swear words before the truck bed settled and the passengers had rearranged themselves. She wondered if the driver was even qualified to be operating the large vehicle.

In the truck's cab, Denton rubbed the back of his head ruefully. "Fourth massive boulder in an hour, Brewster," he said. "Let's not go for five, eh?"

"It wasn't a fucking boulder, it was a little rock in the road. A boulder is big. That was little," Brewster said. "Besides, the truck in front of us hit it and they didn't fucking bounce like that."

"What's it going to take? Are you going to have to see someone come flying out of the back of that truck before you decide they've hit a rock too big for your tastes?" Denton asked.

"Yeah, man, pile it on. We're five miles out. You can bitch and whine about my driving only for a few more minutes. Then it's boat time."

"If the destroyer is even waiting for us. I'm starting to learn to expect the worst."

"It'll be there," Brewster told him.

They were to meet the USS *Ramage*, an Arleigh Burke-class destroyer, in the waters outside of Sharm el-Sheikh, inside the hour. The ship was all that the Naval battle group could spare, but it would be more than enough. There were a little over two hundred soldiers and refugees coming out of Sinai. It would be cramped quarters onboard the destroyer, but it would suffice.

The trucks bounced and rumbled into the deserted town, chugging towards the harbor. The plan was to take a few civilian vessels out to the destroyer, since there weren't any docks large enough to accommodate her at the city's shoreline.

"It's creepy," Brewster said, peering out the side window at the empty streets. The people here had fled weeks before in fear of the disease. "Like a ghost town or something."

"Desolate," agreed Denton.

"Did every single person leave or something?" Brewster asked, furrowing his brow.

"No," Denton said. "I doubt everyone left. There's probably someone left somewhere here."

"Where are they? Aren't they curious about this huge fucking column of trucks going down main street?"

"I don't know," Denton said, eyeing the buildings they were passing. There wasn't a single sign of life anywhere.

The trucks rumbled on for a minute, and both men were silent. They were growing closer to the harbor.

The shortwave radio in the cab squawked and a voice spilled through.

"All vehicles, this is Sherman. We can see the docks. Looks like plenty of civilian craft are available. On arrival, secure a vessel and await further orders. Sound off, over," said the general, voice slightly distorted by static.

"Truck two, roger, over."

"Truck three, roger that."

"Truck four, I copy."

Brewster plucked down the handset from the overhead radio and clicked it on. "Truck five, wilco, over."

"Truck six, roger."

Brewster replaced the handset and spun the wheel to follow the leading trucks down a side street.

"We're close—I've been here before," Denton said, pointing out on the street. "I ate at that cafe once."

Suddenly, a muffled thump sounded from ahead of their truck, and the convoy ground sharply to a halt. Brewster stopped his truck and leaned his head out the window, trying to see what was happening.

"See anything?" Denton asked.

Brewster didn't answer for a moment. Then he swore, slammed the vehicle into park and swung down and out of the cab. Denton climbed out slower, nursing a bruised knee he didn't remember getting at Suez. The passengers in the back of the trucks were peering out cautiously, curious as to what was happening.

"What the fuck, Darin?" Brewster said, spreading his arms wide as the driver from the truck in front of him shrugged.

"Don't know. We just stopped," Darin replied.

"Let's find out, eh?" said Denton, walking past the two soldiers toward the head of the convoy. After looking at one another, the soldiers followed him.

Denton waved a hand at the figure of Sergeant Major Thomas as he approached.

"Sergeant! What's the holdup?" Denton called out.

"Minor snafu," said Thomas. "Lead truck hit a civilian. Jumped right out in front of them at the end of the street."

"*Shit,*" Brewster mumbled under his breath.

The three men walked around the front of the convoy to survey the scene. General Sherman, Colonel Dewen, and the distraught driver of the lead truck were crouched around the prone form of a civilian, who was gasping for breath. He was covered in sweat, and didn't focus his eyes on anything.

"Shock?" Denton asked.

"I didn't hit him that hard! I was slowing down for the turn!" said the driver, holding a hand over his mouth.

Sherman was crouched at the man's side.

"Hold on, son, we've got help on the way," he told the man, checking him over for open wounds. The general turned his head and shouted, "Medic! Let's get a medic up front!"

Sergeant Major Thomas marched to the back of the first truck, yelling back along the street. "Medic up front, pronto!"

In the back of Brewster's truck, Rebecca heard the distant call.

"Oh, crap," she said to herself. "That's me. What's happened?"

She levered herself up from the rough bench in the back of the truck and dropped lithely to the ground below, snatching her bag of ever-dwindling supplies. She didn't know what good they would do her—all she had left were a few antibiotics, some bandages, and a couple painkillers—but it was worth a shot.

Denton and Thomas met her at the rear of the lead truck, talking fast as she jogged towards the wounded man. Denton rattled off, "Lead driver hit a pedestrian—looks okay but he's in shock, don't think anything major is broken!"

"Let me through!" Rebecca said, pushing between Brewster and Dewen to get to the wounded man.

She knelt beside him and checked his pupils, then laid a hand on his forehead. She gasped and immediately fell back, scrabbling away from the man.

"What are you doing?" Sherman said, glaring at her. "He needs help!"

"He's not in shock!" she blurted. "He's burning up! He's sick!"

As one, the soldiers surrounding the man took a few steps backwards as fast as they could.

"Morningstar?" Sherman asked, hand going to the butt of his pistol.

"I don't know," Rebecca said, staring at the victim.

"What do we do? Leave him?" Colonel Dewen asked, glancing at Sherman.

"Fuck him, man, let's get out of here. I'm not getting sick this close to a boat ride home," Brewster said, and was promptly fixed with an angry look from Thomas.

Thomas gritted, "Private, that's the first and last thing you're going to say at this point in time."

Brewster grimaced and shuffled his feet.

Sherman sighed, folded his arms and took a long look at the man. He said, "No, he's right, Thomas. We've got no choice. We have to assume he's infected with Morningstar. I don't know how the disease could have gotten here ahead of us unless he was infected much earlier in the outbreak. If we take him along and it turns out he *does* have it, we're truly screwed. We've got to leave him."

Dewen nodded. "Right. Let's move him out of the way and keep going. We've got rendezvous in forty minutes."

"Leave him some water and food," Sherman said. "If he's not infected, he'll need it."

Sherman, Rebecca, and Denton returned to their trucks and waited for the soldiers to deal with the hapless man.

Brewster and Darin pulled gloves out of their BDU pockets and slipped them on, then grabbed the victim's legs and arms and hefted him between them. They set him down gently on the side of the street, and Darin unbuttoned one of his canteen covers, pulling the canteen free and setting it by the man's hand. Thomas tossed him an MRE from the back of one of the trucks and Darin set it down beside the water.

"Poor bastard," Colonel Dewen said, fanning himself with one hand as he stood in the relative shade of one of the street's many doorways. "What if he really isn't infected? Wish there was a way to tell."

"General's right, sir," Thomas said. "No way to tell. Maybe he's just got a fever. But we can't take the chance."

"Yeah. But it still stinks to—"

Without warning, the door behind Dewen burst open, knocking him roughly into the sandstone-colored wall. He grunted in pain.

Thomas reacted first, snatching his Colt from his holster and bringing the barrel to bear. "Sir, get down!"

Framed in the doorway was another civilian, looking deranged and almost feral in expression. Before Thomas could fire, the carrier leapt on Dewen's back, rearing back with her hands and striking the officer in the back of his head. Dewen lunged about, trying to dislodge the diseased woman.

"Damn!" Thomas shouted, trying to draw a bead on the carrier. Dewen's head and shoulders kept popping into his sight picture as the pair wrestled about. "I don't have a shot!"

Brewster came running over, rifle unslung, and slammed the buttstock full-force into the bridge of the carrier's nose. Her head snapped back and her high-pitched gibberish was cut off with a yelp of pain. She fell off of Dewen's back. That was all the time Thomas needed.

The shot from the Sergeant Major's Colt rang out clearly, and blood spray coated the doorway a gory red. The carrier went limp, falling in a heap on the doorstep. Dewen sank to his knees, clutching the side of his throat.

"Colonel!" Thomas called out, running over to the doorway. Dewen looked up at him and tried to say something, but all that came through was a muffled gurgle. Bright red blood seeped through the Colonel's hands and coated the collar of his uniform. The carrier had done serious damage. Thomas' face went blank.

"Shit, man, that blood's arterial!" Brewster exclaimed, slinging his rifle and digging at the medical pouch clipped to his suspenders. "Get some pressure on it!"

"No!" Thomas replied, holding up a hand to Brewster. "Don't go near him."

Dewen managed a slow nod in agreement with Thomas. He was fading fast.

"He's infected," Darin said, stepping back.

The three soldiers watched, helpless, as Colonel Dewen lay dying at their feet. In the silence, they heard the sounds of feral, hungry moans drifting through the empty streets. Their eyes turned upwards, focused on the cityscape in front of them.

"They must have heard the shot," Thomas said, glancing at his pistol.

"They'll be coming," Darin murmured. "They'll be coming right for us, won't they?"

Thomas was silent for a moment, then turned to face the two men.

"We have to get to the harbor. Get back in your trucks! Now! Move!"

PART SIX:

WILDFIRE

Sharm el-Sheikh
January 10, 2007
1233 hrs_

BREWSTER TRIED TO keep his thoughts in order as he sprinted for his truck. The convoy was in the middle of enemy territory. There were certainly carriers in this town—it had been overrun and the convoy was surrounded. A crude ambush, though not one planned by any sentient tactician. He had been in three firefights in his lifetime, not counting Suez, and one of them had been an ambush. It hadn't been pretty.

Brewster flung open the door to his truck and clambered up into the cab. Denton was on edge.

"What the hell's going on, Brewster?" he demanded. "I heard shots!"

"We're getting the fuck out of here, photo-jockey!" Brewster exclaimed. "Buckle up! We're burning rubber!"

He slammed the truck into drive and floored the accelerator. Denton was flung back in his seat and the passengers in the back shouted muffled protests.

"Wait!" Denton said, pushing himself upright as Brewster took a hard left. "What's happening?!"

"This town's a dead zone, man! We're fucking surrounded by those things! They got Dewen!" Brewster shouted back, grimacing and shifting gears.

"Colonel Dewen's dead?" Denton uttered, surprised and dismayed.

"As a rock," Brewster replied. "Shit!"

He swerved to avoid an abandoned car. The passengers in the back were thrown to one side and crashes could be heard through the cab wall.

"Take it easy, Brewster! You're going to throw out the guys in the back!"

"No can do, partner. We're bugging out, pronto!"

Denton grabbed a firm hold on the dashboard and braced himself as Brewster threw the truck around another sharp turn. As he straightened out the wheel, the harbor came into view. It was below them, less than a mile.

Between the convoy and the harbor were the carriers.

There were a scant few compared to the horde they had faced at Suez. Denton doubted he would ever again cast eyes on a group that large. Nevertheless, they were in the road, shambling or running out into the streets from houses and storefronts, or pulling themselves out of shadowed alleyways.

Sherman's voice boomed through the radio.

"Convoy drivers, we have carriers in the roadway. Do not engage or decelerate. Plow through!"

Brewster nodded to himself and downshifted.

The road was wide enough to allow for some maneuvering room. The trucks drifted out of their convoy formation, giving Brewster and Denton a clear view of what lay ahead. The lead truck, (the one carrying Sherman,) swerved sharply, and jolted. Brewster saw the tattered remains of a carrier twisting under the axles. The truck spat out the body, which rolled to a slow stop in the center of the road.

"Fucking right, man!" Brewster shouted, pointing.

"Watch the road! Watch the road!" Denton admonished.

Brewster dropped his hand back to the wheel. The second truck scored a direct hit and gore sprayed around the sides of its cab. A few drops of blood splattered back onto the windshield of Brewster's truck. A moment later, the second truck wavered, and the terrible sound of rending metal ripped through the air. The truck jolted to a dead stop, decelerating from forty-five miles per hour to zero in less than a second.

It flipped, end-over-end, and landed upside-down on the road, skidding roughly into a storefront. The walls of the store shattered, sending debris flying into the roadway. Brewster raised a hand to protect himself as a beam of wood smashed into the windshield of the truck, leaving a spider web of cracks behind.

"*What the hell?*" Brewster breathed, casting a backward glance at the smoldering truck as they passed.

"Axle locked up!" Denton shouted. "Watch the road! The road, Brewster!"

"There had to be thirty people in that truck!" Brewster exclaimed.

"No time! They're gone! Keep driving!"

The carriers were getting thicker. The noise was drawing them out. Trucks were running over shambling forms left and right—Brewster managed to steer a pair of tires onto the sidewalk, smashing one of the carriers under them. The thump was sickening, but strangely satisfying to the private first-class.

Denton hung his head out the passenger side door, trying to catch a glimpse of what lay behind them. The bulky tan canvas of the truck's bed blocked most of his view as it whipped about in the forty-mile-an-hour wind streaming over the moving truck. Brewster weaved the truck around a jutting curb, giving Denton the glimpse he was hoping for.

"Oh, that's wonderful, eh?! Half the city's behind us!" he yelled, sliding back into the cab and tossing Brewster an exhausted glance.

"Sprinters or shamblers?" Brewster asked.

"Sprinters, mostly. Think maybe this town got hit hard and fast by the virus? Looks like they all got sick with it. Not many wounded."

"Let's worry about that after we leave here breathing, alright?" Brewster said.

A crash from ahead of them drew their attention. The lead truck had crashed through the chain-link gate at the entrance to the city's harbor. The trucks sped into the open parking lot and skidded to full stops close to the docks.

The town of Sharm el-Sheikh was a tourist trap. That would be working to the advantage of the soldiers and refugees in their hurried escape from the Sinai peninsula. Because of all the tourism dollars spent here, there were a number of well-kept speedboats and even a number of luxury yachts moored in the harbor. The parking lot the trucks had pulled into was large and open, terrible for defense, but the dock itself had only three access points: small ramps of wooden planks that ran down to the dock proper.

General Sherman dropped down from the lead truck and squinted out across the harbor. There were more than enough boats for the people in the convoy.

But one problem remained.

"Keys," Sherman said. "We need to find the keys to the boats!"

"Sir," Thomas growled, appearing at the general's side. "There."

Thomas pointed out onto the docks where a boathouse had been constructed. There was a vending machine set out front, and a number of bright signs were nailed to the wooden siding. It had every appearance of the dock's main office.

“Check it,” Sherman said, gesturing with his left hand. His right drew his sidearm. “Everyone else: If you’re unarmed or a civilian, get out on the docks and into a boat! Stay together, and take the largest vessels you find! Soldiers, on me! We’re holding the ramp to the docks!”

Brewster was assisting people out of his truck, reaching up to pull them down one by one. He heard Sherman barking orders and stepped back, unslinging his rifle and charging the handle. He only had one and a half magazines left. He hoped they would be enough.

Most of the civilians had rushed out onto the docks as soon as they were down from the trucks. What few remained on the paved parking lot were hurrying towards the access ramps, which were also quickly being filled by any soldiers still carrying ammo.

“Drag those crates over!” Sherman was shouting. “Form barricades!”

The soldiers were busy dumping anything heavy and solid they could find at the top of the three ramps. Coils of rope, empty coolers, cargo crates, stripped prop engines—all found their way into the rapidly growing piles.

The last refugees pulled themselves over the crates to relative safety just as the carriers began arriving outside the gates to the parking lot.

Sherman cast an eye over the ragtag band and their hasty fortifications. It was clear to him that they couldn’t hold for long. The barricades weren’t high enough to stop the sprinters, and even the undead shambling carriers would be able to pull themselves over given the time. His eyes drifted over to the harbor’s main gates, where the carriers were beginning their run across the parking lot. There were hundreds in total, he estimated, most still out in the streets beyond the gates. They would come at the soldiers in a steady wave until they overran them or were all killed. Sherman wasn’t sure his men had the ammunition and accuracy to win such a fight. His eyes moved south, to the access ramp on which he stood. There was something itching at the back of his mind.

The soldiers were pressed up against the barricades, rifles to their shoulders, eyes against the iron sights. Sweat trickled down their foreheads and their hands shook almost undetectably as they waited for the carriers to move closer.

Sherman's head shot upright. He had remembered what it was that was bothering him.

"The ramps!" he shouted, drawing glances. "These ramps are detachable! You can remove them!"

He had seen similarly constructed docks before. The access ramps could be folded up onto the pavement or down onto the dock itself, or they could be removed entirely. He had no idea what the purpose behind the mechanism was, but the seemingly useless bit of trivia could end up being their salvation.

"Look for pins or bolts! Figure out how to get these things off!" he shouted, holstering his pistol and kneeling quickly, running his eyes and hands along the frame of the ramp.

On the opposite end of the dock, Brewster heard Sherman's idea.

"Shit, yeah!" he said, looking back and forth at the soldiers around him. "He's right! I've seen these things too!"

Brewster flattened himself out, hanging his head and shoulders over the edge of the planks, desperately looking for whatever it was that bound the ramps to the dock.

"They're coming closer, sir!" shouted Sergeant Decker, flicking his safety off. Similar clicks issued from up and down the line of soldiers. "Do we fire?!"

Sherman looked up. The carriers were more than halfway across the pavement, advancing swiftly, spreading out as they got closer.

That, in his opinion, was quite close enough.

"Open fire!" he ordered.

The distinctive staccato chatter of M-16 fire ripped across the docks as the soldiers opened up. Bursts of viral blood sprayed up into the air as rounds drilled through fevered foreheads, dropping the first line of carriers in their tracks. The second line was right behind them, deftly negotiating their way around the corpses of their former comrades and charging straight at the line. They fell a moment later as a second fusillade hit them, but the infected advance had gained a yard.

Brewster cast about wildly under the ramp as he heard the shots. He knew he didn't have much time. His eyes settled on a small steel chain that dangled below the planks. He reached out a hand to grab it, but it dangled just out of his reach. He pushed himself farther, hanging out over the blue water, and managed to snag the chain with his ring finger. With a gasp of achievement, he wrapped his hand around it and yanked. Whatever the chain was attached to, it was wedged in firmly. He pulled in his breath and pulled with all the strength he could muster.

The chain popped free, pulling a stout metal pin with it. The access ramp shifted under Brewster, hanging loose. He grinned in victory and pulled himself to his knees, turning and cupping his hands around his mouth.

"There's a pin at the top of the ramp on the underside! Pull it out!" he yelled. He saw Sherman and Decker on the other ramps look in his direction and nod. Responsibility fulfilled, Brewster grabbed up his rifle and jumped to his feet, taking in the scene.

The carriers had covered three-quarters of the parking lot and were nearly on top of the defenders. Corpses littered the pavement, dozens of carriers lying face-down in pools of blood. It was time to add to the casualty list.

Brewster drew a textbook sight picture on the forehead of a shambler and fired off a round. He watched with satisfaction as the carrier went down, twitching, in a heap. Out of the corner of his eye, he saw Decker rising to his feet on the other ramp, holding a chain and pin in his hands. Two ramps were ready. General Sherman was having difficulty, apparently, as he was still reaching underneath his own ramp.

Brewster picked off another carrier, this one a sprinter. It fell facedown, skidding a few feet as it burned off inertia, coming to a rest in a tangled knot of limbs, a neat hole drilled through its forehead.

"I'm out of ammo!" yelled a soldier, stepping back from the barricade and dropping an empty magazine from his rifle. Brewster moved up to take his position, resting his own weapon on the crate in front of him. The steady firing position gave him some added accuracy—time to put it to good use. Brewster let his training kick in. He acquired a target, drew a sight picture, and fired. Target, sight in, fire. Target, sight in, fire.

The carriers were almost completely on them now. The sprinters were too fast and too numerous. By the time one fell, another had already run around the falling corpse and gained a foot or two. Brewster sensed the situation deteriorating. Sherman had better hurry. He sighted in another carrier and pulled the trigger.

Click.

Brewster swore, pulling himself upright and pinching the button that released the rifle's magazine. He let it drop to the ramp, forgotten, as he slapped in his full—*and final*—ammo magazine. As he did so, Sherman stood upright, waving a pin and chain over his head.

"Everyone back down the ramps, get on the dock!" Sherman yelled.

"Fall back!" Decker echoed, waving his wounded arm overhead. The soldiers pulled away from the barricades, backing down the ramps, still firing.

As the last soldier cleared his ramp, Brewster slung his rifle and dug his fingers between the wooden planks. He pulled, and the ramp rose a few inches before crashing back down.

"Someone help! It's too heavy!" Brewster yelled. Corporal Darin appeared a moment later, grabbing hold of the ramp alongside Brewster. Both heaved, pulling the ramp into a vertical position. It hovered there a moment before wavering and falling back. Darin and Brewster barely had enough time to dive out of the way as the ramp hit the docks. It left a six foot gap between the dock proper and the pavement.

"Hoo-ah!" Brewster shouted, pumping an arm in the air and throwing a taunt at the carriers, who were now grouping around the barricade, pulling aside the obstacles in an effort to get at the men beyond.

Decker and Sherman had also managed to pull their ramps back, sealing the docks off from the parking lot. The soldiers filtered back towards the boats, keeping a wary eye on the carriers as they did so.

Brewster unslung his rifle again, holding it angled down. He decided to conserve ammo—the dead and infected were cut off for the time being.

"Sir!" came a cry. Sergeant Major Thomas appeared in the boathouse door, holding key rings above his head. "I've got 'em! Keys to four of the yachts!"

"Right!" Sherman yelled back. He turned to look at Decker, who stood about ten feet away on the adjoining walkway. He said, "Looks like we'll make it after all."

Darin and Brewster turned away from the mass of carriers on their end of the dock and headed toward the boats. Behind them, with no warning other than an uttered snarl, one of the carriers decided to go for it.

It came barreling through the barricades, launching itself from the edge of the pavement and sailing ungracefully through the air. It hadn't so much jumped as ran out over the water, but it had the speed it needed. It hit Darin from behind, knocking him to the planks, and tried to bury its nails in the back of his neck.

Brewster was shocked into inaction, but the moment passed quickly, and he lowered his rifle with one swift motion and blew the back of the carrier's skull off. The infected body hung over Darin for a moment, then slumped over the side of the dock and splashed into the water below.

Darin, wide-eyed, sat up slowly. "Thanks."

"Don't mention it," Brewster said, resting his rifle on his shoulder. "Come on, let's get out of here before another fucking Evel Knievel wannabe tries his luck."

"Yeah," Darin agreed, backing away from the gap, rifle trained on the staggering infected above.

He didn't take his eyes off of them until they were safely onboard one of the band's commandeered yachts, and pulling away from the harbor.

Open Sea
January 10, 2007
1513 hrs_

The USS *Ramage*, DDG-61, was an Arleigh-Burke class destroyer, the pinnacle of state-of-the-art technology. It was a sub-hunter, a mobile anti-aircraft station, and a long-range cruise missile platform, boasting firepower on its decks that outperformed entire third-world militaries. But it wasn't hunting subs now. It found itself pressed into service as a floating refugee camp.

Cargo webbing had been thrown over the sides of the deck to allow soldiers and civilians to climb up from the moored yachts alongside. The ship itself was operating on a skeleton crew, since most of the crewmembers were working with the USS *Ronald Reagan*'s battle group in the Red Sea. That left it with enough room onboard to accommodate the escaping group, albeit slightly uncomfortably.

Rooms normally left for storage of supplies or briefings were filled with displaced civilians, among them Mbutu Ngasy.

He found that he had had little trouble adjusting to the world falling apart around him, a fact that sat uneasily with him. Maybe adaptation was in his blood. His family, after all, were notorious survivors, moving from region to region in the past to avoid conflict and poverty. Whatever it was, he found he was having fun escaping from the continent on this floating fortress, and the idea made him wonder about his own morality.

People are dying, he thought as he pressed himself against a bulkhead to allow a pair of sailors to pass. *People are dying and I'm enjoying myself. Or, maybe I'm NOT as crazy as that.*

He figured that maybe the dull routine in Mombasa of waking up, going to work, and going to sleep at the end of the day had worn him thin. Maybe a tragedy like the one that had struck Africa was exactly what his life needed—a jump start.

Certainly he had met plenty of interesting people on the journey so far. As an air traffic controller he had had the opportunity to broaden his horizons, talking with pilots and crewmembers of cargo and passenger flights alike, but he had never actually gone to any of their home nations. He had now, in less than a month, been through four countries, and was on his way to his fifth, the United States.

He had just had his picture taken on deck by a man named Sam Denton, a Canadian photographer, as he had helped a soldier aboard.

"I'll make you famous," Denton had said with a grin. "If there are any newspapers left to print when we get back."

If indeed, Mbutu thought. The fall of Suez had left him with a gnawing sense of dread in his stomach. The virus was trampling any organized resistance in its path. Mother Nature was pissed off about something and she was taking heads. He wasn't a pessimist as a rule, but Mbutu couldn't help but feel as if this disease had barely begun its rampage.

Mbutu arrived at his destination, the destroyer's sickbay. He leaned in the doorway and knocked on the bulkhead.

"Hello," he said. "Would you like any help?"

Rebecca Hall was sitting on a metal stool, re-wrapping a wound on a refugee's leg, and glanced up at the sound of Mbutu's voice.

"Oh, hi!" she said, grinning. "Not really. The ship's got a full stock of medical supplies and the sailors have a doctor with them. We're close to wrapping up now."

"Hey, Becky, where'd you want your charts?" came a voice from behind Mbutu.

He stepped aside, allowing a sergeant to squeeze by with a double handful of scrap paper Rebecca had been jotting case notes on.

"Hi, Jack! In my hand would be great," Rebecca said, putting the finishing touch on the leg wound in front of her. She stood, accepting the papers from Sergeant Decker. She turned back to her patient and told him, "You can go. Keep an eye on it. It'll be throbbing for a while, but there shouldn't be any sharp pains. Remember to take the penicillin I gave you. Take one every six hours or so."

Mbutu grinned. The patient probably only understood every third word Rebecca said to him. As the man walked past him, Mbutu grabbed his arm, repeating the instructions in Swahili. His guess was right. The man was from his own home country.

"Asante!" he said with a broad smile before moving on.

"You are welcome," Mbutu said softly, turning back to Rebecca and Sergeant Decker in the sickbay. The pair were talking quietly between themselves. Mbutu may as well have been invisible. Other than him, the bay was empty.

Mbutu smiled. He could take a hint. He cleared his throat and the pair looked over at him.

"I am going up top. Maybe they could use my help," he said.

"Oh, okay. We'll be up once we get this place organized," Rebecca said. Decker waved a hand in his direction.

Mbutu strolled off down the corridor, squeezing to the side once more to allow sailors to pass by, the vague smile still on his face. *No husband*, she had said. Well, a sergeant in the Army was not the worst choice she could make.

Back in the sickbay, Rebecca shoved her charts into a folder, tucking it neatly into a desk drawer, then turned back to Sergeant Decker.

"Well?" she asked.

"Well, what?" he replied.

"Well, there must be a reason you came down here other than to just give me my charts," she told him, coquettishly brushing her hair back behind an ear. "—Not that I'm not happy you did."

"You caught me," said Decker, smiling. "I wanted to talk to you some more."

"Oh, I'm that interesting, am I?"

"Well, you're more interesting than the other people on this ship," Decker replied, leaning his rifle against an exam table.

Rebecca laughed. "Thanks, I think."

"We're heading back home," Decker began, choosing his words. "We should be there in a couple weeks. I was thinking . . ."

"Sergeants think?" Rebecca quipped.

"Ha-ha. I was thinking . . . I don't know, maybe once we got back we could go out sometime. My credit's good. Haven't been able to spend anything for the past couple months on deployment."

Rebecca smiled, looking down at the floor to hide the barest hint of a blush.

"—That is," Decker quickly added, "Assuming there are still restaurants when we get back."

"That's not funny," Rebecca replied.

"Well?"

"Oh." Rebecca took a moment before answering: "I . . . think I'd like that very much."

Decker flashed her a grin. "Me too."

They held the smile and gaze for a pair of heartbeats. As if by unspoken agreement, they leaned in towards each other, faces mere inches apart.

Outside, the ship's intercom buzzed loudly, and they pulled apart, the moment shattered.

"This is the captain. A few announcements before we begin our voyage. Listen up. All civilian refugees and military passengers, be advised. Remain out of areas designed crew only. The only authorized locations for passengers are temporary quarters, mess, and deck. Volunteers are needed in the mess to help prepare meals. General Sherman and staff, to the bridge, please . . ."

Above, Mbutu was just stepping into the hot sun when the announcement ended. General Sherman and Sergeant Major Thomas were standing at the far end of the deck, looking up at the bridge with furrowed brows. Mbutu saw Sherman gesture at Thomas, and the pair began a brisk walk towards the forecastle. Mbutu wasn't entirely sure he liked the look on the General's face. As the pair drew near, he risked an interruption.

"General," he said, "Is everything okay?"

"Things are fine, Ngasy," Sherman told him, brushing past Mbutu without further explanation. Ever-gruff Thomas shot him an annoyed glance. The two soldiers disappeared into the ship.

Mbutu sighed, folding his arms as a warm sea breeze washed over him. His mother, so famous in his mind for her stories of subtle wisdom, had once shared a Western tale of a man named Murphy and his Law. This, Mbutu thought, would be the time when Mr. Murphy would poke his head in, if things kept going at their current rate. He hoped they would be back on dry land before whatever was brewing on the bridge hit. He wasn't much of a swimmer.

Inside the corridors of the destroyer, Thomas drew alongside Sherman.

"With respect, sir, maybe it's not such a good idea to get too buddy-buddy with the civvies," he said.

"What do you mean, Sergeant?" Sherman asked, casting Thomas a sideways glance.

"You'll feel obligated to keep them informed, but still control our intel. That might not be a good idea, considering."

"Considering what?"

"Considering the state of affairs in the world. We should keep our little corner as ordered as possible. The last thing we need is a bunch of RumInt floating around making people nervous," Thomas said, hands clasped behind his back.

Sherman said in his own defense, "Rumor Intelligence is nothing new. No matter how much you try to control the flow of information, it's going to get out in bits and pieces."

"You could have just told him about the radio contacts. It could mean nothing, and solid intel's better than playing telephone like a bunch of grab-assy teenagers at a slumber party. If that guy back there," Thomas said, jerking a finger over his shoulder, "decides to tell someone how he just got the brush-off, you can bet there'll be a baker's dozen conspiracy theories floating around by evening chow."

"You sound truly disturbed, Sergeant," Sherman said, smirking.

"I'm just commenting, sir."

"Comment noted. I'll consider it. Maybe we should hold a meeting tonight, smooth things out and let the people know what's going on."

Thomas nodded once, and the pair moved on in silence. When

they reached the door to the bridge, Thomas reached out a hand and pulled it open. Inside, all was harried business. The bridge was ingeniously designed, with a maximum of efficiency for a minimum of space. Consoles lined the walls, and a wide viewport gave the ship's commanders a panoramic view of the open sea off the ship's bow. Crewmen bustled around, checking instruments, jotting notes, and broadcasting reports.

The Captain of the USS *Ramage* was a stout middle-aged career man named Franklin. He spoke with the slightest of New York accents, vaguely reminding Sherman of Joe Pesci in one of those old gangster films. As they entered, Franklin was hovering over the shoulder of the radio op in the center of the bridge. He looked up as they approached.

"Ah, General. Glad you're here," Franklin said.

"Glad you picked us up, Captain," Sherman replied. "Things were getting pretty sporty onshore."

"That's exactly what we're worried about right now. When you got onboard a couple hours ago I told you we were having problems establishing a connection with our base back home."

"Yes," Sherman said.

"Well, it's gotten worse in the past few minutes," Franklin said, leading Sherman and Thomas over to the radio station. He picked up a written transcript and handed it to Sherman. "We think they've got a down antenna or a pretty bad atmospheric disturbance."

Franklin looked around and leaned forward an inch, dropping his voice an octave.

"Least, that's what we hope it is."

"And you needed me here why?" Sherman asked, thumbing through the transcripts. Most were gibberish.

"You were part of the force tasked with quarantining Africa. I know Suez has fallen, but that was only a few days ago. You've been in contact with the commanders of the naval and air blockades these past couple of weeks. Is there any possibility someone got through? I'd like to know so I can give my men some peace of mind. They can't call home to check on their families, and they're worried."

Sherman frowned, but obliged, wracking his brain for any snippet of knowledge that might be useful.

"No," he said after a moment. "Once we got those blockades set up, nothing and no one got off the continent until Suez was breached."

"*Once* you got the blockades up," Captain Franklin repeated, stressing the first word. "All our reports from home are incomplete, but look on the next-to-last page of those transcripts, halfway down."

Sherman scanned the pages, and found the entry the Captain referred to.

```
VOICE 1: [static] to Mexico for [static] fueling.
[static] isn't [static] Be advised that Brazil
now considered [static] back to Panama. Any ships
[static] to the peninsula. Over.
VOICE 2: Say again. Over. [mumbling?] Losing signal
here . . .
V1: Situation [static] untenable as of [LONG STATIC]
fueling. Over.
VOICE 3: Coronado, your signal is breaking up. Relay
sitrep on hard lines. Do you still need resupply &
reinforcement? Over.
V1: [static]
V3: Say again, Coronado. Over.
V2: Andrews, we have lost signal from Coronado. Are
you receiving? Over.
V3: Negative. Edwards can you recon? Over.
V2: Can't do, Andrews. All flights on strike
missions. Can divert by [static]
V3: Edwards are you reading?
V2: [static]
```

Sherman grunted and tossed the transcript onto an empty chair.

"Could mean nothing," he said. "Cali's been having trouble with brownouts for the past decade. Maybe they've just lost transmitter power."

"They have generators, sir," Thomas said.

"Wouldn't have range on those," Franklin added, agreeing with Sherman. "All the relays would be out."

"Still," Sherman began, leaning on a console, "Edwards mentioned strike missions. They don't have much range either. They're flying over our soil."

"Civil unrest, maybe?" Thomas asked.

"Most likely. With Suez gone, the folks back home will be getting nervous," Franklin said.

"This is worth thinking about. Captain, please continue your effort to contact Coronado. They might come back on," said Sherman. He felt strange phrasing the request as such, and not as an order. Still, decorum had to be followed, and Captain Franklin was in command of this ship.

"Can do, General. We're monitoring their frequency even now."

"What about our task forces around Africa?" Thomas asked. "They picking up anything?"

"Similar reports from them. Britain's broadcasting loud and clear, and Australia's got their beacons lit. They've been taking in refugees—*very carefully*, I should add," Franklin answered. "As far as the Navy is concerned, we're running full steam. Army is holding positions on the ground, reporting minor incidents. This radio snafu is the first really bad news we've had since Suez."

"Let's keep on it, Captain. Can you keep me updated?"

"You'll get regular bulletins, General."

"Thank you. Sergeant, let's finish getting the civvies snuggled in for the night."

"Yes, sir."

Washington D.C.
January 10, 2007
2020 hrs_

Julie had lost track of time. The cell she sat in was windowless and dismal. She spent most of her time hanging on the iron bars that kept her snugly segregated from the damp corridor outside. It felt like weeks had passed, but she knew that wasn't the case. They'd fed her twice. She'd been ravenously hungry for the past twelve hours or so, she estimated, so it had probably only been a couple of days at one meal per day. It would keep going like this, she reasoned. They were wearing her down, trying to wrangle a confession out of her.

They were right, of course. She had betrayed her country's

national security by allowing the documents Dr. Demilio had given her to go public. She'd taken drastic steps to protect her own identity, though, and couldn't for the life of her figure out how they had tracked them back to her.

They're FBI, she mused. *They have ways.*

She almost chuckled then, tossing the thought in the imaginary rubbish bin she usually kept for less-than-stellar copy on the news floor. There was no way these guys were FBI. She'd figured that much out early on.

Firstly, she thought, *there's the matter of this cell and their methods. It's all designed to wear me out. The dampness, the dark, the lack of food, the inch-thin straw mattress—I'm supposed to crack like a piece of shitty porcelain from a budget souvenir store. One thing's for sure—they aren't getting the satisfaction.*

The men had been back to see her four times since they'd dumped her in the cell. They hadn't bothered to open the door since they'd tossed her in, but rather had sat out in the hallway, faces obscured by the dimness and dark shades, and had pitched questions at her. When she refused to answer, they'd pitched other things at her: Buckets of freezing water, generous spritzes of Mace, and half-finished scalding cups of coffee. And they'd been ramping up the pain. On their last visit, they'd brought a cattle prod with them. The methods they used were unconventional, not to mention illegal. There was only one agency that could effectively hide such activities from their overseers for any extended period of time. Judging from the dungeon she was in, they'd been hiding these interrogations for decades, maybe centuries.

And that brings us to the matter of the building itself.

Usually, historic places like the wine cellar she was now entombed in were eventually turned into museums, historic homes, or tourist destinations. This one was being used for a distinct purpose without the public's knowledge. This made her believe that the men who were holding her belonged to a group older than the Federal Bureau of Investigation, and had kept the secret of the rusty dungeon for quite a while. Again, there was only one group that had been around, in one form or another, long enough to have access to such an old facility, if only for psychological purposes.

Thirdly, there was the agents themselves, who were far too cliché to possibly be real FBI agents. As a reporter, she'd met dozens of such federal agents. Most were laid back enough to be considered human, even during interrogations. These guys dressed themselves in suits, ties, and dark sunglasses even in the depths of the dungeon she languished in. They were all business, all the time. They were playing a part—*acting*, if you will. There was only one agency that would go to such lengths to protect its own identity even from the people it arrested.

No Such Agency, Julie thought. *The NSA*.

That went higher than mere treason. If the problem were just leaked information, the FBI really would have come to arrest and question her. Without solid evidence, and her high-profile job, she would have been released within a day or so. With the NSA, one could never really tell. For all Julie knew, the outside world had been told she had died in a tragic car accident.

Despair was getting harder to fight back.

One of the few things that kept her going hour-by-hour was the increasing distractedness of the agents questioning her. It was as if each session their minds were less on prosecuting her for treason and more on events outside, whatever they were.

Perhaps things were coming to a head. Or perhaps they were simply toying with her. From the confines of the dark cell, Julie Ortiz couldn't tell one from the other.

USS Ramage
January 11, 2007
1202 hrs_

Ewan Brewster found that life at sea wasn't as bad as he had thought when he'd turned down the Navy recruiters with an upheld middle finger while the Army reps chuckled in the background. There was plenty of hot chow, the view on deck was spectacular—and, as a ground-pounder, he wasn't expected to do anything more than wait until they made landfall. He expected boredom would quickly become a factor, but he was still in the thrall of enjoying his downtime.

"Got any kings?" asked Corporal Darin, peering over a fanned-out hand of cards.

"Go fucking fish," Brewster said, puffing on a cigarette.

"Hear the latest?" Darin asked, plucking a card from the center pile. Brewster arched an eyebrow at him in silent response. "People are saying we can't raise bases stateside. They think home's been contaminated."

Brewster scoffed. "Fuck that. We've probably had our borders sealed for weeks. There aren't any viruses or illegal immigrants getting in until well after this shitstorm blows over."

"Hope that's true. But, man, what if it really happened? What would we do? Stay out on the water? We can't do that forever."

"Got any aces?" Brewster asked.

"Go fish."

"But to answer your question," Brewster went on, "I guess we could. We'd just go up and down the coast, do a few fuel runs and stay away from the cities if we could, I guess."

"What about food? Water? Drinking water, I mean," Darin added. "And we're packed in here pretty tight. I mean, not cramped like Shanghai tenements or anything, but it's not comfortable."

Sounds like dull thumps from the interior of the ship made them look over their shoulders, but Brewster shrugged.

"Dumbass civvies, knocking shit around. The Captain'll be pissed. But, man, I'll take being uncomfortable over being dead any day of the fucking week," Brewster said, getting back on subject. "Hey, Sergeant Major, what's the news?"

Thomas had been on his way to the bridge when his route took him past the irrepressible private and worrisome corporal. He scowled at Brewster.

"News is the skullfuck palace is open and you're the first customer," Thomas said, continuing on without a backward glance.

Brewster turned to look at the retreating NCO with a wide grin on his face, waving his free arm.

"And you have a nice day too, Sergeant!" he said, then turned back to Darin. "I like that guy. He's friendly."

Darin stared at Brewster with a perplexed look on his face. He was about to say something in response when the belowdecks door slammed open, revealing a sailor half carrying, half dragging a civilian refugee whose clothes were stained with blood.

"Help!" he cried. "Someone down there has it!"

The cry made Brewster's blood turn to ice. The sailor didn't even have to define what he meant by '*it*.'

Morningstar was onboard.

"Shit!" Brewster exclaimed, standing up sharply and knocking over the box they were playing cards on. He snapped up his rifle.

"No fucking way," Darin muttered, recoiling a few steps. A line of sweat had broken out on his forehead. He hadn't forgotten his close call at the Sharm El-Sheikh docks.

"Come on, man!" Brewster shouted, gesturing towards the bulkhead.

In the few moments since the sailor's terrified cry, the deck had begun to swarm with activity like a disturbed hornet's nest. By the time Brewster reached the open hatch, a few more soldiers had already grouped up nearby, standing with their backs to the forecastle wall. Sergeant Decker had been one of the first to arrive. He directed the soldiers with authority.

"Sidearms if you've got 'em!" he said. "Check your targets before you fire!"

It was going to be close combat. Brewster was glad to have an excuse to save rifle ammunition. He only had twenty-nine rounds left. He leaned his rifle against the steel wall of the ship and drew his pistol, holding it downwards at the ready.

The ship's alarms sounded general quarters, the steady *whoop-whoop* driving the frightened refugees even further from the open bulkhead that led below decks. Decker raised his voice to be heard above the din.

"Nobody get separated! Move in teams of two! If you find dead or wounded, you know what to do! Make sure they stay down! Ready?!"

He was interrupted as a figure came running up, breathless.

"Wait!" called Rebecca. "There's wounded up here! I need to get down to medical!"

Decker held a hand up to forestall any protest.

"No. You're staying up here."

Rebecca flashed him an indignant look. "I have to get to medical, Jack—"

"You have to stay on deck, Becky," Decker said, voice steely-edged. "Those things won't take prisoners."

Decker seemed to relent after a moment, gaze softening as he looked at her determined face.

Brewster watched the exchange between the two. His trigger finger was getting itchy.

"Decker, c'mon, man!" Brewster said, tapping his finger along the length of his Beretta's barrel. Decker cast a look at the soldiers, and seemed to make up his mind.

"What do you need from medical? We'll bring it up," he said. "Hurry!"

"Gloves, bandages, antiseptics, morphine," Rebecca rattled off. "I can make do with that!"

"Got it," Decker said. He turned back to the bulkhead, pistol at the ready. "Alright, on my signal."

Brewster tensed, awaiting the command.

"Go!"

Brewster swung into the doorway, scanning for targets. The corridor was empty. He moved inside, pistol held out in front of him. Behind him, the other soldiers began filing in, spreading out, covering one another. They moved slowly, deeper into the bowels of the ship.

When they came to the first intersection without incident, Decker spoke up.

"We split here. Half right. Other half, head left. Move!"

Brewster found himself ahead of Darin, Decker, and a sailor toting an MP-5. They rounded a corner, heading in the vague direction of medical. Brewster had no doubt Decker would want to pick up the supplies Rebecca asked for before they cleared the rest of the level. Ahead of them, a heavy door was hanging open. Brewster pointed at it silently and saw Decker nod in his peripheral vision. The four moved up to it and tensed themselves, then swung around the corner with weapons at the ready. The room was empty, but Brewster's eyes picked up spots of blood on the floor and wall. Something had gone down here.

They closed the door as quietly as they could, aware that any noise could draw unwanted attention. Darin's booted foot kicked up a spent shell casing, sending it skittering down the hall ahead of them.

"They were shooting," he whispered.

"Must have been those noises we heard," Brewster agreed. "And here I thought they were just fucking around in the supply rooms."

"Knock it off and keep it tight," Decker told them as he took the lead.

"Some civvie quarters up on the left," said the sailor, nodding towards another door.

This one, while not hanging ajar like the first, was cracked open, and light spilled out into the cold gray corridor. The four approached silently, preparing themselves to clear another room. Decker took up a position on the far side of the door, peering into the crack.

"See anything?" Brewster whispered.

"Shut up!" Decker admonished, one eye illuminated in the narrow shaft of light as he scanned what little he could see of the room. "Don't see anything. Let's clear it. Ready?"

"Ready," Brewster said, holding up his pistol.

Decker flung the door open, and the four soldiers brought their weapons to bear, sweeping the room for targets as they moved in. Nothing jumped out at them. In fact, the room was mostly empty of even inanimate objects—a couple of bunks, a card table, and a few bags in the corner were all that adorned the space.

"Casualties," Darin said, holstering his pistol and moving ahead of the group towards a pair of fallen civilians. They lay in pools of blood, unmoving, eyes open and vacant. Darin knelt and put his fingers to their throats. He shook his head after a moment. "They're gone."

"Get back," Decker told him, narrowing his eyes. Darin stepped away. Decker leaned over the corpses, holding his pistol point-blank against the heads, and fired twice, splashing gore against the wall and floor. Blood flecked his boots. He hurriedly wiped them along a blanket on a nearby bunk.

"Well," Brewster breathed, surveying the damage, "I don't think they'll be getting up again."

"Oh, goddamn it all to hell and back," Darin mumbled. "You got blood on my shit, too. There isn't a dry-cleaners for two thousand miles."

"Get over it," Decker said. "Let's keep moving. This room's clear."

They filed back out into the hallway, closing and securing the door behind them.

The sailor with the sub-machine gun took point, nodding his head down the corridor. He advised, "Medical's just ahead, around the next corridor."

"Right. Keep it tight. Don't pull ahead," Decker said. The four were off again, keeping close to the walls, tense and ready for anything. They were nearly at the elbow in the corridor when the sailor held up a fist. Darin, Brewster, and Decker stopped in their tracks, holding their breath.

"There's something there," he whispered. "I can hear breathing."

Brewster strained his ears. The metal of the ship's body distorted sounds, but he could definitely hear muffled, labored breathing, almost a wet pant, echoing off the steel walls.

"I hear it too," Decker said.

"It's getting louder," said Darin, glancing furtively back and forth. "It's coming this way!"

Safeties were clicked off and the group tensed, scanning the corridor in both directions.

"Nothing for it, it knows we're down here by now," Decker blurted. "Move! Get to medical!"

The sailor nodded, swinging around the corner. Brewster expected him to open fire immediately, but the sub-machine gun remained silent. The sailor relaxed a bit.

"Clear!"

The three soldiers rounded the corner after him. The door to medical was a dozen feet down the corridor, and there was no sign of any infected. The sounds of the labored breathing still echoed around them, slowly growing in intensity. Adrenaline was rushing through Brewster's veins.

"Whatever's going to happen, let it happen soon," he said.

"Amen," Darin agreed, walking in the rear of the group, facing backwards to keep their rear covered.

"Cover the corridor," Decker instructed as they approached the doorway to medical. "Brewster, you and I grab the stuff Becky needs topside."

"Right, sergeant."

The two crept into medical as Darin and the sailor took up position outside the doorway. Once inside, the sound of breathing reached a fever pitch. Brewster and Decker froze, eyes flicking over the room. It looked abandoned, but whatever was making those noises was very close.

"Clear the room," said Decker.

The pair split, inching their way around the examination tables. As Brewster rounded the first table, he stopped, whistling lightly to Decker. The sergeant glanced over.

"*I got him*," Brewster whispered, aiming his weapon into the corner of the room. "On the ground, behind that shelf."

"I see him," said Decker, taking aim as well.

It didn't appear to be an infected as they had originally thought. A man lay half-exposed in the corner of the room, trying to tuck himself as deeply as possible in the shadows. He seemed half-mad with fright, and clutched his shoulder with one arm. He seemed in terrible pain, clenching his teeth. His breathing was loud and grating.

"Say something, buddy," Brewster said, taking a step towards the man.

"Don't . . ." managed the man before a fit of coughing seized him. He cleared his throat, head rolling back in weakness as he tried again. "Don't come close. It bit me."

"We'll see if we can fix you up," Brewster replied, holstering his pistol and scanning the shelves in the room for anything useful. The labels on the bottles of medicine read like Greek to him. "Aw, fuck, man, I don't know what this shit is. I flunked chemistry."

"Don't bother," said the man. Blood leaked between his fingers as they grasped his shoulder. "You should shoot me."

"Fuck that," Brewster said. "If you go, then I'll shoot you. Not before."

"I'll shoot him," Decker said, stepping forward.

"Whoa, hold it, man!" Brewster exclaimed, putting himself between the man and Decker.

"Get out of my way, private. We're containing this outbreak before it gets to all of us," Decker gritted, glaring at Brewster.

"Let him do it," gasped the man. "I can feel it."

"No fucking way," Brewster said, firmly. "He's still alive."

"Shoot me . . ."

"Out of the way, Brewster!" Decker shouted.

"What the hell is—holy shit," said Darin, stepping into the room and seeing the scene within. "Is he infected?"

"Yes!" Decker shouted again. "And I'm going to deal with him if this bleeding heart motherfucker ever gets out of my way!"

"Hey, fuck you, pal," Brewster said, flipping Decker the bird. "You want to kill a living person, you kill me first."

"Can't one of you idiots shoot me?" choked the man in the corner. "I don't . . . have much time!"

"That can be arranged," Decker said to Brewster, ignoring the man's comment. The sailor in the corridor was looking in at them nervously.

"Whoa, whoa," said Darin, stepping in. "We're safe for now, right? Let's watch him. If he turns, we take care of him. He won't leave this room. Right, sergeant?"

"We should kill him now before he has a chance to spread it around," Decker said, turning his ire on the corporal.

"Shoot me . . . shoot me now!" the man gasped. He coughed—a wet, gurgling, pathetic noise, head slumping downwards.

"Look at him, private!" said Decker. "He's got it! If we don't do what we can to stop it now we could—"

A scream from the doorway caught them all off-guard. Weapons snapped up, eyes following suit.

The sailor, distracted by the argument, had failed to keep an eye on the corridor. An infected clung to his back, hissing in rage and scratching at his face and neck.

"Get it off! Get it off!" the sailor screamed, flinging his arms about in terror.

The infected leaned in and tore a chunk of flesh from the sailor's cheek, garnering a shriek of pain from the sailor. His finger tightened on the trigger of the MP-5 and the weapon fired, sending rounds flying into medical, ricocheting off the steel walls. The soldiers dove for cover as the sailor and infected fell back into the corridor outside. The sailor kept firing, nearly deafening them all with the quick rattle of the weapon.

Darin found himself nearest the struggle as he came out of his roll, and brought up his pistol, firing off a pair of quick shots. One missed, and the second took the infected in the shoulder, knocking it off the sailor. It slumped against a wall, life draining from its eyes. A third shot took it in the forehead, ensuring it wouldn't be getting back up again. It twitched once, and was still.

The sailor rolled about in pain, holding a hand to his torn cheek. As he removed the hand and saw his own blood coating it, though, his shrieking ceased, and a calm seemed to fall over him. Darin, Brewster, and Decker slowly came out from behind their cover, looking out at the wounded soldier. He looked back at them, a kind of peaceful resignation on his face. He flashed them a grim smile, and in one swift motion drew his pistol, put it in his mouth, and pulled the trigger, depositing the contents of his skull on the wall behind him. His body slumped sideways, laying beside the corpse of the infected that had doomed him.

The three soldiers were quiet for a moment. Brewster was the first to speak.

"Fuck me running," he managed, mouth agape.

Darin darted into the hallway, scanning back and forth for more hostiles.

"Clear! Damn," he said as he waved a hand to clear the air. "There's brain mist floating around out here."

"Try to breathe in some intelligence," Decker quipped.

"You're a dick, man," Brewster said, frowning.

"Maybe, but I'm a—"

The man in the corner, forgotten during the firefight, howled, and they spun on him. He had pulled himself to his feet and was clutching his head, face twisted in pain. Without warning, he recovered, head snapping up to lock onto Decker with a rageful stare. He sprang forward, growling in the back of his throat, and was almost on top of the sergeant when Decker's pistol discharged, the round taking the man in the throat and dropping him like a wet sack of meat.

They surveyed the body for a moment before Decker whirled on Brewster.

"That's what I was trying to do earlier," he said, pointing at the corpse. "If you'd let me do it, he wouldn't have had a chance to attack us like that. Grow a fucking pair and open your eyes, private. This is total war. Us or them. The sooner you realize that, the better off you are. Now grab those fucking supplies and let's get out of here."

Washington D.C.
January 11, 2007
2000 hrs_

"She's proving to be a much more stubborn subject than we'd thought," said Agent Mason, sipping on a lukewarm cup of coffee and watching a muted replay of last night's interrogation session on a flickering television set. On the screen, Julie Ortiz mouthed indignant answers to questions she had no intention of answering.

Mason could see himself in the background, looking bored and distracted.

"Impressive, that's for sure," mumbled Agent Derrick, thumbing through a manila folder. "Is there really any point in continuing the interrogations? We already have what we want. Our information is reliable."

"And do what? Let her lie away in a cell for the rest of her life? Wasteful," said Agent Sawyer, shaking his head. "We would do better by managing to extract a confession from her."

"We have testimony against her on file," said Mason.

"It should hold up in court," added Derrick.

"It's not enough," Sawyer said. "We have accumulated enough evidence to convict her, true. But the trial would be public—and messy. There's the matter of fraud."

"We were authorized to identify ourselves as FBI," Mason pointed out.

Sawyer raised his eyebrows and asked, "And will the American people be satisfied with that? A mere authorization to impersonate a federal agent of a different bureau?"

"Perhaps," said Derrick. "They are malleable, and easily manipulated. The right story in the right place should cover us well."

"Maybe we're looking at this all wrong," Mason interjected, furrowing his brow in thought. "Maybe we shouldn't even be worrying about this case. Maybe there are more important things we should be doing."

The silence in the room after he spoke was deafening.

"What did you say?" Sawyer said after a moment, fixing Mason with a stony glare.

"Have you looked outside the window recently?" Mason said. "Do our lives really revolve so much around orders that we don't see the storm on the horizon out there? Things aren't exactly running smoothly. I'm certain the country would find us more useful in another role. They can't be bothered with treason charges at a time like this."

"Our borders are solid. Cases are scattered and few. They will be contained," Derrick said, siding with Sawyer.

"In a month, maybe two, this will have blown over, and then it's business as usual.

"When that happens, they'll begin to wonder what happened to

Julie Ortiz—such a high profile case cannot be kept under lock and key forever," Sawyer said. "And speaking of treason—let's not hear such talk from you again, Mason."

Agent Mason grimaced, taking a final sip from the coffee cup before crumbling it in his hand and tossing it into a nearby wastebasket. He said nothing.

"Well, then," Sawyer said, satisfied the situation had been dealt with, "Let's move on to the business at hand. Any suggestions from either of you? New methods, perhaps?"

"Miss Ortiz's profile suggests a susceptibility to psychological tactics," Derrick answered. "I suggest we continue. Perhaps we should up the moisture seepage into the dungeon, and take the lights down a few more watts."

"The dungeon's settings are optimal. In the fifty years we've been using it it's never failed in its purpose," Mason pointed out.

"That doesn't mean this subject won't set a new standard," Sawyer said. "We'll go with Derrick's suggestion. Agent Mason, if you will?"

Mason sighed and swiveled in his chair to face a small console tucked in the corner of the room, and twisted a heavy metal knob farther to the right. A second, more worn knob, was given a twist to the left. The surveillance monitors showed the dungeon dimming. The agents could see Julie in her cell, huddled against a wall, knees tucked up to her chest. As the lights went down a notch, she looked around, surprised by the change. It would be hard for her to make out the far wall of her cell now that it was even darker down there. The moisture seepage was a well-designed irrigation system, but would take a few hours before any real change was felt by the prisoner. The sum of their actions was merely to make Julie Ortiz that much more miserable, and therefore a bit more likely to tell them what they wanted to know.

Suddenly, the lights in the dungeon went out entirely, as did those in the room the agents were in. The monitors and consoles remained lit, powered by a local generator. After a moment, the lights came flickering back on, illuminating the worried glances of the agents as they looked back and forth at one another.

"That was different," Derrick said.

"This building isn't supposed to have power outages," Mason added. "The systems are redundant."

"Perhaps the grid suffered a brownout," Sawyer offered.

"I hope there isn't trouble out there."

"Once again with the worries," Sawyer admonished. "The military is in position if civil unrest reaches a boiling point and they are more than well enough equipped to deal with anything a shotgun-toting civilian could throw at them. Power is a valuable commodity at the moment. A brownout, nothing more."

"I hope you're right," said Mason.

"For the last time, Agent Mason, we are the most secure building in the most secure city in the most secure nation in the world," Sawyer retorted. "If anything is going to happen, it'll happen to us last. There's no reason to get our hackles up over a power fluctuation."

"And as to the business at hand?" prompted Derrick, gesturing at the monitors.

"Oh, yes. I'd almost forgotten over Mason's constant worrying," Sawyer said, smiling grimly. "We'll increase the frequency of interrogations in addition to the modification of the dungeon environment. Let's begin to throw in items she doesn't know we're aware of yet—maybe that will help throw her off-guard."

"How about a little good cop, bad cop?" Derrick said. "Classic, but we haven't tried it yet."

"We'll need to enlist outside help," Mason replied. "She's far too familiar with the three of us to buy into any overtures of sympathy."

"Oh, at last a helpful suggestion from you, Mason. How kind," said Sawyer. "You're right, of course. I'll contact some people."

"What about our other guest?" Derrick asked. "Do we have any further use for her?"

"No, she's given us what we wanted with little protest," Sawyer said, tapping a finger on the tabletop. "Still, we can't just set her free."

"And we can't keep her here forever, either," Mason pointed out.

"But for the time being, we can," Sawyer replied. "Discontinue interrogations, but keep Dr. Demilio under guard. She may still be of some use in the future."

USS Ramage
January 11, 2007
2122 hrs_

General Francis Sherman knelt beside a crumbled infected corpse in the halls of the USS *Ramage,* grimacing at the sight of the gruesome head wound that had killed it. Around him, soldiers swarmed through the belly of the ship, double-checking rooms and preparing corpses for removal. The firefight below decks had been swift and decisive. Once the soldiers had reacted to the threat, it hadn't taken long to put down all the infected on board—but the victory was hollow. The corpses of victims lined the bowels of the destroyer.

Sherman grunted softly, voice muffled behind the surgical mask on his face.

"How many so far?" he asked, pulling a pair of latex gloves over his hands and snapping them tight.

"Twenty-three, sir," answered a grim-faced Sergeant Major Thomas. "Seventeen refugees, four soldiers caught unarmed, two went down fighting."

A camera flash went off, followed by the thin, thready whine of the bulb charging for another shot. Sam Denton crouched beside Sherman, face also obscured behind a surgical mask.

"How do you think it got started, Frank?" Denton questioned, snapping off another photo of the body in front of them.

"One of the civvies brought it in," said Sherman. "Only found one body without any bite wounds. Had to be the original carrier—It took a few rounds to the chest and two to the head later on that put him down."

"Twenty-three dead because of one carrier?" Denton said, voice filled with awe and a hint of dread.

"We saw it back before Suez," Thomas said. "A good bite turns you in a few minutes, maybe an hour or two, tops."

Sherman nodded in agreement. "The original host onboard probably got everyone in his compartment before he was discovered. One became six or seven within a few minutes."

"*Jesus Christ*," Denton whispered.

"No," Sherman said, turning his head to shoot Denton a bemused glance. "Quite the opposite, actually."

A soldier in thick, stained MOPP gear and mask came walking up. He addressed General Sherman with an edge in his voice.

"General, we've finished securing the area. We've found two more bodies. One civvie, one sailor, down in the engine room. Looks like they made a stand—blood that ain't theirs is all over the place. They didn't make it, though," said the soldier, accenting the obvious at the end of his short report. The soldiers, in their ever-dwindling numbers, were getting accustomed to death.

"Thanks, private," said Sherman. "Secure the bodies and take them topside for burial."

"Yes, sir."

Denton watched the private as he hurried away, then turned back to Sherman and Thomas.

"Twenty-five now," he said. He got a mute nod from Sherman as a response. "Think they'll find any more?"

"I doubt it," Sherman said as a pair of soldiers hefted the corpse up off the floor and onto a gurney. "We've got everyone accounted for now."

A shout came from the direction of medical. Instantly, hackles rose and rifles were trained on the doorway. A soldier backpedaled into the hall, wearing a surprised look on his face. He noticed the rifle barrels trained on him, and raised his hands up quickly.

"No, it's alright, he's strapped down!" he said, gesturing into the room in front of him. "Just startled me, that's all."

"What is it?" Sherman asked, striding over to the soldier and looking into medical.

"The body—it just started moving again," said the soldier.

Inside medical, strapped securely to another wheeled gurney, was a sheet-covered body, twitching randomly under the thin cover. The metal bars of the gurney squeaked here and there as it rocked back and forth under the weight of the reanimated corpse.

"Soldier, dispose of that carrier," Sherman ordered, pointing at the gurney.

"Yes, sir," said the soldier, stepping back into medical and drawing his sidearm.

"No!" Sherman barked, holding up a hand. "You'll just get more hot blood all over the place. We don't want anyone else getting infected. Take it up topside first."

"Yes, sir," said the soldier, sheepishly holstering his pistol and grabbing the gurney to wheel it out.

"Frank," Denton began, coming up alongside the general. "Are you saying *any* exposure, even to dead blood, can trigger an infection?"

"That's the idea," Sherman replied, glancing askew at the photographer. "Standard virology. We don't know how long Morningstar lives in exposed blood. Basic stuff. Didn't you learn any of that in college?"

"No, I know that. But what about the soldiers who cleared these rooms? They weren't wearing any masks," Denton said, eyes widening.

"It's been taken care of," Sherman said, staring hard at Denton.

Denton felt his face fall slack. "You don't mean . . ."

"Yes," said Sherman. "As of an hour ago, they're all under quarantine."

Elsewhere on the ship, grim determination was being replaced by bewildered indignation.

"Let me the fuck out of here, man!" Brewster shouted, pounding on the bulkhead with the flat of his palm. He, Decker, Darin, and a few other soldiers were all locked in a barrack belowdecks, under armed guard. They weren't allowed out for any reason until further notice. "This is bullshit!"

"Give it a rest, Brewster," Decker said, lounging on one of the bunks in the room, idly puffing on a cigarette and staring at the ceiling. "They're not going to open the door. That's why they call it a *quarantine*."

"Fucking quarantining what, man? I'm not sick. None of those fucks bit me. I'm right as the fucking rain, chief."

"They've got to have their reasons. Maybe they're just waiting to check us for bites," Darin said from the corner of the room, where he sat glancing through a ragged Sports Illustrated he'd found under a bunk.

"Nah, we'll be here a while, I think," Decker replied. "They'll want to see if any of us get sick. That could take a few days."

"*Days?*" Brewster mouthed, pounding again on the bulkhead. "I'm trapped in this tiny fucking room for the next few days? That's great, man, that's just A-list material right there. Let me clear my schedule and get ready for the fucking tedium."

"But what other reason would we have to be infected if none of us were bitten?" asked another private first-class named Scott.

"Maybe it's airborne," someone offered.

"Then *everyone* would be infected, dumbass," came a retort.

"The *blood*," said Darin, suddenly, sitting up straight and dropping the Sports Illustrated onto his lap. "It's in their blood!"

"What? Well, thanks, Captain Obvious. Have a bronze star," Decker said.

"Sergeant, we practically waded through it. Oh, shit—the sailor who shot himself! I know I got his blood on me! It was aerosol! Oh, shit, I might have it!" Darin ranted, breathing heavy. The soldiers seated near him subtly began to edge away, eyeing him cautiously.

"Oh, for fuck's sake, Darin, calm down," Brewster said. "That guy had barely been bitten. It couldn't have been all through him by then. You probably just got some old-fashioned regular blood on you."

"But I didn't," Decker said, looking down at his bloodstained boots. "I got some on me when I finished those bodies in one of the bunkrooms."

"Only on your boot!" Darin protested. "I breathed it in, man! Breathed it in! I'm fucked!"

"Now, for shit's sake, keep your head!" said Brewster. "Jesus, any one of us could've slipped up and put our hand in a little blood. No need to go freaking out or anything; we'll just sit tight and wait. Look, Darin, like I said, that guy barely had any virus in him when he shot himself. You're fine. I fucking guarantee it. Decker, you only got it on your boot, so I guess you won't die a painful fucking death. Sorry."

"Eat shit, private," Decker retorted.

Brewster ignored him. "No one else remembers getting any blood on them?"

No hands were raised; no voices piped up.

"Good. Then we'll all be out of this fucking tomb in a few days. Now . . . ," Brewster began, pulling a chair up to the room's small table. "Seeing as we've got some more time on our hands, anyone play Texas Hold-Em?"

PART SEVEN:

HOLOCAUST

2203 hrs_

It obviously wasn't enough that their numbers had dwindled to less than half of what they started with—it wasn't enough that radio contact with the continental states was on the fritz—it wasn't enough that a killer virus was sweeping half the globe.

Just one problem after another, thought Sherman as he surveyed the scene in engineering. The two people found within had put up quite a fight before they had been brought low, but their dignity had come with a price. Bullet holes pocked the walls. Damaged equipment sputtered in protest as it fought against failure.

"They ruptured the fuel pumps," Franklin said over the noise of the engines. "Lost pressure in the lines to two of the plants."

Sherman grunted, resting his fists on his hips, and asked, "How's that translate?"

Franklin glanced askew at Sherman and replied, "Middlin' impact at best, so far. We're trying to patch the pumps now, but we're still managing about seventy-five percent of our maximum drive."

"I thought these ships were more resilient than this, Captain," Sherman said, disappointed at the loss of speed they were going to experience in their long steam towards home.

"Well, usually we're attacked from the outside, sir," Franklin said with a chuckle. "Just bad luck on our part."

"Yes, well, we seem to be having an awful lot of it lately," Sherman replied. "I think we're overdue for a little good fortune."

The fuel pumps chose that precise moment to cough, sputter, and die, leaving the engineering compartment in what suddenly felt like dead silence. The men working on the pumps cast it a disgruntled stare. One threw down a wrench in disgust and kicked the dead pump with a booted foot.

"So much for good fortune," Sherman sighed.

Franklin turned to the men gathered around the pump and asked them, "Can you get it running again?"

The detail's leader let his eyes slide over the fuel pump and slowly shook his head. "I don't think so, Captain. Reuters is the usual mechanic for these pumps. I've only dealt with them a couple times. This could take a specialist, or maybe just a lot of time and effort."

"Where's Reuters?" Sherman asked.

"He's dead, sir. He shot himself after he was bitten."

"Keep on it, sailor," Franklin said. "Do what you can."

"Aye aye, sir."

"How does this change things?" Sherman asked, turning back to Franklin with an anxious look on his face.

"Well, two of our power plants are offline until we can get those pumps running again. We'll be operating at fifty percent efficiency until then."

"Unacceptable," Sherman said, frowning.

"I know," Franklin replied, "But short of finding a port and a skilled mechanic we're shit out of luck. We'll have to steam on half our normal power."

"Now, wait, maybe not," said Sherman, wrinkling his brow in thought. "We're still a day out of the Philippines, correct, Captain?"

"That's right. We should be passing through in around thirty hours. Why?"

"I've got an old buddy who lives there these days. Master Sergeant, retired. Used to be a tank mechanic. He might be able to help us out."

"No offense, but these GE plants are a lot different than tank engines."

"I know, I know, but he runs a machine shop, and he'll have access to the parts and information you'll need to get these turbines running again. Captain, given the proper materials and hands, how fast can this problem be fixed?"

"Master Chief?" Captain Franklin asked, addressing the detail leader working on the broken pumps.

"I'd reckon about six, eight hours, sir," came the reply. "Only if we knew exactly what we were doing, and kept the guesswork to a minimum."

"That time investment's more than worth it," Sherman said. "We'll save ourselves days in the end."

Franklin nodded in agreement. "Full steam would get us there in half the time. We'll lose a day or two from our original schedule, but it's better than losing a week. I'll need to know where this friend of yours is, General, and I'll take the *Ramage* to him. Better let him know we're coming. Don't want to have to wait for the parts to come through on back order."

"I'll get you the port, you plot the course, Captain."

"Very well."

Washington, D.C.
January 11, 2007
2314 hrs_

Escape, Dr. Demilio reasoned, would be impossible. She'd paid attention on the way in and had been examining her cell closely. The facility where she was being held was far too secure—she was more than willing to peg it as 'ultra-modern' in her eyes. The agents responsible for her interrogation used iris and voice identification to access her cellblock, touch pads in the floor recognized her position in the cell, and cameras observed her every move. She deduced the only way she'd be leaving would be if someone actively brought her out, and not before. In the meantime, she was having a bad time of things.

Somehow the NSA had figured out it had been her that leaked the classified aspects of the Morningstar Strain to the public. Though the information was received with skepticism by the people and in the end "disproved" by government officials as hokum, she was still under arrest for treason. She hadn't been allowed access to the outside world since her arrest—No lawyer, no phone calls, not so much as a letter. She wondered if the world had noticed she'd vanished. Surely her colleagues at USAMRIID had noticed, but were probably stifled within a day.

Overall, Anna thought, she wasn't being treated that shabbily. She'd cooperated after the first few interrogation sessions and told the agents what they wanted to know. She thought she would feel worse about giving in to their demands, but they already knew much of what she'd told them. She was doing little more than confirming items they already had a good idea about, and sparing herself unnecessary pain and trouble in the meantime.

Originally they had tossed her in a dark, damp, dungeon-like cellblock somewhere in the bowels of the building, but once she'd cooperated they'd moved her up to more civilized quarters; Brighter lighting, a warm cot, and best of all dry air—no cloying dampness. They'd even begun feeding her three times a day again.

The agents still stopped by now and then with trivial questions.

"What containment measures are appropriate when dealing with a contaminated high-rise structure?" was one question.

"Would basic, subsonic riot control weapons function against the second-stage carriers?" was another, referring to the undead infected.

"What is your approximation of the rate of infection in a host that is contagious, but not showing any symptoms?"

Anna was getting very tired of being left in the dark. She never got a chance to ask any questions of her own, though she figured she wouldn't get much in the way of answers if she had. The agent's questions, on the other hand, were giving her a little insight into what might be happening outside. Lately their visits had become less frequent, and when they did show up outside her cell door their inquiries were concise and anxious.

"If someone is exposed, what is the chance they won't become symptomatic?"

"Will the virus burn out after it's been active within a host for a time?"

She worried that their questions meant real trouble. They always asked, in roundabout ways, for strategies to fight the virus. She figured that meant there were at least a few cases of the disease in the United States—where or how many, she had no way of knowing. The agents didn't seem particularly disturbed, so she guessed the situation was still tenable. There was no guarantee that would last for long, though.

Footsteps in the corridor alerted her to someone's approach. She stood, smoothing out the plain uniform shirt they had given her. The footsteps stopped outside her cell and the small metal panel embedded in the door slid open, revealing the piercing gray eyes of Sawyer.

"Dr. Demilio."

"Afternoon. Haven't seen you in a little while. Everything alright out there?" Anna said, slipping in the question before Sawyer could reply.

The agent narrowed his eyes and expelled a short breath of disgust. Though Anna couldn't see all of his face, she imagined she could see the sneer on his lips.

He asked, "What effect would a chemical nerve agent have on the carriers?"

Anna folded her arms across her chest.

"I don't think so, Serpico," she said. "I've had just about enough of being the one doing all the answering and none of the questioning."

"You're in no position to question anyone, Doctor."

"Oh, come on!" Anna said, raising her voice and throwing her arms up in exasperation. "Who am I going to tell, huh?! I've cooperated with you so far! Throw me a damn bone, here! If the situation's good, that's great, let me know, I'll relax! If it's bad, then it's my world too, and I want to know about it! So no, I won't answer your question until after you've answered mine! I'll ask again: How're things outside?!"

Sawyer didn't say a word, yet seemed to be considering Dr. Demilio's demand. Instead, after a moment, he began to speak slowly and clearly.

"Doctor, you are in this portion of our facility as a gesture of our appreciation for your cooperation. You can always go back to the dungeon and keep Miss Ortiz company."

Taken aback, Anna took a step back, and asked, "*You have her here?*"

"Surprised, I take it? Yes, even though you left her out of your confession, it wasn't hard to find out who you'd leaked the information to. She has not been very cooperative so far. As a result she is not very . . . *comfortable* right now. You could join her, if you want. All you have to do is refuse to answer my question."

Anna turned the threat over in her mind for a moment and decided it was better to retain her dignity this once—if only to piss off Sawyer.

"I don't think so," she said. "You've got my notes. Figure it out for yourself."

Another invisible snarl from the face on the other side of the door.

Sawyer began, "Maybe I wasn't making myself clear—"

Anna interrupted, "No, maybe I was the one who wasn't being clear. I'm not helping you. At all."

"Unless I submit to your little questions," Sawyer said.

"Quid pro quo, Agent Sawyer," Anna said, smiling on the inside. She was beginning to feel a bit like Hannibal Lecter, cooped up in a cell, the only source of credible information that was desperately needed outside.

"Then your usefulness is at an end," Sawyer said, and Anna could see his posture shift, the sound of raspy leather being scraped, and then the barrel of a pistol pointed at her through the panel in the door. "I could kill you now and let you rot in there. They'll have better things to do than fry me for it."

"And if they succeed in stopping the virus, Agent? Would they really just forget it? Even with the tapes to remind them?" Anna asked, jerking a finger over her shoulder and smirking.

Anna imagined she could see his eyes following where her thumb had led them, up to the corner of her cell where the tiny closed-circuit camera rested, red light blinking.

"Not to mention the bugs that are probably recording our conversation now from a couple dozen microphones," Anna went on.

Sawyer hesitated and Anna stared him down, waiting. Suddenly the gun vanished from the panel and Anna heard the weapon slide back into its holster. Sawyer's face pressed up to the door, brow creased in frustration.

"If that's the way you want it, Doctor, that's the way you'll have it. Live, for now. And enjoy the warm cell. You won't be here much longer."

The panel in the door slid shut with a clang, and Dr. Demilio was left alone. She sagged visibly, expelling a long breath of relief. She was certain Sawyer was the type that would actually kill her if he thought she was becoming more trouble than she was worth. She was just thankful he wasn't the one in charge.

Who knows who that is, Anna thought. *And I'm not even sure I would want to know.*

USS Ramage
January 14, 2007
0902 hrs_

"Miserable heat, eh?" remarked Denton, resting his forearms on the steel railing in front of him.

"Quite," General Sherman replied, holding a hand to his brow to shield his eyes from the bright sunlight reflecting off the tropical waters. "But a beautiful view."

The USS *Ramage* was anchored in an inlet that nestled up to a storybook island. Curving palms jutted out over the beaches, and a thick green canopy dotted here and there with a rooftop spread back as far as the men on the ship could see. One small town was the focal point of the island, a tiny wedge of civilization tucked between the dense forests. The sight was a welcome one to the battle-weary men and women onboard, but their presence was attracting a degree of attention that couldn't be all good. Distant figures on the beach gazed back at them with a bit of trepidation in their step, and fishermen gave the vessel a wide berth as they sailed toward the town's docks.

"Does this pal of yours know we're coming?" Denton asked, eyeing the folk onshore.

"No," Sherman said.

"It doesn't look like they're rushing to greet us." He gestured at the people. "Likely we'll be stoned to death before we pull a dinghy onto those beaches."

"I couldn't call ahead. There are only two generators on this island, and one of them powers their radio. They don't leave 'em on all the time, just long enough to catch news every now and then or to call in assistance. I'm banking on Hal firing it up when he hears about the destroyer sitting in the harbor, and maybe we'll get somewhere."

Denton was doubtful. He asked, "How does an entire island go on with only one radio?"

"There are only a few hundred people here, Denton," answered Sherman. "It's all they need or ask for from the outside world. They take care of themselves just fine."

"Well, I hope something happens soon. I'd like to get off this ship and stretch my legs on dry land for a change. I bet half the ship's with me on that idea."

"Let's not go rushing off to shore," Sherman replied. "At least until we're invited, that is."

"I suppose it's too much to hope for that they know anything about what's going on back in good old North America, eh?"

"They know as much as we do, or less," Sherman said. "I'm sure our communication problems with home aren't what we think they are. We've been getting bulletins from almost every other corner of the world for the past couple days. Did I tell you the Brits managed to fight back an outbreak in London?"

"No," Denton said, surprised. "Good for them. Gotta wonder how long that'll last, though."

"They've got a pretty good position on that island, just like the people here," Sherman said, folding his arms across his chest. "Don't jinx 'em. Let's hope for the best."

From behind Sergeant Major Thomas announced, "Sir! Radio contact from the island, sounds American. All he'd say was '*take me to your leader*.' Sounds like Hal, sir."

Sherman grinned. Hal Dorne was a bit of a crackpot, but professional under duress. Sherman had served with him decades ago, before the man had retired and left America entirely, preferring the solitary paradise of the islands. He was a drinker and sometimes prone to childlike acts of mischievousness.

"Tell him it's me, Thomas. I'll be on the bridge in half a minute."

"Yes, sir."

Sherman left Denton leaning on the ship's railing, looking out over the clear blue waters.

"It's a shame," Denton said to himself. "Us being here, in a place like this, and all that shit's just lurking over the horizon. Like the eye of a storm. And to think that the only reason we're here is to gear up to go rushing back out into it."

He sighed, squinting his eyes at the people on the shoreline in the distance, with their sullen movements and cold stares.

"A shame," he repeated softly. "Damn shame."

0908 hrs_

"We've stopped," remarked Scott, sitting up suddenly.

"Whuzzat?" mumbled Brewster, pulling away the thin wool blanket he'd been lying under away. "Stopped? Where?"

"I don't fuckin' know," said Scott. "Do I look like I have x-ray vision to you?"

"You don't look like much of *anything* to me," Brewster shot back.

"Damn, these mattresses are thin," Darin said, pulling himself to a seated position from one of the bunks in the quarantined room. "My back aches like hell."

"Maybe it's the virus," taunted Decker, slowly flipping over cards as he played a round of solitaire in the corner of the room. "Next'll be the fever."

"Fuck you, cockbreath," Darin said, throwing the finger to Decker.

"Knock it off," said Brewster, rubbing his temples. "At least you got a bunk, Darin. I'm sleeping on the damn floor here. You want to talk about a back ache? My whole fucking *body* aches."

" . . . And we're still stopped," Scott repeated, annoyed at being forgotten.

"Yeah, I noticed it a couple hours ago," Decker said, looking down at his cards. "And before that the hum in the ship was a lot quieter. I think we've stopped for repairs."

"The *whatthefuck*?" Brewster said. "The hum? What the fuck is the ship's hum?"

"You know, that noise inside the ship you'd have heard if you weren't constantly flapping your jaw, Private. The ship's generators and engines."

"That doesn't make any sense," said one of the room's other occupants. "Where do you stop in the middle of the ocean to do repairs? A floating service station?"

"Maybe it was—" Darin started, but Brewster interrupted.

"—Fuck this honkey theory shit. Let's just find out."

He hopped to his feet and stepped over to the door. He raised his fist and banged on it, a quick series of blunt strikes. After a moment a weak voice was heard through the metal, shouting to be heard but dulled by the partition.

"Yeah, what?!"

"What's the story?!" Brewster shouted back, certain his voice sounded just as distant to the guard on the other side.

"What?!"

"The story, man! We're stopped! Where are we?! What's going on?!"

"The islands!" came the reply. "We've got a busted fuel pump! Sherman knows a guy here who can fix it, or something! Rumor says we're getting shore leave!"

"Shore leave?!" Brewster shouted. "You motherfuckers are going out to get drunk and nail the native girls and we're stuck in this fucking meat locker?! Shit, man, if that doesn't beat all I don't know what does! Join the army, they said! See the world, they said! Motherfuckers!"

"If we went out there and we were infected—" Decker started.

"Yeah, yeah, we'd infect the island and die and shit. I know," Brewster said. "Spare me."

0938 hrs_

Hal Dorne was a Master Sergeant, US Army, retired—and he knew it. The fishing dinghy he brought alongside the USS *Ramage* wasn't his own, but the fisherman who owned it owed him a favor, and he'd called it in to score a ride. He pulled the faded baseball cap he wore from his balding pate and waved up at the deck of the ship in front of him.

"Frank! How the hell are you?!"

Sherman's face peered over the side rails of the vessel, a wide grin spread across his features.

"Not too bad, considering, Hal."

"I'll say. You're alive. That's about as much as anyone can ask for today. What can I do you for?"

"Never one for small talk, were you?"

"Let's just say I've got a daiquiri and a beautiful lady waiting for me back at the shop and I'd like to get back to both as fast as I can," Hal said from the dinghy, shielding his sunburned face from the sky with his upheld baseball cap.

"We've got ruptured fuel pumps, Hal. We're trying to make it back home ASAP, but on half steam it'll take us a lot longer. Think you can fix it?"

"Well, she ain't an Abrams, but I'll give her a shot. Do I owe you any favors?"

"Not that I can remember," Sherman said. "You thinking of charging me?"

Hal shot Sherman a lopsided grin. "I always charge my customers, Frank. *Retired*, remember? Pension doesn't pay the bar tab. How much depends on whether I owe you any favors. Seeing as I don't, what have you got to offer?"

"Hell, Hal. I'd pay you cash, if you think it'll still be worth anything by the time you get around to spending it."

"Cash? Keep it. I want parts and equipment. We'll barter. Here's the deal—I'll see what I can do for your fuel pumps if you fork over, say, about a hundred gallons of fuel for our generators, some assorted tools, a new radio—and weapons."

"Goddamn, Hal, you drive a hard bargain," Sherman said. "I can't authorize the tools, fuel, or radio, but I can get you weapons. Small arms be okay? Pistols? We're low on rifle ammunition."

"No deal without the fuel and radio."

"I didn't say we couldn't get those, Hal, I just said I can't authorize 'em. I'm not the captain of this ship. Franklin will have to authorize that."

"Well, fetch him out here, let's get rolling!"

"He's on the bridge trying to contact the mainland again. He'll be out shortly. Want to come aboard and have a look at the pumps?"

"Oh, you can't authorize a barter but you can invite me on his little boat, is that it?" Hal said with a grin, reaching out to the netting dropped over the side of the ship.

"That's how it works today, Hal. Climb on up."

Hal was nimble for a man of almost sixty years, and pulled himself up the cargo netting with little trouble, dropping onto the deck of the *Ramage* and firmly shaking Sherman's hand.

"Welcome aboard the USS *Ramage*," Sherman told him. "This way to the engine room."

The pair made their way into the bowels of the ship, heading towards engineering. Hal surveyed the corridors as they walked, taking careful note of the pockmarked bulkheads and occasional dried bloodstain coating the otherwise pristine deck.

"Looks like you guys have seen a little action," Hal said carefully.

"We had an incident on the way here," Sherman replied. "We're ferrying refugees. One of them . . . got sick. It spread quick. We managed to control it. We lost a few good men and women, though."

"I gotta tell you, Frank, the people here won't take kindly to you if they even suspect you're carrying the virus. You should probably keep that under wraps—*tight wraps*, if you take my drift."

"I don't blame them, Hal. Half the world's been contaminated. They've got every right to be suspicious of outsiders. If it'd make them feel more comfortable, we'll all stay onboard."

"Aw, hell, Frank, that's no fun at all. Of course you can bring them ashore. You'd have a mutiny on your hands if you tried to sail away from a paradise like this without letting the boys stretch their legs a little. We've got a great little cantina in town. Tell 'em to bring stuff to trade—most folks around here already think the world's done. Cash'll be useless. I gotta admit, I feel the same way. Just tell your guys to stay off the subject of the virus, keep out of trouble, and they'll be fine."

"Can you really speak for the whole island like that?" Sherman asked, pulling open the heavy door that led to the ship's engine room and letting Hal enter first.

"No," Hal scoffed, stepping into engineering. "But I can speak for most of it. There are a few bad eggs, like anywhere, who want protection at any cost. They think we should just shoot every outsider who drops by, but there's no future in an attitude like that."

"I completely agree," came a voice from ahead of them. Denton was sitting near the broken fuel pumps, scratching notes on a legal pad. His camera lay by his side, back open, film removed. "Sorry for interrupting. I was just getting some work in order."

"Not a problem, Denton. Hal Dorne, Sam Denton. Hal's retired Army, worked with him before. Denton's a photographer. You've probably seen his work in the papers."

"Not really, actually. Paper delivery out here isn't daily," Hal said, shaking Denton's hand.

"So you're the mystery mechanic who's going to get us moving again?" Denton asked.

"That's right. Though why you'd want to leave, I don't know. If I were you all, I'd pull up a parking spot and find a stretch of beach to call my own. No better place to live out the end of the world than the tropics."

"You know," Denton replied, a distant smile on his face, "I was thinking almost the same thing earlier."

"Anyway," Sherman said, kicking the fuel pump with a dusty boot, "Think you'll get her ticking again?"

Hal had barely even looked in the direction of the pump since he had entered, but he fixed Sherman with a gaze and answered, "Hell yes. She'll be on her feet sometime tonight."

"Don't you want to look it over before you make an estimate?" Denton asked, incredulous.

"If Hal says it'll take him less than a day, then that's how long it'll take him," Sherman told him. "He never let me down before. Unless he's slipping. You slipping, Hal?

"Only when I'm drunk."

"There you have it," Sherman said.

"Are you drunk?" Denton asked, a grin creasing his face.

"A little," Hal said with a chuckle. "As it stands, you're in luck. What you've got running here is the General Electric LM 2500-30 gas turbine—real nice model, if you ask me. Little prissy sometimes, but she's a workhorse. How many you have total? Three?"

"Four," Sherman said. "Broken pumps on two."

"Huh," Hal murmured. He walked around the power plant, mumbling to himself quietly. When he'd finished a circuit, he stopped, nodded once, and turned to face Denton and Sherman. "I'm going to need some manpower to go fetch the parts you're going to need from my shop. Some racquet-club yuppie on a long cruise showed up in his thirty-million-dollar custom yacht about half a year ago. It had a busted power plant just like this one. I replaced it with an inferior model and kept the broken plant. Its pumps are fine. We'll use them."

"How much did you take him for?" Denton asked.

"What?"

"The yuppie in the yacht. How much did you take him for?"

Hal chuckled. "I don't take cash. I barter. I got myself a brand damn new Jacuzzi, fresh out of that guy's yacht cabin. Can't really enjoy retirement in the tropics without a hot tub, right?"

Denton laughed. "You're a terrible liar. You only have a generator on that island, no electricity. How can you power a hot tub?"

"I said there were *two* generators, Sam," Sherman said. "One of them powers the radio."

"The other one's mine. And it powers my hot tub and mini-fridge. Can't really enjoy paradise without cold beer and ice, either," Hal said.

Denton cast Sherman a curious glance.

"You run with a strange crowd, Frank."

"I like to think so. Makes life that much more interesting."

"Yeah, yeah—let's get started," Hal said. "Got a crew chief I can talk to? Let's get him to do some prep work on this beast while I head back to my shop and get the parts I'll need."

"I'll have Franklin send him down," Sherman said.

"Need a hand getting the parts here?" Denton asked.

"Yes, actually. A pair of hands, more precisely," Hal said. "And a driver. I don't have any way to strap 'em into the truck. We'll have to ride in the back and hold 'em in."

"Any deuce drivers left?" Denton asked Sherman.

"One, I think. He's quarantined. Or maybe two."

"Oh, Private Brewster," Denton said, nodding his head. "Better to just take someone else then, anyway."

"Troublemaker?" Hal commented.

"No," Denton replied. "He hasn't made any trouble since I met him. Trouble just finds him pretty easily."

"Who are we taking, then?" Hal asked.

"I'll send Thomas," Sherman said after a moment's thought.

"Sergeant Major Thomas?" Hal said, curiosity in his eyes.

"Command Sergeant Major these days, actually. He still answers to Sergeant Major."

"Hell," Hal scoffed. "He'll probably chew my ass for being out of uniform and drunk on duty."

"I'll remind him you're retired," Sherman said, rolling his eyes.

1013 hrs_

The boat ride to shore was swift, and the captain of the tiny vessel, a thin, sun-bronzed fisherman who looked to be around thirty, said nothing to either Denton or Thomas during the journey. He cast nervous glances at them as he tied the boat off to one of the wooden docks jutting out over the water in the inlet.

"Get the feeling we're not exactly treasured guests?" Denton whispered to Thomas, who had cast off his BDU shirt in the heat. The old sergeant folded his arms across his t-shirt clad chest and grunted in reply.

"What do you expect? They think we've brought the virus with us. If I were them I'd shoot us."

Denton shifted uneasily. "Yes, well, let's not give anyone any ideas, eh?"

Hal had already clambered up onto the dock, and the fisherman looked as if he wished Denton and Thomas would follow suit quickly. The pair knew when to take the hint, and pulled themselves onto the sturdy pier. Thomas dusted his hands off and looked around the little town.

"Nice enough place, Hal. Where's yours?"

"Around the coast a ways," Hal said, starting down the pier towards the sandy shore, beckoning for the two to follow him. "There are a few trails cut through this island."

Hal led them to a rusted, paintless pickup truck parked in the sand near the head of the beach. The body was patched in multiple places with scrap metal, spot-welded here and there as if they were afterthoughts, and the engine complained loudly when Hal turned the key, but it caught shortly and purred in tune when he shifted and accelerated.

"She's not much to look at, old Bessie," Hal said, patting the window frame of the truck with a heavy palm. "But she gets the job done year after year."

With Denton perched in the bed, holding onto the roof of the cab, and Thomas lounging in the passenger seat, Hal took them through the village towards the thick forest beyond. Denton took the chance to snap a few pictures, steadying himself with one hand as the other brought up his camera. It still amazed him that the rest of the world was busy fending off what could be the enemy that will deal a mortal blow, but here, life went on more or less as usual. He captured the image of a pair of old men sitting on stools under a thatched canopy, drinking liquor the color of ripened bananas from cracked glasses. He managed one of a storeowner chasing a trio of kids from his shop, and another of a lone woman dozing with a wide hat pulled down over her eyes, lying under a tree, before the truck slipped into the foliage and obscured the town from view.

A deep pothole jarred Denton from his reverie and sent him scrambling for a firm hold on the truck.

"Jeee-sas!" Denton cursed. "Got anything bigger to hit on this island, Hal? I'm still holding on back here!"

"These trails aren't built for comfort!" Hal shot back.

"That's good, because I'm not comfortable," Denton said, kneeling to help banish the sudden feeling of insecurity. The truck jolted off a rock a moment later, and affirmed his caution.

"Don't worry, we're nearly there," Hal said.

"Already?"

"Small island," Hal replied. "Besides, it helps to be close to town, in case I need beer. There it is, through the trees on the left."

Denton tried to look in the direction Hal was pointing, but couldn't see anything through the leaves. Thomas apparently had a better vantage point.

"Nice place, Hal," he said. "How's the cost of living?"

Denton almost chucked. He had barely seen Thomas utter three amiable words since he'd known him, and there were two full sentences, just like that. The truck cleared a short turn and brought Hal's house into Denton's view, cutting his reply short. The retired mechanic lived in what was simultaneously paradise and hell, it seemed.

The house sat up off the ground on supports to keep it dry in stormy weather, and the beach sat behind it through a narrow line of trees. Denton could see a well-worn path meandering off through the forest leading in the direction of the sand. The house itself was picturesque, built of seasoned timber without glass in the wide windows, and skylights dotted the thatched roof.

If one ignored the house and scenery, however, the setting was quite different. Disassembled machinery dotted the yard, and contraptions the likes of which Denton had never even imagined seemed to have been cobbled from the scrapped parts.

"Lord, it looks like the room where rejected props from Tim Burton films go to die," Denton breathed.

"Don't knock my babies before you try them," Hal said, parking the truck and stopping the engine, which breathed a shuddering sigh of relief as it ground to a halt.

"Try what? I don't even know what I'm looking at," Denton said, scratching his head. Something that looked like a cross between a dinosaur and a weed whacker sat in the tall grass by the side of the truck. It was propped up on flat tires from a scuttled wagon whose butchered hide lay in a pile not far away. Denton guessed some of the chopped-up pieces had found their way onto the truck's frame in the patchwork Hal had done.

Hal followed Denton's gaze. "That's my lawnmower. Ain't she a beaut'? Made her from aluminum sheets I twisted around some pipes I got a hold of when they pulled the old plumbing out of a condemned building in town."

"Yeah," Denton said, surveying the waist-high tropical grass that sprouted around Hal's house. "Looks like it does a real good job of things."

"Oh, it works," Hal said. "I just don't use it. What's the use of being retired in paradise if you spend it mowing your lawn? Besides, I'd dent up the blades on all the stuff lying around here I can't even see anymore."

"Yeah," Thomas drawled. "Couldn't be bothered to iron your trousers in the service, can't be expected to mow your lawn now."

"Exactly," Hal said, jumping out of the truck and slamming the door behind him. "Come on. Workshop's around the back."

Hal led them around the overgrown house, down a loose dirt slope and into his backyard—which, after a quick look-over, seemed to be much better kept than the front. Here, the junk seemed almost organized the closer one got to the rinky-dink work shed that butted up against the thin tree line. From the sheer diversity of the things that littered the yard, Denton guessed Hal had been supplementing his pension by doing handyman's work for most, if not all, of the island.

As they walked, Hal pointed out various odds and ends and tried to explain them.

"That's a conveyor system I started to install in the shed to move my tools along with me as I worked. Couldn't figure out a way to power it efficiently. Over there's my garboat—that's a golf cart boat, I mean. I think *garboat* works better. Anyway, stopped using it when I lost the last plastic golf ball I had that would float. All the fun went out of it. Right there by the door to the shed is the EM-15; worked on that for almost twelve years, on and off. Finally gave up not long ago. Moved on to bigger things."

Thomas perked up and showed some interest, running his eyes over the cylindrical piece of metal propped against the side of the work shed. He asked, "Is that the same bastard spawn of science that you stole those car batteries for back in Desert Storm?"

Hal looked impressed. "Hell yes. I can't believe you remembered that. And she still runs on car batteries, too. Sort of."

"What *is* it?" Denton asked, scrunching up his face as he peered at it.

"It's the Electro-Magnet Fifteen!" Hal said, as if expounding on the acronym explained everything.

". . . Eh?"

"It's a *gun*," Thomas grunted with folded arms. "A very, very stupid gun."

"It is not," Hal said, managing to sound both condescending and indignant at the same time. He turned to Denton to explain. "It uses a system of electromagnets to accelerate projectiles down the barrel."

"At about the same speed as you could toss a rock, yeah," Thomas said. "The only thing you'd ever kill with that is a bird, and that's only if you got off a lucky shot."

"I beg to differ," Hal retorted. "You haven't seen the EM-15 in almost a decade. I've made improvements."

"So it works, then—like all your other little projects?" Thomas inquired, sweeping a hand around the yard in an all-encompassing gesture.

"Well," Hal murmured, "Not quite. I'm having a few problems getting the magnets to . . . work in tandem. I can't get the ammo feed to work properly. So it's a single-shot heavy-ass rifle at this point and I'm too old and drunk to be hoisting that son of a bitch everywhere I go. Here she rots."

"You said it works, though—one shot at a time. How?" Denton asked. Thomas scowled. It was plain he wanted to get on with it, but Hal enjoyed the excuse to ramble on about his hobby a bit more, and secretly relished the chance to toss a little discomfort Thomas' way after all the old sergeant had put him through over the years.

"The magnets fire up and push a projectile—basically any piece of metal that fits in the barrel—forward at what I've gotten to be a pretty high speed. She's almost completely silent except for a whistling noise, but plenty inaccurate since there's no standardized ammunition. In short, I have no clue what anyone would ever actually use this model for even if I got it working right, except as a base to work on better ones with. But she's damn fun to play with when I'm drunk and bored. Here, watch this!"

Hal strode over to the EM-15 and pulled it upright with a grunt. What Denton had thought was one irregularly shaped cylinder was actually a folded tripod with the actual weapon welded to the top. Hal snapped out the legs and straightened the barrel, swiveling the weapon towards the tree line. Upon closer inspection, Denton noticed the barrel was absolutely colossal, about as big around a bore as he could form with his thumb and forefinger. Hal stooped and picked up a pair of jumper cables, blew on the contacts, and snapped one pair to the weapon and another pair to a battery lying half-obscured in the grass. The weapon began to emit a dull hum.

"She's warming up," Hal said. "Takes a moment. Here, let's use this."

He reached down into the dirt at his feet and withdrew a bent scrap of iron, reached into a recess in the bottom of the weapon and pushed the piece of metal into what served as the chamber.

"If I had these damn magnets working the way they're supposed to, it'd feed that up there automatically," Hal said. "Alright. She should be ready now. See if this don't tickle your socks."

Hal pushed a button that rested on the back of the weapon. It seemed to jump a tiny bit, and belched almost silently with a rapidly-fading whistle. A small tree, far off across the meadow of Hal's home, suddenly sprang apart, the top half somersaulting into the air while the bottom half stood quivering in the ground.

Hal chuckled out loud as he disconnected the cables from the weapon.

"What was that you were saying about barely being able to kill a bird, Sarge?" Hal said.

Thomas said nothing, and Denton stood with a slightly slack jaw.

"That's amazing."

"Not really. Just my peashooter, when it's all said and done. But what the hell are we doing?" Hal said, shouting the last at a much higher volume and startling Denton out of his reverie. "We're here to get engine parts. They're just inside."

"About goddamned time," Thomas grumbled.

1210 hrs_

Rebecca Hall leaned over the side rail of the USS *Ramage* and stared down into the clear waters below. She could see fish darting in and out of the ship's shadow, where the bulk blocked out the sun and turned a bit of the ocean to twilight purple. Far and away she could hear the shouts and laughter of a group of children on the beach as they ran up and down the sand chasing one another, and closer to her ears were the gentle lapping of tiny waves against the hull. Closer still were the near and dear voices of her comrades.

"Fuck that and fuck you, ass-hat. I'm not doing it."

"Come on, you pussy—what are they going to do? Court-martial you? Out here, *now*? Just do it. Jump. Double-flip gets you a hundred."

"Yeah, come on, man! Who's going to know? Say you looked over and fell."

"Yeah! Vertigo. Happens all the time."

"I don't know . . ."

"One hundred dollars. In your hands. Jump. Do it. You know you want to."

"I don't even know if I can spend that now . . ."

"Then for glory and honor, bro. And the hundred bucks."

"Yeah! Honor. Jump, man!"

For a moment there was no response from whomever the peer-pressured party was, and Rebecca turned back to the tranquil scene in front of her, feeling drowsy with the warm sun on her neck—and then a blurred shape shot past her with a yell of "Banzai!" and she let out a yelp, jumping back from the rail and then rushing forward again just in time to see one of the soldiers cannonballing into the water below.

"He did it!"

"Fuck yeah!"

A more faded call of, "Where's my hundred bucks, motherfucker?" from down below drifted up.

Rebecca shook her head and walked away from the railing. So much for tranquility.

She wondered what Mbutu was doing. It had been a couple of days since she'd last managed to talk with him. She found him interesting and a bit on the mysterious side, sort of like Sherman. Interesting people were one of the few reasons she enjoyed waking up in the morning. Mbutu seemed to have an objective, global view of things, and reminded her of the wise old men in Indiana Jones movies who popped up and said prophetic things then faded away—though Mbutu was certainly not old and probably didn't consider himself wise. Sherman's constitution seemed more attuned to simple worldly pleasures, Rebecca thought. His cigar smoking, the reading of literature, his studying of history. Mbutu seemed to understand the world, and Sherman seemed to know it.

Thinking of them reminded her of a rapidly fading person in her memory—Decker. Sure, he was just fine and in good health below, and almost certainly still interested. Maybe it was the work she was kept occupied with on the ship, or the thought of the virus' spread, or the revealing way he had tried to order her—no, *successfully ordered her*, she reminded herself—to stay, nice and safe, up on the deck when the virus had broken out below. Rebecca knew she would honestly prefer to treat wounds and not cause them, but the incident on the ship had caused her to consider acquiring a weapon at the next possible chance. There were M-16s lying all around the deck and in compartments below, but ammunition for them was very low. Sherman had already ordered the collection and redistribution of rounds to the most proficient marksmen remaining, which reduced most of the soldiers to sidearms and what few sub-machine guns the *Ramage* had onboard.

Rebecca had chuckled when Sherman had explained to her, in civilian's terms, what their weapons situation was like.

"We have enough munitions on this ship to level a metropolis. We have Tomahawk cruise missiles, two 20-millimeter auto-tracking FLIR cannons, anti-air SM-2's, anti-ship Harpoons, sub killers, and six torpedo tubes. But we barely have enough rifle ammunition to fight a platoon to a standstill."

If she were home in the States, Rebecca could go to her uncle's house. The man had four gun cabinets full to bursting with every model of small arms humanity had designed since 1911. She had always laughed at him—sometimes to his face—and chided him for taking his Constitutional rights too far. Now she wasn't so sure she had it right. She bet her uncle was holed up in his house in the woods right now, sipping whiskey and chuckling about the plight of the unprepared world.

Despite her dwindling feelings for Decker and the pressing concerns of the work ahead of her, she found herself wondering how the soldiers in quarantine were doing. She wasn't allowed access to them, of course, and as one of the few trained medics left on the ship, that concerned her. Maybe they couldn't do anything for a soldier even if they somehow diagnosed him as being infected, but they could at least get the uninfected ones out of there to safety. She had bargained, cajoled, begged, and finally simply asked to be let in to the quarantine area, but was rebuffed. Finally she told the soldiers guarding the door that in the very least they could slip a weapon inside to the quarantined men so they could defend themselves if one fell ill. This had been vetoed by the corporal in charge.

"I was an MP for three years," he had said. "I've seen what desperate men will do with a weapon if they think it'll get 'em somewhere—like out of that room and off this ship. No, ma'am, they're unarmed and staying that way."

All that was left for her to do was wait and see what would happen. Keeping busy kept her mind off other things—like the world falling to shit around her—and she hated having to tick time away instead of being proactive.

"Oh, well," Rebecca sighed to herself. At least she'd been hearing murmurs about being allowed access to the town. Maybe she could find a strong drink somewhere.

Washington, D.C.
1225 hrs_

Dr. Anna Demilio prowled her cell nervously, pacing back and forth, casting sideways glances at the heavy door. The facility she was in was modern, but not well insulated enough to keep the sound of gunfire from her ears. It had been going on for almost two hours now, on and off, starting up in a rapid crescendo, then tapering off to nothing—only to repeat minutes later. At first it was the staccato clack of pistols, and now she could hear the basic chatter of automatic fire.

There had been no build-up to this, nothing in Sawyer's face to suggest that the situation was so bad it was at the doors of the facility. Demilio didn't believe—or didn't *want* to believe—that the plague had spread throughout the city. It was, more likely, a small outbreak within the facility itself.

But she couldn't be sure, and that was what made her nervous.

If this was the plague out there now, beating down the doors of the stronghold and holding the surrounding area with infected ranks, the agents wouldn't be able to hold out for long, and she'd wind up dying alone of starvation in a locked cell. That thought scared her more than the idea of being infected did.

Footsteps in the hallway sent her scurrying back to the far end of her cell. If Sawyer was back, she certainly wasn't planning on being helpful. She listened—the steps were lighter than Sawyers, and quicker. It sounded like someone was darting sneakily around the hall, moving in short bursts. She could hear heavy breaths being drawn outside, and the clinking sound of a weapon being slung.

The metal panel in the doorway shot open and a face came into view. It wasn't Sawyer.

Agent Mason reached a hand into the cell, holding a pistol. Anna shrank away, thinking for a moment Sawyer had sent his subordinate to kill their prisoner now that the last stand had come—but it was not to be. The pistol was being handed in, handle-first.

"Come on," Mason said, sweat beading on his forehead. "Take it! Now's our chance!"

"*Chance*?" Anna asked suspiciously, narrowing her eyes. "What chance?"

"Our chance to escape, you idiot! Take the pistol! We're getting out of here!"

"My God," Anna breathed. "The shit is really hitting the fan out there, isn't it?"

"Take the damn pistol!" shouted Mason, glancing cautiously over his shoulder as he shook the weapon in her face. "We don't have much time!"

Anna grabbed the weapon from the agent, the weight of it pressing comfortably into her hands.

"About time," Mason remarked.

The agent disappeared from the window and a moment later, with the heavy sound of grinding metal, the cell door unlocked and slid back into the wall. Mason stood in front of the newly-freed scientist, clutching a sub-machine gun to his chest. He looked bedraggled and battle-weary, with sweat staining the collar of his shirt. He had a Kevlar vest strapped around his torso. He beckoned for Anna to step out of the cell, scanning the hall in both directions as he did.

"Let me guess," Anna said, racking a round into the chamber of the pistol, "You're expecting company."

"Yeah," Mason replied. "They'll miss me in a couple minutes, if they haven't already. We've got to move fast. Follow me. We'll take the catacombs."

Mason took off at a brisk trot, hugging the wall of the hallway, sub-machine gun held to his shoulder in the ready position.

"Wait up," Anna said, running after him. "Catacombs?"

"Network of service tunnels and back entrances that interconnect every major facility in the city, with seven routes that come out beyond the beltway. They built it in the sixties. We call 'em the catacombs. Been expanding construction ever since. Checkpoint! Stop here."

Mason came to a stop at an intersection and knelt down, peering around the corner as Anna caught her breath behind him. Three uniformed guards blocked their exit from the detention block, all armed and armored.

"Fuck," Mason sighed. "We have to get past this checkpoint if we're getting out. Nothing for it—we're going to have to run and gun. Ready?"

"Wait," Anna said suddenly, grabbing Mason's shoulder. "What about Julie?"

"Ortiz? The reporter?" Mason asked. A moment later his face fell, remembering the other captive in the dungeon below. "Oh, damn. I forgot about her—they took me off that detail three days ago."

"We can't leave her here!"

"I know! I know!" Mason said, grumbling. He glanced back in the direction of the checkpoint, then back towards the detention and interrogation cells, trying to make up his mind. "If we go back to get her, we might be doing ourselves more harm than good."

"Then let's do it fast, and if they catch on to us, we shoot our way out," Anna said, holding up the pistol Mason had given her.

He shot her a surprised look and asked, "Are you a scientist or a soldier?"

"Both, remember?"

"Fine, Colonel. We go back, but let's sprint it."

The pair eased away from the checkpoint. When they'd moved far enough that their footsteps wouldn't be heard, they broke back into a full-out run, Anna following Mason through the numerous twists and turns of the confusing facility. All the hallways looked the same—the sterile whitewash, dull hum of fluorescent lighting, tiny placards next to doors that gave vague impressions of what might lay behind them—Anna would have quickly become completely lost if she had been by herself. Mason, however, knew the way perfectly, and it wasn't long before they came to a narrow flight of stairs that descended into the dimly-lit confines of the dungeon.

"There'll be a guard down here," Mason whispered, drawing to a stop at the top of the stairs. "Let me deal with him. I play poker—I'm pretty good at bluffing."

"Right," Anna said, pushing her back up against a wall and waiting. Mason slung his weapon over his shoulder, took a deep breath to steady his nerves, and walked down the stairway. Anna could hear the guard's challenge as Mason approached. She could make out most of the conversation, and listened intently.

"Halt! This is a restricted area!"

"Agent Mason, NSA."

"Oh, thank God. How's it going up there?"

"Not good. I've been sent to secure a fallback position. The outbreak's contained within the facility. We need to empty these cells and start moving ammunition and supplies down here."

"I wasn't notified . . ." the guard began.

"I don't care," Mason said, taking on an authoritative tone. "Open the cell doors. Get the lighting turned up."

"Yes, sir," said the guard. Anna bit back an exclamation of joy. For once, things seemed to be going well.

That was when the guard's radio squawked.

"All personnel, all personnel, be advised, we have escaped detainees in the facility. Be on the lookout for suspicious activity. Possible rogue agent Gregory Mason. Suspects armed. Use of deadly force is authorized and recommended."

Anna's eyes widened. For a moment, there was silence in the dungeon below, and then she heard a quick shuffling, feet scraping cement.

"Don't do it!"

"Drop your—"

Gunshots rang out. Anna swung around the corner, pistol leveled, to see Mason standing over the body of the guard, wisps of smoke trailing from the barrel of his weapon.

"Goddamn it all," Mason said, spotting Anna. "I told him not to draw. He drew on me. I killed him."

"You did the right thing, but now we've got to move twice as fast."

"Right," Mason said, staring at the corpse at his feet. "Cell lever's on the wall."

Anna looked around and spotted the heavy iron lever embedded in the stone walls of the dungeon, grabbed it, and gave it a pull. The old iron cell doors swung open, but Julie did not appear in the hall. Mason was stooping over the dead guard, pulling his utility belt free and stowing the unfortunate man's gear on his own person. Anna jogged down the hall, scanning left and right in the cells she passed, looking for Ortiz. Near the end of the hall, she found her.

Julie was curled up in the fetal position on the thin, damp cot in her cell, arms wrapped around herself, shivering.

"Julie!" Anna blurted from the cell doorway. "Get up!"

The reporter's eyes flicked open and she locked her gaze on Anna's. Her eyes sparked with recognition as she tried to sit up, but fell back onto the cot.

"Can't . . ." Julie managed, a cough wracking her body.

"Jesus," Anna said, "What have they been doing to you?"

"So cold . . ." Julie mumbled.

Anna noticed for the first time that the temperature in the dungeon was more than chilly—coupled with the artificial dampness of the place, Julie was certainly in miserable straits.

"Mason! I need a hand here!" Anna called back to the agent. "Julie's in bad shape!"

Mason ran over, took one look at Julie, and shook his head. "She'll hold us up. We can't afford the risk. We've got to move fast and get out now that they know we're trying something."

"They've got their hands full with your outbreak. We can get her out of here," Anna persisted. "Help me carry her!"

"Outbreak of . . . *Morningstar*?" Julie managed, pulling herself back up into a sitting position, arms still wrapped around her chest. Her face was pale and sickly in the dim light, but she didn't seem injured aside from malnutrition. Another wracking, full-body cough shook the journalist, and Anna mentally added the possibility of pneumonia to the list of her ailments.

"I'll explain the whole thing once we're out of here," Mason said. "*If* we get out. And we won't, at this rate. If we're taking her, fine. Let's go."

Mason moved over to Julie and pressed the dead guard's weapon into her weak hands.

"You might need this," he said. "Cover us if you can while we carry you."

Julie nodded and allowed Mason and Anna to lift her up and support her as she walked along with them. The trio slowly made their way back up the stairs and into the fluorescents of the main facility, heading back towards the checkpoint they'd abandoned earlier.

"How are we getting past the guards?" Anna asked.

"Leave that to me," Mason whispered. "The guard in the dungeon had a few surprises in his utility belt."

They leaned Julie against a wall. She sagged against it heavily, catching her breath and biting back another round of coughs that would have certainly alerted the guards to their presence. Mason kneeled, pulling a blue-tinted cylinder from the guard's belt slung over his shoulder.

"Grenade?" Anna asked, incredulous. "Half the facility will be after us."

"Grenade? Yes," Mason whispered back. "Explode? No."

Anna shot the rogue agent a perplexed look, but Mason yanked the pin and let the spoon fly free without further explanation. Anna ducked and plugged her ears as the man reached around the corner and sent the grenade clattering down the hall towards the guards. She heard surprised yells from the guards, the safeties being clicked off, rounds being chambered—and no explosion. A loud hissing filled the air, and Mason drew his shirt up over his mouth and nose.

The surprised guards' shouts quickly changed from frightened to annoyed, and their yells explained Mason's tactic to a T.

"Gas! Gas! Gas!" one yelled, and Anna could imagine him fumbling for his mask—and in the process letting his guard down.

"Now!" Mason shouted, springing to his feet and rounding the corner. Automatic fire rang out. Anna leaned out from the corner, aiming her pistol. The three guards had been in the process of donning their gas masks when Mason had jumped out and opened fire, catching them momentarily unawares. His first burst had caught one of them in the chest, dropping him to the ground, sending the mask skittering in one direction and the man's weapon in the other. The guard was stunned—the heavy armor he was wearing caught the rounds, leaving him breathless but unarmed and surrounded by rapidly thickening CS tear gas.

Anna fired a pair of rounds, both missing but causing the other two guards to duck for cover and abandon their masks. Return fire lit up the corridor, and Anna retreated around the corner as bullets took chunks out of the walls of the hallway.

"Bravo post taking fire! Man down! Requesting reinforcements!" shouted one of the guards.

Mason fired another burst down the corridor, suppressing their enemies for a moment. The sounds of choking began to reach Anna's ears, and wisps of gas danced through the air as the grenade's contents dispersed. Anna felt an itch in her eyes and mouth and caught the scent of a distant campfire as the first vestiges of the gas reached her nostrils. She clamped her mouth shut and took only shallow breaths.

She knew CS gas was non-toxic. One could spend their days living in a roomful of the stuff and not die—but they would not have a very pleasant few days. Light exposure left one itchy and set one's eyes to watering. A nice lungful started your nose running and the coughing would begin shortly after. A few good breaths and you could expect to deposit your last meal on the floor—followed by whatever was left of the meal before that. She could only imagine the misery of the guards under cover next to the spent grenade.

"Move in!" Mason said, rounding the corner and charging like a madman toward the checkpoint. One of the two remaining conscious guards was doubled over, bile trickling out of his mouth, struggling to breathe. A quick butt stroke to the head knocked the man out and sent him sprawling to the floor. The third was hacking, spitting, rubbing at his eyes and moaning. When he saw Mason coming through the cloud of gas, he reached for his sidearm, but the agent was too fast. A kick to the chest knocked the guard back, and a second butt stroke knocked him out cold.

"Clear!" Mason yelled, coughing. The shirt he had drawn over his face was no substitute for a gas mask, and he was beginning to feel the effects as well. "Come on!"

Anna grabbed Julie around her shoulders and dragged her past the downed guards and through the checkpoint, out of the detention block they had been held in for so long.

Eyes watering and gasping for breath, Mason gestured down a side hall.

"There's a ramp down to the catacombs here. We're almost out."

The trio turned the corner to find the whitewashed walls gone, replaced by bare concrete and utility lighting. Signs said they were entering a maintenance area, but Mason paid them no heed.

"Downtown has sporadic outbreaks. We're losing this war," Mason said between coughs as they helped Julie negotiate the sloped floor that was taking them deep beneath the surface. "These tunnels can take us most of the way out of the city. I wanted to head to Weather, but I don't think that would be advisable. Probably still a heavy presence of military and government there."

Anna said, "Mount Weather, in Virginia? That's dozens of miles from here. Fifty, sixty . . ."

"These tunnels link everything in the region," Mason told her. "We're heading to the suburbs. They'll be on our trail, looking for us. Especially *you*, Colonel."

"*Me*?" Anna asked.

"You're the foremost expert on the Morningstar Strain. They want you for intelligence. They'll come after us."

A vicious yell from behind startled the trio. They didn't turn to see the source—the voice and determination said it all.

"Mason! You bastard traitor! I'm going to kill you, kill your friends, kill your family—Mason!"

"It's Sawyer," Mason breathed. "Keep moving. Hurry!"

The ramp leveled off and the trio found themselves in a tunnel that seemed to stretch on forever. Lit with intermittent low-watt bulbs and flanked by rusting, corroded piping, the access tunnel was certainly showing its age, but it was clean and functional. Four electric carts were parked near the base of the ramp, and Mason made for one of them.

"Put Julie in the back. I've got to open the security gates," Mason said, helping Anna place the weak journalist in the cart. He jogged over to a panel on the wall that looked to Anna like a subway map—tunnels lit with green and red lights, crisscrossing in a wonderful imitation of Perseus' labyrinth.

Mason slapped buttons and switched tracks. Lights flicked from red to green and back to red.

"Our path's clear. Come on!"

Footsteps sounded on the ramp behind them. Their pursuers were gaining on them. Anna and Mason hopped into the cart and slammed it into gear. It took off at a modest rate—no faster than a sprint. Mason pushed his sub-machine gun over to Anna.

"Cover us!" he shouted.

Anna picked up the weapon and swiveled in her seat, taking aim at the ramp just as Sawyer and Derrick appeared, weapons in hand.

Anna squeezed the trigger, sending a fusillade of rounds back at them. The agents were good. They hit the deck, rolling apart from one another and coming up behind the carts they'd left behind, and returned fire. Rounds whizzed through the air, one so close Anna felt it brush through her hair.

Mason sent their cart careening around a bend and braked to a stop without warning.

"What the hell are you doing?!" Anna screamed. "Go!"

"I'm buying us time!"

Mason had stopped them next to another wall panel, identical to the one he had manipulated moments earlier. He slammed one button and a heavy security gate lowered from the ceiling, cutting off the passage behind them. He grabbed the sub-machine gun back from Anna, held it up to the panel, and put a pair of rounds into it. It sputtered, shot sparks, and died, lights dimming to black.

"That should hold them for a few minutes."

As if to enunciate his statement, a furious pounding on the other side of the gate got their attention.

"Mason! You shit! Open the gate!"

"I'm out, Sawyer!" Mason shouted back. "And I'm taking your prisoners with me! We've got to survive! Someone's got to survive! Stay here and die for a cause you think you believe in—I'm leaving!"

Mason got back into the cart and the three took off again, safe for the moment. Behind them, Sawyer's rapidly fading voice chased after them with words of conviction.

"I swear, Mason, I won't forget this! You're a dead man! I'll track you down wherever you go! You can't hide! Do you hear me, you traitor?! You can't hide from me! I'll look down on your body someday, Mason! Mason!"

If Agent Mason was fazed by the threats, he showed little sign. He seemed very focused on the tunnel that stretched out ahead of them.

"How far do we have to go? Can't they cut us off?" Anna asked, grasping her pistol with white knuckles and casting nervous glances behind them as if she expected to see the other agents already catching up.

"No," Mason replied. "Not unless they call ahead to the safe house's operator that we're heading for and tell him to bar up the catacombs—and he won't be answering any calls."

"Why?"

"Because he's not there anymore—they called in the metro cells for backup at HQ. We've got a clear ride for a while."

Anna said nothing for a few moments and Mason glanced over at her—only to see the barrel of her pistol pointing at his chest. He recoiled.

"Whoa! Whoa! Jesus! What's the idea?!" he protested.

"If you expect me to just start trusting you," Anna said, "You're mistaken. You kidnap us, interrogate us, keep us locked up in conditions that could've been deadly,"—Anna jerked a finger over her shoulder at Julie, who was curled up on the back seat of the cart, shivering—"And now, out of nowhere, you're our best friend. Well, fuck you, Agent. I don't buy it. What's your angle?"

Mason barked laughter.

"What do you think, I'm leading you into a trap by killing four of our own guards and having you fire on Agents I've worked with for five years? Or do you think I'm tricking you somehow? Why? What purpose would that serve? Jesus, listen to yourself. You sound like a raving paranoid. What's my angle? I don't want to die yet. How's that for an angle? Three's better than one and like I already said, you're the foremost expert on the Morningstar Strain. I'd say I made a damn fine choice in getting you out of there—*that's* my angle."

Mason took the cart around another gentle bend in the tunnel. He had already driven past several intersections and Anna knew there was no way she'd ever be able to find her way back, even if she had wanted to. To call the network the *catacombs* was oddly appropriate, for they were damp and dim and depressing, but the word *labyrinth* stuck out as even more appropriate in Anna's mind.

"Fine," Anna said, after a moment. She dropped the pistol into her lap, and Mason relaxed a bit into his seat. "Though you didn't seem to have any intention of getting Julie out with us."

Mason fixed Anna with a chagrined look. He said with conviction, "I honestly forgot she was even down there. Sawyer took over her interrogations and I was removed from the case. If you think I wanted to leave her behind because I'm '*cold,*' or felt she would be '*baggage,*' then to hell with your opinions. I'm not Sawyer—I'm a human being. If I had thought of her before I saw my opportunity, I'd have factored it in. So, '*forgetful,*' maybe. Unfeeling bastard? *No.*

But I've had a lot on my mind recently to be expected to remember the status of every detainee I come across in our facilities." He swiveled his head to glance at the journalist in the back of the cart, then added, "She seems really sick, not just worn thin."

"Might be pneumonia," Anna said, watching the flickering light fixtures as they swept past the cart. "I won't know until I can take a closer look at her. I'm not a medical doctor, but I'll do what I can. Now, there's something else I'm curious about. What happened today, back there? What's happening outside, in the city? The world? I need to know. They haven't told me anything at all."

Mason grimaced. "It's not going well."

Anna winced. That was not what she had hoped to hear.

"What you heard today was our own personal Alamo," Mason explained. "The infected control several sections of Washington. There's a war going on in the streets above us. I don't mean martial law or rioting or flare-ups—I mean a *war*. The last time I was on the streets was two days ago and I saw a tank firing into an apartment complex. The entire place had been overrun. I saw a line of soldiers butchering a wave of the infected. And I saw that same firing line get taken from the side and overwhelmed by another wave. There have been air strikes ordered in several of the major cities. Entire blocks have been leveled. Here's the good news: The tactic is at least doing some good."

He went on, "Lots of major cities have been completely overrun already, but none of ours, not completely—not yet. We think the strain hit our shores when asymptomatic carriers came over on planes or ships before the situation in Africa had peaked. Every time we find an outbreak, we burn the area to the ground. We scorch the earth. *Zero tolerance*, if you want to say that. It's slowed the spread of the virus somewhat, but . . . there have been losses."

"*Collateral damage*," Anna echoed, lowering her eyes.

"We estimated one-hundred and ten thousand carriers destroyed and close to ten thousand innocents killed in the process across the nation."

"In all this time?" Anna asked, hope brightening her face for a moment. As callous as it sounded, the numbers were much smaller than she expected. Maybe the USA would hold out after all. Then, as quickly as it arrived, hope vanished.

"No," Mason said. "That's yesterday's estimate. *Just yesterday.*"

"And back there? Today's attack?"

"Our stand. They'll make it through today, I think. We have enough firepower to hold off the infected, and headquarters is a fortress. The strain will have a hard time driving us from our home ground. I figured the confusion was enough to cover our escape—I don't know when or how they realized what was going on, but they're good at what they do. Which means we'll have to be extremely careful if we're going to make it very far from here. Like I said, they'll be after us."

"How far are we going to get with two weapons and no food or water?" Anna asked.

Mason smirked. "We're heading to a safe house in the suburbs, remember? We'll find whatever we need there."

"Will there be any medical supplies for Julie? I'd like to get her taken care of as soon as possible."

"Doc," Mason said with a grin, "When I say whatever we need, I mean it. Another five minutes and we'll be there."

Washington, D.C.
1830 hrs_

Agent Mason had not been lying. The safe house was a wonder of modern espionage. There were several at any given time in and around every major city in the world, Mason had explained. They had been built and stocked for one purpose: to equip an agent on the run. Naturally, they weren't meant to be used by agents who'd gone rogue on the company, which was why each safe house had an operator stationed inside. The operator was meant to keep the gear secure and maintained, and also to keep up a semblance of normalcy to the neighbors and keep suspicion at a minimum. Luckily for the three escapees, the operator of the safe house in the suburbs was long gone to answer the call at headquarters. Once Agent Mason had picked the lock on the door that led into the house from the catacombs, they were home free.

The door opened into the basement of the house. Anna thought for a moment they had stumbled into an office building—the basement was fully finished, with sterile white walls and a carpeted floor.

Heavy lockers lined the walls. An expansive computer terminal sat in one corner, screens scrolling information faster than the human eye could read. One wall had a number of hooks screwed into it from which dangled suits of riot gear that looked like they'd been collecting dust for a year or more. Another wall held maps of the area—topographical maps, street maps, utilities, every possible variant seemed arranged neatly next to one another for reference.

Mason made a beeline for the computer terminal, quickly punching keys and bringing up a set of windows that showed scenes of suburban normalcy: a deserted street outside, a frost-covered back yard, an empty front porch. The house had its own security system and Mason was arming it piece by piece.

"I'm locking us down," Mason explained. "Don't even touch any of the outside windows or doors. The knobs are electrified and we have a video-assisted targeting program running on a turret 'bot in the foyer. Make a wrong move and this computer will think you're an intruder. It'll light you up."

"Is there food here? Water? Medical supplies?" Anna asked, looking over Mason's shoulder at the screens. Julie leaned heavily against the map-covered wall behind them, coughing into her arm.

"Right there," Mason said, jerking a finger over his shoulder at the nearest locker.

Anna went over and pulled the bulky double doors open, revealing stacks upon stacks of neatly-packed MREs and pre-packaged first aid kits. There were heavier surgical kits strapped to the doors of the locker, boxes of latex gloves and sterile hypodermics, gauze pads, splints, suture silk, iodine and other necessities.

"Good God," Anna said. "There's enough here to run a MASH outfit for a month."

"One stop shopping," Mason replied, eyes still glued to the screens. "Everything you need right at your fingertips."

"How about clothes?" Anna asked. She and Julie were still clad in the thin prison clothes they had been issued.

"Locker next to the riot gear should have shirts and pants."

Anna pulled a couple of medical kits from the locker and tucked them under her arm, then yanked a couple hypodermics as well. She set her bounty on one of the folding tables that occupied the middle of the room. She opened the other locker and found herself staring at piles of neatly-folded uniform clothing. Black BDU pants, white, gray, and black t-shirts, boots, and even a few pairs of dress shoes and button-down shirts that dangled from hangers. The clothing on the hangers looked like the rejected props from a bad costume drawer. There was a vest with a few shotgun shells in loops on the chest, a faded Hawaiian shirt, a cowboy hat—all seemingly at random. Anna realized they were probably items left here by agents stopping in to change into uniform gear. She pulled two pairs of BDU pants free as well as a pair of the gray shirts, and then, as an afterthought, yanked down the vest as well. She figured the pockets might come in handy.

"Alright, Julie," Anna said, piling all of her goodies together and scooping them up. "Let's go upstairs, get changed into more suitable clothes, and see if we can get you fixed up."

"Sounds good," Julie managed, choking back a cough. "Too bad there weren't any Ludens in that locker."

"Don't wander far," Mason advised. "And for God's sake, stay away from the outside doors and windows. And don't turn on any lights. And don't touch anything you don't recognize."

"Yeah, yeah."

The safe house underwent a magnificent transformation as Anna and Julie stepped through the door at the top of the stairs and entered the main floor. It was, to all appearances, a completely and benignly average home: A few family pictures lined the walls, change had been left lying out on a table, a coat was tossed across a chair. It looked as if the family had just stepped out for a few minutes.

"*Creepy*," Julie commented, standing in the doorway.

"Tell me about it," Anna agreed. "Come on, let's hurry so we can go back downstairs. I don't like it up here much."

"Seconded."

1902 hrs_

It was mostly official: Julie had pneumonia. Anna guessed it wasn't that bad of a case though, and gave the reporter some antibiotics from the medical kit as well as a small dose of morphine in her arm to distract her. It wouldn't take too long for the medicine to start working, but for a little while Julie would be second string.

They had retreated back down to the clean room in the basement and locked the door at the top of the stairs with its heavy deadbolt. The shutters had been closed in the catacombs below and the door had been barricaded with a locker, giving them two steps of protection either way an enemy could get at them. There were a small number of CDs scattered around the computer, and Mason had found that one of them was a collection of Beethoven. The three were lounging around the room as his Moonlight Sonata filled the air.

Mason sat in the chair by the computer terminal, feet propped up on the desk, cleaning an Uzi he had taken from the armory's worth of weapons the room held. He swabbed the barrel and peered down it with a practiced eye, nodding slightly and swabbing again.

Julie sat on the floor, head leaned up against a locker, using her prison uniform as a pillow. She dozed in and out of sleep. The morphine had stopped the cough for a while.

Anna stood in front of the maps on the wall, looking at what lay outside their safe little room. Any way one cut it, they were going to have one hell of a time getting the rest of the way out of the city. She saw there were three different ways via the catacombs—but all three led to installations that were likely still staffed with people who would ask all the wrong questions when they came popping out. Too many troubles, not enough breaks.

They were safe for a while, though. They had food, water, and protection. They were doing much better than most folks outside the four white walls of the room. However, Anna knew they would have to leave and join the war soon enough. But first it was time to rest and regroup—and wait for a break.

PART EIGHT:

BURNOUT

USS Ramage
January 19, 2007
1545 hrs_

Private First Class Ewan Brewster was beginning to worry about his health prospects. He wasn't ill with the strain now, but that was no guarantee he'd even be in one piece in a few hours. The situation in the quarantine zone was reaching a boiling point. Brewster had kicked a folding chair to shreds hours before and pulled a wickedly-shaped club of bent metal free from the wreckage. He'd backed himself into a corner of the room and kept a close eye on the other occupants, waiting for one to make a move.

The problem wasn't that they didn't trust each other—Trust was pretty well established in a group that had already been through as much as they had. The problem was that they didn't know who was going to turn, and it had become damn near impossible to even tell who was beginning to feel ill—because everyone in the room had contracted a nasty stomach flu around the same time, two days earlier. Rebecca had said it might have been food poisoning, which was possible, considering the men all ate the same rations. It was as if God himself had decided to pull a fast one on the soldiers.

Normally it would have been easy to spot someone beginning to slip under the influence of the strain. They would cough, shake, run a fever, maybe vomit, and eventually turn in the midst of their sickness. Now, with the introduction of the flu, everyone was coughing, running fevers, and vomiting into whatever receptacle lay nearby. And since cabin fever was also rampant—the occupants had been in the same room together for a week—hostility was noticeably higher. In the end, after a particularly nasty shouting match, they had decided to back off and simply watch one another.

Brewster didn't rank his chances of survival very high, being unarmed and possibly in the same room with a carrier. He had his money on Decker; the sergeant had been even more irritable than the others today. Brewster ran the back of his hand across his brow, and shook his head to ward off drowsiness. He hadn't slept in over a day, going on two. It was too dangerous to sleep.

"Feeling fatigued, Brewster?" Decker asked, laying back on a bunk, arms folded across a sweat-stained t-shirt, breathing heavy. "Feeling like you can't go on?"

"Fuck you, ass-hat," Brewster growled from his corner across the room, brandishing the club and hunkering down once more.

"Little hostile for someone who's uninfected," commented Decker.

"Lay off him, Sarge, he's tired. We're all tired," said Scott, laying near the door with his back against the wall.

Decker grunted a barely audible response, and shrugged.

Tension was high. Scott was less worried about the strain than he was about the other soldiers tearing each other apart out of stress. If any of them had the strain, they'd be turning sometime soon, within . . .

" . . . Within zero to twelve hours," said Rebecca Hall, at her makeshift work area halfway across the ship from the men in the quarantine zone. She was checking up on a soldier's broken arm as General Sherman listened from across the room.

"So if after twelve hours has passed . . ." Sherman started.

"Better make it a full twenty-four to be sure," said Rebecca. She hated keeping the men under quarantine any longer than was necessary, but in this case, safe was much better than sorry.

"Okay, have it your way. After twenty four hours has passed, if none of them have turned, they're all safe?" Sherman finished.

"I'd say so, aside from any recent trauma they may suffer at each other's hands before they get out of there," the medic added, dismissing the soldier and swiveling on her stool to face Sherman. "They're getting ready to kill each other out of sheer paranoia."

"I don't blame them," Sherman said. Seeing the look on the medic's face, he quickly added, "What with the flu hitting them like it did. No way to tell now."

"How far are we out?"

"Not far at all. We'll know how it's going to turn out in there before we make landfall, but just barely," Sherman said, fishing around in a chest pocket for a cigarillo. He must have remembered he was in a sickbay, and let the cigarillo go.

"What's the Captain doing? Calling ahead to let them know we're coming?"

"He's been trying. I'm worried about what we're going to find when we get there," Sherman admitted. "He's been getting lots of radio traffic, so there's plenty of souls alive and kicking in San Fran—but they're spooked. Panicked. The Strain's definitely there."

Rebecca felt as if the wind had been knocked out of her for a moment. If the virus was in California, it was probably elsewhere, just like the rest of the world. There was no running from it. It was the alpha and the omega, borderless, primal, and pure.

She carefully asked, "How are they doing?"

"On the whole," Sherman began, picking his words, "We're holding on. Just the same, I've asked Captain Franklin if he wouldn't mind moving our arrival point a bit north so we can avoid the major cities."

Rebecca nodded silently. It was a prudent move, but there was another question that begged asking.

"And where are we going once we're on land?"

Sherman grimaced. "I'm not quite sure. One part of me wants to rush to the nearest town and reinforce the efforts they've got going. Another part of me . . ."

"What?"

"Another part of me wants to find a nice, quiet spot, and sit back for a little while and see how this plays out. Maybe the cities will hold on. Or maybe not. Either way, there's no infrastructure for a while, I'm guessing. There'll be rioting. Looting. We might be doing our world the best service by staying alive and keeping as many others alive as we can."

"What about the military? Won't they come looking for you?"

"Maybe someday," Sherman said. "They have bigger problems at the moment."

A radio clipped on Sherman's belt chirped. He clicked the talk button.

"Sherman here."

"General, it's Franklin. We just received an e-mail, sir, from someone who says she knows you."

"An e-mail?" Sherman barked into the radio. "What happened to the radio?"

"Nothing, we're still trying to raise someone. This just . . . arrived for you when we got back in range."

"I'll be right up," Sherman said, straightening up from his relaxed lean. "We'll finish our conversation later, Rebecca."

"Sure, Frank."

Sherman had an idea about who may have been behind the e-mail. He made his way directly to the bridge of the ship where Franklin was waiting for him.

The Captain had pulled up the message and had it on the screen when Sherman came onto the bridge.

"Just received it a few minutes ago when we came in range," Franklin said. "Makes me wish we had more satellites flying—we'd have been able to get this when it was first sent. Looks like it's been waiting a couple of days."

"Let me see," Sherman said, eyes scanning the text on the screen.

Frank,

It's Anna. Been a while since I've written. That's because I've been a political prisoner up until a few days ago. It's a long story. I'll get into it when I see you next, but for now, let's talk business. Last report has you bugging out of Suez. I don't know where you are or if you'll even get this message, but here's hoping you do. I've been set free by an NSA agent named Mason, along with a reporter named Julie Ortiz. We're holed up in a safe house just outside the beltway in DC. It's secure enough (that's an understatement!).

Okay. SitRep.

Washington is fucked. At least, that's my professional analysis. The city center fell yesterday as far as we can tell. A general retreat was sent out and there's a call to fortify around the outskirts of the city to fend off the carriers. Needless to say, I don't put much stock in their efforts. Besides, I've got reports right here in front of me detailing the state of the major cities here—every single one has reported outbreaks. There are several smaller cities with outbreaks as well. Currently rural areas of the States are unaffected, but civil unrest is everywhere.

Like I said, we're safe here, but we're alone and aimless. Where are you? What are your plans? We'll have to move eventually and when we do, I want it to be with a purpose. We have access to the Internet here, as well as all kinds of government resources from food to fuel to intel. Get back to me.

Lt. Col. Anna Demilio,
of no particular institution at the moment

"Hot damn, she's alive," Sherman said. "I had a feeling she'd make it through this."

"What?" Franklin asked.

"It's from Colonel Demilio of USAMRIID. She's the world's leading Morningstar expert. She's holed up in a safe house outside of DC with a couple other people. Situation's grim on the home front, it seems."

"Figured as much," said Franklin. "Should we scrap our plans to make landfall at San Fran?"

"Not yet," Sherman replied. "Let's get a little closer and see what we can learn. Don't go too far in—I don't want to be committed to any course of action unless we're sure it's the one that'll keep us alive and kicking."

"We'll step up monitoring of—"

"Sir?" said one of the crewmen, holding a red phone to his shoulder. "It's belowdecks calling up. There's a situation in the quarantine room."

"Goddamn," Sherman said, standing up quickly. "Morningstar?"

"Yes, sir—there's a man down already. Guards want to know if they should go in."

"No! Don't open that door!" Sherman barked, grimacing on the inside as he spoke the order. He hated leaving those men to fend for themselves without so much as a pistol. "The guards are to wait outside until the situation has resolved itself."

"Yes, sir," said the crewman, relaying the order over the phone.

"I'm going down there," Sherman said. "Reply to that email, if you will, Captain. Tell her we're safe and sound, more details later."

"You've got it, General."

Sherman ran at full speed through the bowels of the ship toward the quarantine room—and he was quite fast for a man of his years. When he arrived, the guards were clustered outside the door, holding it shut. Furious pounding on the other side threatened to burst the door into the corridor. Faint voices could be heard through the bulkhead.

"Open the fucking door, you shits! Goddamn it! Slide in a gun or something!"

"Hold that door, soldier!" Sherman shouted, pointing a finger at the hatch. "Nothing comes out of that room!"

"We can't hold them off much longer!"

They? thought Sherman. *More than one carrier?*

The sounds of combat were also apparent as Sherman closed in on the room. He could hear muffled shouts, threats, the thump of flesh meeting fist or club.

Sherman blurted, "The soldiers on the other side of the door—*They're* the uninfected ones?"

"Yes sir, but the carriers are right on the other side of them!"

"Open the panel in the hatch."

"Sir?"

"Open it!"

There was a small panel in the door which they had been using to serve the soldiers' meals. The guard Sherman had addressed threw it open, and Sherman reached a hand in the room, holding his own sidearm.

"Take it!" he shouted, shaking his arm around to get the soldier's attention. He felt desperate fingers grab the weapon away, and a moment later there were two shots, loud and clear in the metal bowels of the destroyer—and then silence.

"They're down," came a weary report from inside. "And the rest of us are clean, no bites. Can we come out now?"

The guards looked over at Sherman for approval. He shook his head silently, bending down to look through the panel in the door.

"How many of you turned?"

"Two," came the reply, as a face appeared on the other side. It was Brewster. "Darin and Scott. I got 'em both. Thanks for the pistol, sir."

"My pleasure," Sherman said. He stood upright. "Open the door."

"Sir? They might still be infected . . ."

"Open the door. They're clean. They've been in there long enough."

"Yes, sir."

"Oh, no, you don't!" came a new voice. Rebecca came jogging up to the group at the door. She had seen the guard reaching for the latch when she'd let fly with her own orders: "Not for another day!"

A collective groan issued from the surviving quarantined men on the other side of the door.

"Don't listen to her, man, don't listen," said Brewster, pressing his mouth up to the panel and creating an almost ridiculous picture of talking lips. "Open the door, man. I can taste that fresh air now."

The guard started to pull the latch open again, but stopped a second time as Rebecca spoke.

"We haven't given it enough time!" Rebecca exclaimed. "You want to open that door and maybe let another carrier out into the ship? Give it some more time."

"Now, wait, Rebecca, those guys have been in there over a week. They just had to kill two of their own fellow soldiers. They've earned a break."

"At the expense of the rest of the ship, possibly?" Rebecca asked, arms akimbo.

"Open the door, corporal."

"Yes, sir."

"I think this is a very bad idea," Rebecca said, stepping back from the doorway.

"Noted," Sherman replied as the door swung open, revealing a gaggle of very weary-looking soldiers. Brewster returned Sherman's pistol, butt-first. The General nodded in appreciation and holstered the weapon at his side. "Before any of you go anywhere, get checked out by Becky."

"First woman I've seen in over a week," Brewster said, snickering. "She can check me out all day long—getting out of this room is just a fringe benefit."

Rebecca scowled. "I prescribe a cold shower."

"Oh, harsh."

"Knock it off, soldiers, and get in—"

"Get down!" came a cry from one of the guards, fumbling for his weapon. A feral-looking figure had risen up behind the group of soldiers at the door, bile dripping from its mouth as it hissed a battle cry. The strap of the guard's rifle had caught on his webgear, snagging it up. The figure managed to plant both hands on Brewster's shoulders and was inches from closing its jaws around his neck when its head snapped backwards, an empty hole where its eye had been. It flopped backwards onto the deck, twitching randomly.

"Holy shit!" Brewster yelped, jumping into the corridor and grabbing his neck where the carrier had touched him. "That was close!"

Rebecca stood shock-still, holding the pistol that had dropped the carrier in front of her, a blank look on her face. She had snatched the weapon from Sherman's loose holster and fired it in one smooth, instinctive movement. She didn't even know she was capable of such a thing, especially when one considered just who the carrier had been.

"Fuck me, I knew Decker was one of 'em," Brewster said with an impassive expression, leaning over the corpse of the sergeant. He absentmindedly rubbed his shoulder where the carrier had grabbed at him. "Bastards."

"See?" Rebecca said, still staring at the body. "I told you more could turn."

"*Damn*," Sherman breathed, grimacing and pulling Brewster away from the corpse of the sergeant. His eyes scanned over the rest of the room, from the overturned bunks and strewn mattresses to the other two corpses—one lying face down in the middle of the room and the other slumped in the corner, a splatter of blood on the wall behind the hanging head. Darin, Decker, Scott. Three more had bought the farm. "I want the full story, soldiers. But tell it to me from your new room—I'm convinced you should be watched a little while yet."

If the newly-freed soldiers were disgruntled, they hid it well, and allowed themselves to be slowly led away from the room by the guards, casting the odd glance back at the room they'd just spent a full week in, the bodies of their fellow soldiers lying unmoving in the wreckage inside.

Sherman turned his attention to Rebecca, who still grasped the pistol with white-knuckled hands. He reached out to retrieve the weapon from her and said, "I think I'll have that back now."

Rebecca drew away.

"No," she murmured. "I think I'll hold on to it."

Sherman looked undecided for a moment, then smirked.

"I don't blame you," he admitted. "We'll get you a pistol belt and some ammunition to go with it."

"Thanks," she said, nodding almost invisibly, eyes still locked on the corpse lying in the quarantine room.

Sherman followed her gaze.

"You did the right thing," he said.

"I know," she replied.

1730 hrs_

Sherman was seated on one side of a doorway in the bowels of the destroyer and Ewan Brewster was seated on the other, relating the events of the day's violence to the general.

"Darin turned first," Brewster said, speaking loudly but hesitantly through the door. "We didn't even notice. He could be a real quiet guy sometimes and we weren't paying any attention to him. Scott went a couple minutes later while we were trying to hold back Darin—that was a trick, trying to fend off two of those sprinters with just clubs made out of busted furniture. We ended up backing up against that door and staying tight. I don't know if we could have won if you hadn't passed that pistol through, sir. It's like they didn't feel pain, or at least didn't mind it. Poor Darin—last week I was playing cards with that guy. This week, he's a carrier. It's fucked up, sir."

"I understand," said Sherman. "But he wasn't your ally anymore. You did what you had to do. We'll have you out of there within a day or so, I guarantee."

"Thanks, sir."

Sherman sat silently in the corridor a moment longer, thinking over the events of the past hour. Though he wouldn't have used such a crude summation as the enlisted man, Sherman had to agree they were fucked up. And he felt terribly about overriding Rebecca only to discover that she had been right. To add insult to injury, he'd had to re-confine the soldiers he'd just freed to make up for it. Soldiers killing their friends, a general who is successfully second-guessed by a medic in her early twenties—and on top of all that, a very uncharacteristic thought kept creeping into his mind. It involved holing up once they made ground fall—going AWOL.

He was distracted, and he knew that could be dangerous.

Best to make a decision and be done with it, he figured.

But what to do? If he committed himself and his men to the government's containment efforts and they faltered like the defenses at Suez, more would die. There was always the chance they'd be successful, however slim that chance might be.

Or . . .

Or he could lead his men away from the fighting, away from the cities—find some small town on the coast and ride out the storm. And maybe be hunted as a deserter.

Decisions, decisions. There wasn't much time left to make up his mind. Soon they would be close enough to the coast that they would have to commit to one course of action.

Due east to aid the cause . . . or north to freedom?

Brewster leaned on the opposite side of the wall, equally caught up in thought, but of a more dreary nature. The violence in the quarantine room had happened in what felt like an indistinct blur to him. Days with little to no sleep, the adrenaline of the moment—it was all beginning to sink in. Relating what he could remember to General Sherman had brought back some unpleasant images.

Brewster couldn't believe he had shot two men he'd grown to know very well over the past week—Darin especially. He'd known the corporal since before Suez. The worst part was that he knew Darin had been fearing he was infected more than anyone else in the quarantine room. He'd complained frequently of symptoms before he'd even shown any, certain that it was his fate to become a carrier.

He turned out to be right in the end, it seemed.

And the medic—what was her name, Brewster wondered. *Hall.*

Rebecca Hall. She'd shot Decker. For all his bluster in front of the young woman before, Brewster knew she had to be hurting a lot. He didn't know how far Decker had gotten with her—he suspected not that far—but having to shoot him like that was enough to disturb anybody.

Brewster shook his head. Focusing on the girl had taken his mind off Darin and Scott for a while. He rubbed his temples wearily, leaning forward and trying to keep his train of thought off the bloodshed.

They would be getting close to land now. Brewster wondered what he'd be doing once they arrived. Maybe rounding up civilians and keeping order at an aid station somewhere, or patrolling the suburbs. The last word they'd had before the violence had erupted was that the strain had hit the home front, but was being held at arm's length. For how long, though, no one knew, and few would even venture guesses.

Ewan Brewster wasn't much of a praying man, but he prayed that he wouldn't be forced to stand in another battle line against a flood of carriers like he had at Suez and Sharm El-Sheikh. The infected were completely fearless and utterly relentless. They just kept coming and coming until there wasn't a round left for the defenders to fire, or until all the carriers were destroyed. And there were always more carriers to fill in the ranks.

Brewster knew he could always run. Once they hit ground and he was carrying a full pack—weapons and ammunition—he could hit the trail; find a nice valley in the pacific northwest somewhere and wait out the pandemic.

And leave behind all of his comrades?

"Fuck, what comrades are left?" Brewster muttered under his breath. "The General? I respect him but I'm not dying for him or some lost cause in an infected city center. Denton? Maybe he'd run, too. *Nah*—that Canuck'll want his pictures. Fuck me. Looks like it's Brewster looking out for Brewster."

What would he have to do?

It would be easy enough to slip away once they were on land, but he'd better go properly prepared. He'd snag a few MREs for his pack and button pants pockets. Some nine-millimeter ammo for the pistol—a couple boxes at least, whatever he could get his hands on. A rifle would be nice, but unless they came across an armory on land all he had was the Beretta. It would have to do.

A few clean t-shirts and skivvies from the quartermaster, maybe a knife, some assorted sundries—he'd be good to go in the wilderness for a while. Maybe he could even scrounge enough to get by comfortably. He almost regretted not going to Ranger school when the Army had offered it to him.

Brewster hid a faint smile behind a week's worth of stubble. He felt like he had a plan now. Something to hold on to and hope for. It felt good—better than he'd felt in over a week.

Despite his assessment of what comrades he had left, he'd see who he could get to come with him. Maybe one of the other fellows in the new quarantine room would want to come along. God knew they were all sick and tired of being controlled by their leaders, and maybe it was time to take their fates into their own hands.

It would be easy living in the wilderness. There would be plentiful sources of food, water, and shelter. Most importantly they would be away from any sources of the Morningstar Strain. None of the violence and bloodshed would be haunting his dreams for a while, just the open sky above and nature all around. A pleasant change from the dreary interior of the Navy vessel.

On the other side of the wall, General Sherman was still lost in thought as well, and didn't notice the pair of men who came sauntering up, sober expressions on their faces. The guard at Sherman's side stepped forward, but General Sherman, finally noticing the newcomers, waved him off.

"Heard there was a bit of a to-do down here, Frank," Denton said, keeping his expression neutral.

"Anything we can do to help?" added Mbutu Ngasy, at Denton's side.

"No, thanks for coming down, though," Sherman said. "It's all over and done with. We're having a funeral service later this afternoon."

"Are you doing alright?" Mbutu asked. The air traffic controller was proving very adept at reading moods. "You seem stretched thin."

"I'm fine, I'm fine. Just got a lot on my mind, you know?" said Sherman, sighing and folding his arms. "We're going to be busy soon."

"Yes," Mbutu said. "We'll all have our hands full onshore. We've been wondering about that too, General."

"That so?"

"Yeah, that's so," chimed Denton. "Now, we know you and the other soldiers have your responsibilities to deal with, but the refugees and I wouldn't mind being let off somewhere safer than a downtown harbor, if you know what I mean."

"I know how you feel, more than you might think," Sherman said.

"Then you wouldn't mind dropping us off somewhere along the coast a bit more out of the way before you head in, Frank?" Denton asked.

"I don't see why it should be a problem. I'll assign you a few riflemen as guards."

"That won't be necessary. We can handle ourselves," Denton said. "Just issue us a few sidearms and we'll look after ourselves."

Sherman nodded, a wistful smile tugging at the corners of his mouth, and said, "Seems like our little group is all set to break up.

All this time spent together since Suez . . . Seems strange to be planning on parting ways."

Denton cast a glance at Mbutu, who shrugged. Denton grimaced, turning to face the General. He didn't want to insinuate anything the old officer might have to take official notice of, but it was worth a shot.

"We were wondering if you might be cajoled into coming with us, Frank. Not just you, I mean. All of you. The sailors and soldiers."

Sherman barked out a rough laugh, earning him a surprised look from the others.

"Frank?" Denton asked.

"I was wondering if you'd get around to asking that," Sherman said. "I think I've about made my decision, too. I've got a friend on the east coast I'm going to need help to get a hold of, and you all could use a good escort on land. So yes—let's join up when we hit land. See what we can do to make our own difference."

"No repeats of Suez."

"No goddamn repeats of Suez, that's right," said Sherman, chuckling. "We've got work to do if we're going to ride this out our own way."

Denton grinned. "I'll get the interested parties on deck."

USS Ramage
January 20, 2007
1021 hrs_

Mbutu Ngasy stood on the deck of the destroyer, clipboard in hand, going over a checklist of supplies. He, Denton, and a couple of other refugees with initiative had dragged up all the goodies that Franklin had decided he could part with. The captain of the destroyer had unequivocally denied any interest in their plan to make a run for it once they hit land. He said that he and his sailors would stay at sea aboard their vessel, safe and secure in their own way.

"Two rifles, M-16A2," Denton said from across the folding table they had set up, placing the weapons on the tabletop as Mbutu marked them off. "Rifle ammunition, two magazines, sixty rounds."

"That's all?" Mbutu asked, frowning at the meager amount of ammunition Denton placed by the rifles.

"It's all Franklin could spare," Denton explained. "We'll give them to our best marksmen and hope they can make 'em count." He then began listing off the smaller arms. "Twelve pistols, Beretta 92FS. "We've got ammo for these puppies—nine-millimeter, five boxes of a hundred rounds, five hundred rounds total, with twenty-six magazines."

Mbutu made a note on his clipboard. "That's much better."

"Yeah, looks like most of us'll be armed. And there's a few more things: One sub-machine gun, MP-5, with two full magazines, sixty rounds. Grenades, fragmentation, twelve. Grenades, white smoke, six. Grenades, tear gas, four."

Mbutu made the necessary notations, frowning at the grenades.

"What?" Denton asked.

"Have you noticed how Franklin has been giving us supplies only in even numbers?"

Denton cast an eye over the table. "You're forgetting the MP-5. Only one of those. Besides, it's probably just the military in the guy. Everything's got to be squared away."

"With two full magazines of sixty rounds total," Mbutu countered.

"Heheh," Denton chuckled, digging through the cardboard box in front of him. "Oh. Gas masks, two."

"See?" Mbutu said, grinning.

"Knock it off. There's some assorted MOPP gear in here. Looks like two or three full suits."

Mbutu scratched a note on the clipboard. He admitted, "I wrote it down, but I don't know what MOPP gear is."

"It's clothing designed to counter biological, chemical, or nuclear threats to a soldier's life," Denton explained. "It's thick, with a charcoal layer between the cloth to catch particulates. Very hot to wear in the summer; doesn't breathe well. But someone wearing this could be standing under a Sarin mortar and be just fine."

"Like a space suit," Mbutu said.

"Yeah, I guess you could make that comparison," Denton conceded.

"What's next?"

"Oh, ah, looks like a box of spare clothing. Call it . . . damn, just write down '*box of clothes.*' I don't feel like sorting through it all."

"Very well, box of spare clothes," Mbutu said, checking it off on the clipboard.

"Gentlemen," came a new voice. Mbutu and Denton looked over to see Sherman approaching from across the deck. "How's it coming?"

"Pretty well, General," Denton answered. "Franklin's given us enough gear to be comfortable once we make landfall. How's our approach?"

"We're only a few hours out. We'll make landfall around seventeen hundred hours this afternoon."

"What's the procedure once we hit?"

"Franklin's decided he's going to sail in and offer what help he can to the defense efforts. I've tried to convince him otherwise, but he's adamant. He's also said he's not going to say a word about us, so we're in the clear. He'll make landfall north of where he wants to be, drop us off, and sail south. We'll head inland from wherever he lets us off."

"Can't really blame the captain. He's got a mobile island and enough firepower to see himself through to the end," Denton said.

Sherman nodded in agreement. "He's a good man. He just can't run. It's not in him. I've seen enough, though, and it's high time to look out for number one, if you know what I mean."

"Damn right," Denton agreed, chuckling.

"So what have you got here?" Sherman asked, gesturing at the table.

"We're listing all of the supplies Franklin has given us," answered Mbutu, handing the clipboard to Sherman, who gave it a cursory scan with his eyes.

"Looks pretty solid so far," Sherman commented. "Get some canteens and other water storage containers—and medical supplies. I don't see any listed here yet."

Mbutu took the board back from the General and looked it over again.

"He's right. There isn't a single bandage in here."

"I'll get Rebecca to round up what she thinks we'll need," Sherman said.

"Is she coming along?"

"I assume so," said Sherman. "I doubt she'll want to stay on this ship after being cooped up on it for so long. But I'll ask to be sure." He paused a moment, then continued, "Another thing we'll need is a complete manifest of all the people who are coming with us as opposed to those staying with Franklin and heading south. Get us a solid number and make sure you mark down who's a trained soldier and who's a refugee so we can distribute these arms accordingly."

"You've got it, Frank," Denton said.

"There's one thing I'm still unclear on," Mbutu said, raising a finger.

"Yes?"

"Where are we going once we're on land?"

"East," Sherman said. "More specifically . . . well, I can't get more specific. I've got a friend on the east coast who's sent me an e-mail. She said she's looking over courses of action for us, doing a little research. In the meantime, we'd do well to head for the midwest. Population is spread out enough there we should have a decent shot at moving undetected, not to mention moving safely. No hordes of infected people following in our wake."

"And to get there we have to make it through a more densely populated region," Denton noted. "Gotta love it, eh? Our very own Catch-22."

"I never said it was a flawless plan," Sherman said defensively. "For example, we need vehicles. Better find out if any of the men coming along can hotwire a car. Otherwise it looks like we'll be burglarizing some dealerships along the way."

"I'll finally be able to get my Viper," Denton said, grinning.

"Would it be wise to commit theft?" Mbutu asked, a slight frown creasing his features. "I mean, the breakdown of order is certainly far from complete. Law is still in place. We may find ourselves on the wrong side of that law."

"That's a calculated risk we'll have to take," Sherman said. "There are certain supplies and gear we'll need that we just can't requisition. We'll have to take what we can, where we can. It's the nature of survival."

"I agree," said Denton. "Besides, we can weigh the risk against the benefits once we're in those situations. We won't pull a smash-and-grab if there's a Johnny Law parked across the street directing traffic."

"In the end, though, I think we'll have to take a few choice items," Sherman said. "Well, I'm going to get back up to the bridge and write a reply to Doctor Demilio. Maybe we'll have a more concrete plan from her before we disembark."

"We'll continue organizing our gear, General," Mbutu said.

"Good. On second thought, mark off one of those sidearms," Sherman said, picking up one of the pistols. "I gave my other pistol to Rebecca. She didn't have one."

"Grab a couple magazines while you're here," Denton said, gesturing at the ammunition. Sherman nodded and picked up a pair of full magazines and tucked them away.

"Remember, keep close reins on those rifles," Sherman added, jerking a finger in the direction of the firearms. "They go to the most skilled. Issue 'em when we're about to hit land."

"You've got it, Frank."

Washington, DC.
1206 hrs_

Like the cities far to the east, Washington was beginning to burn.

There had been sporadic fires downtown for over a day now. Mason and Doctor Demilio had risked going up to the second story of the safe house to get a better view of the surrounding area and had first spotted the plumes of smoke from there. It appeared to be several small blazes as opposed to one massive firestorm, spread out across the city. That was fortunate. They would most likely remain safe where they were for a while yet.

The lack of solid information regarding what was happening less than a few miles away was frustrating Anna. Even though a wealth of intelligence was available to her now compared to when she was cooped up in her cell, she still felt in the dark about much of what was happening outside. The fugitives knew that the martial law situation was deteriorating. Whereas the military had once held total control, the remainder of the civilian population was growing bolder now that they felt they had nothing to lose.

Anna was glad for the security cameras that were positioned around the safe house. They allowed her and her companions to monitor activity in the streets from the safety of the basement room. They'd seen no less than four groups of rioters running down the street outside, armed with bats, rifles, and Molotov cocktails. They were smashing car windows, setting fire to front lawns and taking whatever struck their fancy. So far, none of them had approached the house that Mason, Anna, and Julie were hiding in, and if their luck held, they would remain undiscovered.

As it stood, if a group of rioters did approach, chances are they wouldn't live to regret it. The three were armed better than ever before now that Mason had gone through the lockers and picked out a few choice items for each of them.

Still, it wasn't the rioters that really worried Anna. It wasn't even the fires, though those might smoke them out if the wind shifted in the wrong direction. It was the carriers. For every rampaging citizen they'd seen outside, they had identified two carriers. They were easy to tell apart from uninfected people—they twitched spasmodically, drool dripped from their limp jaws, and they gnashed their teeth as they walked or ran with uncertain movements down the darkened streets. With every passing hour, the carriers added more and more citizens to their ranks. The wails of the injured and dying penetrated even the thick walls of the basement safe room.

The balance had definitely tipped in favor of the Morningstar Strain.

Anna tried to keep her mind off the living hell outside in the streets. She assisted Julie in taking her dose of antibiotics, tipping her head back and chasing the pills with a sip of water.

"How is she?" Mason asked, sitting with his back to the two women at the computer terminal, punching keys absentmindedly as he scrolled through screen upon screen of recent reports.

"I'm fine," coughed Julie, scowling at Mason's back.

"I think it's in remission," said Anna, referring to Julie's pneumonia. "We caught it just in time. Any longer in that dungeon and she'd be a lot worse off."

"Good," Mason said, nodding.

"What are you reading?" Anna asked, closing the box of medical supplies she'd been using.

"Action reports," Mason told her, tapping the screen with his finger. "We've got casualty tallies, safe zones, hot zones, quarantine areas, recommendations, plans, and orders here. Pretty much anything we'd like to know about what's going on out there that can be written down. Funny."

"What's that?"

"How the world can be crashing down all around us, and people are still filing reports, like the higher-ups are still going to be reading them Monday morning."

"Force of habit."

"Force of stupidity," scoffed Mason. "Look at this. A post-action report filed by a battalion commander in Florida detailing the amount of ammunition expended and the estimated cost of the action, in dollars, rounded up. As if the dollar is worth anything these days."

Anna stopped for a moment, struck by a thought. She'd filed hundreds of reports to her higher-ups at USAMRIID detailing each day of her research. There was data in those reports that might be very useful to a group of people working to stay safe from the Morningstar Strain.

"Can you tap into the USAMRIID database from here?" she asked, walking over to stand behind the agent.

"Yeah," Mason said, looking over at the doctor. "If you've got an account I can use to access it. I'm no hacker."

"I have an account," Anna said. "But will it still work? I've kind of been arrested the past couple weeks."

"I bet it will," said Mason. "They probably figured you wouldn't be near a terminal to even try to access the database. They probably left your account open. Why? Got something you want to look up?"

"Yes. I've been thinking: Before I was arrested, I was working on the Morningstar Strain, trying to figure out how it works so I could, basically, reverse-engineer a vaccine or a cure. Same basic principle we've used dealing with Lassa and Ebola and any number of other nasty bugs. Maybe I can download my research and get back to working on it now that I'm free again."

"You actually believe you'll find a cure?"

"By myself? Without my lab and staff? Not really. Even with that, the chance is slim. But there *is* a chance."

"Okay, I'll buy it," said Mason. "Here, give it a shot."

Mason slid out of the seat and let Anna take his place. As she had a thousand times before, she brought up her login screen and typed out her username and password. She hit enter, and waited while the computer talked to the database.

```
>ERROR: Invalid username/password. Please try again.
```

Anna growled. She re-typed the password, being certain each key was hit in the correct order, and hit enter again.

```
>ERROR: Invalid username/password. Please try again.
```

"Damn it all," Anna mumbled. "They got me."

"Let me have a shot at it," Julie said from behind the pair. She came walking over, a wool blanket draped around her shoulders, looking weak but determined.

"What are you planning on doing?" Mason asked.

"You might not be a hacker," Julie said to Anna, "But I sort of am. Used to be an investigative reporter before I got my anchor position, remember? I can hack into that database."

Anna didn't have a ready answer, but she was impressed. She merely blinked, nodded, and slid aside, giving up the chair to Julie.

The reporter sank into the desk chair with a heavy sigh, slowly cracking her knuckles.

"This may take a while," Julie said. "Get comfortable,"

She began typing.

"Handy," grinned Mason.

"Bet your ass," Julie managed, biting back a cough. "Glad you brought me along now?"

Mason chuckled. "I'll be more impressed if you manage to get in. Remote access has been tightened up since that kid hacked the Pentagon in the nineties. If you can, though . . ."

"I've got to earn my keep somehow, huh?"

USS Ramage
1834 hrs_

Brewster drifted in and out of a fitful sleep. He couldn't get comfortable. He tossed and turned in the narrow bunk he lay upon, throwing off the blankets in exasperation.

"*Fuck it,*" he whispered, clasping his hands behind his head and staring at the bottom of the bunk above him. A sailor had pinned family photos to the underside of the mattress, and Brewster let his eyes play over them.

A knock came on the door. Grateful for the distraction, Brewster glanced over.

"What is it?" he asked. No answer came. "Stop fucking around out there. What's going on?"

The door began to swing inward, creaking loudly.

"Who's there?" Brewster asked. The door finished the long swing, coming to a stop against the wall. Framed in the doorway was the stooped silhouette of a soldier.

"Who are you?"

"Don't remember me?" the soldier said, stepping forward into the light.

"Darin?" Brewster asked, sitting up in the bunk. "*What the fuck?!*"

"Don't remember your old buddy?" Darin repeated, walking slowly towards Brewster. "Don't remember the guy you killed?"

"*I had to,*" Brewster protested, drawing back. "You were infected."

"That's right," Darin said, flashing a feral grin. His teeth were coated in blood. As Brewster watched, the blood began to fill the corporal's mouth, running out across his lips and down his face, dripping to the floor with a steady *plip-plip-plip*. "I was infected."

The corporal's eyes seemed to glow with an inner light, and Brewster felt terror welling up in his chest.

"Stay back, man," Brewster told him, recoiling.

"You killed me without a second thought," Darin said, voice distorted behind the blood in his mouth. "I'm here to return the favor!"

Brewster noticed for the first time that Darin held a pistol in his hand. The corporal raised the weapon and aimed it directly at Brewster.

The blast was deafening.

Brewster came awake in a flash, sitting upright and slamming his head on the bunk above him.

"Fuck!" he yelped, wiping a hand across his forehead. It came away covered in sweat. The nightmare had been incredibly real.

Another knock sounded at the door. Brewster remembered the gunshot in the dream and realized it must have been the knocking.

"Up and at 'em, soldiers!" came a voice from outside. "We're about to make landfall. Quarantine's over. You're cleared to leave."

The other soldiers in the room with Brewster whooped with joy, slapping high-fives and grinning. Brewster ran a hand through his close-cut hair, heaving a massive sigh. He was relieved to be allowed out of the room—but more than that, he was relieved they were about to get off the ship. Before he had even tried to sleep, he'd made his decision. The first chance he got, he was going AWOL. He had no idea what the situation would be like on land, but he bet if it was anything like the other infected areas of the world he'd have plenty of opportunities to get away.

The door to the quarantine room swung open and the soldiers gratefully piled out into the hallway.

"Assemble on deck in five minutes," ordered Sergeant Major Thomas, who stood against the far bulkhead directing the half-dozen freed soldiers. "Gear'll be issued shortly, then General Sherman wants a word with you all."

Grateful to have something to do besides sit around in a bleak room, the soldiers made their way through the winding corridors of the destroyer to the deck, with Thomas trailing behind them.

Brewster was now even more dead-set on making a break for it once they hit land. He was still a bit shaken up from his dream as the soldiers walked out into the sunlight for the first time in a week. Still, Brewster couldn't help but stare at the view in front of him. The ship was coming up on the west coast of North America, and the rocky, tall shore sat off in the distance, partly concealed in thick, cottony fog.

"*There it is*," Brewster murmured. "*Home sweet home*."

"Fall in!" came the order from Thomas, who had pushed his way through the soldiers to stand in front of them all. "Fall in!"

The soldiers scrambled to obey, forming straight rows, standing at attention. Brewster found himself in the front row with Thomas no more than a few feet away.

"Dress right—dress!" Thomas ordered. The soldiers' right arms shot out to the shoulder of the man next to them, and the lines evened themselves out into even neater rows. "Ready—front! At ease!"

The soldiers relaxed, folding their arms behind their lower back and spreading their feet shoulder-width apart. Brewster noticed Sherman for the first time. The General had been off on the side of the formation, talking with the photographer, and now came walking in front of the formation of men. Brewster followed him with his eyes.

"Gentlemen," Sherman began, "In less than an hour we'll make landfall. The reason we're having this talk is because when we hit land, you are all going to have something you don't normally get in the service: a *choice*."

Brewster perked up a bit.

"As many of you know, the situation on land is mostly a mystery to us. Communications have been disrupted. We've been receiving conflicting reports. But for all intents and purposes, we'll assume that North America is indeed an infected zone."

The soldiers glanced back and forth at each other, but said nothing.

"Captain Franklin has graciously decided to assist the quarantine efforts to the south. I, however, have a different plan of action."

Sherman stopped for a moment, gathering his thoughts. He then went on, "I've been in the service for a long, long time. There are few things I haven't seen, almost nothing I haven't done. But I realized that I don't want to die trying to keep a dead city from falling. I'd rather live to enjoy a retirement. Therefore . . . I'm submitting my resignation."

The soldiers again shared a glance back and forth, and here and there came murmured comments.

"That doesn't mean I'm done here," Sherman clarified. "I have a plan. I've been talking back and forth with an old colleague who happens to be one of the world's leading experts on the Morningstar Strain. She's trying to engineer a cure. It's a long shot, but it's better than sitting in a city waiting to be bitten by one of those godforsaken carriers. To that end, I've decided to head east—maybe find a nice unpopulated area in the Midwest and wait for news. I'm here now to ask you all which you would prefer: to go on with Franklin and help the defense efforts, or go AWOL with me. Measure your decision wisely."

Brewster somehow knew that the General wasn't joking, but he still couldn't believe his ears. He was being saved the trouble of running. Even more incredible was the General himself making the same decision a lowly PFC had—even to the point of their similar goals. It wasn't much of a decision for Brewster. He'd already made up his mind, but some of the other soldiers were not so lucky.

"Sir?" came a voice from the formation. "What happens if this blows over and we've gone AWOL?"

"Then we're in trouble," Sherman admitted. "Anyone who goes with me runs that risk. That's why I want you all to weigh your choices very carefully before you make your final decision. Personally, I've got to admit I don't think much of the chance of this blowing over. I think the Morningstar Strain is here to stay. Perhaps the passing of time will prove me wrong. I hope it does. But I don't think it will."

Washington, D.C.
January 20
1845 hrs_

The streets were mostly empty in the waning evening light. *Mostly.* Here and there an abandoned car sat with doors hanging open, and the dim sky was lit periodically by fires in the distance. The rioting that had been going on for days was long gone.

A man sprinted down the wide, open avenue, gasping for breath, clutching his chest with one hand and wielding a pistol in the other. His hair was unkempt and he had a wild look in his eyes. As he turned onto the street, he stopped for a moment, brandishing the weapon and squinting into the darkness. Sighting nothing, he took off again, running full-tilt, dodging the abandoned vehicles. His eyes scanned the houses as he moved, reading the address numbers silently to himself.

"*Christ, where is it?*" he said aloud, gasping as he managed each word. He'd almost run the length of the block before he stopped again, noticing a small, two-story house set back off the street. The windows and porch were dark, but the number on the mailbox was the one he had been searching for.

The man's run had been with a purpose. He'd been forced to use an old car on this journey and the junker had broken down a mile back. There was only one safe place nearby—the house he stood in front of now. It had been designed to be used in a situation just like the one he found himself in: A refuge for legal fugitives. A safe house. The agency took care of its own.

The man didn't approach the house with the same haphazard manner he'd run down the block. He knew that the place had its own defenses and it would do him no good to set off every alarm in the house and perhaps get himself ventilated with lead. He walked cautiously up the brick path to the front door, nervously keeping an eye on the shadows around him, worried that they might hold a carrier of the Morningstar Strain, or—*just as bad*—a civilian out for blood.

He climbed the stairs one by one, the wood creaking under his feet. His breaths were heavy and loud in the silent twilight as he reached a hand out to the knob on the front door.

His fingers stopped inches from the knob. His eyes had caught sight of a blinking red light through the window panes in the door. The alarms were indeed active. He took a step back. Even though he was the cautious type, the man hadn't expected to find anyone at the house. It had supposedly been vacated almost a week before.

This bore investigation.

It was a good thing he had a high-level security clearance and had been briefed on the safe houses. Otherwise he wouldn't have known that the kitchen window wasn't alarmed. The idea was that an agent could still access the house if he or she needed to, even without the proper security codes. Still scanning the darkened street, the man walked around the side of the house, heel to toe to keep the noise to a minimum. He pulled a small flashlight from his pants pocket and twisted the end to turn it on. He shone the beam around the frame of the kitchen window, checking to see if any additions had been made to the house's security. Seeing nothing, he turned the light off and pocketed it, exchanging the tool for a pocketknife.

Hearing something behind him, the man swiveled, holding out the pistol, and let his eyes scan the area. For a moment he neither moved nor breathed. When nothing sprang out of the shadows at him he relaxed, turning back to the window. He fit the blade of the knife under the window, pushing it along until it kicked up the old-fashioned latch. He used his free hand to retract the blade and then lifted the window silently from the sill.

He was in.

He took one last look around the yard, then stuck the pistol in his waistband and lifted one leg through the window as quietly as he could. When he felt his foot touch the linoleum on the other side, he shifted his weight and pulled the rest of his body into the house.

He spun, quickly but carefully sliding the window shut behind him.

He had already heard voices from deeper in the house. The pistol reappeared in his hand. Better safe than sorry. He knew there was always the chance he'd stumbled on a few of his colleagues taking shelter, in which case all his caution would be for naught, but there was an equal chance that the people in the house had no business being there.

He moved past the refrigerator covered in crayon drawings that looked like they were done by a child and the end tables displaying pictures of a family that didn't exist, through the hardwood-floor hallway towards the door that led to the basement safe room. The door was mostly shut, but hung open a half an inch.

The man slid the barrel of the pistol in the gap and used it as a lever, very slowly pushing the door further open until he could see down the stairs. The second door—the one at the base of the stairway that was meant to be secured in a crisis—had been left hanging open, and a shaft of light shone through. The voices were much clearer now. It sounded like at least one woman and a man. He couldn't make out their words.

The angle of the stairway would afford the man a view of the room if he descended a few steps, but he had no desire to put his weight on a creaky board and be discovered. Besides, he already had more than a vague idea of who was below.

His control had sent out a bulletin, telling everyone in the city to be on the lookout for a rogue agent and two escaped fugitives. They could be anywhere, the report had said, because they had escaped into the catacombs below the city.

The man knew for a fact that the catacombs connected to this safe house. He had a feeling he'd found the escapees. He slid back from the door, once again using the pistol to close the door behind him. He slipped back through the hall and into the kitchen where he could relax somewhat.

There was a hard line telephone in the upstairs bedroom, just like there was in every safe house in the city. He could make his call from there. Soon—*hopefully*—the fugitives below would be dealt with.

Down below, in the basement safe room, Julie was busy at the computer terminal.

"Goddamn, this security is thick," she said.

Mason leaned over her shoulder and asked, "Making progress?"

"Yeah," she told him. "But it's going slow. There's multiple layers of security. I have no clue how many, but I've gotten through three already."

"Wish my login was still working," said Anna. "Would've saved us a lot of trouble."

"What's the payoff we're looking at?"

"Pretty much all of my research," Anna replied. "*Years' worth.* Everything from data on the strain to the behavior of the infected. Once we get through we can burn it onto discs so we won't have to barge into the system again."

"Just how many discs are we talking about here?"

Anna looked defensive. "Hey, when you write daily reports and have to save high-definition x-rays and RNA samples you end up taking up more than a few gigabytes of data."

"I had no idea what we were getting into when we started on this," Mason said. "I really didn't want to stay here this long, much less another day or two or however long it's going to take Julie to get through the security. We're taking a big risk."

"I'm not going to get caught," Julie countered. "I'm too cautious for that."

"It's not you I'm worried about, though if you *are* caught that'd fry us just as well," said Mason. "No, what I'm worried about is Sawyer. There's a lot of exits to the catacombs, and he'll have his hands full with the infected, but it's not out of the question that he'd track us down. And I'm sure he's going to try. That guy just couldn't accept that the world's spiraling down the shitter. He'll see it as his patriotic duty to bring us in, even if there's no one left to care."

"Relax, Mason. He's got an entire city to search," Julie said.

"Maybe that sounds like an intimidating job to you," Mason replied, "But it's his job to gather intel and track people down. Once the outbreak at HQ is contained, he'll be right on our asses. I bet there's already an APB out on us."

"We'll be long gone," Anna said. "Once we get my research downloaded we can head out."

Mason nodded. "Good to hear. I'll leave you to it, then. I'm going to finish getting our gear together. Maybe focusing on that will help me relax."

The agent stepped back from the terminal and turned to the folding table in the center of the safe room. He had already laid out three backpacks and packed them with food, spare clothes, and tools. As long as they were within the city limits he wouldn't be able to let his guard down. He felt as if they were in enemy territory—a *double threat*, as it were. One from the infected mobs roaming the city streets and the other from his ex-comrades at the agency. Perhaps, if they were extraordinarily lucky, one would take care of the other. He wasn't going to put his money on that chance any day soon, though. Sawyer could handle himself as well as Mason, and the infected were more likely to die than the agent was.

Upstairs, the house's uninvited guest was finishing up his telephone call.

"Two, maybe three," he whispered into the phone. There was a moment of silence as the person on the other end spoke. "No, it's just me here. I didn't even know they were here. Just stumbled onto them. No way. All I've got is six rounds in my sidearm. I'm waiting for backup."

There was another moment of silence.

"Hey, I'm not committing suicide to take in three fugitives this late in the day. In case you hadn't noticed, the world isn't exactly standing on its own two feet at the moment."

The man sighed as he took another earful from the voice on the other end.

"Look, this has been a courtesy call from me to you letting you know I've found the people you're looking for. As for me, starting a half hour ago, I'm looking out for number one. That being *me*, in case you couldn't guess. Right now I'm going to hang up, go back downstairs, and get the hell out of Dodge. You want these people, you come and get them. You've got the address."

The man hung up and heaved another heavy sigh. Eight years to pension and the agency falls to shit, thanks to the Morningstar Strain.

At least he could take an early retirement. He checked his sidearm and silently left the room, gliding towards his window exit.

USS Ramage
2034 hrs_

Night was beginning to fall when the *Ramage* came into sight of the mainland. Soldiers and refugees had gathered on the deck, looking out at the rocky shores half-obscured in evening mist. Captain Franklin had taken his ship north of the nearest city to give those who were leaving a better chance at getting away without being discovered by carriers or hostile uninfected.

Franklin's sailors had begun ferrying the departing soldiers and refugees to the shore in a small dinghy. It was relatively slow going, as the little boat could only hold a few people at a time, and twenty-eight of them were still waiting to be taken in to dry land.

Brewster and Denton stood near the bow of the ship. The issuing of equipment had just been completed, and Brewster was idly loading nine-millimeter rounds into a clip.

"Goddamn, I wish I had my rifle back," he muttered.

"Can't be helped," Denton said. "Not enough ammunition to go around."

"I know, I know," Brewster replied. "I just hate the idea of going in there and not being able to take a shot at range. It'll be hell if we have to let 'em get close enough to use these peashooters."

As if to emphasize his point, Brewster raised the pistol up and fell into a shooter's stance, peering along the iron sights at the mainland. He squeezed the trigger and dry-fired the weapon, then nodded, slapped in the loaded clip, and holstered it.

"Out of curiosity," Brewster said after a moment had passed in silence, "Who was issued the M-16's?"

"Didn't you hear?"

"Hear what?"

"Sherman gave 'em over to Franklin. Said there wasn't much chance of finding ammunition for 'em as we go along, and the Captain might need 'em in the city to the south."

"Bloody fucking hell," moaned Brewster. "So we're nothing but close-range snacks for those walking pus-bags out there?"

"Well, we've got the MP-5's. Those things can lay down a pretty solid sheet of lead. We're better armed than most folks'll be."

"Next landing party, board the dinghy!" called one of Franklin's sailors, waving an arm at the group of folks waiting to be taken to shore. Another six—three armed soldiers, three civilian refugees—began to board the small boat.

"We're up next," Denton said, looking down at his watch. "Wonder what the plan is once we're all back on terra firma. Think we'll make camp for the night?"

"Hell no," Brewster scoffed. "First thing I learned in the Army is, just because it's night doesn't mean we stop working. Sherman'll probably have us get a move on. Cover of darkness and all that."

"Too bad. I feel like I haven't slept in the last couple days."

"Tell me about it," Brewster said, shuddering inwardly at the memory of his disturbing dream.

"But anyway," Denton began, "Thinking in the long-term, I wonder what the plan is. Sherman said something about having a friend he was keeping in touch with. Heard anything about that?"

"Just RumInt," Brewster said, using the military abbreviation for *Rumor Intelligence*, widely respected as the fastest means of transmitting information in the world. "People are saying it's a woman doctor, someone who knows a hell of a lot about the Morningstar Strain. Maybe she's got a cure or something."

"A cure? For *this* virus?" Denton chuckled. "When was the last time you heard of a virus like this getting cured?"

"Well . . ." Brewster murmured, wracking his brain. "Polio?"

Denton flashed the infantryman a bemused grin. "AIDS? Lassa? Hanta? Ebola? Marburg? None of 'em. Viruses are tricky bastards, and this one's a lot more diabolical than most. I don't think we're after a cure, personally. I hope I'm wrong."

"So do I," Brewster said, then, catching Denton's glance, added: "No offense."

"None taken."

A moment passed in silence.

"Hey," Brewster said after a few seconds, changing topics faster than an obsessive-compulsive changed underwear. He turned around and scanned the crowd. "You know who I haven't seen in a while? That medic girl."

"Rebecca?"

"I guess. Don't think I ever actually met her. Is she coming with us?"

"I think so. Not sure. Last I saw of her she was in medical below, packing up supplies. She seemed kind of shaken up."

"Oh, right! Of course!" Brewster exclaimed, slapping a hand against his forehead.

"What?"

"Decker!" Brewster said triumphantly. "She shot Decker!"

"What, that sergeant who turned out to be infected?"

"Yeah. If you ask me, there was little something between those two. Don't know if it went anywhere, though. Still, damn good reflexes on her part. You shou=ld've seen it. She yanked Sherman's pistol and blasted that fucker right before he bit me. I guess I sort of owe her. Hope she's coming along so I can repay the favor someday."

"Next landing party! Time to move out!" called the sailor near the dinghy.

"Well . . . that's us," Denton said, shouldering his backpack. "Ready?"

"More than ready," Brewster said, grinning. "Let's do this."

Washington, D.C.
2213 hrs_

Julie was definitely feeling better. As she worked, hunched over the keyboard, eyes locked on the glowing screen, she murmured to herself, taking mental notes of her progress. Anna tuned out the chatter easily; working in a busy lab most of her adult life had taught her to ignore the conversations around her and focus on whatever work demanded her attention. Mason, on the other hand, had been trained and conditioned to pay attention to every little change in his environment, and Julie was beginning to drive him mad.

He did a wonderful job of hiding his annoyance, if only to maintain civility in the little group.

Julie had been at work for hours, and still hadn't managed to access Dr. Demilio's backed-up research. Finally, Mason could stand sitting in the basement no longer. He stood, throwing his coat over his shoulders and holstering a sidearm.

"I'm going up," he said. "Maybe have a look outside, see what's cooking."

"Is that a good idea? What if you're spotted?"

"I'm not going out the door," Mason said, rolling his eyes. "I'll stay inside. That's what windows are for. No one will ever know."

Mason trotted up the stairs and entered the darkened hallway on the first floor of the safe house. He glanced back and forth, making sure the front and rear doors were still secure, and walked leisurely into the dining room. He ran a finger along the tabletop. It came away covered in dust. Whoever had been taking care of this safe house wasn't big on housekeeping. Mason let his eyes play over the fake pictures on the wall as he entered the kitchen.

He opened the refrigerator a crack, peering inside. He allowed himself a small grin as he pulled out a can of beer, then popped the top and took a long, satisfied drink.

"*Ahh*," he breathed. He'd needed that.

Mason froze as he lowered the can. Something wasn't right. He switched his focus to scan the countertop.

"*What the hell?*" he murmured, walking over and peering down at the surface. There were clear shoeprints on the window sill and countertop, and one equally dusty print on the linoleum flooring. Mason narrowed his eyes as his sidearm appeared in his right hand. His left hand set down the beer can and reached out to the window, checking it. It was unlocked.

"*Shit*."

Mason wheeled away from the counter and planted his back against the wall of the kitchen, listening intently for any noise in the house. All he could hear were the distant, muffled keystrokes and murmured commentary by Julie in the basement.

Someone had come in through the window, that much was obvious. Whether they were still in the house—that was another matter. Best to do a sweep.

Mason considered fetching Anna to help, but decided against it. No need to worry either of them. This was one of his specialties.

He sank to a squat and peered out into the hallway, eyes darting left, then right. Clear. Mason rose to a hunched stance and—walking on his toes—moved silently down the hall towards the stairs. When he reached the foyer, he swept the dining room and living room once more with steady eyes. Both rooms were empty. He mounted the stairway, going slowly. The fourth step creaked heavily under his foot and he winced, not wanting to give anyone in the house even a moment's notice he was approaching. After waiting a few seconds to see if the noise would kick up any proverbial quail, he continued.

The first upstairs room was made up to look like a child's bedroom, though no child had ever lived there. Mason looked around the room, opened the closet, checked under the bed, and, satisfied it was empty, returned to the hall, closing the door behind him. He swept the other three rooms in a similar manner. By the time he reached the master bedroom he was starting to relax. If someone had come into the house while they were in the basement, it seemed they had already left.

The master bedroom was empty as well. Mason sighed, holstering his pistol. The footprints were worrisome to an extent—but chances were they belonged to a looter who'd bolted the moment he realized the house wasn't empty.

Still, why would a looter go to all the trouble of trying to enter so silently? Why wouldn't he have just smashed a window and come charging in?

Something about it set Mason's nerves on edge.

He decided there was nothing more to be done about it except to be on guard. He retreated to the basement as quickly as he could, shutting the doors behind him and slamming the deadbolts closed. Anna and Julie looked over at him with curious gazes.

"You're acting like you've seen a ghost," Anna said.

"A spook, maybe," Mason replied. Under any other circumstances, he might've chuckled at his play on words, but he wasn't in the mood for lightheartedness. "Get your things together. We should leave very soon."

"What? I'm almost through, just wait a little longer," Julie said distractedly, pointing at the computer screen.

"Maybe we've got lots of time. Maybe we don't. I don't know. All I know for sure is that someone has been in the house. I found footprints in the kitchen and a window was unsecured."

"One of your old friends?" Anna asked.

"Like I said, I don't know. Maybe it was just some civilian looking for a place to hole up, but I'm not taking any chances," Mason told her, walking over to the folding table in the center of the room. He had already spent time preparing packs for each of them filled with food rations, water pouches, changes of clothing, ammunition, and assorted sundry items they might need on the move. Mason exchanged his sport coat for a plain black windbreaker and slipped his pack on.

Anna watched with interest. "You really are spooked, aren't you?"

"Quiet! I'm concentrating!" Julie admonished.

"Hey, I'm just looking out for our best interests," Mason said. "If you let your guard down, you'll probably—*wait*. Did you hear that?"

Mason looked at the ceiling above them, head cocked to one side.

"Hear what?"

"Shut up and listen!" Mason said, holding up his hand. The sound of squealing brakes drifted to their ears. "*Oh, shit.*"

Mason ran over to the security terminal that sat next to Julie's computer and turned on the screens. There were three cameras that watched over the house. One was pointed at the back door, one at the front, and one in the hallway watching the entrance to the basement safe room. Mason tapped a finger on the screen of the camera that was aimed out front.

"Look," he said. "Headlights. They're here."

Anna cursed, snapping up one of the MP-5s that lay on the folding table.

"I can't believe these bastards are coming after us when they've got an infected city to deal with," she said, resting the sub-machine gun on her shoulder.

Mason drew his sidearm and laid a hand on Julie's shoulder. "We've got to go—right now!"

"But I'm not in yet!" Julie protested.

"Would you rather have the research and be dead or go without it and live?" Mason challenged.

"Buy me five minutes! I'm almost there, really!"

"That's what you said a half an hour ago!"

"I mean it this time!"

There was a furious pounding upstairs—a heavy, solid boom that repeated itself every couple of seconds.

"They're battering down the front door," Mason said, watching the security terminal screen.

"Five minutes!" Julie pleaded.

"*Damn it*," Mason cursed, casting a glance at the stairway that led to the first level of the house. "I'll put a few rounds in their direction, make 'em duck their heads—but when I come back down here, we are leaving! Doctor, get the gear picked up. We'll try to head out through the catacombs, maybe that'll throw 'em again."

"Right."

Mason opened the locked doors and ran to the top of the stairway, peering around the corner. Flashlights were being shone in the darkened windows. Mason guessed Sawyer had brought six or seven men with him—More than enough to deal with one rogue agent, a virologist and a half-sick journalist.

One of the flashlight beams spotlighted Mason's face and he quickly tried to withdraw. However, a shout from outside told him he'd been spotted.

"Mason!" Anna called up from the base of the stairs. "Be loud! There are infected all over this neighborhood—we saw them earlier on the monitors, remember?! Make some noise! They'll come running!"

"Nice thinking, but I'm way ahead of you!" Mason called back, yanking a flash-bang from the pocket of his jacket and pulling the pin.

He tossed the grenade out into the hallway and let it roll down the hardwood floor toward the front door. His timing had been off—he had hoped they would manage to bash through the door at roughly the same time the grenade exploded, but heavy oak and quality hinges both stood up to a battering ram rather well. Still, the grenade had the intended effect. The flash and deafening blast rattled the cabinets and frame of the safe house, making the pictures on the walls do the jitterbug before hanging off-kilter on their nails. Mason heard muffled curses from outside. Apparently, some of the men had been looking in the windows when the grenade had blown, half-blinding them.

More importantly, anything infected—or undead—within three city blocks would have heard the explosion. Judging from the actions of the infected in the past, it wouldn't be long before there would be dozens swarming the house.

Mason didn't wait for the men outside to recover. He leaned out and fired off five, six, seven rounds in rapid succession, peppering the door and letting in stray beams of light from the cars parked outside. He didn't hear any cries from wounded men and figured all the rounds had missed, but for the moment the battering ceased. Return fire shattered the front windows and bullets ripped into the hallway floor and walls. Mason ducked back into the stairwell as his enemies fired. When the barrage ceased, he leaned back out and emptied the rest of his ammunition into the door.

A flashlight beam danced across Mason's back, casting a shadow in front of him, and he darted back just in time to avoid being shot by a man who'd circled around to the rear of the house. Mason slapped in a second clip and sent a pair of bullets out the back door, shattering glass. The front door shuddered under another heavy blow from the battering ram and the frame cracked noticeably. A couple more hits and they'd be in.

The picture window in the living room—already broken by gunfire—was further smashed out by the barrel of a rifle. A gloved hand reached in and cleared away the sharp debris. Mason fired at the figure, but the rounds went wide. A pair of men jumped in through the broken window, rolling into crouches with weapons at the ready. Mason had seen them begin their leap, however, and was ready.

His first round caught the lead man in the throat, dropping him to the carpet where he rolled around, clutching at the wound and gurgling helplessly. The second shot, meant for the man's partner, missed completely as the enemy jumped to the side and returned fire.

The front door took another heavy pounding and began to separate from the frame. One more blow and it would fly free.

Time to get the hell out of Dodge, Mason thought, firing a few more rounds for good measure before retreating into the stairwell, slamming shut and bolting the heavy doors once he was through. Anna was waiting for him at the base of the stairs.

"What's going on up there?"

"They're in the house," Mason said, breathing heavy. "I got one of them. I don't know how many more there are—Six, seven maybe."

"Julie? Ready?"

"Just about!" she said, slapping a CD into the empty tray and pushing it shut as quick as she could. "I'm in—just copying data!"

"Copy faster!" Mason growled. Above them, the basement door took a heavy hit from the battering ram.

"Look!" Anna said, tapping on Mason's shoulder. "The monitors!"

Mason glanced over. The front door had been knocked clean off its hinges and they had an unobstructed view of the front yard through the security camera's eye. Activity at the bottom of the shot showed the intruders in the hallway, but beyond them, out on the grass, new figures were taking shape. Some shambled along, jaws hanging slack, eyes devoid of humanity. Others ran past them, a feral look on their faces, sweat and blood streaming down their skin.

"Here they come," Anna whispered. "*Carriers.*"

"Dinner time for the sick fucks," Mason said.

The first of the infected reached the front door, fixing the startled intruders with a frenzied glare before being cut down in a hail of gunfire. Though the monitors didn't capture sound, they heard the blasts all too well through the ceiling above them. Before the first infected had even hit the ground, another had appeared to take its place. This one, too, was gunned down—but there were plenty more still coming. The intruders fanned out, one stationing himself in front of the broken window, another pair guarding the door. The heavy blows of the battering ram continued all the while.

"It's working. They're splitting their attention," Anna said.

"Glad these bastards are good for something," Mason agreed. "Let's get into the catacombs before they bust through these doors."

"I'm right behind you!" Julie shouted, fumbling for a jewel case and stabbing a finger at the CD tray's eject button.

Mason heaved open the heavy door that led down to the tunnels below the house. Behind him, Anna shouldered her pack and tossed a third to Julie, who quickly stuffed the discs in the half-open top before shoving herself away from the terminal and rushing to catch up.

Mason ran in a full-out sprint down the gently sloping ramp. Ahead of him was a narrow entryway that widened into the tunnel proper beyond. Their electric cart was still parked, waiting for them to make their getaway. In his hurry, Mason made a mistake.

He didn't notice the second cart.

As he ran through the entryway an arm shot out of nowhere, clothes-lining the rogue agent. Mason slammed into the concrete floor with a grunt of pain. He looked up in time to see a polished shoe descending towards his head. He rolled to the side just as the foot hit the ground where his temple had been a moment before. Mason sprang up, holding a hand to his chest and struggling to pull in breaths.

"I knew you'd come back this way if I sent men in the front door," said his attacker, falling back into a ready stance. "Like rats fleeing a sinking ship. You're too predictable, Mason."

"*Sawyer*," Mason uttered, spitting on the floor in front of his adversary. He risked a glance down the tunnel, looking for other agents—but there was no one else. "Where's your backup?"

"I came this way alone," Sawyer said. "I wanted to finish you off myself. I'm not even armed."

He stepped back and showed a wide grin. He then spread his coat open, proving that he indeed carried no weapons.

"Mistake," came a voice from the entryway. Sawyer flicked his eyes over in the direction of the sound and saw himself staring down the barrel of a sub-machine gun wielded by Anna Demilio.

"Doctor. It seems we were in this situation once before, only then it was I who held the weapon."

"*Don't*," Mason told her, holding up a hand. "*Let me*."

Sawyer nodded almost imperceptibly. He'd expected nothing less from Mason.

"Oh, bullshit," Anna said, clicking off the safety on the weapon. "Let me kill him now, before they get through the doors."

"No, hold your fire. Sawyer here might be a worthless pus-fuck, but I did run out on him. Call it a . . ."

" . . . Debt of honor, perhaps?" Sawyer said, finishing Mason's sentence for him. "I figured. Like I said, you're too predictable."

"And you're too overconfident," Mason retorted, shedding his jacket and tossing his weapons to the floor.

The two agents squared off, circling slowly and watching one another for the telltale signs of an attack.

"This is ridiculous!" Anna called out. "We don't have time for this!"

Neither man responded. Their eyes were locked on each other. The agency had made hand-to-hand combat a major part of their training regimen. Like the armed forces, both men worked on a solid base of boxing and jiu-jitsu. It might lack the poetry of karate, but it was more than effective.

It was Sawyer that threw the first punch, a quick jab that flashed out so fast Mason didn't have time for a block. The blow landed on his chin, staggering him back a half step. Sawyer wasted no time in pressing the attack. A flurry of punches came at Mason—a second jab, which he slapped aside handily. A roundhouse came next, but Mason ducked his head, and Sawyer hit only air. The next attack was a brutal uppercut, and might have ended the fight right then if Mason hadn't leaned back just enough. Even so, Sawyer's fist clipped his chin, jarring his head for a moment.

As Sawyer followed through with the uppercut, Mason saw an opportunity. He stepped in, throwing a quick one-two combination into Sawyer's unguarded stomach. The agent expelled breath in a pained gasp and fell back a half step. Mason took a chance, throwing a roundhouse of his own aimed directly at Sawyer's right temple. Sawyer raised an arm, stopping the punch before it reached him, and stepped forward, slinking one leg behind Mason's and planting a hand on his chest. He shoved hard, sending Mason sprawling to the ground. The takedown was considered one of the most basic combat moves. Mason would have berated himself for opening himself up to it if he'd had time, but Sawyer was already hovering over him, raising a leg to stomp the agent as he lay on the ground.

Mason kicked out hard, nailing Sawyer in the kneecap. He grunted, falling to his knees, and Mason leapt up, full-body tackling Sawyer.

For a split second, Mason flashed back to his hand-to-hand class. The instructor's first lesson was a simple one.

'*Almost all fights start with both combatants on their feet*,' the instructor had said. '*But you'll find that in almost every case, both fighters will be on the ground within seconds. From there, it's like chess: the endgame. Every move must have a purpose, or you're dead. It's as simple as that.*'

Mason had an advantage. He found himself on top of Sawyer. He wasted no time, wailing mercilessly about the agent's head and neck with a furious flurry of punches, bloodying Sawyer's nose and mouth within moments.

Sawyer was helpless to block the blows, but he wasn't done yet.

He locked his leg around Mason's, reaching up with one hand to grab at the fabric of his shirt. Mason felt the grab and knew what was coming—but the move was already set up. Sawyer heaved. His positioning gave him plenty of leverage. The pair found themselves rolling, and when they came to a rest, their positions were reversed—Sawyer sat on top and Mason was pinned beneath.

Sawyer managed one or two heavy blows before Mason flat-palmed him in the chin, cracking his jaw back and sending spit and blood flying through the air. While Sawyer reeled, Mason pushed back on his chest, freeing himself from the pin. He attacked again as Sawyer recovered, quickly locking both legs around his opponent's chest from behind and working an arm up around his throat, his other arm holding Sawyer's forehead back.

The fight was over. Mason knew it, and Sawyer knew it. From his position, Mason could snap Sawyer's neck in one quick movement.

But Mason did neither. Combat simply ceased with both agents locked in their hold on the cold concrete floor.

"*Do it,*" Sawyer croaked. "*Finish it.*"

"If I did that," Mason said, whispering in Sawyer's bleeding ear, "I'd be no better than you, you piece of shit."

Instead, Mason tightened his hold, closing off Sawyer's air supply. The agent choked and gasped, struggling for air, beating his elbows into Mason's ribcage, but the blows were weak, and grew weaker by the moment. It took no more than twelve seconds for Sawyer to slump into unconsciousness. Mason released his grip, letting his opponent fall face-first onto the floor.

The pain of Mason's injuries started to creep into his mind as the adrenaline rush of the fight began to wear off. He felt weak, shaky, and the thought of lying down and taking a nap was very appealing. He might have actually considered it in his foggy state of mind if Anna's MP-5 hadn't started chattering out rounds one after the other. Mason sprang up, looking back in the direction of the safe room. The attackers had battered down both doors and Dr. Demilio was giving them something to think about before they went poking their heads in.

"It's clear!" Mason called, picking up his own weapons and rushing to join the renewed fight. "Get in the cart! Quick!"

He hammered down, taking Anna's spot and providing suppressing fire. Julie had already climbed in and started up the little buggy while glaring over her shoulder impatiently at her two compatriots. Anna jogged back to the cart and jumped in the back, pointing her weapon back in the direction of the safe room, covering Mason's retreat.

The agent skipped backwards, sending rounds like raindrops in a spring shower back into their formerly safe hideaway. Return fire began to come in his direction from weapons held blindly around the corner, bullets ricocheting off the concrete and zipping around the concrete tunnel. One hit the only bulb in the entry ramp, plunging a section of the catacombs into darkness. Mason used the opportunity to turn tail and bolt for the cart. He jumped over Sawyer's prone form, still moving full-bore, slamming into his seat and barking at Julie, "Go! Go! Go!"

They took off. The cart wasn't a speed demon, but it moved at a pace that would keep up with your average human sprinter. As an afterthought, Mason turned around and fired again, this time sending his rounds into the second cart that Sawyer had obviously arrived in. Sparks flew from the cart's panel and a plume of oily smoke rose up from the ruined board. Satisfied, Mason nodded to himself and turned forward once again.

Anna was still firing, forcing the men in the darkened corridor to remain covered. Even still, as the entryway receded in the distance, bullets chased after them. One winged the back of the cart with a loud crack, making Julie jump in the driver's seat.

"Save your ammo," Mason said to Anna. "We'll probably need every round."

The cart careened around a corner. Julie had taken a random turn, which was probably for the best; it might help throw off the pursuit that would most certainly be following. Mason allowed himself to fully relax. For the time being, they were safe enough.

Anna shouldered her weapon, then shoved Mason hard in the shoulder.

"Hey," protested the agent. "What the hell?"

"You almost got us all killed back there!" Anna yelled. "If you'd taken ten more seconds with that stupid fight with Sawyer we would have been run down by those guys coming in the front door!"

"Oh, come off it," Mason groaned. "First of all, there're always a ton of '*ifs*' in combat. For example, Doc, *if* those carriers hadn't shown up and stalled that assault team, we'd have been killed for sure. *If* I hadn't seen those footprints we wouldn't have had any warning at all. *If* Sawyer hadn't been such a pompous bastard in thinking he was going to take me down unarmed and by himself we would have been dead too—so don't shove that crap down my throat. Besides, we're alive."

"Yeah, *for now*," Anna replied, unconvinced.

Back at the entryway, the five remaining members of the assault team struggled to secure the safe room. The house above was packed to bursting with carriers of the Morningstar Strain. Every blast from a weapon had been like a dinner bell to them, beckoning them to the noise that meant warm, uninfected bodies, and since the doors had been battered down there was nothing hindering them. The remaining members of the assault team were doing the best they could, holding the broken door up in its frame and pressing against it with their body weight. The door shuddered under the blows of the carriers on the other side, but they could hold it for a while longer.

One of the assault troopers had clicked on a flashlight and was searching the entry tunnel. The beam landed on Sawyer's unconscious form.

"*Damn*," breathed the trooper, chuckling under his breath. "Asshole had it coming to him."

He kneeled next to the agent, holding a pair of fingers to Sawyer's neck. Finding a pulse, the man's eyes widened. He hadn't expected the rogues to let him live. Shrugging to himself, he slapped his hand on Sawyer's cheek.

"'Ey. 'Ey. Wakie-wakie, sir," he said.

Sawyer coughed, groaning and rolling his head to one side, batting the man's hand away.

"Want an aspirin?" chuckled the trooper. Sawyer glared at him, holding up a hand to his bruised throat.

"What happened?" he croaked, voice brittle and weak after Mason's strangulation.

"They got away. We could have gotten 'em if we hadn't got some company of our own," said the trooper, jerking a finger over his shoulder at the three men holding the door up. The angry moans of the carriers and undead beyond were evident.

Sawyer sat up and pulled himself to his feet, gritting his teeth.

Mason had been right. He'd been too overconfident. Well, that wasn't a mistake he'd make again. He tossed one regretful look at the tunnels where Mason, Anna, and Julie had made their escape, then strode briskly into the light of the safe room. The trooper followed slowly, weapon at the ready.

Sawyer cast about, looking at the disturbed equipment and splintered door panel. He was a seasoned agent—looking for leads was a big part of his job. His eye fell upon the computer and the open CD tray in the tower.

"*Hmm*," he breathed, walking over to the terminal. He was seemingly uninterested in the peril they were all in with the carriers on the other side of the flimsy doorway. Single-minded, as always. He cracked his neck slowly, reading over the data on the screen. In her rush, Julie had left the browser open. His stare drifted downwards, until it reached the last few lines of text.

. . . *in closing, findings indicate a tendency toward metabolic restructuring in most hosts. Until further information is available, suggest allocating resources to study this effect. All data classified top secret/eyes only. Further reports should be sent to CRF, Central Research Facility, Omaha, Nebraska.*

Sawyer grinned widely.

"*Got you.*"

PART NINE:

CINDERS

Oregon Coast
January 22, 2007
0830 hrs_

THERE WERE FORTY-FOUR survivors who had elected to join Sherman on the trek inland. They'd been on the move for almost two full days, rarely stopping except to eat or catch short, fitful naps. Sherman had them sticking to the side roads, walking in the tall grass on either side of the pavement. Every time a car or truck came rumbling by, the group would hit the dirt. Better to be safe than sorry.

Out in the forested wilds of the west coast of North America there were few carriers, if any. They'd seen a half dozen uninfected persons driving by, but no victims of the Morningstar Strain. Sherman had spent his last several hours on the *Ramage* studying maps and finally decided their destination would be a small town inland where they might be able to find themselves some transportation.

Of the forty-four, only twenty or so were armed. These men and women spread themselves out along the line of travelers, eyes scanning the underbrush and road for any sign of attack. The group had been undetected so far.

As the sun rose on the morning of their second day, they came upon the village Sherman had been aiming them towards.

Brewster, Denton, and Thomas crouched at the edge of a thicket, peering out across an open field towards a group of buildings in the distance. Thomas held a pair of binoculars to his eyes, studying the hamlet. The smaller towns were holding out well, it seemed. The lower windows of the buildings were boarded up in a ramshackle fashion and wrecked cars had been moved to blockade the streets that led in.

"Looks deserted," Denton commented, scratching his chin.

"They're in there," Thomas grunted, handing the binoculars to Denton. "Got themselves buttoned up tight. Don't think we should go walking up to 'em."

"Why not?" Brewster asked, shifting his weight, eager to do something besides march. "We're friendly and we're armed. They should welcome us."

"They don't know that," Thomas replied. "Besides, read that sign they've got nailed up."

"Where?" Denton asked, peering through the binoculars.

Thomas pointed and Denton swiveled his focus. There was a wire mesh board set up with a nicely printed sign:

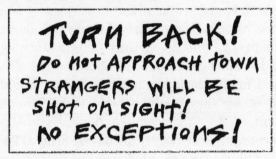

Hyattsburg
Pop. 910

Below that hung a sheet of plywood on which thick red paint had been smeared, spelling out a warning:

TURN BACK!
DO NOT APPROACH TOWN
STRANGERS WILL BE
SHOT ON SIGHT!
NO EXCEPTIONS!

"*Damn*," Denton sighed. "What now?"

"Next town's more than twenty miles away," Thomas said. "We can try to make contact or start walking."

"Fuck that, let's show 'em a white flag," Brewster suggested.

Thomas half-turned to glance at the private, quirking an eyebrow. "That's a first," he grunted.

"What is?" Denton asked.

"The Private just made a halfway decent suggestion," Thomas said. "Maybe we can get close enough to parley. They look holed up. Doubt they want to go anywhere. Maybe they'll be able to get us some vehicles."

"If there's anyone left," Denton noted, still peering through the binoculars. "I still haven't seen a single person."

"Let's go," said Thomas, standing and shouldering his MP-5. "We'll let the General make the call."

The three pulled back from the edge of the thicket, crouch-jogging through the underbrush to where the remainder of their group was quietly waiting.

"How's it look?" asked Sherman as they approached.

"Town's there," Thomas answered. "But they don't look like they want visitors."

Sherman said, "Well, we've only got enough food for a few more days, and we can't keep walking around in the open like this. We've got to try to get some transport and supplies."

"If they're in there, let's send out a couple guys to try and make contact with them," Brewster suggested.

"The white flag idea," Thomas added.

"Think maybe they'll be willing to deal?" Sherman asked, scratching at a couple days' worth of beard stubble.

"Don't know," Thomas stated.

Denton shrugged, and Brewster coughed.

Sherman glanced at the three, then nodded his head once. "Alright, it's settled. Private . . . *Brewster*, isn't it? Pick two men and see if you can get the locals to come out of their houses."

Brewster sat up sharply, looking left and right.

"Who, *me*? Shouldn't an officer do that, or something?"

"Shit rolls downhill, private," Thomas said. "Besides, it's your idea."

"Yeah, but we're not exactly in the Army anymore, Sarge," Brewster tossed back, earning a cold stare from the Sergeant Major.

"Call it a favor, then," Sherman cut in before Thomas could rip into Brewster. "We'll be right behind you. First sign of trouble and we'll come in shooting."

Brewster frowned, scratching a pattern in the dirt at his feet as he mulled it over.

"Alright," he said slowly. "I want Krueger and Denton."

"You want *me*?" Denton muttered. "Oh, hell."

"Good choices. Denton, you're a smooth talker. Krueger's a great shot with his pistol," Sherman said, nodding in approval. The soldier had already done more than his fair share, walking point in two twelve-hour shifts on their trek inland.

"Now all we need's our white flag," Brewster said.

Sherman unslung his pack and dug around inside until he found a clean t-shirt. He handed the garment to Brewster.

"Thread that on a stick. It'll do."

It took ten minutes to relay the plan to the forty-odd people in the entourage and for Brewster, Denton, and Krueger to get their gear in order. When they were ready, they stepped out of the underbrush on the road that led into town, Brewster holding aloft the t-shirt flag, Denton and Krueger holding their arms out and to the side to show they held no weapons. Behind them, in the foliage, crouched close to twenty armed men and women, keeping well out of sight and watching carefully for any sign of ambush or violence.

The three emissaries walked forward slowly and steadily until they neared the blockade in the road. There they stopped, casting glances at all the boarded-up windows.

"Starting to get a creepy feeling here," commented Krueger. He was a compact little man, but all muscle, and had been with the survivors since Suez. "Shouldn't we be getting shot at by now?"

"Was thinking the same thing," Brewster said back. He cupped his free hand around his mouth and yelled out, "Hello! Is there anyone there? Hello!"

The three stood silent and unmoving for a full minute, waiting for a response. None was forthcoming. The windows remained buttoned up, and the streets stayed empty.

"Okay," Denton mumbled, taking a step back. "Maybe this isn't a good idea."

"No, wait," Brewster said. "There's got to be *someone* in there."

"There!" Krueger suddenly shouted, pointing up at one of the unboarded second-story windows of a nearby brick warehouse. A lone figure had stood silhouetted in the glass a moment, but as Denton and Brewster looked up, the figure vanished.

Brewster yelled up at the window, "Hey! Come on! We just want to talk! We're not infected!"

Whoever it had been showed no sign of responding. The window stayed dark and empty.

"Call the others in," Denton suggested. "If there's only a couple people left, looks like we've got ourselves a free lunch—maybe there's a car dealership we can hit on our way through."

"Right," Brewster said. "Sign must've been a bluff. Looks like most of this town evac'd."

Brewster turned around and waved his arms over his head, telling the rest of the group it was safe to approach. They broke cover and began jogging the several hundred yard-run to the three at the town entrance.

"What's the score?" Sherman asked as he jogged up.

"Nada, sir," Brewster informed him. "There's someone in that building, but no one else that we can see."

Mbutu Ngasy, though one of the unarmed members of the group, ambled over to add his thoughts.

"I don't like this place," he said. "It's . . . *cold.* We should go around."

"*Nonsense,*" said Sherman, slapping Mbutu on the shoulder. "We should be able to get whatever we need here. Let's move in, but let's keep our guard up. Krueger, Brewster, try to get that civilian to open up. Thomas, tactical column on this street. Keep an eye out for automotive dealerships, convenience stores, any place that might have gear we could use."

"You got it," Brewster replied with a nod.

"Yes, sir," Thomas said. He turned to bark out orders. "Tactical column! Civilians in the center, soldiers on the flanks! Be on the lookout for any useful storefronts!"

"Hoo-ah!" came the automatic reply. The group worked its way around the crude blockade and entered the town proper. Total silence greeted them. Here and there a piece of trash drifted about in the morning breeze and a few wisps of fog still clung to the ground as they moved down the road. Brewster and Krueger ran up to the door of the warehouse where they'd seen the figure earlier and pounded on the door.

"Open up!" Brewster shouted, banging the butt of his pistol against the heavy wooden door.

"We know you're in there!" Krueger added. "We just want to help!"

The banging continued for half a minute before they got their first furtive reply.

"Go away!" came a voice from the other side of the door. "Stop shouting! They'll hear you, dammit, they'll *hear* you!"

"What?!" Brewster yelled back.

The column of troops and civilians had moved about a block away, leaving Brewster and Krueger behind, but the pair focused on getting the man inside to open up.

"You don't understand!" the man shouted. "There's no one here to help you! And there's nothing you can do to help *me*! Just leave me alone!"

"Come on, buddy! Where is everyone?!" Krueger asked.

"They're . . . still here!" came the frightened reply. "Get out! Get out while you can!"

Brewster's eyes widened in comprehension. His gaze met Krueger's, an equally concerned look on his face.

"*Oh, shit*," Brewster whispered.

Down the street, Sherman nervously looked back and forth at the boarded-up buildings. Something wasn't adding up. The town seemed clean once one got past the barricades on the outer streets, but here and there was a knocked-in door or shattered window. Riots, perhaps? Or something worse?

"Used car dealership, sir," Thomas said, breaking Sherman out of his reverie. Thomas pointed down the block at a small corner lot filled with older model cars and pickup trucks surrounded by a neck-high chain-link fence and a massive banner proclaiming the best quality used cars at the lowest possible interest rates. Sherman nodded.

"Let's head for it," he said.

Mbutu had stuck close to Sherman and had been watching the General closely. He saw the older man's nervousness and it mimicked his own. He took a chance at speaking up again.

"General, I think we should leave, fast," he said again. "This place . . . it reminds me of the town in the desert."

Sherman stopped walking. That was it. That was what he had been trying to place in his mind—the factor that didn't add up.

"*Sharm el-Sheikh*. It's exactly like Sharm el-Sheikh."

That was when he heard shouts from Brewster and Krueger. Sherman spun to see the two soldiers running at a flat-out sprint towards the column, waving their hands in the air.

"What in the name of Buddha are they yelling about?" Thomas grunted.

"They're here! They're here!" Brewster screamed. "It's a trap!"

"*Can't be* . . ." Thomas started, but his voice was cut off as the first scream of pain washed over the street. A soldier fell to the ground, tackled roughly by a carrier that had launched itself out of one of the darkened windows of a storefront.

Sherman felt himself paralyzed in shock for a brief instant. These were not the tactics of a brainless enemy.

—This was an *ambush*.

Carriers poured out of the stores and apartment doorways, crawled out of dank alleyways and moved with single-minded determination towards the column of men and women.

"Fire at will!" Sherman shouted, drawing his pistol and dropping a carrier with a single shot to the head.

Shots rang out all along the column, mostly single shots from pistols, here and there automatic chatter from one of the sub-machine guns. The living carriers seemed to far outnumber their undead cousins. Sprinting infected tore into the lines, tackling those defenders who couldn't drop them in time.

"Get to the car lot!" Thomas bellowed. "Get inside! Close the gates behind you!"

Brewster and Krueger caught up with the column, pistols blazing. Brewster lined up a shot and caught a carrier in the shoulder, spinning the infected and dropping it to the ground where it began to pull itself back to its feet. A second shot to the forehead sent it to the ground forever.

The unarmed civilians ran with the speed only panic and adrenaline can produce, heading for the car lot. The soldiers played rear guard, forming a decent skirmish line and firing into the ranks of the carriers, whose numbers seemed to increase with each passing second as new ones launched themselves from their dark dens within the buildings of Hyattsburg.

Mbutu found himself cut off from the group of retreating civilians. A dead soldier, throat torn open, lay on the ground in front of him, pistol hanging from nerveless fingers.

He scooped up the weapon.

A snarling carrier jumped in front of him, baring her teeth in a feral expression, saliva and sweat dripping from her chin. Mbutu aimed the gun at her and pulled the trigger, drilling a neat hole where her right eye used to be.

Thomas came running by and grabbed Mbutu by the arm.

"Let's get a move on!" he shouted, running towards the chainlink gate.

Screams from behind the skirmish line caught the soldiers'

attention. A second group of infected had come running from the opposite direction. Some had already penetrated the relative safety of the chain-link fence and the unarmed civilians were doing their best to fight them off with little more than rusted pipes, wrenches, or whatever other bludgeons they could find—but their best was not nearly good enough. As Mbutu watched, a pair of survivors were brought down by a half dozen of the infected, crushed under the weight of gnashing teeth and scratching nails.

"Fall back! Fall back!" Thomas shouted.

Sherman and Denton managed to get into the entryway of the dealership and were blasting away at any of the carriers who thought it might be a good idea to charge the lot.

Brewster took a final shot at the mass of carriers charging up the street before dropping an empty magazine and slapping in a fresh one. He turned and sprinted, followed closely by Krueger and the other remaining soldiers. They managed to pull back into the lot and slam the gates home by flipping the simple latch. The carriers remaining in the lot were put down in moments, but outside the fence the infected built up their numbers, shrieking inhumanly and grabbing onto the fencing, shaking it back and forth, threatening to tear it loose.

"We don't have much time," Sherman said, reloading his own weapon and surveying the scene. "They'll break through real soon. Shoot any of them that try to climb over! Brewster! Thomas! Get in that office and find us keys!"

"Right, sir!" Thomas replied, jogging over to the door of the used car lot's office and busting it down with one fierce kick. He burst in, followed directly by Brewster.

"Check behind the counter. I'll get the office," Thomas said. Brewster nodded, leaping over the countertop and casting about for the ubiquitous rack of keys every dealership had stashed somewhere, the master set for all the models on the lot.

"I've got some here!" Brewster yelled, pulling out a clipboard with six sets of keys nailed to it. "Trucks, looks like!"

"Got some here, too," Thomas said. "Bullshit minis and coupes. Take the truck keys. Let's get out there and find which ones they start!"

"No worries—plate numbers are written on the keyrings!"

Brewster said, yanking the keys off the board and cradling them to his chest with one hand.

"Hurry up in there!" came a yell from outside, punctuated by the sound of gunfire. The carriers were climbing on each others' shoulders, trying to get over the fence.

Outside, Sherman leveled his pistol at one of the snarling carriers and fired, blowing the creature off the top of the chainlink fence. It cawed as it fell backwards, landing on the shoulders of the other infected, knocking a small cluster of them to the ground.

Sherman had done a quick tally in his head as the survivors had straggled into the lot. Twenty-nine. Fifteen lost.

That was a stupid mistake, Sherman thought. *The live ones like to wait for their prey if they aren't chasing any. Should've remembered Sharm el-Sheikh—Should've listened to Ngasy*.

Sherman fired another round, cursing as the weapon ran dry. He fumbled for another magazine, scowling as he drew out his last one. He slapped it in, glancing left and right at the defenders.

The remaining soldiers had quickly lined up along the inside of the chainlink fence, firing whenever one of the infected started to pull itself up and over. The tactic was working for now—but there were at least fifty or sixty carriers who had death grips on the fence and were shaking it back and forth. It was starting to wobble, and at their rate they'd have it torn up soon enough.

Sherman saw Rebecca out of the corner of his eye. She was behind the line of soldiers, standing near the knot of remaining civilians, holding the very same pistol she had snatched from Sherman while they were on the ship.

Denton was right up alongside the soldiers, taking careful aim before firing at any of the carriers. He didn't waste a single round.

Brewster and Thomas burst out of the office, holding up a few sets of keys.

"We've got some!"

"Outstanding! Get those vehicles up here!"

"Right, sir!"

Brewster tossed one of the sets of keys to Thomas, who caught them deftly with one hand and took off sprinting towards the line of small trucks parked on the side of the lot. Mbutu came up alongside Brewster, snatching one of the remaining sets from his hands.

"I've been driving stick-shift since I was six," he said, grinning before following after Thomas.

Brewster ran after the pair, glancing down at the set of keys in his hand, quickly reading off the license plate number and scanning the line of vehicles for matching numbers. He spotted it: a flat-painted brown Ford pickup. He shrugged, unlocking the door and clambering into the driver's seat.

Thomas pulled out in front of him as he started up the truck, driving a modified utility worker's truck with a heavy box-like rear bed. Brewster pulled out behind him as Thomas' truck groaned to a halt in front of the chainlink gate.

"Think this baby can ram through that gate just fine, sir," Thomas growled out a half-lowered window at Sherman. He pointed at the carriers. "Better get in before they do."

"Right!" Sherman said. He holstered his pistol and cupped his hands around his mouth and yelled, "Everybody get on a truck and hang on! We're going to try to force our way through 'em!"

Mbutu pulled up behind Brewster, bringing up the rear of the little convoy.

One by one the soldiers fell back from the fence, turning and bolting towards one of the three trucks. Rebecca ushered the frightened civilians over to the vehicles, shouting and pointing.

Denton slammed the door shut on the back of Thomas's utility truck, closing up the people inside, then bolted back to Brewster's truck, opening the passenger door and jumping in.

"Just like old times, eh?" Denton asked, grinning.

"Yeah, except we had assault rifles that time," Brewster fired back. "And my truck was a lot bigger."

"But you didn't have a CD player, or AM/FM radio."

"Yeah, well, there's a shortage of leather interiors and heated seats in the Army, ok?"

Brewster tapped a finger on the dashboard impatiently, whistling an uneasy tune to himself as people climbed into the bed of the truck, settling in and holding on tight to anything solid. Brewster glanced down, going over his own mental checklist. Weapon? On the seat, ready to fire. Passengers? Ready to move. Gauges?

Gauges?

"Shit," Brewster cursed, eyes going wide as he stared down at the dash. He thumped a fist off the plastic a couple times, staring intently at the gauges with a look on his face that screamed murder. He rolled down the window as fast as he could manage, then stuck his head out and shouted, "General! Hey! We've got a problem here!"

Sherman was in the middle of climbing into the passenger's seat of Thomas' truck, but he halted, turning to face Brewster.

"What is it?!" he yelled back.

"I'm running on fumes here, sir! No gas in the trucks!"

Thomas had stuck his own head out the driver's window to listen, and then cursed, ducking inside the cab again and looking down at his own gas gauge.

"He's right, sir, got a little less than an eighth of a tank here," Thomas said, shaking his head and reaching into a BDU pocket to pull out a crumpled pack of cigarettes he'd been saving. He lit one up as Sherman ran up and down a litany of swear words.

"We can get away on that much!" Mbutu yelled from his own driver's seat. "We don't need to go on a cross-country drive—just away from the carriers!"

"Then what?!" Sherman yelled back. "We'll just be stranded somewhere else!"

"Much better than being stranded here," Mbutu countered.

"Agreed!" Sherman shouted, climbing into the cab of Thomas' truck and shutting the door. He pulled on his seat belt, buckling it and tightening the straps. Across from him, Thomas did the same, strapping in securely. He glanced over at Sherman.

The General nodded.

"Hold on to your ass, sir," Thomas murmured, shifting into gear and flooring the accelerator. The truck's tires squealed and thick white smoke whirled up around them before gaining traction, slamming the vehicle forward. It smashed through the fence, sending the infected standing on the other side sprawling. A pair were hit head-on by the truck and flung back into the street, skidding across the pavement until they came to a rest, bloody and unmoving. The gate bounced off the windshield of the truck, sending a spider web of cracks through the glass and causing both Thomas and Sherman to flinch. The truck roared through the mess of infected, tearing off down the street.

Brewster was right behind them. The soldiers on the open bed of his truck leaned over the cab, firing at the infected that had started to move over from the fence when Thomas' truck had broken through the gate. The truck rolled over the remains of the carriers floored by the first charge, and skidded a bit on a piece of the torn-down fence, but Brewster straightened it out with a wrench of the wheel, earning muffled curses from the passengers struggling to hold on in the back.

"Which way did Thomas go?!" Brewster yelled.

Thomas' truck was nowhere to be seen; they'd made a turn somewhere.

"Left! I saw him go left!" Denton shouted, pointing wildly at the street and hanging on to the door handle with a clenched fist.

"Left it is!" Brewster said.

The soldiers on the back of Mbutu's truck covered their escape as Brewster's had done, firing into the infected, who had spread out considerably, some taking off after the retreating trucks while others tried forcing their way into the gate to get at the last vehicle.

A carrier fell, drilled neatly through the head by a pistol round, and Mbutu edged to the side as he burst out of the gate to avoid the corpse. His truck slammed into yet another, knocking it to the ground. It went under both sets of wheels as Mbutu swung the front end around and accelerated away from the car lot and the mess of infected.

Then he slowed a bit, furrowing his brow.

He cursed under his breath.

Where had the other trucks gone?

Two streets over, Brewster squealed tires around a corner, just fast enough to catch a glimpse of Thomas' truck making a right turn three blocks down.

"Where the hell is he leading us?" Brewster asked.

"No clue," Denton said. "Maybe Sherman is back-seat driving?"

"Ha," Brewster managed, concentrating on the road. Here and there an abandoned car dotted the streets, and Brewster wove skillfully between them at speed, making for the turn he'd seen Thomas make.

He turned the wheel, bringing the truck around the corner and right into—

"Jesus! Look out!" Denton yelled.

Brewster had time to catch a glimpse of a group of a half-dozen infected that had wandered away from the entrance to a nearby building in pursuit of Thomas' truck before he slammed into them going forty-five. The bodies collided with the trunk and bounced up onto the windshield. A skull smashed into the glass, taking a chunk out of it. The steering wheel jerked out of Brewster's hands, and the truck spun sideways.

Brewster felt the world twist as the truck rolled end-over-end before slamming into the side of a building. He felt his face smash into the driver's side window, and his vision went bright white for a moment before everything crashed into nothingness.

Edge of Hyattsburg
0912 hrs_

Sherman braced himself as Thomas took them around their third turn, exhaling in relief as he saw open road ahead. They'd cleared the town. The truck passed the last brick store and apartment building and rolled off into the countryside. Sherman sat back as Thomas slowed the truck to a cruising pace, loosening his seat belt as he did so.

"Jesus," Sherman muttered. "I really screwed the pooch on that one."

"How do you mean, sir?" asked Thomas, taking a long drag on the cigarette that had sat, forgotten, between his lips during the entire flight through the town. Ashes tumbled off the end and onto his lap, but he either didn't notice or didn't care.

"Did you hear Mbutu before we even went in there? He smelled that ambush. Should've listened to him. Got good people killed."

"First of all, sir, this is war. People die. Secondly, you really think these pus-bags have the foresight to plan an ambush? Nah, they were just lying in the shade until some food walked by—then they came at us."

Sherman grunted, but after a moment looked over at Thomas with a curious expression. "They waited until we were in the middle of town and then jumped us all at once. I'd call that an ambush, Thomas."

"They jumped us when Brewster and Krueger started yellin'

like retards in heat while running down Main Street, sir," Thomas replied.

Sherman took a moment to consider, but before he could offer his opinion, Thomas swore loudly and slammed on the brakes. Sherman braced a hand against the dash as the truck slid to a stop on the pavement.

"What is it?" Sherman asked.

"The other trucks aren't behind us," Thomas said, concern on his face. He opened his door and dropped out of the cab, looking back in the direction of Hyattsburg.

Sherman snapped his head around to the side-view mirror. All he saw was the off-white paneling of the truck and open road behind them, the little town off in the distance through the leafless trees.

"Where are they?" Sherman asked, incredulous, taking off his own seat belt and jumping down out of the truck. He circled around the hood to where Thomas was standing, peering off down the road, scratching his chin with one hand.

"Maybe they're just delayed," Thomas growled over his shoulder. He glanced down at his watch. "Let's give 'em a couple minutes."

Sherman nodded, then reached up a hand to his epaulette and the radio that hung there. Franklin had given them twelve, enough to outfit the soldiers who were left as well as Denton.

"Ghost Lead to any personnel, respond, over."

There was no answer. Only static issued forth from the radio.

"I say again, Ghost Lead to any personnel, please respond. If you can't talk, click the handset twice."

They waited. A minute passed, then two. Each felt like a granite hour. Every second that passed without the trucks appearing behind them weighed down on Sherman's shoulders like the Earth must have done to Atlas.

"No, something's very wrong," Sherman said after five minutes had passed with no sign. He spun on his heel suddenly and walked back around the truck, clambering up into the passenger doorway and looking over at Thomas with resignation on his face. "We have to go back."

"Sir, that place is crawling with infected," Thomas said.

"I know it."

"Are you willing to risk more lives to rescue people that might already be dead?" Thomas asked quietly.

Sherman looked over at him with an icy expression. He gritted, "*Yes*. We don't leave anyone behind."

Thomas grimaced and tossed his cigarette to the concrete and snuffed it out with a worn boot heel. He suggested, "Try the radio again."

Sherman nodded, reaching his hand up to the radio once more.

"Ghost Lead to any personnel, anyone left in there, over?"

Moments passed in silence as they waited for a response. Sherman frowned, then shook his head at Thomas.

"It's a no-go. Either they can't answer or they aren't getting my signal."

"You're well in-range," said Thomas. "Battery power up?"

Sherman held the radio out so he could look down into its tiny LCD screen. The battery meter showed two of four bars.

"Half-power left. Should be plenty," Sherman replied.

Suddenly, the little radio squawked, catching both Thomas and Sherman by surprise.

" . . . Can't tell if . . . thing on?" came a female voice.

"Say again, over?" Sherman asked through the radio.

" . . . push the button to talk, like this. Hello? Hello?" came a second voice, this one male.

"This is Ghost Lead. Identify yourselves, over," Sherman replied.

"You with the guys in the truck?" came the male voice again.

Sherman hesitated a moment before he realized the man on the other end was finished speaking.

"Yes, I am. Identify yourself, please. And for God's sake, man, say '*over*' when you're through so I know you're done talking, over," Sherman said, shaking his head at Thomas. He lifted his finger off the handset so it would stop transmitting and said to the Sergeant Major, "Gotta be civilians."

"Name's *Ron*, Ron Taggart, here with Katie Dawson in the old theater. One of your trucks took out the infected outside, but they wrecked pretty big in the process. Who's this? Uh, over."

Sherman looked over at Thomas with dread on his face.

"*Crashed,*" Sherman uttered.

Thomas nodded. "I heard."

"Never mind who I am. How are my people, over?" Sherman asked.

A sound like a heavy sigh drifted over the radio before Ron spoke again.

"Well, we counted eleven. Four survived. The truck ran right up against the building! Just smashed—totally smashed. We saved who we could and got back inside before those things showed up again. Think they were following you from wherever you were running from. Oh, yeah—over."

Sherman slumped against the roof of the cab. Seven more dead. He'd lost more people in one morning than he had since the Battle of Suez. He'd underestimated the strength of the infection, that was for sure.

"What shape are the four in, over?" Sherman asked after a few seconds.

"Banged-up, but decent. Got three people and a soldier. Two of 'em are awake; got thrown out of the bed before the truck hit the wall. Cuts and bruises on them. We pulled two more out of the cab who lived, but they're both out cold. One's got a broken arm. You want to pick 'em up? Because it'll be tricky business right now. There's about twenty of those things out in the street, over."

"Think we can handle twenty?" Sherman asked Thomas over the roof of the truck.

"Sir, I doubt we can handle ten with our ammunition situation. Not to mention—there's probably five pistols between everyone in this truck. Most of us would just be bait."

Something tickled at the back of Sherman's mind, an idea, perhaps, that struggled to rise to the surface of his thoughts, but before it developed, it faded away. Sherman shook his head a little to clear the sensation that he'd just missed an important bit of data.

"I hope you're not thinking of charging back in there the way we are now, sir," Thomas went on. "We still need you to lead us away from here when the day's done."

There it was again, thought Sherman. That prickling sensation was back.

"Hello? Still there?" came Ron's voice through the radio.

"Yes, we're here. Hold a moment, over," Sherman said. "Thomas, what did you just say?"

"I said, '*We still need you to lead us away from here when the day's done.*'"

"No, before that," Sherman said, making a tape-winding motion with one finger.

"Uh, I think I was saying most of us would just be snack food at this point in the engagement, sir."

That was it, Sherman thought. *That's what I was missing*.

"Ron, if I was able to get those infected out of the way, would you like to get out of there, over?" Sherman asked.

Thomas fixed the General with an inquisitive stare.

"*Would I?*" came the reply over the radio. "'Course, you'd have to get rid of them first, and I'd like to see that happen, over."

"Sit tight, son. I've got an idea."

Old Theater
1845 hrs_

Brewster awoke with a start, sitting up in a burst of motion, gasping at a half-memory lodged in his brain. He immediately regretted it, hissing in pain and holding a hand to the side of his head. Instead of a wound, his fingers touched the soft fabric of a bandage.

"It's not that bad of a cut. Wish I could say the same for some of those other people out there," came a voice.

Brewster looked up into the friendly face of a man a year or two older than himself. He was perched on the edge of a desk in a dim room, sipping on a flask. There were a couple of large projectors set up, and a far wall held a rack of thick reels. Brewster noticed a box of canned vegetables lying half-empty in the corner, surrounded by several empty cans.

"What do you mean about the others? And where am I?" Brewster asked, voice scratchy. He cleared his throat, wincing at the pain it caused in his head.

"You're in the old theater. We pulled you and a couple others in after you crashed. The rest we couldn't help."

"Who are you?" Brewster asked next, pulling himself to his feet, using the cinder-block wall as a support.

"Good question. Name's Ron. You are . . . ?"

"Brewster's fine."

"I see. Well, Brewster, sorry about your uniform—we tossed it in the furnace downstairs. There was blood on it—figured we'd better not take the chance any of it was infected," Ron said, standing up off the desktop and pocketing his flask. Brewster noticed he wore a heavy machete on his belt.

"Don't worry about it. You saved my ass, I guess. I'm not going to sweat a uniform," Brewster said. He glanced down at the nearly-new pair of jeans and plain t-shirt he'd woken up in, and asked, "Where'd you get these clothes?"

"Theater joins with the thrift store next door in back. We ducked across a while ago and brought over some things. Haven't been any infected in the alley yet, but the only way out of it is straight through the mob in the street outside."

"Well—thanks."

"Don't mention it," Ron said. "Come on, you're the last one to wake up. The rest are downstairs in the lobby."

Ron led the way down a narrow staircase, resting a hand on the hilt of his machete and talking all the way.

"This place was built back in 1934. Lots of old architecture in it, but it's solid. No windows on the lower level, and the doors have nice old iron bolts, and they're solid oak. We're safe enough inside. Hell, we've been safe here since the virus hit."

"When?" Brewster interrupted. "I mean, when did you start getting sprinters popping up? We really didn't expect the infection to have spread this far or we'd've been a lot more careful before we came in here."

"About a week, maybe a week and a half ago," Ron said, shaking his head. He and Brewster came to the bottom of the staircase and headed through the theater past rows of seats toward the lobby. He continued, "It was . . . *terrifying*. It spread so fast we barely knew what hit us. The first infected was a cop who'd gone to Portland to volunteer with the relief and refugee effort there. He came back with it. I'd say twelve hours after he turned the city was pretty much up shit creek with no paddle. You've got to understand, it's not that we couldn't defend ourselves, it's that we didn't get together to wipe out the things early, before they got a foothold. We boarded up our houses to wait it out, and they picked us off pretty quick, house-by-house."

"You guys made it through alright," Brewster commented.

"Yes, but there's only two of us."

"There's another guy boarded up in a warehouse on the other side of town, too."

"I'm sure there are others who fended them off, but the truth is, we're fighting a losing battle. We can't live holed up in a theater for the rest of our lives. We've got to try to bust out. That's where your friends outside come in. They're cooking up some sort of a plan. We're still waiting for them to get back to us."

"Who? Sherman?"

"Sounded like an older guy on the radio. Oh, yeah, sorry, I took it off of you when he started transmitting. Here it is," Ron said, reaching into a pocket and withdrawing the small radio. He handed it to Brewster.

"So we're going to run? Where's my gun?" Brewster asked. "We might need some firepower."

"You weren't carrying one when we brought you in," Ron told him, shrugging.

Brewster cursed. He'd left it lying out on the seat of the truck. It was probably sitting out in the wreckage somewhere.

"Is that all you're packing?" Brewster asked, nodding at Ron's blade.

"Yeah," Ron replied. "We've been wanting to get into the sporting goods store a street over, but it's too dangerous. Besides, it's probably been picked clean by now. Anyway, the machete works."

Ron demonstrated by unsheathing the blade in one quick motion and holding it under the dim light in the theater. Brewster saw brown, dried bloodstains coating the steel. Brewster nodded in silent appreciation, and Ron sheathed the machete as they approached the doors that led to the lobby. He reached out a hand and pushed the squeaking door outward. Though there were no windows on the lower floor, the lobby's ceiling extended far above to the top of the building, and an overlarge picture window centered in the building's facade was letting in the light of the evening sun. Brewster held his hand up to his brow to shield his eyes.

"Hey. Welcome back," came Denton's voice.

Squinting, Brewster took a few steps forward until he was out of the sun's rays. He saw Denton leaning against the far wall, and nodded at him before letting his gaze sweep the lobby.

The theater was certainly old—the paint on the walls was beginning to chip and crack, and some of the posters were nearly twenty years out of date. It appeared functional—right up until the Morningstar Strain hit, naturally. The concessions stand was stocked full, the walls were solid brick, and the main door was thick, heavy wood, barred with iron bolts. Brewster was beginning to see why Ron had run into this particular building when he'd had to hole up.

Beyond the secure door, however, came the sound of blows raining down on the wood, accompanied here and there by a guttural growl of frustration as the infected in the street tried in vain to break through.

Ron explained, "We've been under siege here basically since the virus hit the town."

"But we're doing a lot better than most," added a young woman as she walked from around the back of the concessions stand. She held out a bottle of water to Brewster, who accepted it gratefully, downing half in a few quick gulps to soothe his dry throat.

"This is Katie Dawson, my girlfriend," Ron said. "Aside from a few others, we're pretty much all that's left of this town."

"Pleasure," Brewster said. "Hey, didn't you say there were four of us you pulled in? There's two here."

"They're up on the roof doing a little recon on the street," Denton answered, pointing up at the ceiling.

"Who is it?" Brewster asked, wincing a little bit as his head throbbed.

"Shephard and Mitsui, the contractor."

Shephard was an aid worker who had been cooking meals for refugees when the Suez line had fallen. Mitsui was a general contractor from Japan who had been on hire in the Middle East. He'd hitched a ride when the retreating convoys had come through the small town he'd been working in.

"Goddamn it," Brewster said, scowling. "And everyone else was lost?"

Ron nodded.

Brewster shook his head slowly.

Denton, as if trying to read his mind, spoke up: "It wasn't your fault. Those infected came right out in the street, and that was a blind turn."

"Yeah, I know," Brewster said.

"I mean it—"

"So do I!" Brewster shouted, then lowered his voice. "Sorry. It's just—look. I'm starting to think maybe we're fucked."

Denton raised an eyebrow and said, "What, and how many times—*precisely*—have we been in imminent peril just as badly as this in the past month or so? Can't count it up on two hands, that's for sure."

"Just being aware of the situation," Brewster replied, gesturing around them at the walls as he spoke. "This place can't hold out forever. Now, Ron says that Sherman's out there getting a plan into action to move us out of here, but that'd mean going outside, which brings us to the next problem—we don't have any guns, man! We'd be going out into that war zone with one big-ass knife and a couple of sporks to fight with."

"Sherman and whoever's with him will have weapons."

"Man, didn't you hear all those rounds popping off at that car lot this morning? I bet they've all got half a mag' apiece, and only half of the people with him will even have a weapon to begin with. Damn it all—we clusterfucked ourselves this morning. And I have a really fucking bad headache."

"Jesus, you're dour when you've got a concussion. Just have faith. Sherman's got a sound head on his shoulders. I'm sure whatever he's cooking up will be worthwhile," Denton said.

Ron and Katie were hanging back, letting the two go over their options and listening in silence.

"Come on. Tell me what I've said isn't true," Brewster said, shoving his hands in his jean pockets and waiting. Denton sighed and shrugged. "See? I knew I was making a valid point. Besides, look, even if we make it out of here, how long are we going to last with nothing more than pointy sticks to defend ourselves with?"

"I'd be more worried about having enough food to last, but you know, to each their own," Denton said. "I guess you do make a decent point, though."

"Hold it, hold it," Ron interrupted, face impassive, stepping forward with his hands held up as a gesture of truce. "Brewster, we can kill those things with blades. It'll be tough, buy there's a chance we can—"

"—And if you get the blood on you? On your face? In a cut? What then? You going to turn that blade on yourself before you go apeshit?" Brewster retorted, arching an eyebrow at Ron. "No thanks, man, I'll stand back a good ten feet—at least—when I'm killing infected. That or be wearing a MOPP suit."

"MOPP?" Katie asked, quirking her mouth. "I think you're losing us."

Denton and Brewster looked at each other and sighed. Both were used to military jargon and explaining it all got old quickly.

"Like a space suit," Denton said dryly.

His explanation was blunt and to the point. He gave it no further thought, and turned his efforts back to thinking of a way to guarantee their escape.

Brewster leaned against the concessions stand and rubbed his chin. He then said, "Maybe we could . . . I dunno . . . throw rocks off the roof into the alley. Maybe that'd distract them, make 'em go check out the noise and leave the front clear, or mostly clear."

"Won't work. We tried something like that earlier with a tape recorded voice. Somehow they know it's not a real living person. It gets their attention—for about five seconds. They just sort of looked in that direction, then went back to banging on the door. I guess they still hear like uninfected—you know, you hear a rock hit concrete, and you know it's a rock hitting concrete and not a person. Guess they've got enough brain left to figure out stuff like that."

"Hell, animals can do that," Brewster said scornfully.

"But it does show *thought*, whether it's conscious or not," Denton countered. "Well, that might not help us, but it's info we might be able to use."

"*How?*" Ron, incredulous, asked from beside the popcorn popper.

"I don't know," said Denton. "But remember that inventor you Americans had . . . don't remember his name. Anyway, he tried to make something work about a thousand times. None of the prototypes worked. So people called him a failure, right? All he said was '*I didn't fail, I found hundreds of ways not to go about this.*' Maybe in the future it'll come in handy to know that."

"That was Benjamin Franklin, dumbass," Brewster said. He looked over at Ron and Katie while jerking a finger over his shoulder at Denton. "Sorry. He's Canadian. Should've told you before you let him in."

Ron managed a grim smile.

"Good to see you've got part of a sense of humor left," Ron said. "That's all too rare these days."

"Humor? I wasn't being funny. I really mean I'm sorry you let this Canuck in here. Hear that, Denton?" Brewster said menacingly, but after a silent moment, flashed a wide grin and chuckled. "Naw, fooling, natch. We'll need you around to take pictures."

"Out of film," Denton said, shrugging his shoulders. "Used the last in the islands."

Brewster's face seemed to fall a moment, as if he were truly disappointed.

1910 hrs_

Sherman and Thomas had tallied and counted every resource available to them and their truckload of personnel. The only thing that wasn't in short supply, it seemed, was apprehension. Ammunition, weapons, even food and water—all were running dangerously low.

"Well, this is about as fun as an FTX in the July rain," Thomas drawled, shaking his head slowly.

There were nine of them total that had made it out of the city in the truck. Two-thirds of the survivors were still left in the town down the road, and Sherman's plan to rescue them was looking less and less feasible as they went over their supplies.

"Got four full magazines, if you want to consolidate what ammunition is left," Thomas said.

"That's enough to cover the point man if we decide to go forward," Sherman replied. "But it's a lot less than I'd like to have in case things go south on us."

"And that's more than likely, given our track record," said one of the soldiers.

"Out of curiosity, sir, you've only given us a few hints about this idea of yours. If we knew more, maybe we could help out," Thomas said. "Care to share?"

"Well, it's not much of a plan, per se."

"So what? It's not much of a world we're living in these days, either," said Thomas.

Sherman sighed. "Very well. Something you said gave me the idea—you mentioned *bait.*" He knelt and began scratching pictures in the dirt to illustrate, and went on, "Every time we've encountered the infected they've behaved in an almost predictable pattern. They're usually dormant until someone comes too close—then they attack. They're totally single-minded about getting to their victims, as we saw at Suez. They'll tear themselves to pieces if it means moving an extra meter closer to their target."

"And?"

"And we can use that against them," Sherman said. "We send in a runner. Someone quick. They move into position near the theater, where Brewster and the others are trapped. When the infected see him, I'm sure they'll give chase. The runner retreats, draws the infected away, and meets up with an armed escort somewhere outside town. We'll leave the truck with the escort to give them the edge of speed. They kill or lose the infected, and the people trapped in the theater meet up with the rest of us while the front door is clear."

For a moment, no one said anything. They studied the little dirt drawing Sherman had sketched out, rubbing their chins thoughtfully.

"Well, it's . . . risky," said one of the soldiers.

"Risky? That's damn near suicidal," said another.

"Watch it," Thomas admonished.

"No, it's alright," Sherman said, holding out a hand to stop Thomas. "All opinions are welcome."

"I don't think it's that bad of a plan at all," said a third soldier. "I mean, it's not a great idea. But it might work. And it's not like we have a ton of options available to us at this point, right? But it seems to me there's one really sticky issue, sir."

"What's that?"

"Who's going to be the runner?"

Again a pall fell over the group, and sideways glances were cast back and forth.

"Yes, that is a problem, sir," said Thomas. "Supposing we draw straws?"

"No," Sherman said. "We need the fastest runner we've got. Those infected—the ones still alive, I mean—will be moving like the wind. I'm not sending a slowpoke in there because he drew the short straw."

"Don't suppose anyone here wants to volunteer?" Thomas asked, raising his eyebrows and letting his gaze move over the circle of survivors.

No one met his eyes.

Sherman sighed. “Alright, people, listen up. This isn’t the old Army. We’re down to the line here. I won’t lie to any of you. All of us are assets in each other’s survival. We need to work together whenever we can. Don’t hide your talents from the group. Putting your neck on the line now might not seem that appealing, but down the road someone will certainly do the same for you. So I ask you all: *anyone here a runner*?”

The soldiers sighed and scratched their chins. Sherman looked at them expectantly, but when no one answered he shook his head in disappointment.

“Guess we’ll have to do the straws after all—” he started to say.

“—Wait,” said one of the soldiers. “I’m a runner. Old hobby. Not a sprinter, more of a distance guy—but I’ll give it a shot, sir.”

“Outstanding,” Sherman said, while Thomas nodded in appreciation behind him. “What’s your name?”

“Stiles, sir. Mark Stiles.”

“Okay, Stiles, that’s what I like to hear. Then we’re all in agreement? We’ll give this plan a shot?”

The soldiers, looking relieved that someone had stepped up to the task of being the runner, nodded and murmured their consent.

“Good. Thomas, distribute the remaining ammunition. I’m going to try to get the theater on the radio and tell them what we’re cooking up. Let’s set a time and hope for the best.”

☆ ☆ ☆ ☆ ☆

Brewster slapped a stack of paper cups off the top of the concessions stand with one hand, sending them skittering across the floor.

“Fucknuts!” he swore, a thick scowl creasing his features. “What the hell does he think he’s going to get done besides kill a couple more of us?”

“I don’t know, but Sherman’s got a solid head on his shoulders,” Denton said, shrugging slightly from across the lobby.

“Oh, alright. Tell you what—you be the first guy to stick his head out those doors when they say it’s all clear,” said Shephard, one of the other survivors of the crash.

“What other real choices does he have, eh?” commented Denton.

"Low on ammunition, low on personnel. He's got to improvise. It's not a bad plan, really."

Sherman had managed to get in touch with them on the radio, and had explained what they were going to attempt. They'd set the time for the next evening, when the dimming light might help the runner evade the infected, or maybe give him the edge in preventing more from picking him up as he ran. Brewster's reaction had been immediate and quite negative. He'd denounced the idea as idiotic.

"And did he even ask us if we'd come up with any ideas? Hell no," Brewster said, scoffing.

"He's a *General*," Denton told him. "His type aren't used to asking opinions."

"I don't see any other way to get out," Mitsui said. His English was excellent. As a foreign contractor, he'd picked up several languages through his career. "Even if we try Brewster's idea to get to the sporting goods store, we're still going to be trapped in this theater."

"Yeah, man, but we'd be trapped with ammunition—better than sitting around defenseless. It'd give us a little more power when we figure out how to bust out of here. Hell, think of how different Sherman's plan would be if he had a couple thousand rounds backing him up."

"You can't eat bullets," reasoned Mitsui.

"Jesus, I'm surrounded by civilians," moaned Brewster.

"But I'm right, no?" Mitsui said, raising his eyebrows at the private.

"No, you're not. I mean, *yes*, but *no*. Look, let's just say for a second we were trapped in a supermarket, right? Plenty of food—but nothing to defend ourselves with. What happens if the infected manage to bash that door down? Or some other survivors show up and decide they want what you've got? Huh?"

Mitsui shrugged almost imperceptibly.

"Man, I'll tell you what'll happen—you'll be evening chow for the infected or a corpse to the raiders."

"Alright, alright—seems to me what we've got is two ideas that actually complement each other. Why haven't any of you thought to get the two to work together?"

"What, like send the runner Sherman's got through the sporting goods store while the infected are trailing behind him?" Brewster asked.

"No," Ron said, rolling his eyes slightly. "Like get back on that radio and give the store's address to the General. They might be able to sneak in and get what they can before they send in their runner. That'd be safer than trying to get one of us past the infected out there, and give Sherman a fighting chance if there's anything left to be had there."

Brewster seemed to consider this a moment, and his expression revealed he thought there was merit there. Shephard looked over at Denton, nodding his head in approval, and Katie smiled from her perch on the edge of the stairs that led to the projection booth.

"Damn," Brewster said after a while. "And I was all psyched up to run, too."

"Oh, you'll be running," Denton said. "Just hopefully without that many infected after you."

"So it's decided, then?" Brewster asked, holding out the radio. He let his eyes pan over the occupants of the theater.

Seeing no disapproving stares, he clicked the handset.

"Ghost Bravo to Ghost Lead, come in, Ghost Lead, over."

Brewster relaxed his finger and waited. After a few seconds of static, he repeated the request.

"Ghost Bravo to Ghost Lead, come in, please—over."

The radio crackled and Sherman's voice came through.

"Ghost Lead here. What's the sitrep, Bravo, over?"

"We've got an addendum to that P.O.A., sir. Recommend you scout a sporting goods store one street north of our pos. Possibly ammunition and weapons there, over."

The radio went silent again for a few moments. Brewster could imagine Sherman discussing the suggestion with Thomas and a couple of the other soldiers before making a decision. Finally, his response came through.

"Thanks for the intel, Bravo, but it's a negative. We don't have the manpower or gear to attempt a superfluous recon, over."

Brewster sighed heavily.

"See?" he said to the group, wiggling the radio in front of them. "These guys always do a risk-benefit calculation before they try anything new."

"Just call him back," Denton suggested. "Tell him what we're thinking."

Brewster scowled, but lifted the radio up again.

"Ghost Lead, we strongly recommend you scout the sporting goods store. Ron believes the infected in the area are either dormant or already focused on an objective like the theater. A small group of one to three should be able to remain undetected long enough to see what that place might have to offer. Even if it's nothing, sir, it's worth a look. How far can we expect to get with a few rounds of pistol ammunition and barely any food, over?"

Again, a drawn-out silence as the group outside of town mulled over the proposition. Brewster scratched at three-day beard stubble, and Shephard idly kicked around one of the fallen paper cups with the toe of his boots. Outside the door, the sounds of bare fists pounding on heavy oak was as steady as ever. The infected, in their single-mindedness, were swiftly becoming the only predictable element in an unpredictable world.

"Ghost Bravo, Ghost Bravo, wilco, over."

Brewster's head swiveled around to the radio, a look of surprise on his face.

"What?" he asked, incredulous.

"What?" repeated Ron, unsure of what he had just heard, with genuine curiosity in his voice.

"He said he's going to do it," Denton said, the beginnings of a grin working at the corners of his mouth.

"About damn time the Army listens to a grunt's suggestion," said Brewster. He picked up the radio to send a response. "Ghost Lead, reading you five-by-five. Standing by for updates. Out."

Hyattsburg streets
0134 hrs_

Mark Stiles, the soldier who had volunteered to be the foreman in Sherman's plan, now found himself stalking through the shadows of the small buildings of Hyattsburg. Sweat had beaded on his forehead despite the cold temperatures, and his eyes flicked back and forth, triple-checking every dark corner and debris pile for threats. He held one of the remaining nine-millimeter pistols pointed downwards at the ready, safety off and a round in the chamber.

When the call had come in from the people stranded at the theater recommending that someone check out a sporting goods store, he'd been the natural choice to investigate. It would be folly to send in all of the remaining troops—that much noise would certainly draw unwanted attention. Instead, Sherman had elected to send one man to scout the place. Since Stiles had already volunteered once, he didn't see any harm in raising his hand a second time.

Besides, it'd give him a chip to bargain with the next time someone was needed for a suicide mission—That is, if he survived his current one.

According to Brewster's source, the storefront he was looking for was only a street away from the theater itself. Apparently, the survivors in the theater had been planning on sending a runner of their own. That would have been even less advisable—Stiles had no clue as to how they'd expected to get past the dozen and a half infected pounding at the front doors.

The moon had swung out from behind scattered clouds and was nearly full, bathing the street in diffuse blue light. It was bright enough to cast indistinct shadows—an advantage for Stiles, who never really had much night sight to speak of in the first place. The moonlight gave him just enough to see by and navigate the cluttered streets of Hyattsburg without tripping over refuse and alerting any infected.

He crouched on one side of a deserted intersection, back against the red brick of a building, and raised his pistol. He slowed his breathing, and slowly scanned the street. It was empty, save for a few gutted automobiles and overturned trash cans.

"*Fucking ghost town*," he whispered under his breath, shivering slightly—and not due to the cold air.

Down the street, about three-quarters of a block away, he spied the outline of a carved wood sign in the shape of a fishing pole. That had to be the sporting goods store. He'd have to cross the intersection and leave himself completely exposed for a few moments if he was going to make it.

"*No use wasting time*," he mumbled, and took off from his crouch, sprinting like greased lightning across the street with his boots slapping on the pavement. When he reached the other side, he slammed his back against the nearest wall, sinking into a crouch, pistol out and aimed. He sighted down the barrel, scanning the street once more for activity. The only sounds were that of his heavy breathing and the metallic clicking of the pistol in his shaky hands. He'd made it across without being spotted by anything.

Still in a crouch, he hopped around the corner of the building and back into the shadows. Then he relaxed a bit, rising into a half-bent over stance, still low but mobile, and jogged down the sidewalk. Each time he came to an alley or recessed doorway he halted, flattened himself against the wall, and peeked around the edge for a split-second to check for carriers.

The store before the sporting goods shop was a laundromat, obviously marked with cartoon figures of a washer and dryer and the slogan, '*A quarter gets your clothes clean*!' The front picture window had been knocked out completely and broken glass littered the sidewalk.

Stiles halted as he approached the building. He cocked his head to one side and held his breath, remaining as still as he could manage. He thought he'd heard something. Five, then ten, then twenty seconds passed, and Stiles still didn't move or breathe.

Then it came again—the sound of a footstep crunching on glass. Stiles swiveled around, putting a stoop between him and the broken-out window. He'd had a feeling he wouldn't make it to the store he was looking for before a carrier got in his way—and it sure as hell wasn't a healthy human standing in the broken-out window in the middle of the night. Anyone living had better sense than that these days.

"*Shit, shit, shit,*" Stiles muttered.

There was no other way to get to the sporting goods store except to cross directly in front of the laundromat's window, unless he wanted to backtrack and circle the block—and who knew how many more infected might be blocking that route?

Using his pistol was out. It was a last-resort defensive weapon. He knew it. He had fifteen rounds to cover a blown attempt's escape. Shooting the carrier would not only waste a precious bullet, but also alert every infected on the street to his presence.

Mark Stiles wasn't the type of person to be hasty or reckless when it didn't suit his needs. The fact that he'd survived to reach home soil after Suez, Sharm el-Sheikh and the battle on the *Ramage* was evidence enough of that. He reached down to his belt and holstered his pistol, snapping it securely to his side.

Then, the same hand reached around and popped a button, slowly drawing forth a tool most soldiers in *This Man's Army* rarely used anymore: his *bayonet.* He'd kept it even after he'd run out of ammunition for his M-16. A knife was always a handy tool. Stiles had another use for it tonight besides impaling opponents. He'd spent an entire day months before polishing one side of the bayonet until it shone as clear and bright as a mirror—exactly what Stiles had had in mind. Originally, he'd thought he'd have to use it clearing buildings in the burning desert sun. Being able to look around a corner without exposing yourself could keep you alive if someone was waiting with a machine gun just around the bend.

Stiles stretched out on the ground, laying flat on his stomach, and low-crawled around the stoop to the edge of the busted window, moving slowly but deliberately. He stopped just short of the broken glass and flipped himself over onto his back. Ever so slowly, he raised the polished edge of the bayonet over the lip of the window, turning it gently between his fingers. The moonlight was just bright enough to illuminate the inside of the laundromat.

It looked like someone had tried to make a stand here. The machines had all been unplugged and dragged to the center of the floor, forming a kind of makeshift fort. It hadn't held. Even in the darkness, Stiles could see dried bloodstains running down the white-painted sides of the washers and dryers. It might have made an interesting forensic study if his attention hadn't been grabbed by the sight of a pair of feet barely two meters from where the bayonet was poking up.

There was definitely a carrier here—luckily, it was only one. Stiles could see by the way the head was moving around, (almost curiously, as if surveying its surroundings,) that the carrier was a sprinter, not a shambler.

That would work to his advantage.

He'd seen enough of the carriers to know how they worked. Their basic tactics, their physiology—a soldier always made mental notes as to what their opponents' capabilities were. It helped keep them alive. In this case, Stiles knew one thing: a sprinter was still a living thing. Thus, a sprinter could be killed.

Shamblers were dead. He'd known that much for a fact when he'd seen a carrier with a nice grouping of bullet holes in its chest open its eyes and pull itself to its feet. The only way to kill them was to put a round through their brains, or take their head off somehow. A *sprinter*, on the other hand . . . well, one needed only kill them like any other living foe. It took a while before they would reanimate.

The carrier in the store used to be the owner. He still wore a bloody plastic nametag that read "DON," along with the laundromat's slogan in neatly printed cursive underneath. If any shred of consciousness remained in him, he showed no sign besides aimlessly walking the rows where his store had been.

If Don had been facing the street, he might have seen Mark Stiles rise up from beneath the broken-out window and step silently onto the linoleum inside. If Don hadn't been slightly entranced by the silently rotating fan in the air vent above him, he might have seen Stiles' reflection in the glass shards on the floor as the soldier snuck up behind him, bayonet held out and ready. He noticed none of these things. The first clue he had that he was not alone came when Stiles' hand reached around and held back his forehead while the other slid the razor-sharp blade across his throat.

Don gurgled, trying to yell out in fury and attack, but other than the sound of bloody bubbles, nothing came forth. He tried to spin and sink his teeth into his assailant, but Stiles held him firm as his blood drained out onto the floor. Don slowly went limp. His eyes closed and his body slumped in Stiles' grip.

Stiles quietly laid the carrier down on the floor, wiping clean his bayonet on the man's shirt and sheathing it, careful to not touch any of the infected blood. He let loose a shuddering breath. He'd barely been breathing as he snuck up on the carrier, desperate to make as little noise as possible.

Odd, Stiles thought to himself as he looked down at the body. He didn't feel any remorse—any regret. The objective part of his mind told him he'd just killed a living, breathing human being. The subjective part told him that this man was aligned with the enemy. Either way, he felt as if the body at his feet was feral, *animal*—not even human. He wasn't sure if the lack of emotion was a good thing or a bad thing.

With the threat dealt with, Stiles retreated to the street, stepping through the broken glass carefully. The next building down was his objective—the sporting goods store.

He repeated his drill when he reached the building. It had a recessed doorway and four large-paned windows to display product in. Stiles could see in the windows that the store had already been ransacked. Display cases were tipped over and a trio of bullet holes had sent webs of cracks running through the glass here and there. The door itself hung open, squeaking slightly as a nighttime breeze pushed it hither and to.

Unlike the open laundromat, the sporting goods store was nearly pitch black on the inside. High shelves and no side windows kept most of the store in shadows. Stiles had no flashlight, but he reached into the cargo pocket of his BDU's and withdrew a pair of chemlights. He snapped them and shook them with one hand to get them glowing brightly, then he quickly palmed them to keep himself from standing out like a lighthouse in the fog.

Stiles crept up to the open door and tossed the chemlights in, one as far back as he could manage, the other closer to the doorway to give him a marker once he was in. As the first flew through the air, Stiles caught glimpses of taxidermied animal heads arrayed on the walls. They gave him a start, and he silently rebuked himself for being so jumpy.

Stiles waited a few seconds, but was reasonably sure the store was clear of infected. If there had been any carriers inside, the chemlights would have drawn them out into the open when he'd thrown them. Still, he took no chances, and drew out his pistol once more. He toed the door open with his foot, reaching a hand up to silence the bell that was tied to the frame, and slipped inside.

Still holding out the pistol, he reached up with his other hand to the radio.

"Ghost Recon here—I'm in."

He cleared the aisles one by one, staying as close to the exit as he could. When he was sure he was alone, he closed the door and snapped the lock shut behind him so he wouldn't be surprised. He holstered his pistol, unslung his pack, and got down to business.

The shelves closest to him held camping supplies. The survivors could have used almost everything that was left, but there was no way Stiles could carry even half of it. Instead, he ripped a small flashlight from its plastic case and snapped it on, illuminating the store further.

"*Damn*," he said softly. "*Someone's had a field day here.*"

It was true. The place had been looted half-clean. The only truly untouched shelves held fishing rods, targets, and novelty t-shirts with printed paintings of bucks and trout on them. Stiles caught a glimpse of a rifle rack near the rear of the store, and quickly hopped over a small pile of abandoned woodland camouflage trousers and jogged over.

"Shit," he said, feeling disappointment in his gut.

The guns had been looted clean. There had been a pistol display in the countertop, but someone had smashed the glass and pulled every firearm from within. The racks on the walls that once held bolt-action hunting rifles, shotguns, and home defense weapons were empty.

Stiles let his flashlight beam play over the shelves near the racks, and he nodded slightly in approval. There was plenty of ammunition left. It looked as if whoever had grabbed the guns swept a few boxes of each ammunition type into a bag and then had bolted. Boxes of nine-millimeter rounds lay spilled on the floor, mixed in with shotgun shells and 30.06 ammo. Stiles could see pristine boxes of .357 and .38 caliber ammunition left untouched directly under the empty rifle racks.

"*Now if only we had something to shoot this stuff with*," he muttered, unzipping his bag and dumping armloads of the nine millimeter rounds into it. Unless he could find more firearms, all they needed was pistol ammo.

Stiles held the bag open on the floor and used his free hand to sweep loose rounds that had scattered on the boards into the opening. Even without guns, this was more of a haul than he'd expected. He closed up his bag and stood, pulling it over his shoulders and shrugging it on evenly with his flashlight held securely in his teeth. He plucked the light out after snapping the bag's straps across his chest and let it play over the walls one last time. He strolled along the back of the counter with slow, solid footsteps.

Near the end of the counter he stopped, sighed, and shook his head.

"*Well, that was a lot better than I thought it'd be,*" Stiles murmured. He clicked off the flashlight and stepped out from behind the counter to head for the exit—then suddenly halted. His last footstep had echoed.

The flashlight clicked back on, illuminating Stiles' perplexed expression. He slowly lowered the beam until it lit up his dusty boot. He stomped twice more, just to test his memory. Sure enough, the sound of his steps echoed slightly. He stomped his other foot—no echo.

Stiles dropped back down to his knees, twisting the end of the flashlight to narrow the beam. He brushed away at the sawdust and dirt that coated the floorboards. His fingernail quickly caught on an edge and he leaned over it, blowing out a quick breath and sending dust spiraling into the air. Stiles' curious expression was quickly replaced by one of eager anticipation.

"A *cellar*," he said, blowing out another breath and clearing the edges of the trap door.

Stiles clamped his jaw around the end of the flashlight, keeping the beam on the floor, and drew out his bayonet once more. He slid the tip into the crack in the edge of the trap door and pried upwards. The door popped open, and Stiles caught it with his hand, shoving it loose and tossing it aside. He stood, sheathed the bayonet, and aimed the flashlight down the hole. Wooden steps led down to the basement of the building. He leaned his head inside, letting the beam play over the space inside.

Stiles felt his jaw drop open slightly, then whistled quietly to himself. He pulled the radio Sherman had given him free of his epaulette and clicked it on.

"Ghost Recon to Ghost Lead—I'm going to need a bigger backpack."

Stiles didn't bother waiting for a response. He wasn't going to get one, anyway—Sherman had told him that they would maintain radio silence and assume he didn't want any noise other than his own while on the scouting run. He shifted his feet around the opening of the cellar door and stepped down the first few wooden stairs. The angle gave him a much better view of what he'd thought he'd seen from the entrance—and the sight was no less welcome.

A slow smile spread across the soldier's face. He'd found the owner's private storeroom. Stiles heard cloth scraping his boot as he reached the bottom of the staircase, and glanced down at the floor. It seemed someone had been here since the beginning of the outbreak. A couple cardboard boxes lay on their sides, half-empty, with the remainder of the contents scattered along the floor. Along one wall of the surprisingly clean and dry basement were obviously handmade shelves filled to the point of bursting with still-full cardboard boxes. He couldn't make out the labels on all of them, but it was clear at least one shelf held several cases of tinned foods. The nearest was spiced deer jerky—Stiles needed to know no more. There was enough food here to feed the remaining survivors for the next week or two.

The shelf above that was stacked with heavy outdoor clothing—waterproof jackets, parkas, jumpsuits, all bagged in thick plastic. If the soldiers hadn't already been wearing the extra layers Captain Franklin had given them, he would have been quick to add them to his list. It was neither the clothing nor the food supplies that got Stiles' immediate attention, however. It was the pair of angular free-standing gun racks in the center of the smooth concrete floor—racks that were not empty.

Stiles was too grateful to whatever deity was bestowing the find upon him to mourn the spaces on the racks that didn't have rifles in them. There were still a baker's dozen left, of many makes and models. From the look of the room, it seemed someone—likely the owner—had already taken what rifles he or she could carry.

"*Now that's a sight,*" Stiles whispered, walking over to the racks and brushing a hand along the polished walnut stocks and plastic hand guards. He spotted at least four shotguns right off the bat—distinctive as they were. Most of the others were hunting rifles. There were a few bolt-action 30.06 rifles as well, scopes already mounted on the rails.

Stiles reached down and gently retrieved a beautifully-kept Winchester repeating rifle from one of the racks. He cradled it in his hands almost reverently, a soft sigh escaping his lips.

"*Beautiful,*" he whispered to himself, turning the weapon over and running a finger along the intricate engravings on the receiver and hand-carved patterns on the stock. Stiles knew his weapons well enough to realize this was not something you left on the display rack in the window. Older Winchesters fetched prices of tens of thousands of dollars in certain circles, and even though many were close to or over a hundred years old, they were still as deadly and practical as they were on the day they were manufactured. This had been more than the owner's storeroom—it had been his showroom.

Stiles decided then and there that the others could decide who got what—but the Winchester was his. Call it hazard pay.

He worked the lever action—the swift clack-clack echoed in the basement room, and Stiles nodded in appreciation. It had definitely been well taken care of. It even had a sling. He leaned the rifle back up against the rack while he took stock of the remaining items in the room.

Stiles stepped around the gun racks, shining his flashlight along the walls.

Suddenly, out of the darkness loomed a bloody face, eyes wide open and locked on the soldier.

Stiles jumped an inch in the air, skidding backwards and slamming into the wooden shelves, knocking boxes loose. He tore his pistol from its holster and aimed it at the assailant, finger on the trigger. After a moment, when he realized the bloody body wasn't charging him, he relaxed, though the adrenaline pumping through his veins made his hands shake and his breath come in gulps.

He let the pistol drop to his lap, and he breathed a deep sigh of relief. The body was just a body. It wasn't getting up any time soon.

After a few moments, he pulled himself to his feet and walked closer to investigate, kneeling in front of the still form and shining the flashlight at it.

It was the body of a middle-aged man. He was dressed in hunting camouflage and wore a watch cap. Black face paint had been smeared under his eyes. It was obvious he'd intended to survive, but something had changed his mind.

In his limp hand was a long-barreled .357, barrel coated in gore from when he had stuck it in his mouth and fired. The back of his head was M.I.A., and black, dried blood coated the otherwise bare wall of the cellar corner behind him. Stiles presumed this to be the owner of the store. For a moment, he wondered why the man had chosen to kill himself. Maybe the situation had just seemed too hopeless to him.

Stiles reached out a hand and gingerly removed the magnum from the man's hand, careful to clean the blood from the gunmetal—just in case. He shoved it securely into his pistol belt.

"Sorry," Stiles said to the dead man. "We need this more than you do now."

He was about to stand when he noticed a barrel protruding from behind the man's back. For the first time, his eyes registered the black plastic strap running around the man's shoulder. The dead owner had gone well-armed in life. Stiles leaned the man forward, grimacing at the stiffness of the corpse, and slipped the rifle free. It was a simple but deadly Ruger Mini-14, a compact civilian carbine that Stiles didn't ever remember hearing a bad word being spoken about. He'd add that to the windfall of other weapons.

Only one real thing remained to deal with: how to carry all the newly-acquired items back to Sherman and the other survivors.

Stiles pondered this a moment, and even looked around the basement for a larger backpack. He chuckled inwardly—no backpack was large enough to carry a dozen rifles as well as the ammunition he'd found upstairs. And that wasn't even taking into account the cans of food on the shelves, which was something else they needed badly. He'd have to make more than one trip.

"I'll be damned if I'm sneaking halfway across this town five more times and get myself killed in the process," he said to himself.

It would have been best if he'd had five more people with him to haul the stuff back. He decided the best thing to do would be to take what he could and leave the rest for later. They'd have to drive back with the truck to pick up the remainder, especially the boxes of food. Stiles knew he could carry enough of the weapons and ammunition to attempt such an operation, especially since they now knew exactly where to go and what to do. It would be a lot different from the first time they came into the town—it had to be.

Stiles took the straps off of the Ruger and one of the .30-06's and laid them parallel on the ground. He pulled a pair of shotguns from the racks and laid them on the straps, then topped the pile off with the Ruger and a scoped hunting rifle. He tied the bundle up tight, and hefted it onto his shoulders. He looped the ends of the straps through his webgear and tied them off as well. He shifted his weight, testing his makeshift carrying device. It was a bit cumbersome and more than a little awkward, since it made his shoulder width a couple feet wider than it normally was, but it would do.

He scooped up the Winchester and jogged back up the wooden stairs, poking his head up through the trapdoor and scanning the store in case any unwelcome visitors had made their way in. When he deemed the way safe, he rose up, but was yanked back down as the rifle barrels and stocks caught on either side of the wooden doorway.

"*Damn it*," Stiles cursed under his breath, sinking back down and twisting his shoulders until the weapons slipped through. He made his way back over to the bank of half-empty ammunition cases and chose a few boxes of twelve-gauge shells, some .30-06 rounds, and a few .357 magnum rounds for the revolver. Stiles looked around as if expecting someone to be watching as he shoved three full boxes of .45 rounds for his Winchester into his pack as well. He fully planned on picking up at least another three if and when they returned for the remaining gear. No use in having a beautiful weapon if there wasn't any ammo for it.

Before retreating to the store's exit, he kneeled and took a moment to load up his new rifle. He worked the lever, chambering a round, and nodded in satisfaction.

They'd be back.

And they would be ready.

Outside Hyattsburg
0631 hrs_

It was an abnormally cold morning, even for Oregon in late winter. Fog blanketed the countryside, reducing visibility to what seemed to be a matter of yards. But it wasn't the cold or the oppressive, stifling fog clouds that were wearing on the survivors that had stayed behind with Sherman that were making them uneasy. It was the lack of the presence of long-overdue scout Mark Stiles. The last report they'd received from him had been around 0200, in the middle of the night, and after that—*silence*.

Even Sherman was beginning to feel that something awry had

happened on Stiles' return trip. He knew the soldier was highly competent—he not only showed initiative in volunteering, but his manner bespoke of someone who was willing to do his duty, no matter the cost, and no matter how distasteful he found that duty to be.

Finally, as the sun began to find its way through the clouds and fog, a cry went up from one of the sentries Sherman had posted around their makeshift camp in the leafless woods.

"Halt!" came the challenge.

The reaction among the soldiers and refugees was immediate—they sprang up from dozing slumber, grabbing for what few weapons remained. Some of the civilians, mostly Arabs and a few Africans picked up after the disaster at Suez, had spent their time fashioning spears from tough tree branches—primitive, but much better than nothing. Sherman was glad he had a group of aware and cautious people with him. They were ready for anything.

The guard's challenge continued.

"Identify yourself!"

A weary, exhausted-sounding voice drifted through the fog.

"Private Mark Stiles, returning from recon!"

"Advance, and be recognized!"

Sherman felt a knot in his stomach untie. It could have been a carrier—and one of their battle cries, standard reaction from them when they spotted prey—would certainly have drawn unwelcome reinforcements. The fact that Stiles had spoken had saved him from receiving a bullet from the sentry's pistol.

"General?" came Stiles' voice from the fog.

"I'm here, son! Come on in, grab what's left of the grub. Hot chow, cooked over a campfire. You deserve it, whatever you found!"

"No can do, General. I'll be staying where I am."

Sherman frowned, then looked aside at Thomas, who was scowling. He and the Command Sergeant Major were apparently sharing the same thought.

"What is it, son?" Sherman asked, pronouncing his words softly, with comfort and a touch of apprehension.

"I'm done, sir. I fucked up. A shambler bit me on my way out. I'm not coming any closer to camp than this."

Sherman opened his mouth as if to reply, but closed his lips.

What do you say to a man who knows he's going to die, and seems calmly resigned to his fate?

"Make him comfortable, sir," Thomas said, grimacing. For all his bravado, no man reaches the rank of Command Sergeant Major without knowing and caring about the men under him. Not to mention it seemed as if he was once again reading Sherman's mind.

"Stiles! Advance far enough for us to see you, at least! And we'll send Rebecca out to take a look. We can make your time pass well—you don't have to be alone, son."

"I don't know, sir."

Sherman frowned. Time for a little coercion.

"Get the hell up to the line, son. That's an order. Even if you've been bitten, it'll take a while for it to catch up to you. Let Becky check you over, give you some painkillers and a good meal, and we'll talk over your options."

For a full minute there was nothing but silence, and Sherman was worried Stiles had cut and run. He realized his respect level for the soldier had shot up another full notch or two—or ten. He wasn't flying off the handle. He wasn't despairing. He was still looking out for his brothers and sisters, even though he'd received a certainly mortal wound.

"Yes, sir," Stiles said. "I'll come in. Against my better judgment, sir."

"Noted. Now get in here, soldier!"

Ahead, out of the mists, loomed a strangely-shaped figure. Most of it appeared human, but bulging packs dangled from webgear and a long, cloth-covered bundle was slung across the man's shoulders. He limped, favoring his left leg, and was using a brightly polished rifle as a crutch. Half of Sherman wanted to run up to the man and tell him he'd be all right—and the other half, he noted with displeasure—remained professional. If Stiles had found a rifle, he must have found more. That shot up the survival chances of everyone else considerably. Stiles had not only kept cool in an otherwise hopeless situation, but he'd also completed his mission to the letter.

Thomas was already shouting for Rebecca Hall to grab her medical supplies and move up front. She'd been nearly silent since the incident with Decker and the other infected onboard the USS *Ramage,* as if consumed by inner ghosts, but like the rest of the survivors she was already hardened enough to know when business meant business.

She came jogging up alongside Sherman as he approached the wounded soldier. Stiles saluted, and in return Sherman snapped off one of the neatest salutes he'd given since he received his commission.

"Welcome back, soldier."

"Thank you, sir."

"Report?"

Stiles nodded, unslinging his heavy gear and ALICE pack and slumping to the ground, utterly exhausted after his all-night foray. Rebecca held up a finger to silence both of them.

"One moment. Bitten in the leg?" she asked, spying blood seeping through Stile's BDU pants.

"Yeah. Some laundromat freak named Don. I killed him, but was a little too hasty in getting out. Forgot the bastard would come back as a shambler. He crawled out and grabbed me without me even noticing him coming. Got in one good bite before I offed him. Sorry I'm so late, too, sir—when I fired on him, I had to spend a few hours evading the other infected that came out to see what the hubbub was about."

"Not a problem, Stiles," Sherman said as Rebecca used a pair of sharp scissors to cut the legging of Stiles' pants free, exposing the wound. Sure enough, a neat bite mark scored the soldier's skin. It hadn't ripped any flesh, but teeth had punctured in a few places.

Rebecca sighed and got to work, dropping iodine into the wound to sterilize it. Stiles gasped and gritted his teeth against the sting.

"Well, sir, here's the lowdown—and I think you'll like it," Stiles said, watching Rebecca work. "The main floor in the store was looted damn near clean except for ammunition. I got us enough nine-mil to last a good while. I thought that's all there was, but I found something."

Sherman nodded. "I remember the broadcast you sent. '*Going to need a bigger backpack*,' I think it was."

"Yes, sir. And we do. Several backpacks, I think. I found a storeroom in the basement that looked like it doubled as the owner's private collection of firearms and surplus gear. I know the guns are important, but there's also a full shelf of T-rations down there.

With all of us, it's about a full week's supply if we eat three squares a day—we can stretch it to three weeks if we need to."

"And the weapons? If they're all as beautiful as that, we should be in for a treat," Sherman said, nodding at Stiles' antique Winchester.

Stiles chucked somberly, picking up the rifle. "Ain't it a crime. I finally get one of the rifles I've always wanted, and I get bit two minutes later on my way out."

"It's yours, soldier, even in death, if I have my way. You've certainly earned a few perks. Speaking of which . . . Rebecca?"

"Already on it, Frank," Rebecca said, glancing up at Sherman. "Morphine, anyone?"

"Oh, God, yes, please!" Stiles answered, managing a genuine grin. "If I'm going to go nuts, might as well go comfortably, right?"

"What else did you find?"

Stiles didn't answer vocally. Instead he reached over as Rebecca stuck a syringe full of morphine into his thigh and picked up the cloth-wrapped bundle. He untied one of the leather straps and let the rifles he'd brought spill out. Sherman whistled under his breath, then reached down and picked up one of the 12-gauge shotguns. He hefted it in his hands and smiled.

"You did real good, trooper," Sherman said, still grinning. "Real good."

"And there's more where those come from, sir," Stiles added, laying back against a tree trunk and half-closing his eyes as the morphine began to take effect. "There's about a dozen more, assorted calibers, mostly .30-06 and 12-gauge."

"Ruger Mini-14," Sherman said, looking over the weapons. "And a Winchester model 70. Beautiful! These rifles even have scopes mounted—there's our long-range supporting fire. That gives our new runner an even better chance."

"Uh, sir?" Stiles said, shock on his face. "Your *new* runner? I'm your runner, still."

"No, you relax, Stiles—you've done all of us a great service."

"With all due respect, sir, blow it out your ass," Stiles said. Sherman was taken aback a moment, but realized the remark was not meant to be offensive. Stiles elaborated, "Look—I'm dead anyway, and I can still run like mad if Becky here gives me another shot of that painkiller before we head out. If I get killed—so what? I'm a dead man either way. The way I see it—I might have been your best choice before, but now I'm the perfect choice."

Sherman raised his eyebrows, then slowly nodded. Once again Stiles proved to be a sound thinker.

"Very well, Stiles. May I say something?" Sherman asked. Stiles nodded, eyes still half-closed.

"If we were still technically in the Army, I'd see to it you got the Medal of Honor for this. I mean that."

"Hell, sir, I'd settle for a discharge and partial pension," chuckled Stiles. Even lately-morose Rebecca cracked a smile at that. "Is there anything else, sir? Getting pretty tired . . ."

"One last question. You said there were more weapons in that store?"

"Yes, sir . . . trapdoor behind the counter . . . gotta pry it up . . . guy down there . . . he's dead, don't mind him . . . get the food and more ammunition . . . especially food . . ." Stiles voiced drifted off and his head lolled to the side in sleep. The morphine and exhaustion had caught up to him.

Sherman reached out a hand and clasped the sleeping soldier's shoulder. "You did real good, son. Real good."

Then he stood, Rebecca still kneeling and collecting her supplies, and yelled to the survivors.

"Group! School circle! We've got a new plan to work out!"

With the exception of the sentries posted around the main makeshift camp, all the men and women grouped around Sherman, Thomas, and Rebecca, who took a few steps back, not wanting any real attention to fall upon her.

"Alright, listen up!" Thomas declared, looking directly at the soldiers and skipping his eyes over the civilians, who he still felt he served and wouldn't presume to order about. "There's been a minor change in our rescue attempt. We've acquired a pair of long-range, high-powered rifles. What we need now are two of you—civilian or soldier—who has exceptional marksmanship skills. Their new job will be to cover our runner, Stiles, as he tries to drive the carriers away from the siege at the theater. Be warned—your shots will draw attention. Be ready to break and run if you find you've got unwelcome company. Despite that, we're also assigning our sniper volunteers a rifleman with our new Mini-14 to cover them at close range. That leaves us a handful of pistols, a revolver, and a shotgun for our main defense and rescue crew—and just for your information, that's every last one of you who isn't assigned to drive or snipe. If you're without a firearm, you'll still be sticking to plan one—hang back and wait to withdraw when the rescue squads are leaving the city."

Sherman stepped forward to add his piece: "It also seems the sporting goods store we scouted last night holds a few more items we can use. First and foremost—we'll be eating tinned foods for the next couple weeks—old T-rations."

"Better than nothing, sir, and a damn sight better than the scraps we've been getting," sang out a soldier. The rest chorused in with a muted, but still morale-boosting, 'Hoo-ah!'

"Second—and just as important—Stiles has reported there are at least another half-dozen to dozen rifles left in the store that he couldn't hump back with. We'll be adjusting our escape plan. Our runner, snipers, and covering-fire rifleman will *not* have vehicle support to evac them once they're clear of the city. You'll all be running. I'm sorry to whoever else has to join Stiles, but we need to get that gear or risk starving to death—and I want every possible person armed. Once again, this is not the kind of decision I like to make, but I feel it is in the best interests of the group at large. Mark Stiles has already gone above and beyond, and despite being wounded, he's still up for being the runner. I suggest all of you do your best to imitate the ideals he has selflessly set for himself."

"*Oi*, General, I heard he was bit. That true?" asked one of the refugees, an Australian welder named Jack—he refused to give his last name. "Should we be letting him hang around?"

"Yes, for the time being," Sherman said. "A bite that small means he's got five, maybe up to ten or twelve days before he turns. He knows he's a dead man. I expect all of you to show him proper respect for the manner in which he's handling this. Is that clear?"

"Don't have to tell me twice, sir," said Thomas. His eyes, sweeping the crowd, addressed once again the soldiers that remained. "Kid reminds me of me at that age—only then getting wounded meant stepping on a scatter mine, not being bitten in the leg—and you at least had a chance to survive the mine."

"So what'll we do once we re-raid that store?" asked a soldier, raising his hand.

"Take what's left of the weapons. Load up all the food. Grab any gear that might be useful once we're into the countryside. I don't want to go into any more towns unless we can clearly see they're uninfected, or if we're so low on supplies that we have no choice."

"Sounds like a damn fine idea, sir," growled Thomas. "I can deal with a banzai charge, but those infected get me all uneasy. Too quiet. Too . . . *inhuman*. I, for one, wouldn't mind never seeing a city again after this and Sharm el-Sheikh."

"They're deathtraps," chimed Rebecca, speaking for the first time since treating Stiles. "They build up in there, relax when there's no more prey, then jump out when they see you walking in."

"Seemed an awful lot like an ambush to me," Sherman agreed. "They all struck at once."

"I've been thinking a lot about it," Rebecca said, moving forward again to the center of the circle of people, standing next to Frank. "I don't think it was really an ambush. I think it was . . . *instinctive*. You could say that, like, those dinosaurs—*velociraptors*—might have been pretty smart. They lull you into thinking you're safe, then while you're focused on one of them, a buddy strikes from the side. I remember that from Jurassic Park—the book, not the movie. The movie sucked. Anyway, these guys don't have any tactics. They're just dormant . . . then they hear you, and they all come rushing at once. I think it's the growl."

"The *growl*?" chuckled one soldier. He earned a glare from Rebecca so icy that he shut his mouth, pursed his lips, and looked down at the pothole-filled road.

"Their cry. Haven't you noticed it? When they see you—the living ones, anyway—they scream at you and then run at you. I think the scream draws all the others in the area. Back there in town, the first one that came out gave that growl, and suddenly they were all around us. They're not smart, they're just . . . *pack hunters*. Yes, that's it. That's what I was trying to remember. They work together—I don't know if they know what they're doing or if it's just coincidence. But get spotted by one, and let it get that growl out, and you're swamped."

"She's right," came a weak, shaky voice. It was Stiles, re-awakened by the discussion, looking over at the group with glazed eyes. "Only one of those bastards came to look for the gunshot I had to use, but right after he saw me they were pouring out all over the place. They're instinctive. Single-minded. We've all got at least a hundred IQ points on these pus-bags—if they're even self-aware. But the apple pie was good."

With that, he drifted back into a semi-slumber, shivering slightly in the morning cold.

"That was interesting," said Jack, the welder. "Think that was the drugs talking?"

"The apple pie comment was the morphine," Rebecca said. "I didn't give him enough to make him go sideways on us. Just a babble dose. Nah, I think he's right."

"So do I," Sherman began, "But until you gave your opinion, Becky, I was starting to think they were actually coordinating ambushes. Now I'm starting to really wonder. But one thing's non-debatable: go into a city, get one little piece of bad luck, and you've got a thousand carriers on your six. Thomas!"

"Yes, sir!" bellowed Thomas, snapping to attention. The other soldiers were slipping back into semi-civilian attitudes, but for Thomas, the Army was his life.

"You will not be part of the rescue mission. I have a much more important task I need taken care of."

Thomas scowled, but quickly wiped the expression from his face and straightened back up. "I'm ready, sir."

"Go on foot. Take one man, and a pistol for both of you. Find a gas station on the outskirts. You have two objectives: first, see if there's any fuel left for our truck. Second, find us batteries for our radios and—*this is the big one*—a road Atlas of the West and Midwest. When you get back here to the rendezvous, start plotting routes that'll take us to our destination and keep us out of any big towns. Hamlets, villages—those I can risk, or go around. But nowhere—*nowhere*—that brings us close to a large-population area."

Thomas smiled. This wasn't such a bad assignment after all. He loved recon in his younger days.

"Yes, sir. Krueger! On line!"

Krueger, the sharp-shooting shortie who had gone with Denton and Brewster when they first approached Hyattsburg, trotted up and fell back into parade rest. Like Thomas, he was still clinging to military tradition.

"Sergeant Major?" Krueger asked.

"Grab us each a pistol, five magazines apiece now that we've got ammo. Get moving—I want you geared and ready to move out in five."

"Hoo-ah, Sergeant Major," nodded Krueger, spinning neatly on a heel and jogging over to where a pair of soldiers were laying out Stiles' haul. He selected a nine-millimeter for the Sergeant Major, then halted. There, on the table, was a pristine chromed .357 magnum revolver. His eyes widened, then flicked left and right to see if anyone was watching. Grinning, he quickly holstered the weapon—a tight fit in a holster designed for a Beretta—and pocketed the speed loaders that had already been laid out.

"Finally, a bit of good luck," Krueger commented, strolling over to his webgear laying next to his dew-dampened bedroll. He clicked it across his chest, double-checked his remaining equipment, and ran back up to Thomas with a full minute to spare. He handed the Beretta, butt-first, to the Sergeant Major, whose eyes were locked on the bright and massive long-barreled magnum the Private carried.

"Nice weapon choice," growled Thomas. "Have fun reloading it in a firefight."

"Don't expect to get shot at, Sergeant," quipped Krueger. "Plan on doing some shooting, though—and this will be a fun thing to do that shooting with."

Thomas turned away and headed off on the trail to hide the half-smile on his face. The world was falling to shit—but some people still managed to find a bit of pleasure in life.

The pair didn't have very far to hike, as it turned out. There were several small roads that led out of Hyattsburg in almost every direction. They traversed an open field, grass comfortably low and crunchy underfoot in the cold day. Beyond the field lay a stretch of trees, sloping down through a gulley, and the two men wound their way around the trunks, stepping slowly and carefully between fallen branches and dried leaves. Through the trees they could already see the next road.

They slid down the incline that had been carved out of the gulley to make room for the road. Both dropped into crouches in the drainage ditch and jogged lightly toward town, moving out of sight around a distant bend.

Back at the truck, Sherman got busy marshaling the remainder of the survivors for the foray into Hyattsburg.

"Alright, empty the back of that vehicle to make some room!" Sherman ordered, gesturing at the truck. "Anybody who isn't getting ready to head back, settle in. We'll be gone until just after nightfall, if all goes to plan."

The handful of unarmed refugees had already scouted out a nice thicket off the edge of the road to hunker down in while the soldiers raided the town. It would afford them at least some protection from detection if an infected were to wander by. It wasn't likely. So far they hadn't seen so much as a single shambler once they'd left the town—but that was not a guarantee one wouldn't mosey past.

"Sir, those of us that are armed are ready to move," reported one of the soldiers.

"Better see if we can get Stiles on his feet," Sherman said, looking in Rebecca's direction. "Get him into the truck. He can ride until it's time."

"He'll be woozy," she warned. When Sherman only nodded in reply, she shrugged and shook the soldier's shoulder. Stiles waved an arm and batted her hand away, wrinkling his forehead in annoyance without awakening. She tried again, and this time he caught her forearm in a lightning-fast move, eyes blinking open.

"Don't do that," he said.

"General's orders. He wants you in the truck," Rebecca said, jerking a thumb over her shoulder at Frank. "Can I have my arm back now?"

"Yeah. Yeah. Sorry," Stiles said, letting go of her wrist. He leaned heavily against the tree behind him as he unsteadily rose to his feet.

"Need a hand?" Rebecca asked.

"I'm fine."

Stiles limped over to the off-white utility truck, still using his rifle as a crutch. He grimaced as he put weight on his wounded leg, and looked back over his shoulder at the medic.

"Not complaining about the morphine, but you got anything that's more of a local?" he asked, trying to smirk.

Rebecca didn't reply.

"Alright, saddle up!" barked Sherman, waving an arm over his head. He wanted everyone who was going into Hyattsburg to be in position well before dusk. It was still a good twelve hours before the sun would fall below the horizon, but that would only give them more time to scout the town before moving in.

The truck left the camp first, driven by one of the soldiers with another riding shotgun and Stiles sitting up in the back. It would move to the town's edge and park to conserve what little fuel that was left. The rest of the men shouldered or holstered their weapons and moved out after it, walking in twin columns on either side of the road.

Sherman knew that he was being forced once again to risk the lives of many to only possibly save the lives of a few. It was true soldier's work, the kind not every person was cut out for in life. He knew of plenty of officers who froze up when presented with such decisions—not that he blamed them. A person had to have very thick skin and a lot of rationalizing power to cope with the knowledge that their plan or call was the direct impetus behind death—on whichever side. Sherman thought of it simply: to make an omelet, one must break eggs. It sounded callous and shallow when he said it to himself, but he always reminded his conscience that it was as true as any other common-sense adage.

It was a curious human condition that led people to be willing to die to save the life of another. How many times had he read in the newspaper of events like a lost hiker in the mountains? Dozens, if not hundreds, would rush out of their homes and jobs to search for the victim, possibly becoming lost themselves. Often, he'd heard of civilians—people not often credited with much honor by soldiers—who lost ten, twelve, fifteen people in a search effort for just one lost person.

Yes, if you want to do a rescue—or make an omelet—you break some eggs.

He'd be damned if he let his people—even the civvie refugees—stay stuck in a godforsaken movie theater to slowly starve to death when he had a chance to make things different.

And Stiles had given them a fighting chance once they finally left Hyattsburg. The town's name left a sour taste in Sherman's mouth even when thinking it silently. He'd lost less people here than he had at Suez or Sharm el-Sheikh, but it felt more personal now. Then, there had been hundreds of them. In Hyattsburg, maybe fifty. And now, less than a dozen—unless by some miracle they located Mbutu's missing truck. They still hadn't gotten so much as a peep out of the radio from him. Sherman hoped for the best—but deep down he believed if they hadn't come by yet, chances were they hadn't made it.

Sherman was tossing his attack plan for raiding what remained in the sporting goods store when the civilian Jack came up alongside him. He was one of those left unarmed, but he'd jogged up silently, leaving the rest of the unarmed folk in their hideaway.

"General," he said, nodding.

Sherman looked over, still caught up in thought, and nodded in reply. He then performed a near-perfect double-take, grimacing when he glanced down at Jack's bare belt.

"You have no weapon. Get back with the others," Sherman said, a bit more aggressively than he'd meant to. Jack held up a hand and made a peace sign, grinning lopsidedly.

"Don't really like sitting, Sherm," he said. Sherman might once have gotten more angry at the civilian shortening his last name, but it seemed almost endearing from the friendly, sensible fellow. "I'd like to do something. I heard your little speech yesterday about volunteering—well, my hands are empty. Think maybe you could use them carrying things at that store while someone armed keeps an eye on my back."

"Don't know," Sherman said, shrugging. "It's always best to rely on yourself in close-quarters like we'll be facing in town. If you go around a corner first—"

"I know, I know—it's a risk. But the soldiers here take the same risk every time they go out. I don't mind. Gotta earn my keep."

Sherman looked the man up and down, pretending to evaluate him. Truthfully, the moment Jack made his proposal he'd decided to bring him along—but it was good to make folks sweat now and then. It kept them sharp.

"Alright," Frank said slowly. "But like I said, don't go around any corners first. Let my boys clear the way."

"It's a deal. So, what do they call you at home, General?"

"Frank. Feel free to use that. I'm getting a little tired of being addressed by rank after all these years."

"You got it, Frank. Thanks for letting me come along. Much appreciated. Don't worry—I won't get in your way. I'll leave you to your thoughts," Jack said, performing a slight bow with his head and slowing his stride.

Sherman pulled away from him, fighting the temptation to grin again. Almost every day the people he was with found some small way to impress him. It was strange—before Morningstar had decimated the so-called civilized world, he'd been disgusted on an almost daily basis with people in general. Now, those he knew had earned nothing less than total respect from him. Odd how tragedy, death, and violence brought out the honor in people. They were finally seeing what a lot of fighting men had already learned—that life was a lot less complicated than people make it out to be. In the end, it's down to whether you have to die—and if you do, the method in which you check out.

He had a grim feeling at least some of those with him on the road would have to make that decision soon.

Edge of Hyattsburg
2134 hrs_

Night had fallen a few hours before. Sherman had noticed at dusk that the street lights were still operational, as well as a few of the automated floods that kicked on as night approached. He'd confirmed with a soldier who hailed from the northwest that the power supply came from a rural town that relied on the plant for most of their jobs—chances were decent they were still alive and kicking. The infection seemed to spread from the edge of the West coast and the edge of the East coast inland in both directions. It was an odd pattern, but Jack, the civilian welder, offered a rather intriguing and plausible theory:

"Well, it's cheaper to fly on shorter flights, right? So wouldn't it be shorter to fly into la Guardia or BWI or Dulles than it would be to fly to Oklahoma? Bet half the infected that started the Morningstar plague here came in as cheap and quick as they could when they ran outta Africa back in the early days."

Sherman agreed. It might not be a one-hundred percent accurate theory, but he figured Jack had gotten at least part of the solution down.

For now, though, their worries were not global—they were quite local, and very personal.

With the addition of the streetlamps' glow, Sherman had delayed the operation by a few hours to allow them to work in total darkness rather than the half-illumination of twilight. It was easier to shoot in the dark than at dusk. Not to mention half the carriers who heard them might not see them—and their escape route when they were done would be well-lit by the yellow incandescence of streetlamps. For once, Lady Luck—or God or Karma—seemed to give them a small break.

The soldiers' raiding party had crouched on the edge of the town in thick, young vine growth. Though there were little leaves on the vines in the dead of winter, they still wound around each other so thickly it was easy to remain hidden behind them. Once Sherman was satisfied the town was quiet and quite settled for the night, he'd raised a hand and signaled for the men to move out. All of them knew the location of the store as well as the theater, and all had been well-briefed on their primary and secondary objectives.

Sherman played back the briefing in his head as the men silently padded in towards Hyattsburg, double-checking himself to make sure he hadn't forgotten a thing—just in case.

"Men, let's review," he had said as the soldiers kneeled in a school-circle around him after a quick half-ration snack two hours earlier. "Here's a short rundown: primary objectives. You have two. The first is the procurement of additional weapons and chow. Both of these items are of equal importance. Use your common sense. Recover equal loads of both, and rotate what you grab in each trip to the storeroom Stiles found. One trip, weapons and ammo. Next trip, food. I don't want to hear about anyone calling dibs on the firearms, either. They'll be distributed based on your individual backgrounds and talents. Second primary objective—though some of us will head back with what we recover from the store, the rest of us will relocate to the alley behind the theater and prepare to launch a rescue on our men stuck inside. Remember—those of you who are coming—silence is key. Absolutely *nothing* must distract the infected and their dead cohorts from Stiles, our runner. Wait until the main doors are clear before sweeping out into the street. Secondary objective—only one, this time, and this is it. Triple check everything. And I mean it."

Sherman remembered pacing back and forth, shaking his head as he'd spoken, remembering past fatalities that could have been prevented if they'd been more cautious.

"What I'm trying to say is—remember the fight on the destroyer? If we'd checked every last refugee for the slightest cut, and done a bit more quarantining, we wouldn't have lost good men in battle. Think an alley is clear? Triple check. Think your weapon is ready to fire? Triple check. Think that corner is safe? Triple check the fucking thing."

Sherman had stopped again, cheeks actually darkening to what might have been considered a blush. He almost never swore, especially around those under his command.

"Other than that, you know the drill. Watch your buddy's back. Play smart. Play safe. And maybe, with a bit of luck, we'll all make it out of this dead zone and get to see the Rocky Mountains before the month's out. Hell, maybe we'll camp a couple days. Raid a store for some beer, maybe. You'll have earned it if you pull off this op tonight."

At this, the soldiers had sensed the review was over. As one—but quietly and subdued—they chorused: "Hoo-ah!"

Sherman remembered nodding with satisfaction.

"Tonight it's game time, men. Get ready."

As the soldiers stepped over the cracked curb, they settled into their professional habits, fanning out, holding weapons at the ready with barrels pointing so they overlapped each others' fields of fire. They moved to opposite sides of the street, using the stoops, steps, corners, and lampposts as pieces of cover. None of them so much as brushed against any circle of light cast from the few automated bulbs—they stuck to the shadows.

Jack and Sherman stuck together in the middle of the wide street, the nearest soldier a good ten or fifteen yards away. It was actually the safest place to be. To get to the two, a carrier of Morningstar would have to break through the columns on either side. Sherman had his pistol drawn, the safety off, held at the ready. He was no hypocrite—he had triple-checked the weapon himself.

They almost made it to the sporting goods store without incident. Sherman looked ahead, and made out the sign denoting the laundromat where Stiles said he'd been bitten. Signs of battle were still apparent, even though it had happened almost a full day before. The corpses were tough to miss—five of them, in and around the storefront. All had been dispatched with quick shots to the head, except for a corpse wearing a work uniform, lying face-up on the sidewalk. His skull looked as if it had been half-smashed in by a rifle butt. His nametag read DON. Sherman guessed this was the one that had gotten Stiles. The soldier had probably instinctively smashed the reanimated carrier with his Winchester a few times before getting enough of his wits back to put a bullet through its eye socket. Sherman grimaced when he saw Don's sliced throat, again flashing back to Stiles' full account of his foray. The smallest slip-up, the tiniest piece of carelessness—that was all it took. That was all it *ever* took.

The rest of the corpses seemed to form a line leading towards the edge of town. Sherman's mind's eye saw the scene: Stiles retreating on his wounded calf, firing as he hopped backwards, carriers running out of the darkness at him. Must have been hell.

The store had been left in good shape by Stiles. He'd closed the door and set an ashtray upright in front of it. It was still standing—that told Sherman nothing infected (and brainless) had opened the swinging door since the scout had left.

Good thinking, soldier.

"Right column!" Sherman stage whispered, getting a column's attention. Five sets of eyes flicked over to him. He hand signaled for them to move in on the store. They worked silently and efficiently, shining lights in the windows, scanning the rows and alleys, and then turned, crouching and forming a small, hemispherical defensive perimeter around the main entrance. "Left column!"

His second set of hand signals sent the left-side column jogging towards the entrance. The only sound, besides Sherman's whispers, was that of rubber boot soles on black pavement. The left hand column filed quickly into the store, spreading out, scanning the rows again. They cleared the store in less than a minute. A corporal appeared in the swinging door's frame and signaled the all-clear to Sherman.

"Alright," Sherman whispered once he'd gotten to the doorway. "Get to work! You men inside—load up your packs! Quickly, now! Two of you out here, get in that storeroom and pass the gear up the steps! Go, go! Work fast!"

They knew what to do. They could have done it without Sherman's orders—but his presence definitely boosted their confidence. They didn't take more than five minutes to load six ALICE packs to the brim with ammunition and cans of food. It was enough ammo for months, but only enough old rations for a few weeks. Three, maybe four, tops, if managed properly. Sherman was pleased enough. They'd scrounge fresh food where they could to save the rations. The tins wouldn't go bad until Jesus decided his beard wasn't fashionable and shaved it off—or when Hell froze over. Both were equally unlikely.

Sherman, still standing in the open doorway as the squad finished, nodded simply. He directed the soldiers with full packs back they way they'd come. They'd be near useless when they had to run after the rescue—best to get them out and secure their new gear. They nodded, one or two whispering a furtive hoo-ah, and dog-trotted down the street, moving as fast as they could without making too much noise. Sherman had confidence they'd make it if they didn't draw attention to themselves.

He turned, surveying those left around him, and scowled. Near one of the perimeter guards, he spotted Jack—the civilian welder. He'd worked fast and hard in the storeroom, throwing whole boxes of rations up and out of the basement to the soldiers above. He seemed to have missed the bus out of town, though. Sherman ran over to him.

"What in the name of Saint Peter do you think you're doing, guy? Next move's combat for sure. Get the hell after that squad that just left!"

"No can do, sir. Armed now. Still gotta be useful—and I had no pack to carry stuff out. What's better? An empty-handed civvie, or an extra gun?" Jack held up a small pistol, grinning impishly. Sherman looked perplexed. Stiles hadn't said there were any more pistols. Jack seemed to sense his confusion and explained, "Someone must have dropped it. It was on the floor just inside the door, half under one of those shelf units. Nine-millimeter. Looks Polish or something. It's a gun, though, right?"

Sherman knew the last comment was rhetorical, and probably laced with undetectable sarcasm.

"You know how to use that?" he asked, raising his eyebrow.

"Yeah. This end points at the bad guys," Jack said, pointing at the barrel. When Sherman fixed him with a disapproving glare, Jack grinned, then quickly ejected the magazine, checked the chamber, reinserted his ammo, and chambered a round in one long, fluid motion. "I've fired a few in my time, Sherm."

Sherman couldn't resist a tenth of a second chuckle. Another go-getter.

"Alright, fine. But you'll take orders like my soldiers," he told him. He then turned and called to one of his men: "Corporal!"

"Sir?"

"You've got Jack, here. His standing orders are to remain behind you and watch your back. If he runs past you, tackle him. If he runs off, shoot him in the leg. He'll be good bait for the carriers—maybe help us get away."

"Yes, sir."

The corporal's response was automatic—emotionless, nothing more than a quick acknowledgement. To Jack, it probably sounded cold, calculating, and deadly serious. Sherman wasn't, though—his orders would be followed, but he was now certain the welder would stay safely behind the soldier—now that he feared the man would shoot him. Psychology was a semi-hobby of Lieutenant General Francis Sherman. It came in handy on the battlefield—and when confronted with his often-naughty grandchildren.

That thought gave him pause. He wondered how they were doing. He quickly dismissed it—no use worrying now.

"Alright, men, let's get into position," he whispered. He glanced at his watch. "Twelve minutes to game-time. Let's kick some carrier ass, soldiers, and all head out alive and in one piece! Hoo-ah?"

"Hoo-ah!"

A light breeze had begun to blow as the soldiers helped each other clamber over the tall brick wall that blocked the alley behind the theater from the street.

"Come on, come on, get over! First two on the other side, cover the end of that alley! Overlapping fields of fire!" Sherman stage-whispered the orders as the men began to drop silently to the pavement in the alley behind the theater.

They could already hear the sounds of fists beating on the heavy wooden doors in front of the building, and the scuffling noises of shoes being dragged across asphalt. There were definitely a number of carriers on the street. They had no idea how many, but from the sound of it, there were at least a baker's dozen, maybe two.

Sherman swung his legs over the edge of the wall, dropping down with a heavier thud than the rest of the men and groaning inwardly as his ankles and back complained.

"*I'm getting too old for this,*" he muttered.

Arthritic pangs were the last thing he wanted on his mind at the moment, though. He turned and looked over the soldiers. A pair of them had taken up position where the alley made its sharp ninety-degree turn towards the street, crouching at the corner, weapons held tight to their shoulders. One wielded a newly-purloined shotgun; the street-sweeper would be excellent to have in the close quarters of the alley if the infected decided to charge them here. The other was taking more careful aim with his .30-06, breathing shallowly as he peered through the scope mounted on the rails.

"Got anything?" Sherman whispered as he edged over to them.

"Couple contacts, three shamblers—haven't even looked over yet," said the soldier with the .30-06, watching the infected at close range thanks to the magnification of the scope.

This was what the soldiers had been psyching themselves up for over the last few hours. They were more than ready. The thinly veiled excitement permeated the air thicker than the damp, cold fog beginning to form in the winter night.

Sherman remembered being at an officer's training class earlier in his career. One of the speakers had been a behavioral analyst. He'd said that a particularly strong emotion seemed to have a contagious effect—in short, a dictionary-perfect definition of morale. Though the men who were headed to free the besieged folk in the theater were facing possible death—or *infection*, which was even worse—they knew this was not only their duty, but their privilege as survivors. They were all running on adrenaline now, and the '*fight or flight*' instinct in their brains were all switched firmly to '*fight*.'

Sherman glanced down at his watch, which he'd synchronized with Stiles and his backup crew before they'd left. Stiles was due to appear on the street in two minutes. Sherman had no doubt he'd be punctual. He hadn't let the surviving group down yet. Once most of the infected were clear, they'd try to break through and get back to the thick hedges that lined the forest by the edge of town.

"Two minutes," Sherman whispered, holding up a pair of fingers above his head. The soldiers, except for the two watching the alley, nodded silently and Jack nervously held up his pistol in a white-knuckled grip.

Sherman watched the hands on his clock as they ticked away, feeling his own anxiety grow with each passing second. What if something went wrong? What if the whole thing turned into a clusterfuck worse than the Bay of Pigs? What if this all would go down for nothing?

Sherman shook his head, frowning. He berated himself for a second in his head.

'What the hell kind of thinking is that? It's the waiting that's doing it. Just nervous. Stay frosty—you've been in worse scrapes and come out shining. Adapt and overcome.'

It turned out Stiles' watch must have gained five seconds since they'd synchronized. Just before Sherman gave the order to move forward, they heard his screaming voice in the street, echoing slightly off the brick walls off the alleyway.

"Hey! Pus-heads! You! Yeah, you, the shamblin' pukes! This way! Hey, look! Fresh meat!" came Stiles' voice. Sherman imagined he could see him in the middle of the street, waving his hands over his head and jumping.

The response from some of the infected was immediate. A couple of sprinters turned around, lightning fast, and issued low, guttural growls from their fever-inflamed throats. One of them actually began drooling as it looked at the soldier. The others, as if responding to an order, stopped beating on the theater door one by one and turned to look at Stiles. Once they'd all turned, there was a moment of complete silence. None of the carriers moved. They just stared, hissed, and growled. The shamblers swayed slightly back and forth, moaning pathetically.

What are they doing? Sherman mused. *Measuring him up?*

Just as he completed his thought, the pack took off. The sprinters lived up to their name once more, running flat-out at top speed straight towards Stiles.

"It's on like Donkey Kong, fuckers!" Stiles yelled defiantly. His voice began to fade as he continued to shout, indicating to Sherman he'd begun his retreat. "Keep it coming! This way! This way, you dumb fucks!"

Next went the shamblers, one by one, stumbling past the alley's entrance, arms out in front of them, reaching for their prey—which was probably two blocks away already.

"Alright, team, go, go, go!" Sherman ordered, speaking louder now that silence wasn't an issue. The two on guard sprang forward, running at a half-crouch to the alley's mouth, sweeping the barrels of their weapons back and forth to check the street. The man with the shotgun fired almost immediately. A shambler had been just around the corner. It must have been one of the last to catch on. The blast took it full in the chest at nearly point-blank range, lofting it off its feet and dumping it in the gutter a few yards away. It almost immediately began struggling to get up, but the soldier packing the rifle swung the barrel around, took a moment to aim, and put a round through its skull. It went limp.

"Thanks," said the soldier with the shotgun. "Fired by reflex. Should've aimed."

"Don't talk tactics—get to work!" Sherman barked. "I want defense! Keep a sharp eye! Don't let any get close, and hit any sprinters first—shoot 'em in the legs if you can't get a clear head shot. That goes especially for you, Private."

"Hoo-ah, sir," said the soldier with the shotgun. The wide spread of the buckshot might let him knock down a couple runners with one shot.

Behind them, the side door to the alley burst open. Brewster and Denton had been told to expect to hear shooting in the alley—that was their signal to go. All of the theater occupants poured out. Brewster was brandishing a nice chunk of wood he'd pried from a banister, and a man Sherman didn't know held a bloody machete in his hands. A young woman stood behind him, unarmed. Behind them came Denton—also unarmed—and Mitsui and Shephard filed out last.

"Thank God!" exclaimed Ron. "The front doors were just about ready to come off their hinges when you showed up!"

"Seconded. Good timing, General," Denton said, throwing Sherman a loose, half-serious salute.

"Contacts!" said the shotgun-soldier in the alley mouth. "Multiple! Five—no, seven—sprinters, heading this way from downtown!"

"Armed personnel, skirmish line in the street! Open fire and retreat! Jack, myself, Ron, and you—Private Enders—form a ring around our unarmed ones! Step lively!"

The armed soldiers ran out into the street, abandoning stealth. Their earlier shots and Stiles' yells would no doubt have alerted half the town's infected already. Now was the time for speed. Shots rang out as the soldiers fired at the oncoming infected. Three fell almost immediately. None were head shots, but they were fatal ones. They'd be down for a while before they reanimated. Good enough for retreating purposes.

The shotgun blared, and blood flew from peppered kneecaps. Two more sprinters stumbled and fell to the pavement, howling reflexively in pain.

"More contacts, sir, from behind us! Some of Stiles' group must've headed back!"

Sherman turned to look. Seven or eight more were heading back towards them. All were shamblers, slow-moving but deliberate—and shooting one in the kneecap or chest wouldn't put it down.

"Riflemen, to the rear! Headshots on those shamblers—clear us a path! Pistoleers, shotgunners—keep on the sprinters!" Sherman barked. The soldiers shifted immediately. He was impressed to see that Jack the welder also ran to the defense, firing quickly and reloading efficiently alongside the trained infantrymen.

"Sir! More contacts! They just keep coming!" shouted a corporal firing shots from his issue Beretta. He pointed with his free hand in between shots. More sprinters were coming towards them from the center of town. It appeared to be the same mob that had ambushed them near the car lot when they'd arrived. Indeed, as Sherman watched the crowd turn the corner onto the theater's street, he recognized a carrier that he'd shot in the shoulder wearing a very ugly plaid flannel nightgown. If it was the same group, there were probably a hundred more just about to turn that corner, half of them sprinters.

"Break and run for it!" Sherman ordered, feeling bile rise in his throat. They had plenty of ammo—maybe enough for all the carriers here—but they'd be overwhelmed and annihilated before they could get those rounds fired off. Sherman shouted again, re-issuing the order he liked the very least: "Full retreat! Disengage and retreat!"

The soldiers took one last shot apiece, spun on their heels, and ran. The riflemen dropped a couple more shamblers that were near the center of the street, clearing the group a small path of safety. They dodged past the slow, decaying carriers and headed for their rendezvous, where—Sherman hoped—their stolen utility truck would be waiting to whisk them out of reach of the infected.

"Gotta go faster, gotta go faster!" Brewster said as he ran, chanting it like a mantra over and over. He was hanging back, running slower than the slowest of the group, which happened to be the Japanese contractor, Mitsui, who was more than a bit portly. "Pick it up, man, you can do it, we can do it!"

Brewster's words seemed to edge the man on. He picked up his speed, but it wouldn't be enough. The group as a whole was losing ground to the sprinters. The infected ran with fevered determination, and the survivor group was already exhausted, weak from half-rations and carrying gear.

Denton spared a glance over his shoulder as they made it past their fourth block. Five more and they'd be free from the town—but he, too, could see they weren't going to make it. The sprinters had closed more than half the distance to the group.

Sherman knew it too. He knew if they stopped, they'd be overrun. But if they kept running, they'd be tackled from behind, one by one. That was no way for a soldier—for *anybody*—to die.

He heard the words playing in his head as he realized what his next orders must be. He stopped in his tracks.

"Life's but a walking shadow," he said, drawing his pistol and turning to face the oncoming carriers. The others slowed, turned, and looked. They knew they weren't going to make it. "A poor player, that struts and frets his hour upon the stage . . ."

" . . . And then is heard no more," Denton said.

"It's a tale told by an idiot, full of sound and fury—signifying nothing," Sherman finished.

"Be glad to go out with a bit of sound and fury, General," Denton said.

"Me, too," Jack added, walking over to stand with them. The rest of the group filtered over, weapons ready. Safeties clicked off and Ron held out his machete, whispering to Katie to stand back and run if she could. She took one step backwards—but no more.

The line was drawn. The sprinters sensed their prey wasn't going to get away, and the frenzied intensity in their eyes gleamed even more brightly. They'd be upon them in ten seconds.

"Give them hell, brothers and sisters," Sherman said. "Make 'em pay!"

Fingers tightened on triggers, but just before the first round fired, a screeching noise drew the attention of all on the street, infected included. A pair of headlights had appeared behind the mob of carriers, and the sound of a roaring engine cut through the air. With a sickening, fleshy crunch, the vehicle plowed into the mob, knocking carriers left and right. Some got caught under the wheels and were twisted and broken when they were spat out behind it. The vehicle rammed its way through the line, speeding up to the survivors and skidding to the side, tires smoking. A familiar-looking face leaned out of the driver's side window.

"I thought we had lost you for all time!" yelled Mbutu Ngasy, flashing a bright white smile. "Quick! Get in! Fastly, fastly, fastly!"

Sherman's eyes boggled, and his jaw dropped a bit, but he heard Mbutu's words and reacted. He was right next to the cab, so he swung open the passenger door and nearly dived in head first. The rest of the group clambered into the truck bed, fit so tightly some were laying on other's legs and laps. None of them cared—this was a *miracle*.

"Punch it!" came Brewster's voice from the truck bed. "All bodies onboard!"

Mbutu slammed the truck back into gear and burned rubber. The tires caught traction and the truck shot forward just as the leading edge of the half-broken carrier mob reached the bumper. Shots rang out as the soldiers in the bed picked off some of the closer sprinters.

"Where in the name of the Holy Ghost and Satan's Cookies did you come from, Ngasy?! We thought you'd bought it in the ambush!"

"So did we!" Mbutu yelled over the sound of the roaring engine and gunfire. "We doubled back when we lost you and holed up in that warehouse we first passed! Guy was a lot more helpful when your men threatened to blow the door off its hinges! Been hiding out there since!"

"How'd you know to come now?!" Sherman shouted back.

"Heard the gunfire! Saw the cursed ones heading out—we knew something was up! We would have radioed, but no one on my truck had one that still had power!" Mbutu explained. He'd taken the first right turn he could, then a left, followed by another left to throw off the mob of carriers, and was swinging a hard right back onto the street they'd started on as he spoke. Some of the carriers were still there, a block back, and started after them again, but the majority had taken the decoy street and didn't see them.

"Nice thinking!" Sherman said as he realized what Mbutu had done.

"Air traffic controller, remember? I have a good sense of timing and direction—comes with the work. Should've gone a little slower though, then the rest would have been out of sight, too."

"Good enough, friend, good enough. A dozen's better than a hundred," Sherman said, clasping Mbutu's shoulder warmly and staring in the rearview mirror at the diminishing forms of the carriers.

They passed the city limit sign, still bright and cheery, reading, *'Thank you for visiting historic Hyattsburg! Come back soon!'*

Sherman doubted very seriously he'd ever come back, and smirked inwardly.

We've done it, he thought, as buildings and streetlights became trees and shrubs.

"Oh, damn it all," Sherman said, frantically fumbling for his radio. In the excitement of Mbutu's last-moment rescue, he'd forgotten about the rendezvous team and Stiles. He needed to tell them to get out, and that they were safe and sound. He clicked the transmit button.

"Ghost Lead to Ghost Evac, come in, Ghost Evac," Sherman said.

The response came back in a scant moment. They'd been waiting for word. "Good to hear you, Ghost Lead—we heard shooting. Sitrep, sir, over."

"Bug out, Ghost Evac, we're clear of the town. Ngasy showed up in the third truck. Bug out to original location and regroup. How'd Stiles make out, over?"

"Stiles is gone, sir, over," came the static-laced reply.

Sherman put a hand on Mbutu's arm, silently directing him to stop before they moved out of range of the handheld radios.

"Dead?" Sherman asked, feeling a bit despondent all of a sudden.

"No, sir, not dead—gone! He took off down a side street instead of coming to us! Took all the carriers with him, too. We think he didn't want us to get infected, sir. We think it's a kamikaze run, over."

Sherman sat still for a moment, then heaved a breath. He'd seen it a couple of times before. Wounded men who were certain they were dying would do heroic things that would end in their death. The same psychologist who'd explained group moods mentioned that it was called Doc Holliday syndrome, after the famous gunslinger. He'd had tuberculosis and knew he was dying—so he took risks any other man would run away from—after all, he was going to die anyway. Stiles had done the same thing. The infected had probably killed him by now, and he'd be reanimating as a shambler soon, somewhere in the town. But he'd accomplished what he wanted to. He'd led the infected far from the survivors.

If there was still a working government, Sherman would have put him in for the Medal of Honor—or if that was denied, the Distinguished Service Cross. That was dedication. For that matter, Mbutu should get one, too—if he were in the Army. Or at least a United States citizen.

The truck interrupted Sherman's train of thought as the engine suddenly began to sputter. It coughed twice, turned over one final time with a pathetic wheeze, and died.

"What the . . . ?" Sherman said, frowning.

"This truck is out of fuel," Mbutu told him, tapping the dashboard meter. "It was on the red-line all through town as it was—I am amazed we made it this far."

"It made it far enough," Sherman said, opening the door and hopping out. He pointed back at the town, looking up at the people in the truck bed. "Dismount, folks! This vehicle's FUBAR for now, until we get some gas. Riflemen, cover the road. Might have a couple curious infected coming through to see if we're nearby."

Sherman didn't say so, but he was a hundred percent sure there'd be infected on them in a few minutes. At Suez they'd followed a truck halfway across a desert just because it occasionally popped into sight across the dunes—they'd definitely walk a couple miles after a truck full of dinner to see if it had stopped. "Stay alert. Use your ears more than your eyes—those streetlights have us all night-blind for the next few minutes."

The people piled out of the truck, soldiers kneeling in the cracked, old roadway, a few laying prone in the ditches alongside it. The bushes rustled, and a couple of the soldiers reflexively swung their weapons toward the noise, but it was just the civilian refugees they'd left behind. Their original spot—where they'd planned the whole rescue—had been only another hundred yards up the road. The refugees must have decided to head for the headlights of the truck. The looks on their faces said they were amazingly relieved to see friendly armed people nearby again.

Sherman clicked his radio.

"Ghost Evac, are you bugged out yet, over?"

"Sir, yes, sir—should be seeing our headlights in ten seconds, sir, over."

They heard the utility truck about the same time they saw it. The driver had taken a shortcut, cutting through a dirt access road that ran across a barren winter wheat field. A good choice—taking the street through town would've brought more carriers after them.

As the utility truck drew near, Sherman tried the radio again, this time trying to raise Thomas and Krueger. They'd need gas if they wanted to make good time—not to mention riding would be a lot better than walking on Sherman's slightly arthritic knees, about which he'd never tell a soul.

"Ghost Lead to Thomas—come in, Thomas, over," Sherman said. He'd forgotten to assign a call sign to Thomas and Krueger.

Oh, well—not like it matters, he thought.

It took a short while before he got a response. He didn't have to call again, but Thomas must have been in the middle of something, because Sherman's finger was on the transmit button to give it another shot when the Command Sergeant Major's voice came through, heavily distorted by static. He was just barely in range, apparently.

"We're here, Ghost Lead. Mission is a SNAFU. We found a gas station—plenty of fuel here, too. Problem is we've wasted all our ammo clearing the place of infected—it was crawling with 'em, sir.

Lots of cars here, too. Most have keys and are in good shape. Looks like people lined up to gas up before leaving and got jumped by a group of infected—half the people left in the cars have been torn apart, sir. It's not pretty here. Over."

Sherman nodded. Thomas didn't know they'd succeeded in getting more weapons and ammunition and probably thought he'd just used half the remaining rounds the group had. He hadn't just done a SNAFU'ed op, he'd done quite well. Almost exactly as Sherman had wanted it to go down, in fact.

"Excellent. We're at the original sortie point on the road outside town. We're nicely armed now—about half of us have rifles and we've got tons of pistol ammunition waiting for you here. Get another car, gas up, and bring as many cans of fuel as you can with you, over."

"Wilco, sir. That's good news. How'd the rescue go, over?"

"Beautifully, Thomas. All personnel made it back without a scratch—except Stiles. He took off down a side street, led most of the horde of sprinters with him."

"Damn, that's a crying fucking shame, sir. He was Sergeant material, if I may say so."

"I agree, Command Sergeant Major. Now move out—we've got to extract Ngasy's survivors from a warehouse and beat it, over."

"The air traffic controller's still alive? I thought he wrecked in town and bought himself a farm," Thomas said.

Static nearly drowned out the transmission, but Sherman managed to pick up the words. He'd used much worse field radios twenty years before. These sounded crystal-clear to someone who was accustomed to ten-pound models that only transmitted a couple miles in the best of conditions.

"Alive and kicking—he saved our butts. But I'll tell you the rest when we're far away from this place and better protected, Thomas. I'm out for now. Move fast. We need that fuel."

"Roger that, sir. Way to hammer down, sir. Thomas out."

Sherman dropped the radio and let it hang from his shoulder epaulette. He clasped his hands behind his back. The utility truck had parked and the three men who had been assigned to cover Stiles climbed out of the cab. The back had been loaded with the gear and food plundered from the sporting goods store, and the soldiers who'd lugged it out of town were clinging on the ladder racks on the sides of the tall rear end of the vehicle. They had also already dropped off and walked over to the main group.

"Alright, folks, here's the situation!" Sherman declared, loud enough so all could hear, but at a volume just below shouting. "As we all know, the rescue's been accomplished with almost no hitches. A few close calls—but that was about it. The only personnel lost was Stiles, and he went out honorably, according to our rendezvous detail."

The men who had been in the utility truck's cab nodded somberly.

"In case any of you newly arrived folks haven't noticed, Mbutu and his truckload of people *did* in fact survive the ambush in town, and he showed up just in time to save our sorry butts from infection. We'll have to go around the town and pick up his people—they're holed up in the warehouse we passed just as we entered."

"Sir, how?" asked Brewster. He'd acquired a brightly polished double-barreled break-action shotgun, and had just snapped it closed after loading a pair of shells into it. "We've basically got fumes in both vehicles. We'll never make it there and back without running the risk of gettin' jumped by those pus-fuckers again. Not that I'm against saving them—hell, you saved us. I say go for it. But *how*?"

Sherman answered the question, but managed to phrase it as if the Private First-Class hadn't said a word: "I've also just received word that Thomas and Krueger succeeded in securing us plenty of fuel, and another vehicle. It's just a car, but we can use it for cargo—and that means we'll be riding, and not marching. Can I get a hoo-ah for that?"

Even some of the civilians joined in the staccato chorus of acknowledgement.

"Question," said Jack the welder, holding up a hand like he was in a classroom. Sherman nodded at him. "Where are we going? I mean, once we're out of here?"

"I'll tell you that once we've got everyone together. Before we left the USS *Ramage,* I contacted an old friend. She's an expert on the Morningstar Strain, and she's got a couple ideas, and a nice meeting location in mind. I'll tell you the whole deal when we're on the road."

Some of the people looked back and forth at each other, nodding in anticipation and appreciation. An expert on the Morningstar

Strain? A person like that would be a wonderful addition to their little team of rogue survivors.

Off in the distance, they heard the sound of a rattling car engine. It was definitely a smaller vehicle than either of the trucks. Thomas and Krueger had found a back road, half-paved, half-gravel, that led them to the rural road the group was gathered on. They watched with satisfaction as a blue Mercury Topaz turned in their direction. The headlights from Mbutu's truck illuminated the form of Krueger, leaning out of the passenger window and waving a hand over his head in greeting, a wide grin on his face. The group could see red and yellow plastic gas cans piled nearly to the roof of the old car, all probably filled to the brim with precious fuel. There had to be a hundred gallons stashed in there. No wonder the windows were down—the fumes were probably overwhelming.

The Topaz ground to a halt near Sherman, who stood with his arms folded in the middle of the cracked, deteriorating road, hiding a smile under his calm, blank expression. They had now recovered their lost personnel, (with the exception of those in the warehouse,) and plenty of weapons and food and enough fuel to get all three vehicles to the great Rocky Mountain chain, if not through it into the open plains of the Midwest.

"Command Sergeant Major Thomas reporting back, sir—mission accomplished," said Thomas as he approached Sherman. He snapped to attention and threw a picture-perfect salute. Krueger was too busy jackballing with the excited enlisted men to salute, but Sherman didn't care. Military doctrine was going out the window—no use for parade rest and forward march and dress right dress in a world where staying alive was the only real concern. Sherman returned Thomas' salute, then stepped forward, chuckling, and shook his hand firmly. "Looks like we'll live to fight another day, Sergeant."

"Looks like it, sir. What are we doing about the warehouse folks?"

"We'll find side roads that lead us around the town, not through it. The building's right outside the town proper. Shouldn't be much trouble. We'll send a crew in Mbutu's truck, fully armed, and the utility truck behind it, with the bed empty to load 'em up in. Stow the gear wherever you can—we can tie some on top of that piece of crap you got at the filling station."

Sherman paused a moment, regarding Thomas' new car.

"Out of curiosity, Sergeant . . . why'd you pick such a junker? Nothing better there?"

"It was the only one left without half a body stinking it up, sir," Thomas said bluntly. "It runs. That's all that matters, really."

"Guess you're right. Alright, men," Sherman said, turning to the group. "A few of you go unload that truck of the gear inside. Stack it by the road for now. Volunteers for our warehouse rescue?"

If finding a volunteer for the first rescue was hard, this time it was at the exact opposite end of the spectrum. Almost every hand shot up, save for the unarmed civilians. Mbutu's hand wasn't up, but he was already clambering into the driver's seat of the truck he'd driven.

"I have a feel for this truck, now," Ngasy said, leaning his head out of the half-lowered window. "I better drive. Can someone loan me a pistol?"

One of the soldiers pulled his sidearm and passed it in the window to Mbutu. He was already carrying one of the high-priced showroom-quality hunting rifles they'd pulled from the store, and figured the pistol wasn't a huge loss.

"Alright, since we're all so eager, the first six in Mbutu's truck bed go—and I want them all to be carrying rifles," Sherman said. There was a bit of a scramble among those carrying long arms, and when they'd settled in, Brewster, Jack, the two soldiers who'd guarded the alley, Thomas, and Krueger were all in the truck. Thomas had calmly climbed in the passenger side while the other enlisted men pushed and shoved at the tailgate. He had no rifle, but had a look of determination on his face that told Sherman not to say a word. He was probably pissed he missed the rescue mission while looking for gas. Krueger had traded his .357 for a pump-action shotgun on the promise they'd trade back once he returned. He wanted some more action, too.

After they'd fueled up the trucks with some of the gas from the car, they rumbled off down the side road Thomas and Krueger had used to approach. Sherman watched the tail lights until they disappeared around a bend, then turned, sat down on the rear trunk of the blue Topaz, and heaved a sigh. He suddenly realized he was utterly exhausted. There was little for him to do at the moment, and his brain was sending him signals he couldn't deny.

Rebecca was watching him from the group of unarmed refugees. She walked over and sat down next to the older man, eyeing him closely. She was either clairvoyant or an excellent medic, because she idly asked him if he'd like to take a short nap.

"You do look tired, you know. You've been a couple days without sleep," she added.

"I've gone longer without sleep—or *food*, for that matter," Sherman told her. It was true. You never knew when you'd have a moment of peace in the middle of war, and Sherman had been on more than his fair share of long campaigns.

"All the same, you should catch a rest. If anything comes through on the radio, I'll wake you," Rebecca said, reaching out and plucking the radio from Sherman's shoulder before he could reach his hand up to stop her. He *was* tired. Usually his reflexes were much better than that. "You can trust me. I'll wake you the moment we hear something new."

"I know I can trust you. I just don't feel like I want to sleep—let my guard down, I mean," he said. Despite his words, he felt his eyelids growing heavier and heavier.

"You're surrounded by people who'd probably die to keep you alive, you know," Rebecca said suddenly and bluntly.

It was the truth. Sherman had kept the group together so far. Without him, they wouldn't know who to turn to. Thomas? Probably. He had just as much experience as the General, but lacked his charisma. He could issue orders, and they'd be followed, but fights would certainly pop up. Who else? Denton? He had the charisma and some experience, but didn't seem the leader type.

At any rate, Sherman seemed to take her words to heart. He leaned back slowly, resting his head and shoulders against the rear window of the car, and closed his eyes. Rebecca sat next to the Lieutenant General for a few minutes until she was certain he had fallen asleep, then eased off the trunk and wandered over to the pile of gear the soldiers had unloaded from the utility truck. She picked up a few plastic-covered items and walked into the darkness of the woods, staying in sight of the group, but hidden from their view.

She stripped down, removing the dirty, stained clothes she'd been wearing for weeks now, and shivered as her body was exposed to the cold, northwestern winter air. She quickly tore open the packages she'd taken from the pile, pulling a set of camouflaged boxer shorts from one, wondering inwardly as she pulled them on why in the hell anyone would need camouflaged underpants. The next item she pulled free from its plastic wrap was a medium-thick hunting jacket, also in woodland camouflage. She had abandoned her bra, but the jacket would do the same job nicely once she buttoned and zippered it up. Woodland camouflage trousers came next, almost exact duplicates of what the soldiers were wearing, except theirs were still desert camouflage, tan and brown. Hers were dark brown, black, and evergreen. Fully-clothed once more in clean, warmer gear, she squatted next to the other boxes and plastic-wrapped items she'd snagged and began rummaging through them.

Fifteen minutes later, she re-emerged from the bushes wearing a pistol belt that sported a brand-new fabric holster for her pistol, the same one she'd taken from Sherman when she'd shot Decker. The pistol was a kind of comfort item for her after that incident—she'd killed someone she could have possibly been deeply involved with by now, shot him right between the eyes. The memory made her simultaneously want to vomit and jump for joy at her own primal reflex when she'd pulled the pistol and fired. She'd saved at least one life with that shot. And—as she thought about it—Decker was already dead in a way. He had been infected.

She'd also gotten a backpack from the stack of items, as well as a few MREs. She'd eaten her share on the *Ramage* on their trip across the Pacific. They weren't as bad as people made out. Some of the entrees were actually decent. And some tasted and smelled like cat food—but she'd sorted through the box and picked out a few of her favorites and stuffed them in the pack before returning the rest to the pile, which was slowly being loaded into the Topaz. She saw Sherman was still asleep on the back trunk. A pair of soldiers were quietly arguing over whether they should wake the General so they could get into the trunk.

"I ain't doin' it," said one, with a heavy rural West Virginian accent. "I reckon he's beat. Best to let the guy get some sack time."

"Hell, man, let's just get him to move to the front seat. He can even recline it a bit. Better than laying on the trunk," said the other, this one with a touch of New York in his voice.

"Like I said, I ain't doin' it. You wake him up."

"I'm not waking him up. What if I piss him off? I could get picked for some shitty detail because I interrupted a good dream," said the other soldier.

Rebecca pushed her way through the two arguing men, walking straight for Sherman.

"I'll do it," she said, then turned her head and grinned at the two men. "*Pussies.*"

If the soldiers were angry, they didn't show it. More likely they were relieved someone else was crazy enough to wake a sleeping General. Rebecca climbed onto the trunk, squatting down on her knees, and reached a hand out to Sherman's shoulder. The moment she touched him, his eyes snapped open and his hand grabbed her wrist.

"*Whazzit?*" he slurred, still confused and half-asleep—though his reflexes had obviously improved after the short nap.

"The men want to get into the trunk, Frank," Rebecca said, throwing a thumb over her shoulder at the two nervous-looking Privates.

"Oh. Oh, I see. No problem," Sherman said, sitting up with a slight groan and sliding off the trunk. "I'll sleep in the front seat."

"See? I told you that would be a good place," said the soldier with the New York accent.

"Shove it," said his companion.

Sherman settled into the car and was asleep again the moment his head hit the seat. He had definitely pushed himself to the limit since they'd made landfall. Even with all the bumping and swaying from the soldiers shoving in boxes of food and gear, he didn't crack an eyelid or so much as stir. Rebecca looked in at him with an expression on her face that was a mix of pity and admiration. She felt a tap on her shoulder, and turned to face a girl about her own age, maybe a year older. She didn't know her, and guessed she must have been one of the folks in the theater.

"I'm Katie," said the girl, extending a hand. "You're, like, the only other woman here that's my age. Figure I should make some contacts. Network. That sort of thing."

"Rebecca. You can call me Becky, if you want. Medic with the Red Cross. What do you do?"

"I worked at a restaurant in town. Waitress. Until this shitstorm happened, of course—then me and Ron ran to the theater," Katie replied. "Red Cross, eh? Must have been exciting."

"You could say that," Rebecca said, expressionless, reliving the hell of Cairo on fire, the dead children she'd seen, the blood on the walls in the corridors of the *Ramage*—shooting Decker in the face, watching his brains . . .

She cut herself off in mid-thought.

Katie sensed she'd said something wrong, and changed the subject adeptly.

"You've got a good leader, I see," she said. "Almost everyone in infected areas just breaks and runs. No organization. Half the military bases on the West Coast had to deal with hundreds of deserters—least, that's what we heard on the radio. But you guys—you work like a real team. And you're still alive. I'm glad we've run into you all."

Rebecca smiled as a reply, but said nothing.

Katie kept going, "Where'd you get those clothes? Did the Red Cross issue them? I'd love to change out of this stuff." She picked at her dirty long-sleeved shirt with a pair of fingers, quite gingerly, treating the fabric like it was crawling with spiders. Rebecca knew how she felt. None of the survivors had had a shower since they left the *Ramage,* and there was no shower room in a theater, either—Katie and Ron had probably gone without a decent bath since they holed up there—possibly weeks.

Rebecca grinned again. She said, "I can help you in that department. The Cross lets you wear whatever you want, but we just got an entire load of winter gear from that sporting goods store you guys tipped us off about. Let's go get you some new duds."

Katie had just vanished into the woods to change into her new woodland camouflage clothes when the rumble of engines alerted the group. They weren't coming from the back road—they were coming from the town. They must have hit trouble and had to take a more direct route.

"Soldiers! Get ready to bug out, pronto!" shouted a corporal, the ranking soldier at the moment. Rather, he was the ranking *awake* soldier.

Rebecca sprinted away from the shrubs, where she'd been standing guard to make sure no one disturbed Katie while she changed, and knocked on the Topaz's window. Sherman didn't wake. She opened the door and gingerly touched his shoulder. He awoke as fast as before, this time more alert.

"What's happening?" he asked.

"They're back—but it looks like they've got company," Rebecca said, talking fast. The trucks were about twenty seconds out, and closing at high speed. As they rounded the last bend, Sherman reached out his leg and tapped the brake on the Topaz, and at the same time flicking on the flashers. He didn't want a truck barreling into any of the survivors. It was a good decision—the lead truck immediately slowed. Mbutu had apparently thought he'd had further to go. He could have accidentally rammed the car or one of the refugees.

The trucks pulled to a sharp halt, and none of the soldiers got out. Mbutu rolled down his window.

"Medical! We need medical here!" he shouted. Apparently his otherwise excellent grasp of English didn't extend to the word '*medic*.'

Rebecca was ready. She'd already grabbed up her bag of supplies after she woke Sherman. It was bulging since she'd raided the *Ramage*'s sickbay. She unslung it from her shoulder and dashed over to the truck.

"Who's bit? And where?" she curtly asked Mbutu.

He managed a small smile and replied, "*Me*. I'm not bitten, though. I've been shot—an accident."

"Get out of the truck and let me see," Rebecca said, her voice taking on a hard edge. She wasn't asking. She was ordering Mbutu now.

He obeyed, opening the door and swinging his long legs out, but remained seated. His right leg had a number of small entrance wounds, but nothing on the other side.

"Shotgun wound?" Rebecca guessed. She was getting better with firearms every day—and the wounds they caused on carriers and the living uninfected.

"Yes," Mbutu said. He obviously had no intention of telling who fired that shot, but he didn't have to. Brewster popped up behind Rebecca, a concerned look on his face.

"I'm sorry, man, I'm so sorry—that shambler was crawling right toward you—I should've let someone without buckshot take him out. I'm so sorry, man!" Brewster went on and on, brushing his short hair back and pacing slightly. He leaned in, face next to Rebecca's. She could feel his breath on her cheek, fast and shallow—a sign he was still running on adrenaline from the sortie, or a sign he was honestly worried about Mbutu's well being. She figured it was both.

"Friendly fire, man. What a bitch! I mean, shit, I could've accidentally *killed* you, man! He's going to be fine, right? I didn't, like, hit his femoral artery or any shit like that, right?" Brewster asked, betraying once more that he was a bit more educated than he let on most of the time.

"He's fine," Rebecca said. "Back up. Your breath stinks, and you're in my way. All he needs is a bandage and a small dose of painkiller right now. We'll try to operate later."

"*Operate?*" Brewster asked, eyes going wide. "You mean, like, surgery? You're not even a doctor! You're just a volunteer medic! Oh, goddamn it, I killed Mbutu! This is it, man!"

"Would you shut the hell up?" Rebecca asked, voice deadly calm. "All I have to do is get the buckshot out. Not a problem. I could literally do that blindfolded. But first we've got to get somewhere safer."

Thomas had been busy conferring with Sherman while Rebecca had been taking care of Mbutu's wounds, filling him in on what had happened. They had acquired not only the lost crew of Mbutu's truck, but a couple more rifles and another pair of hands—the man who had refused to open the door when they'd first arrived in Hyattsburg. He had readily agreed to come along when a group of about fifteen sprinters and just as many shamblers had spotted the soldiers boarding the truck. He knew they'd never leave the warehouse door if he stayed. It was a deathtrap. He'd jumped aboard Mbutu's truck as it was pulling away, bringing with him a pack full of canned food and two rifles, both measly .22 calibers—but they were guns, and in the right hands they would do the job just as well as a .30-06.

The group was assembled, and Sherman called for them to gather round the car.

"Group! School circle!" Sherman called. "Time to tell you where we're headed. It's east. We're heading due east. Our destination is Omaha, Nebraska. There's a research facility there, top-secret. Only brass and base personnel know it exists. Its purpose is to study possible uses of deadly viruses. It is a fortress—and I do mean *fortress*. We'll get there, meet up with my old friend—her name is Colonel

Anna Demilio. She's got PhD's in virology, epidemiology, and general surgery. I have confidence that she'll be able to do something about this situation. She might not be able to fix it—in fact, I doubt she can. But she might be able to help, and we'd be safe waiting there. She should be on her way there now. Does anyone think they've got a better plan or place in mind? Speak up, if you do! I want to hear ideas! We're a democracy now, not the military!"

People looked back and forth at each other, but no one spoke a word. A few who were kneeling in the front row shifted from foot to foot, eager to get moving.

"Alright, then, group. We've survived Africa, Suez, we won the fight on the *Ramage,* and we pulled off a picture-perfect rescue in Hyattsburg, Oregon. We'll do just fine, I think. Now mount up! Let's get a move on! To Omaha! Hoo-ah?"

Everyone, in unison this time, replied loudly and clearly. Some of the civilians shouted "Alright!" or "Yeah!" or "Let's rock!" among exclamations in other languages from some of the foreign refugees. Even those who didn't speak English among the survivors felt the excitement, and knew they were in a good position—for now.

The trucks and car were loaded for bear with people and gear. Mbutu was driving his truck, Thomas was in the old car, and Krueger had taken over the utility truck.

Brewster sat in the bed of Mbutu's truck, casting glances at the big man's bandaged leg and cursing his absentmindedness that had almost killed him several times since the whole shitstorm began.

Sherman sat across from Thomas in the Topaz, seat leaned back, snoring slightly as he enjoyed the first real night's sleep he'd had in days. Thomas was similarly exhausted, but his eyes were locked on the road ahead. He was soldier through and through. No rest until the mission was accomplished.

Rebecca was in the back of the utility truck, checking her medical supplies. She felt proud of herself—the way she'd managed to snag herself the new clothing, the way she'd handled Mbutu's wound, and the way she'd made fast friends with Katie Dawson, who sat across from her, head lolling on her shoulder as she drifted in and out of sleep.

They were doing well, for now—heading East, through the forests of Oregon.

EPILOGUE

THREE FIGURES CRESTED a hilltop near the edge of Washington, D.C. They wove their way through the debris-strewn street, avoiding the burning husks of abandoned cars and stepping gingerly over prone forms that lay unmoving on the pavement. Near them, a fallen power line spat sparks, sporadically lighting the road, and a few blocks away, a house was burning.

The air crackled and rumbled as a low-flying jet passed overhead, sending a shockwave through the air. The figures turned, following the jet with their eyes.

"They finally did it," commented Mason, mouth turned down in a grimace. "Air strikes. It's all gone by now."

"It couldn't last forever," said Julie, hefting her MP-5 to her shoulder with a sigh.

The jet banked around to its left, slicing low through the air, and released its ordnance. A dull red light lit the faces of the three survivors as the firebomb hit and detonated. Miles away, they imagined they could still feel the heat off the explosion.

"Like a dream," said Anna. "Still feels like a dream."

"—And we're still waiting to wake up," Mason finished for her. "But I'm starting to doubt that's ever going to happen. It's a brave new world, Doc. We'll have to make the best of it. *A brave new world.*"

Behind them, another pair of jets streaked in, and dull reverberations in the air signaled the detonation of more firebombs.

North was no good. Nothing left there. South—no good either. East was the Atlantic. There was only one way to go from the burning, overrun ruins of the capital of the United States.

The figures turned westward, shouldering their weapons and shifting the heavy packs on their backs, scanning the shadows for carriers.

HISTORY IS DEAD

A ZOMBIE ANTHOLOGY EDITED BY

KIM PAFFENROTH

“*History is Dead* is a violent and bloody tour through the ages. Paffenroth has assembled a vicious timeline chronicling the rise of the undead that is simultaneously mind-numbingly savage and thought provoking.”

—Michael McBride, author of the *God’s End* trilogy and *The Infected*

ISBN: 978-0-9789707-9-6

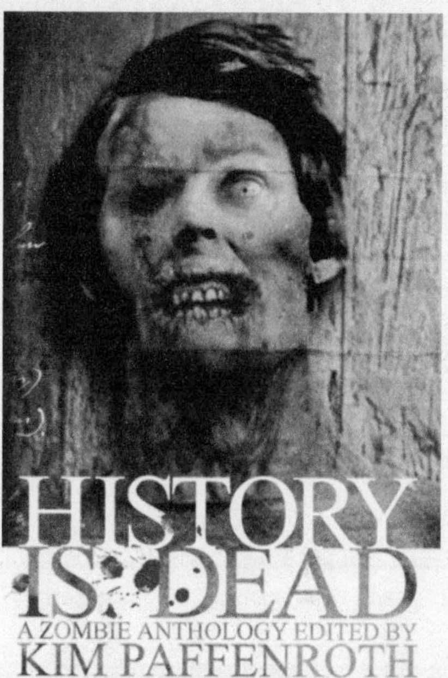

THE WORLD IS DEAD

A ZOMBIE ANTHOLOGY EDITED BY

KIM PAFFENROTH

“A STUNNING COLLECTION OF STORIES.”

—David Moody, author of *Hater*

“THIS COLLECTION SHOWS WHAT WE ALL KNEW THE ZOMBIE STORY WAS CAPABLE OF BECOMING.”

—Joe McKinney, author of *Dead City*

ISBN: 978-1-934861-25-7

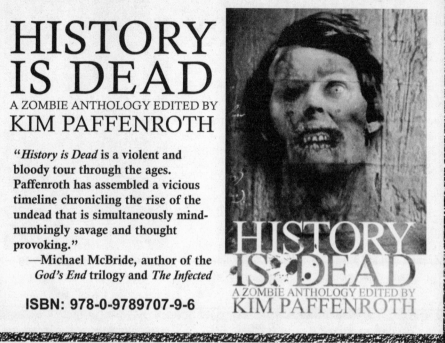